Chasing the Sun

USA *TODAY* BESTSELLING AUTHOR
LENA HENDRIX

Developmental editing: Paula Dawn, Lilypad Lit

Copy editing: James Gallagher, Evident Ink

Proofreading: Julia Griffis, The Romance Bibliophile

Model & Discreet cover design: TRC Designs by Cat

Model cover photography: Ren Saliba

To every woman who has every been called "difficult," just know that you're exactly Callum Blackwood's idea of a good time.

LET'S CONNECT

When you sign up for my newsletter, you'll stay up to date with new releases, book news, giveaways, and new book recommendations! I promise not to spam you and only email when I have something fun & exciting to share!

Also, When you sign up, you'll also get a FREE copy of Choosing You (a very steamy Chikalu Falls novella)!

Sign up at my website at www.lenahendrix.com

AUTHOR'S NOTE

Thank you for coming along with me into a new town. This place is part swoony, small town, part ghost story, and FULL of heart and heat.

Inside you'll find deliciously dirty mouths, deep yearning, rivals that like to argue, and blurred lines between annoyance and arousal.

Don't ever forget that you're not hard to love. Maybe you've just been giving yourself to people who haven't learned how to hold it.

Trust me, Cal can hold anything you've got to give.

ABOUT THIS BOOK

He wants me to stay out of his way. I want to get under his skin.

One look at single dad Callum Blackwood, and I know I messed up. I never meant to save a farm—or steal it from under the grumpy innkeeper who had already claimed it as his future.

Now I'm the woman who swooped in on a whim and left him seething.

Trouble is, I have no idea what I'm doing.

Every smirk, every biting comment, is a reminder that he's waiting for me to fail. But I don't back down from a fight—*even when the fight comes with a jawline that should be illegal and a scowl that sets my pulse racing.*

Tempers flare, but when the lines between rivals and lovers begin to blur, I start to see him in a different light. The longer we go toe-to-toe, the more I understand the man behind the scowl. The one who loves his kid fiercely, who carries the weight of the world on his shoulders, who looks at me like I'm the reason the sun rises.

Cal's wrong if he thinks I'll give up on this farm. He's even more wrong if he thinks I'll give up on him.

But holding a man like him is like chasing the sun—brilliant, blinding, and bound to set your entire life on fire.

ONE

CALLUM

IF I HAVE to get another rabies vaccine, I'm flipping a damn table.

My jaw flexed as I quietly pushed the front door open with the toe of my boot. The hinges groaned as I peered around the corner into the dark, musty cottage. My ears pricked at the faint sound of scurrying, and my instincts from my time in the Army sparked to life. My nostrils flared at the damp, stale air. My heart pounded as I listened.

Nothing.

Shouldering open the front door, I peered into the dilapidated home. I assumed at some point the house had been quaint and perfect for a small family just starting out. Now it was nothing more than an abandoned shack with rotting wood and a raccoon infestation.

A discarded candy bar wrapper caught my eye.

"Levi," I called into the dim, early-morning light, my voice low but firm. "If you're in here, kid, get your ass out. Now."

When I had returned from my 5:00 a.m. run, I had peeked into Levi's bedroom, only to find it empty, so I'd gone in search of him. I listened again, hoping for any sign of my fourteen-year-old son. A shuffle caught me off guard as two baby raccoons scampered across my boot. I bit back a yelp, knowing their mama wouldn't be far behind. Sure as shit, the large raccoon hissed at me, baring her rabies-infected teeth before following her kits outside.

A shiver ran down my spine. "Fucking overgrown rats," I murmured. I stayed rooted to the spot, heart hammering. She waddled her furry ass across the porch like she owned the damn place, before disappearing beneath it.

Assured that Levi wasn't hiding out in the cottage again, I pulled my phone from my pocket and dialed his number. My blood pressure climbed with each unanswered ring.

I gritted my teeth when it went to voicemail. Levi's voice came over the line. "Hey, it's me. You know what to do." *Beep.*

My grip tightened on the phone. *You know what to do?* Yeah, I did. I knew exactly what to do. I just didn't want to do it—track his ass down, drag him home, and try to talk sense into a kid who'd rather dodge me than listen.

"Where are you?" I pinched the bridge of my nose, trying my best not to completely lose it on the kid. "We talked about this. You cannot roam around without letting me know where you're going first. It's the last week of school. We made a deal."

Frustrated, I pocketed my phone and exhaled. I loved my kid but he was going to be the death of me. A moment later, my phone buzzed, and I looked down at the new message.

LEVI

I'm getting in the shower. Chill.

Chill.

A low growl vibrated in my throat. It would be a hell of a lot easier to *chill* if my kid didn't insist on getting himself into so much trouble. I simply needed him to pass eighth grade and have a fresh start in high school.

Maybe things would be a little easier for him then.

I glanced at the time, noting that Helen should already be at the inn. As I looked across the overgrown lawn, my eyes landed on the Drifted Spirit Inn in the distance, and the knot in my chest eased a bit.

The layout of the land was simple: long ago, Stan's land and my property had been one larger parcel of land. His dilapidated cottage hugged his property line and the Drifted Spirit was less than a hundred yards away with a post and rail fence dividing the grass between them.

Helen was already at the inn, keeping the place running. Keeping me running, if I was being honest. I wasn't sure how much longer she'd put up with my shit, but if she ever left, I was royally screwed.

Helen was a saint and the only reason we didn't go completely under after Levi's mom died five years ago. Her self-appointed title of *concierge* was grossly inadequate for all the hard work she put in to help me ensure that our little inn ran like clockwork.

After my time as a Delta Force operator came to an end, running a successful inn in Western Michigan hadn't been on my radar, yet there I was. I looked to the east and watched the first rays of June create streaks of magenta across an inky morning sky. For the briefest moment, I closed my eyes and imagined the warm June rays hitting my face.

I have shit to do.

Standing around, enjoying a sunrise simply wasn't an option. With a sigh, I pulled the front door to the cottage closed and stepped across the rickety porch. On the second step, the wood buckled under my weight, and my foot crashed through the rotting boards. I caught myself, palms slamming onto the worn planks.

"Careful now, Cal." My eyes whipped up to see Stan Stafford's amused grin. "Been meaning to patch that up."

"Yeah? You planning to do that before or after the raccoons unionize?" I grumbled with a halfhearted laugh and hauled myself up before traversing the rest of the porch and standing beside the old man.

I wiped the dirt from my palm and held out my hand. "Stan."

We shook, and he thumped me on the back. "To what do I owe the pleasure?"

Stan's property butted up to the parcel of land that Drifted Spirit Inn was on. Long ago, the Victorian and the adjacent farm had been part of the same parcel of land. Over time, pieces had been divided and my acreage split from the rolling hills and dune-lined cliffs of Star Harbor Farm.

At one time, Stan's farm was at the center of the Star Harbor community. It had once been a highlight for passing tourists, but in his old age, the farm had fallen into disrepair. The fields that once held abundant crops were overgrown with weeds and wild grasses. The apple orchard's scraggly trees looked more like something out of a horror movie than a place where produce thrived.

It was a mess, but that didn't stop Stan from walking his property every single day.

"I was looking for Levi. I thought he might have snuck out here this morning," I said, stuffing my hands into my pockets.

Stan shook his head. "Kids will be kids. Plenty from

town seem to find their way out here and have a bonfire or two, sneak a few beers, and maybe even sweet-talk a pretty girl into a kiss."

I shook my head and groaned. "He's fourteen, Stan."

Stan chuckled and patted my back. "You're in the thick of it now."

I stretched my neck, looking out onto the vast property that was once Star Harbor Farm. It was sprawling, and its gentle rolling hills led to an impressive dune cliff to the west. Soft waves of Lake Michigan glittered in the morning light.

"That leg okay?" Stan asked, pointing to the boot that had created a new hole in his front porch.

I nodded. "It'll be all right." I glanced at the old man. He was the only millionaire I knew who still wore threadbare denim and a Pioneer Seed hat from 1972. "You know, I could help clean up the place. Last thing you need is a tourist wandering around chasing ghost stories to get hurt."

I walked alongside Stan as he continued his morning route that ran along the fence line where our properties met. I had replaced the old chain-link fence with stylish cedar posts and rails last spring.

Stan met my pace, step for step. "It was a lot easier to keep up when I wasn't going it alone. When Karen passed . . ." He blew out a breath at the mention of his late wife, looking out across the property. The couple never had children, so when she passed, he was truly on his own. "Guess I just didn't really see the point anymore."

His words hit harder than they should have. I knew what it was like to lose the thing that made a place feel like home. To let something die with the person who'd kept it alive. Hell, I was never supposed to be here running an inn.

That was my late wife Mary's dream. I was just . . . keeping it together.

Barely.

Stan's wife, Karen, had been a kind and gentle woman, always smiling and laughing. She was the heart of Star Harbor Farm, and without her, Stan had spent the last few years alone, living at their main residence and letting the farm die alongside her.

"I could help," I offered. "Patch things up and mow the grass . . ."

He eyed me. "You have the free time?"

Fuck no.

I was up to my neck in my own projects, but I didn't have the heart to tell Stan that his neglected property was starting to negatively affect my business. Recent reviews reflected the poorly maintained neighboring farm. It was an eyesore, and plenty of people assumed the sprawling land was a part of Drifted Spirit Inn.

My silence stretched and Stan shook his head. "That's what I thought." Stan's eyes went wistful as morning sun slanted over his shoulder, highlighting the deep lines on his face. "Some days I'm ready for it all to be over," Stan said, exhaling as he looked out over the fields.

I blinked at the old man. *Ready for it to be over?*

He'd said it before, in passing—*I'm too old for this. Guess it's about time to think about letting it go. It could be yours if you wanted it.* Hell, I wasn't even sure when he'd started saying it, but Stan letting go of the farmland had been in the back of my mind for years. I'd never been interested in farming, but the land? The space? That was interesting.

Maybe it was finally time to make something happen.

My jaw clenched as we walked in silence, and the possibilities rolled around in my head.

Taking time to fix his property would be stupid. Reckless. Just another thing to add to my already overloaded plate.

But buying it from him? Claiming this land as my own?

There was no denying that land itself could be useful. I could clear out the brush, renovate the barns, and create more guest spaces. Expand the Drifted Spirit beyond the main house and give visitors a full Star Harbor experience— fresh air, walking trails, maybe even a farm-to-table restaurant. If I played this right, I wouldn't just be running the best inn in town, I'd be running a destination—a legacy for Levi instead of another thing left to rot.

I could finally open my own restaurant.

That felt more like my dream than simply running a glorified bed-and-breakfast.

Helen had been badgering me for years to expand—with enough sweat and hard work, Drifted Spirit Inn had been making more than enough money. But the thought of a second location seemed daunting. My days were already filled with maintenance, staff schedules, dealing with guests, and Levi.

Something less than a hundred yards away . . . now that could be an idea worth considering. I let the possibility roll over me, walking in companionable silence with my old friend.

We reached the bend in the road where Stan would continue on, and I needed to get inside the inn to make sure breakfast went off without a hitch.

But for the first time, I wasn't just thinking about today's to-do list.

I was thinking about what came next. The possibilities

of expanding the inn and having my very own restaurant on-site burrowed into my chest. For the first time in my life, I let a tiny spark of hope ignite.

I turned, holding out my hand. "Tell you what—if you ever decide you're ready for those changes, you tell me first, how about that?"

His eyes smiled as he shook. "You'll be the first to know." Stan's grip was strong, and he didn't let me go. "You should also think about coming with me to BOLD. We meet next week." His eyebrows bounced alongside the offer.

I bit back a grimace. Stan had been hounding me for the last few years to join his widow/widower support group.

BOLD: Brave, Optimistic, Living Dynamically.

Even if it wasn't designed for the over-sixty crowd, it was a hard pass.

"You could meet a nice lady," he continued with a hint of mischief in his voice. "One who won't even care about the scars."

I suppressed a wince and tried to ignore the phantom pain in my shoulder.

I mustered up a smile for him, knowing the old man was meddlesome but always meant well. "I've got my hands full with a fourteen-year-old who thinks he's twenty-five. Thanks for the invite, though."

Stan nodded, knowing full well there was *zero* chance I would be hitting up BOLD.

My thoughts flicked to Mary and the gaping hole she'd left in Levi's life. On the long list of ways I had failed her, Levi's latest struggles were the hardest to ignore.

Much to Mary's dismay, despite her unexpected pregnancy at twenty-two, I had never planned to leave the Army. Sure, I had agreed to marry her, but I had been selfish. I'd joined the Delta Force operators as soon as I was eligible and had been gone more than I was home. Her brother, Wes, was one of my best friends and a fellow operator.

When Mary died, he was the sole reason I managed to hold my shit together as a man who had no clue how to raise a son alone. Sometimes I wondered whether Wes ever regretted bringing me home to Thanksgiving that time and introducing me to his little sister.

With heavy shoulders, I dipped through the cedar fence and walked across the yard toward the Drifted Spirit Inn. The old Victorian stood proudly against the stark magenta sunrise. The three-story house had been built in the late 1880s and had survived various renovations over the past 140 years, but the goal was always to retain its historic charm. Mary had begged to take over the inn, saying she was a lot less lonely when I was gone if she was surrounded by people.

I preferred my solitude.

Still, in my absence, Mary had worked hard and made the Drifted Spirit Inn what it was today. Every room, every board in that place, was hers. When her tragic car accident and unexpected death had forced my retirement from the Army, the inn had been yet another saving grace. The settlement from her accident was more than enough to make sure Levi was taken care of for a long time. Any amount that was left, I poured into making her dream a living, breathing thing.

It was my penance for not being the man she had deserved.

I walked through the side entrance of the Drifted Spirit, entering the kitchen. After my detour to the cottage from hell, I was already behind schedule. I grabbed my apron off the hook and slipped it over my head. I tied it in the back as I read over the detailed notes I'd left myself last night.

The morning's breakfast menu included German apple pancakes with whipped maple sour cream, glazed breakfast sausages, scrambled eggs, and pineapple carpaccio with mint sugar. It would feed eight to ten people and take me about forty-five minutes from start to finish.

I looked around the kitchen. In the bustling chaos of an inn, the kitchen was my sanctuary. Everything had a place. A timeline. A result. Helen could handle the guest requests for extra towels or recommendations for the best ghost walk in town, while I could disappear into the kitchen and keep to myself.

Learning how to cook was easy compared to worrying about how to raise a kid who barely knew me. I had never seemed to shake the times as a child when I went hungry. Not having something as basic as food sticks with you—cooking for others eased a bit of that ache of a scared little boy I had once been.

Over time, I'd found my rhythm with both food and Levi.

As I measured the ingredients and placed them on the large island in the center of the newly renovated kitchen, my son came sauntering in.

"Where were you?" I asked, glancing up. He was freshly showered, and his brown hair looked nearly black with the water clinging to it. He needed a haircut, and I mentally added that to my to-do list.

"Out." Levi barely looked at me as he rummaged through the industrial-size refrigerator.

I whipped the eggs with more force than necessary. "Breakfast will be ready in about an hour. Then I'll drive you to school."

He turned, grabbing a muffin I'd baked yesterday off the island. "I'm fine."

"You like it here, don't you?" I asked, watching my son leave his garbage on the counter.

"I guess." He shrugged, then paused. My breath caught in my throat as I waited for him to give me *anything* else. "It's just . . . not the same without her."

Mary had been gone for years, but her absence still haunted us. I swallowed past the rocks in my throat. "I know."

I struggled to find words of comfort and wondered where my bright-eyed little boy had gone. More and more the easygoing Levi I once knew was disappearing right in front of me.

Was it trouble with friends?

Girl problems?

Drugs?

"Good morning," Helen singsonged as she pushed through the door, breaking through my spiraling thoughts.

I bit back a curse as batter sloshed over the side of the bowl. I wanted to finish my conversation with Levi, but when I looked up, he was already gone.

Helen was in her sixties, with warm brown skin and a smattering of freckles across her nose, like shadows of the sun. Tight coils framed her face, neatly styled in short twists that brushed her temples, streaks of silver threading through the black. She was always smiling, a hint of mischief sparkling in her deep-brown eyes.

"The couple who checked out of 2A just called and said they accidentally left a box of . . ."

I glanced up when she paused.

Holding back a giggle, Helen pressed her lips together,

failing miserably at looking professional. "Um, *special items*. They're hoping to get those back."

My eyes closed. "Jesus Christ." I exhaled, fighting my own smirk. *Special items* most definitely meant sex stuff—it always did.

"Oh, well you're going to love this next part." She leaned in with humor dancing in her eyes. "They said they're pretty sure the big one rolled under the bed."

I dropped my head back. "I don't get paid enough for this shit."

"You should ask the boss for a raise," she offered, knowing full well *I* was the boss in charge of salaries.

I held up my fist, ready to rock, paper, scissors Helen in hopes of getting out of sex-toy recon duty. It was how she and I settled most disagreements these days.

We pumped our fists, and when her rock beat my scissors, I let that curse fly. "Fuck."

Helen laughed. "Have fun. Wear gloves . . . maybe a hazmat suit."

I waved her off and focused on finishing up breakfast before I lost what was left of my patience.

How the hell was this my life?

TWO

ELODIE

Transaction declined.

Two little words that punched me straight in the pride.

I blinked at the cashier as she swung the screen back toward herself, her acrylic nails clacking against the keyboard with the kind of irritation that said she'd already decided I was a problem.

A whoosh of embarrassed laughter escaped me. "I am so sorry." I rubbed my credit card against the material of my slacks, hoping that it might help, and held the card up. "Can you try it again?"

Her bored expression had my heart rate ticking higher, but she sighed and clacked the keyboard. "Okay."

"Great. Thank you. I swear there's no reason it should be . . ."

Declined.

I glanced over my shoulder as the line in the café grew impatient. The business card always worked. I was Elodie Darling, for fuck's sake—top dog at one of the most exclusive PR firms in the city. My boss, Amy, had founded the company, but we were practically partners. She never made any decisions without my input.

I attended events with open bars and people whose teeth probably cost more than my rent.

And yet there I was. Broke. In line at a café and contemplating grand larceny over an overpriced chicken Caesar wrap. I swiped a palm down my thigh.

Oh, for the love of espresso shots and emotional stability, please don't do this to me today.

The woman's beautifully manicured eyebrow crept higher. "Maybe you have cash?" she said, slow and patronizing, like I was a toddler learning shapes.

My face twisted. *Who in the world carries cash?*

With a tight smile, I dug through my purse, hoping the incessant foot tapping to my right wasn't meant for me. Before I left the office, I'd decided to surprise Mel, our firm's eternally loyal receptionist, with lunch. She was an unsung hero at the office, and the thought of doing something nice for her made me feel lighter.

A tiny act of goodness in the world.

I pulled out my personal debit card. "Just use this one."

I stared at the card as it moved in slow motion across the counter, praying it would go through.

Maybe the bank was randomly flagging the purchase? Maybe Amy forgot to move money around? Maybe my late-night "treat yourself" shopping spree for my corner office had finally caught up to me?

I mean, surely not that last one.

The cashier tapped my card against the screen and forced a smile. I brushed an unruly curl from my face, my mind already running through the possibilities.

There was no way I was actually *broke* broke.

Sure, my personal checking account was usually only

one bad decision away from overdraft, but I wasn't *that* irresponsible. Maybe I had hit *add to cart* like a feral little goblin a few too many times this month, but happiness wasn't about money.

Except, you know, when you needed money to buy things that made you happy. Like food.

Transaction declined.

Heat prickled at my hairline as my armpits began to sweat.

What in the twilight zone is happening here?

My eyes pleaded with her. "I swear, I have no idea what's going on."

Unimpressed by my internal meltdown, the cashier simply stared. "It's thirty-eight dollars and sixty-five cents."

My mouth popped open at her complete lack of empathy. "No, I understand. I just don't have any cash, and I don't know why the cards aren't working. Are you sure it's not a system error or something?"

"It's not." She sighed, reaching for my chicken Caesar wrap and sliding it toward her like I might snatch it and run.

In her defense, the thought *had* occurred to me, but I would never do that.

Probably.

I mean, if I just grabbed it and ran, what was she going to do? Chase me? Tackle me over two eighteen-dollar sandwiches? Unlikely.

Would that make me the kind of woman who committed mild deli-related crimes? Also unlikely.

I sighed. *Fine. No lunch. No good karma.*

Resigned to go the rest of the afternoon hungry, I apologized profusely to her *and* the long line that had formed behind me. I gathered what was left of my pride and walked out of the café empty-handed.

As soon as I hit the sidewalk, I called Amy, but it went to voicemail. "Hey, do you know if we got hacked again? I tried to pick up lunch, and the card was declined." I left out the part about my own card also being declined. Leave it to me to not realize my checking account was dangerously low after some late-night retail-therapy sessions.

"Anyway," I huffed, "I should be back uptown in a few minutes. My toes are *killing* me in these heels. I can't believe I let you talk me into them. They are hot, though . . . okay, I—"

The phone cut off my rambling, and I made a face at it. Undeterred, I sucked in a cleansing breath and took in the sunny June afternoon.

This is fine. Everything is fine.

Downtown Grand Rapids wasn't New York or LA, but it had the same overpriced coffee shops and overpriced people. Amy and I had met sophomore year of college and become fast friends. After graduation, we had created the most successful event and PR consulting firm in the city. Together we'd built it from the ground up, and that was something to be proud of.

She was the brains behind the operation—always a shark circling the waters, finding new opportunities—but I was the closer. As a team we specialized in planning and promoting high-profile events, brand launches, and charity galas in the city. I knew what our clients needed before they did and could sell any idea, no matter how ridiculous.

A millionaire heiress who was obsessed with her dog? Boom. A pet fashion show where the ultra-rich dressed their pets in custom couture and walked them down the runway for charity? Nothing said *giving back* like a Yorkie in Gucci.

A lonely high-profile influencer with a tragic haircut? Not a problem. The *I Can Fix Him* charity date auction had been one of our most profitable events last year. Guests bid on "fixer-upper" bachelors—guys with bad haircuts, questionable fashion choices, or chaotic dating histories. All proceeds went to a relationship wellness nonprofit, and just last month our client got engaged to his date.

I *lived* for the high of nailing something that seemed just slightly out of my reach. Granted, the fake smiles, endless networking, and crisis management left little time for an actual life, but that was totally fine.

My boyfriend, Brandt, was an up-and-coming attorney, and he was completely unbothered by my late nights and long weekends at work.

By the time I gave up on my heels and hailed a cab, my failed attempt at lunch was all but forgotten. Double Trouble PR had become my entire world, and the occasional nagging sense of unfulfillment was worth it.

I pasted on a smile as I walked into the office building. "Thanks, Ron." I waved at the elderly doorman as he held the door for me. The ride up to the twentieth floor was quick, and I winked at our receptionist as I sailed past, promising myself I'd surprise her with lunch tomorrow.

"Oh! Ms. Darling!" Mel scrambled out of her chair and chased after me.

"Hey, Mel." I smiled and kept walking toward Amy's corner office. "I'm just popping in to see Amy. Something is up with the business card."

She made a squeaking noise and placed herself between me and the door. "Ms. Fields is busy!" She looked panicked, and her attention flicked over my shoulder.

I tracked her gaze and noticed a few pairs of eyes pretending not to stare from behind their keyboards. I laughed. "It's fine, Mel. I'll be quick."

I eased past the receptionist, pushing open the opaque

glass door to Amy's office, then stopped dead in my tracks. Before I looked away, all I saw was Amy bent over her desk, ass in the air, while some guy pounded into her from behind. His slacks were pooled at his feet, and his necktie was flipped over one shoulder.

"Oh!" An embarrassed giggle shot out of me as I turned away. "Shit. Sorry, Aim. I can come back."

"Ellie." The strangled voice caught my attention, and my head whipped back around.

"Brandt?" I shrieked, unable to make sense of the scene unfolding in front of me. My stomach caved in on itself, like the bottom had been ripped out of my entire reality.

It wasn't just any man, but *my* man.

Brandt. My boyfriend. My *everything-was-fine* safety net—currently balls deep in my best friend.

Time slowed. My stomach lurched. My brain short-circuited. I mean, sure, I knew men cheated—I had a whole PR client list that proved it—but my boyfriend? With my best friend? In our office?

I was frozen as they both stood taller. Amy tried to pull her tight pencil skirt back over her ass, but it was bunched around her waist, and the thong wrapped around her ankles restricted her movements. She fumbled against her desk as she attempted to fix her clothing.

"What the actual fuck?" I demanded, not caring that I was likely drawing an audience just beyond the frosted glass of Amy's corner office.

Rumpled, and still fumbling to button his pants, Brandt took a step toward me. "Ellie Belly, I can explain."

"The only thing I need you to explain is how you thought screwing my best friend in broad daylight was the best way to round out the morning." I held up my hand and shook my head. "You know what? Never mind."

I couldn't even *look* at him. My empty stomach rolled.

My eyes flashed to Amy. "How could you?" Betrayal stabbed me in the chest at the realization of what they'd done. I sucked in a breath as my temper flared. "How long?" I demanded.

Brandt attempted to look stricken, and I imagined freezing his balls off with an icy glare.

They both talked over each other, trying to placate me. "It was a mistake," she said as he mumbled, "A while."

Humiliated. The word rattled around in my chest as my cheeks flamed.

"I thought I could surprise you. I brought you lunch." He weakly lifted a brown paper sack and had the audacity to smile at me.

My molars clenched as I fought back tears. "Well . . ." I huffed a humorless laugh. "Color me surprised. And fuck off with your lunch. This is over." I turned toward the door.

"Ellie, I'm so sorry," Amy started, but I whipped around, my finger pointed directly at her.

"Don't." I swallowed back the betrayal with bile hot on its heels. "I can't even look at you."

The genuine hurt that flashed across her face was an ice pick to my heart. I lifted my chin. "I quit."

I glanced at Brandt as a fresh wave of embarrassment washed over me. My stomach grumbled, and my eyes landed on the brown paper bag, still in his hand. I reached forward, snatching it out of his grasp with more force than necessary.

"Ellie, there's no need to quit. You're being asked to step down," Amy called to my back as I pushed through the office door.

I spun on my heels, eyes slicing toward her. "What?"

Amy lifted her chin. Her eyes took on an icy glare.

"Look, I didn't want to do this here—and certainly not in this way—but you're leaving me no choice. You're amazing, there's no denying that, but sometimes . . ." Her eyes darted away.

"No, go ahead." My hands planted on my hips. "Say it."

Her eyes were sharp when they met mine. "You're one hell of a closer, but you're also kind of a flake. I need someone who can follow through, not just get excited about the next project."

Guess now I know why the business card was declined.

The truth in her words stung more than I wanted them to, embarrassment flooding my system.

I bit back hot tears as her eyes pleaded with mine. "You'll get a nice severance package, I promise."

Pushing open the door, I looked around the office space —the office *we* had built from the ground up after college. As expected, we'd drawn quite the audience, and they scampered back to their desks without making eye contact.

My shoes pinched my toes as I stomped toward the exit. I held out my arm, clutching the brown bag like I could strangle it, before opening my fist and letting it drop onto Mel's desk. "That's lunch for you. Please know that the next few sentences out of my mouth are not directed at you."

My chin lifted as I glared at Amy. "I don't want anything from you." I turned, raising my arm high above my head, my middle finger on full display. "Everyone here sucks! Consider this my resignation letter, assholes. Signed, sealed, and aggressively delivered."

I sank deeper into a buttery leather chair.

The apartment view was perfect. Or at least that was what I had told myself.

Below me, the city stretched out in a tangle of lights, glittering in the early-summer dusk—all sharp angles, penthouse rooftops, and the kind of expensive cocktail bars where you paid twenty bucks for a drink that barely got you buzzed. It was the kind of view that should've made me feel successful.

Instead, it felt like staring at something that didn't quite belong to me.

The apartment had never really felt like mine either. A year ago, I had moved in with Brandt because it was the logical next step, not because I actually saw a future here. The cold modern furniture, the sleek gray countertops, the obnoxiously expensive coffee maker that required an engineering degree to operate—it was all very *his*.

I swirled the wineglass in my hand, watching deep-red legs crawl down the crystal. It was some ridiculously expensive merlot—a thank-you gift from a client who assumed my life was as put-together as my Instagram grid made it seem.

Fake it till you make it, right?

I exhaled, rolling my shoulders, trying to shake off the exhaustion curling at the edges of my mind. A very specific kind of exhaustion—the kind that comes from knowing your bank account is holding on for dear life, but you still hit *add to cart* with reckless abandon.

The kind that whispers maybe happiness wasn't about money, but also, money would sure as hell make happiness easier.

I reached for my phone again, scrolling mindlessly.

Three unread texts from Brandt.

A voicemail from the credit card company.

An email reminder about an automatic payment I definitely did not have the funds for.

I swiped them away. *Future Elodie's problem.*

I had spent the last year chasing something—though I wasn't entirely sure what. A feeling. A spark. A reason for why I was still living paycheck to paycheck in designer heels.

Something had to click eventually, right?

I tossed my phone onto the couch, but a second later it buzzed again.

I groaned, rubbing my temples, but when I saw the name on the screen, I sighed and picked up.

"Finally decided to call me back?" I teased my sister.

"I was at work," Selene clipped. "Unlike you, I don't have time to drop everything for a midday scandal."

I snorted. "Oh, so you did read my texts."

"Oh, I read them. Twice." She exhaled, long and slow. "And I'm still trying to wrap my head around the fact that they didn't even bother to lock the damn door."

"I mean, really," I continued, words spilling out like I'd been holding them in for too long. "What kind of idiot gets caught *that* easily? Office sex is, like, the oldest cliché in the book. At least have the common decency to get creative about it. Frankly, I'm offended."

"So, just to be clear," Selene said, her voice thick with amusement. "You're not mad that he cheated—just that he sucked at it?"

I groaned. "No, I'm mad that Amy was the one he cheated with. I'm mad that I gave *two years* to a man who just—" My voice cracked before I could stop it.

Selene softened. "Hey. It's okay to be sad . . . about all of it."

I dropped my spoon into the now-empty pint of black

cherry chocolate chip ice cream. "To be honest, I didn't know what felt worse—the shock or the sheer *humiliation.* Losing Brandt? I know I'll live. Losing the company I helped build from scratch? I'm gutted."

Selene grumbled at the mention of my cheating bastard of an ex-boyfriend's name. "Has he tried to call you?"

I sighed and didn't have the heart to tell her the contents of the final text message that had come through earlier in the day.

BRANDT

I'm sorry for what you saw, but I've been unhappy for a long time now. I will stay at Travis's house for a few days while you pack your things. You're beautiful, and I love you. I just don't think I like you anymore.

Oof. Twist the knife, why don't you?

The nerve. The unmitigated gall. The pure, unfiltered testosterone-induced stupidity of this man.

"He texted, but I have no interest in talking with him." I groaned and pressed a hand into my stomach.

That second pint of ice cream was definitely a bad idea.

"You're not stress eating again, are you?" When she needed to, Selene had a knack for sounding exactly like our mother.

I frowned. "Of course not," I lied. "In fact, I am about to jump on the treadmill and think up all kinds of witty comebacks while I rage-run."

It wasn't a *bad* idea.

"Well . . ." Selene sighed. "I guess it was a good thing you two were always too busy to bring him home. That way Mom and Dad couldn't get too attached to him."

I let out a humorless chuckle. Our parents loved *every-one.* "Amen to that."

"So this means you're coming to Winnie's birthday party, right?" she asked.

A genuine grin spread across my face. My niece Winnie was one of the coolest kids on planet Earth. Selene had been single-momming it for a while now, but Winnie was pure, chaotic sunshine.

The two of us were kindred spirits.

I looked around Brandt's apartment. We had lived together for a year, and there wasn't much there that really felt like home anyway. I could always find a new apartment. "Yes, I'm in. Text me the details and I will be there. Do you mind if I stay with you for a few days? Just until my murderous rage subsides a little?"

Selene chuckled. "Sure. I can fix up the couch for you. And don't do anything that'll put you in jail. My advice is to make sure your revenge is nearly undetectable. Split the seams in the seat of his pants. A little hair remover in his shampoo. Glitter bomb the vents in his car."

I chuckled, feeling lighter already. "You are diabolical." I loved seeing a wicked side to my typically buttoned-up older sister.

Selene laughed again. "I have no idea what you're talking about."

I sighed. "I really love you."

We said goodbye, and a sly grin spread, slow and easy. I had some work to do before I headed home to Star Harbor.

THREE

ELODIE

My hometown was only about sixty miles from Grand Rapids, but without a car or a boyfriend who had one, I had to rely on a rideshare just to get home. Nothing says *thriving* like fleeing your city in the back seat of a stranger's Toyota Corolla, marinating in the scent of stale air freshener and crushed dreams.

Thankfully, I could talk to just about anyone, whether they wanted me to or not. My driver Jeb was more than happy to make the drive for an obscene price, so conversation was his penance.

It only took seven minutes into the drive before he was telling me all about his wife of thirty years and their new grandbabies.

What can I say? It's a gift.

Truth was, hearing all about Jeb's recent squabble with his wife, Rita, was the distraction I needed. I'd have to find an apartment, a new job—my wine-induced headache was back with a vengeance.

"And there I was, watching my favorite bass fishing videos on YouTube when she's chewing my ear about some grocery list nonsense," Jeb continued. "I told her it could wait. So, you tell me . . . am I wrong?"

One corner of my mouth tugged up for poor, clueless Jeb. "Sounds to me like she was simply making a bid for connection. Sure, her timing could have been better, but I'm certain she didn't mean to interrupt *Bass Masters*."

"*Busters*," he corrected. "*Bass Busters*."

"Right. You've gotta make it up to her, Jeb." I shook my head. "Show her that she's more important to you than *Bass Busters*."

"Well, of course she is!"

"Jeb . . ." My voice lowered: "What was the last thing you did, just for Rita? Took something off her plate or reminded her that you've only got eyes for her?"

His pale-blue eyes flicked to mine in the rearview mirror as he grumbled.

"That's what I thought." I dug through my purse, pulling out a business card and handing it to Jeb. "Tell them Elodie Darling sent you, and they'll handle everything—a premium bouquet, handwritten note, the whole 'husband of the year' package. The owner owes me a favor."

"Really?" Jeb accepted the card with a wide smile. "Thank you. Truly."

I patted his shoulder. "It's my pleasure. But flowers are a Band-Aid. It's up to you to make sure Rita knows she's still your girl."

Jeb smiled. "Are you a therapist or something?"

I laughed, sinking back into the cloth seats. "No. I just know people."

He nodded, and we continued on in companionable silence, occasionally making small talk about his grandkids or the weather. My attention focused on the tree line that zipped past as we got closer and closer to my hometown.

The wide curve in the highway brought the Lake Michigan coastline into view. The fresh water glittered and was much clearer than the river that ran through the city. I cracked the window open and pulled in a deep breath of warm, Michigan air.

The scent of fresh water, sand, and the faintest trace of pine wrapped around me like an old sweatshirt—familiar, comforting, impossible to shake. No matter how much I tried to outgrow this place, it still fit.

Blueberry fields whizzed by, and slowly the towering dunes crept higher and higher. Billboards along the highway enticed tourists to shop local, visit a distillery, or experience the local legends for themselves.

"Have you ever seen her?" Jeb asked after passing a billboard advertising a local ghost tour.

I hummed, knowing exactly what he was asking.

"The Lady," he clarified. "Surely someone born and raised there is bound to have seen her."

The Lady of the Dunes.

Our entire town revolved around the mysterious legend. A ghostly woman, dressed in a billowing white dress, who walked along the sandy dunes, carrying a bouquet of wildflowers. She was believed to be searching for her lost love who'd disappeared in a shipwreck in the early 1900s, but he'd been lost in the storm.

People swore they'd seen her—floating through the dunes at twilight, barefoot and heartbroken, her white dress glowing in the moonlight. Some believed she was searching for her lost love. Others claimed she was searching for vengeance. The tale had twisted and morphed with time until no one knew for certain who she was or why her spirit had been tethered to Star Harbor.

Our town's entire existence hinged on the mysterious woman in white.

"I'll tell you this." I leaned forward, lowering my voice just enough to make Jeb's knuckles go white on the wheel. "If you stay long enough, Star Harbor has a way of making a believer out of you."

Just ask my brother Hayes.

A dull ache for my oldest brother bloomed under my ribs. The entire town may think him cursed by the Lady, but really it was just shitty luck.

It had to be.

A visible shiver rolled down Jeb's back.

"Just keep your eyes open and your hands on the wheel," I warned, biting back a playful grin.

His attention remained laser focused on the last few miles of the drive. Slowly, the rolling highway gave way to rural country roads, and houses were interspersed with farmland.

We cruised past the old cemetery, and I shook my head, noting the wrought iron fence was still bent and rusted from where Hayes's accident had damaged it. It had been nearly seventeen years ago, but that night still haunted him.

Literally.

We drove past Star Harbor Farm and a shocked *aww* escaped me, drawing Jeb's attention.

I pressed my finger against the window, my heart squeezing at the sight of it. Star Harbor Farm used to be magic—hayrides, pumpkins, apple cider doughnuts so good they should've been illegal. Now the farm looked like it had simply been forgotten.

"I used to love that place," I murmured. "Mrs. Stafford had a farm stand where she'd give out samples of the best apple crumble ever—like, life-altering crumble.

People would drive in from three towns over just to get a bite."

Jeb huffed a laugh. "Doesn't look like much now."

I watched as the overgrown farm faded into the distance. A strange sense of loss washed over me—some long-forgotten childhood memory that would forever live in the past. "Yeah . . . that's too bad."

Jeb's GPS brought us to the residential street where my sister lived. He rolled to a stop in front of Selene's duplex. Jeb got out to retrieve my suitcase from the trunk, and I thanked him with a handshake as he climbed back into his car.

I playfully pointed two fingers at my eyes and then to his. "Look out for ghosts."

Jeb chuckled and closed the door before driving away. I turned, staring up at the duplex where my sister and niece lived. It was a pretty European-style two-story house split right down the middle. It had been built to accommodate multiple families, with her place on the left and another residence on the right.

The front door opened, and Winnie bounded down the porch steps. "Aunt Ellie!"

While Selene's hair was more of a lighter shade, Winnie had the same deep brown as me. She launched herself into my arms with all the force of a wrecking ball in a sparkly tutu. A very unladylike grunt rolled out of me.

"Happy birthday, bestie." I squeezed her and rocked, sharing in her birthday excitement. "How old are you now? Twenty-seven? Forty-two?"

Winnie giggled and squeezed me back. "*Five.*"

I held her at arm's length and narrowed my eyes to slits. "I knew it. You *are* an old lady."

"I think I'm the only old lady around here." Selene

sighed, wiping her hands on a dish towel. Her hazel eyes looked tired, but I guessed that was what happened when you were a single mom with a shithead ex-husband and a daughter with buckets of energy.

"Thirty-six isn't that old, Mama!" Winnie squinted against the sunshine and called up to her mother.

Selene's soft smile was always stunning. "Well, that's a relief," she joked.

I grabbed my rolling suitcase and hauled it up the shared porch steps. Under the covered porch, my head dipped toward the adjacent home. "Got a new neighbor yet?"

"The Jeffersons moved out a few weeks ago, but no one new yet." Selene wrapped me in a side hug. "But thank goodness, because I was getting tired of hearing them have wild sex every night," she whispered.

"Tired or jealous?" I teased, which earned me a hip bump from my sister.

Heads together, we laughed, and a warmth spread under my ribs. Maybe being back at home for a while wasn't so bad after all.

Inside, Winnie's party was just getting started. I stashed my suitcase in the entryway closet and walked toward the voices in the back of the duplex.

Selene had decorated the entire lower level in hot pink, black, and gold. There was a glittery balloon arch, and a huge banner strung across the entryway to the kitchen read, *Vegas, Baby!*

I paused, my brows pinched down.

"Don't ask." My sister shook her head and laughed. "She could not be dissuaded."

Selene unhooked the velvet rope that led to the kitchen,

and I slipped through. "You're not going to even card me?" I teased.

Selene scoffed. "You're thirty-three, and I can see you're not using retinol."

I snarled at her before sticking out my tongue.

A few of the people were milling about in the kitchen, but the majority of the guests were hanging outside on the back deck.

"Bottle service is there." Selene pointed to the giant ice-filled tub of juice boxes and soft drinks. "All-you-can-eat buffet in the dining room and casino games on the back lawn. But I'll warn you, they're all rigged."

A shotgun burst of laughter erupted from my chest.

"Winnie said, and I quote, 'The house always wins.'" Selene's love and affection for her daughter was unparalleled.

I looked out the back windows to see my niece giggling and running around with her friends. "I seriously love that kid."

"That's because she's you in a different font," she said.

I blinked innocently, pressing my hands to my chest. "Completely lovable in every single way?"

She pinned me with a flat look. "Wildly optimistic and slightly unhinged."

I shrugged, selecting a juice box from the tub. "Same thing."

Together we walked out onto the back deck. I smiled and hugged old acquaintances. Selene left to wrangle the kids just as my little sister Kit walked up.

I wrapped her in a hug. "Skittle." I squeezed, using her childhood nickname. She was shorter than me by more than a few inches, but her personality was larger than life. The sunlight caught the fiery red strands in her chestnut hair, matching my little sister's firecracker personality perfectly.

"Surprised you decided to grace us with your presence," she teased with a hip bump.

Guilt for not taking the time to visit more often flickered over me, but I swept it away. "Hey, at least I'm better than Clara."

A short, disgusted noise rattled in the back of Kit's throat. "Ain't that the truth."

Our sister Clara had gone to college but if you asked me what she studied, I couldn't tell you. While I was designing and *running* events, she found her happiness attending them. Her fiancé's thriving tech company did more than enough to keep her social calendar completely booked. On social media she seemed more than thrilled with the direction her life had taken her.

Not that we saw her often enough to know for sure.

"Where are Mom and Dad?" I asked, looking around and taking a sip of my juice box.

I could see Kit fighting a smile. "Uh . . . Magic Mike was having a wardrobe malfunction."

The juice shot out of my mouth, landing in a splatter at her feet.

Kit's chestnut waves bounced as she chuckled. "Relax. Different Mike. This one is *actually* a magician. Mom was convinced she could fix his cape in time for his performance, so . . . we made do." Her chin jutted toward the back.

I looked across the yard to see my brother's best friend running across the lawn with a squealing child in a fireman's carry as the rest of the kids chased him. "Is that why Brody is fighting for his life over there?"

Her hands spread wide with a shrug, but her eyes moved over him and paused.

We watched with humor as he lost his battle with the tiny terrors and they tackled him to the ground. Brody worked for the local police department, so it was nice to see him having a little fun.

"Where is Hayes?" I asked, looking around for my moody oldest sibling.

Kit sighed and leaned against the deck railing. "You know how it goes with Hayes. He texted, saying he got a flat tire on the way over. He'll be here soon."

I shook my head. Poor Hayes. He literally had the worst luck of anyone I had ever met. We didn't *actually* believe he'd been cursed by the Lady, but sometimes it was hard to ignore that his luck was absolute shit.

"I'm going to go rescue Brody before the feral children stage a coup." Kit grinned and bounded down the stairs.

Sitting alone at a table on the side of the yard was old man Stafford. My heart rolled for him and the dilapidated farm that once held so many of my childhood memories. With a smile, I walked toward him.

The metal of the chair was cold against my palm. "This seat taken?"

He looked up, his blue eyes smiling. "Not for a pretty girl like you."

I curtsied and plunked down into the chair, my legs stretched in front of me and crossed at the ankles. "So what do you know, old man?"

He chuckled, a deep and friendly sound. "I know it's been too long since I've seen you around here, Miss Elodie Darling."

I scrunched my nose. "I know. Work had me so busy."

He shook his head. "No work is more important than

family and friends." He tapped the side of his nose. "That I do know."

His words landed somewhere deep in the part of me I didn't like to poke at too much. Because once upon a time, I had known that, but then I got too busy proving I was important, too busy proving I could keep up.

And now? Now I was back home, unemployed, drinking a juice box at a Vegas-themed birthday party for a kindergartner.

Deep down I knew Stan was right, and I wasn't sure when work had eclipsed how much I loved being home, but it had happened all the same. In that moment everything felt aimless, like I didn't know what I was going to do. It was much easier to shift my attention to the kind old man who was sipping pink lemonade out of a plastic martini glass.

"I drove past the farm today." I leaned forward, planting my chin on my hands with an exaggerated pout.

Mr. Stafford's eyes grew wistful, the spark dimming as he took another sip. "It's a sad thing when time passes and life changes on you."

I sat back in my chair. "I remember coming to the farm as a kid. It was the heart of Star Harbor—the pumpkin patch, the haunted forest walk. Mrs. Stafford's cider doughnuts were legendary."

At the mention of his late wife, Mr. Stafford perked up and smiled. "They were tasty."

"The *best*," I agreed. I closed my eyes and could almost feel the cinnamon-sugary outside on my tongue as I bit down on the pillowy fried doughnut.

Stan sighed. "Over the years, people stopped coming. Flashier tourist destinations popped up in nearby towns and drew people away. Now it seems the only time someone comes around is when they're trying to get a glimpse of the Lady walking the dunes."

My brain was spinning. *How could anyone just let the coolest place in town fall apart and be forgotten?*

Frankly, it kind of pissed me off. Stan looked so sad. There had to be something I could do for him.

And then the perfect idea hit me.

"You know what you need?" I sat up straighter, my brain firing on all cylinders. "A full-blown, family-friendly experience. Hayrides, haunted barns, spiked cider for the parents. People love taking selfies with scarecrows and buying homemade jams. The key is creating a social media–worthy vibe. If you make it fun, people *will* come back."

My attention returned to Mr. Stafford. The sparkle was back in his eyes, but he shook his head. "Hard to maintain a profit when you're only taking in money for one season."

I scoffed, undeterred. "One season? Who said that? You've got three other seasons to explore—people need Christmas trees. They already love apples. What about flowers and weddings? Oh!" I clasped my hands together. "A wedding! The top of that dune cliff would make for the most amazing photos."

The lines deepened on his face. "You really think people would come to something like that? Even after all these years?"

I grinned, knowing I had hooked him. The heady rush of closing a deal zipped through me. "Absolutely. People are obsessed with fall nostalgia these days. Plus, families are looking to get off devices and make *real* memories. You don't have to make it perfect—just make it fun. I would be happy to help you brainstorm."

"My Karen would have loved this." Mr. Stafford slapped the table. "You've got the vision, Miss Elodie, I'll give you that! There was a time I had considered selling the place, but what you're saying . . . well, that sounds like Karen's dream come true. I think we should do it."

I grinned but quickly recovered as his words fully registered. "Uh . . . *we?*" I let out a nervous laugh. "I mean, I was just spitballing, Mr. Stafford. Brainstorming. Thinking theoretically."

He nodded. "Yes, of course *we*. I can't do anything without a visionary like yourself. I'm just an old man." He gestured toward himself. "I can't pull this off without some help. If you've got ideas, I've got the space—and plenty of money to make it happen."

He winked and I was utterly charmed. "Um . . ." I tried to think on my feet. I needed a way out of this, to gently let the sweet old man down, but I came up blank.

"I mean . . . I am kind of in between projects at the moment," I hedged, suddenly feeling like I had stepped onto a conveyor belt moving at full speed. "But I'm only staying with Selene for a few days. Just a quick pit stop before figuring out my next big move."

Caught between guilt—I *had* made it sound amazing—and my childhood fondness for the farm, I was stuck.

"Don't you worry." He patted my hand.

Oh, I was very much worried. I had come home for a temporary emotional reset, not to accidentally sign up for a full-scale farm restoration. But somehow Mr. Stafford had me by the metaphorical balls.

And worse? A tiny, traitorous part of me was . . . *intrigued.*

I imagined the farm, picturing it the way it used to be—families wandering the pumpkin patch, the smell of fresh cider doughnuts, bonfires crackling in the cool autumn air. The idea shouldn't have been so tempting.

But, damn it, it was.

"I've got the perfect place for you," he continued smoothly, like a man who had *absolutely* just hustled me. "And I'll pay you handsomely. What do you say?" His eyebrows did a little bounce, and he was fully aware he had me backed into a corner.

A spark of excitement zipped through me, fast and electric. The idea shouldn't have felt this tempting, but there was no denying it—it did.

I wasn't staying, obviously. This wasn't my life. But maybe, just maybe, helping out for a little while would be good for me too.

Besides, what harm was a fun little distraction until something more serious came along?

Laughter bubbled up in my chest, bright and unstoppable, as I stuck out my hand. "You, Mr. Stafford, are a dangerous man. But hell—why not? Let's save a farm."

FOUR

CALLUM

Losing sucked.

Losing after a god-awful ninth inning where my best teammate let a ground ball roll straight past him? That was downright infuriating.

The guys and I played every Wednesday night for the Remington County men's twelve-inch, slow pitch softball league. Sure, we were the second-oldest team in the league, and our postgame ritual almost always included icing sore muscles and creaking knees, but we loved it.

Losing was a serious hit to our collective pride.

"I swear, Hayes," I muttered as I yanked off my baseball cap and dragged a hand through my damp hair before putting it on backward. "Did you not see the ball? Were your eyes closed?"

Hayes Darling, former town golden boy and reigning champion of bad luck, slumped against the dugout bench with a groan. "You think I wanted that to happen? I got caught in the sun." He held up his glove. "Besides, the stitching tore out of this fucking thing."

He threw his busted mitt into the dirt and pushed it farther away with his shoe.

Brody Shepherd scoffed, unwrapping the tape around his wrists. "Sure, buddy. The sun—the same sun that's been here all season?"

Hayes shot him a glare. "You wanna say that again, Shep?"

Brody just grinned at his best friend, always happy to poke the bear. "I'm just saying, if you need me to buy you some sunglasses, just say so."

"Boys, boys," Wes drawled, his voice full of mock wisdom as he leaned on his bat. "It was an early season game. Nobody's getting a championship ring here."

I shot him a glare. "Yeah, and yet I don't see you giving up your MVP beer at the Lantern when we do win."

Wes grinned. "Never."

Brody snorted. "Oh, don't act all high and mighty, Wes. You were two seconds away from chucking your glove into the dugout like a toddler when you struck out."

"A toddler with dignity," Wes corrected with a scowl.

The best part of our season included celebratory beers at the local dive after the game. Unfortunately for us, tonight they had become consolation beers, but I didn't mind. I needed a break.

"Anyway, I think we need another player," Brody said, tossing his mitt into his bag.

He wasn't wrong. Our team consisted of us four plus a few others, but because of work commitments, most of them were designated subs.

"I could always ask Austin," Brody offered.

A collective grumble of agreement rippled through the group. Having Brody's half brother on the team would certainly be an advantage. Austin was young, eager, and athletic.

Maybe he could run his ass into the ground without getting winded.

"Did Austin find an apartment?" I asked, unlacing my cleats and stuffing them into my gym bag.

"He's still looking," Brody said, shrugging. "He's couch surfing until he finds his own place, but I know he's itching to do something besides work at the marina. He was a decent baseball player in high school."

Hayes snorted, rubbing his shoulder and moving the arm in a slow circle. "Yeah, so was I. Look how that turned out."

"Anyway," Brody dragged out the word. "Beers at the Lantern?"

A round of grunts and nods signaled our agreement. Losing might've sucked, but postgame beers were always a win.

THE LADY's Lantern wasn't just a bar; it was a Star Harbor institution.

As we stepped inside, the carved wooden lantern sign flickered, casting a warm glow over the entrance. Inside, it smelled like old wood, whiskey, and history. The walls were plastered with relics of the town's obsession with the Lady of the Dunes—framed newspaper clippings of supposed sightings, grainy black-and-white photographs of a ghostly figure by the water, and, in one corner, a glass case housing what was allegedly a piece of her original wedding veil.

Tourists ate that shit up.

Even the drink menu played into the legend. The

Lady's Lament—a fancy gin cocktail that Brody once described as "tasting like a perfume bottle." The Sailor's Doom—a whiskey drink strong enough to knock out a grown man.

Ask me how I know.

As we slid into a booth, Wes stretched an arm along the back of his seat, looking around the packed bar. "Look at this shit." He gestured with his bottle to a group huddled around the veil taking selfies. "Never ceases to amaze me." His attention landed on me, eyebrows bouncing. "When's the Drifted Spirit finally going to live up to its namesake?"

My eyes flicked to Hayes as he slipped out of the booth to grab another round. Talking about the Lady always seemed to get under his skin.

I took a sip of my beer, the cold liquid cutting through the summer heat still clinging to my skin. "Never. The whole thing is ridiculous."

"Ridiculous or profitable?" Wes asked, tapping the Lady's Love Lock Fence pamphlet left on the table.

Brody smirked. "You have to admit, the Ghost Run 5K was fun. A bunch of idiots in glow-in-the-dark outfits running from an imaginary dead woman?" His hands spread wide. "Come on. That shit's funny."

I ignored them, swirling my beer. Sure, the legend made money, but I never once actually believed there was a ghost haunting the streets of Star Harbor.

Conversation shifted to work and women as Hayes reclaimed his spot in the booth. Eventually, the sting of the game faded. I paid my tab and headed home.

The inn was quiet when I pulled up. The soft glow of the windows was stark against the cloudy, starless sky. A few guests were sitting out back, enjoying a small fire as I headed toward the side entrance. I raised my hand to be friendly, but exhaled a sigh of relief as soon as I slipped into the kitchen. It still smelled of the afternoon chocolate chip cookies I made and Helen baked every afternoon. The thousands of positive reviews proved that my idea of afternoon cookies was well received.

Besides, what monster doesn't like cookies?

Fresh irritation rolled over me as I looked at my phone for the third time. Levi was supposed to have checked in with me when he got back from hanging out with his friends.

Of course, he hadn't.

Levi was officially done with school for the summer, which meant I had three full months to keep a teenage boy out of trouble.

I wasn't sure how the hell I was supposed to do that.

Inside, I peeked into his room and smirked. He was sprawled across his bed, one foot hanging off the side, headphones over his ears, the bluish glow of his phone illuminating his face.

At least he was here this time. That was my bar now—he made it home in one piece.

I exhaled. He had been slipping lately—staying out late, skipping school. The kind of behavior that had warning bells blaring in my head.

The last thing I needed was Levi becoming *me* at his age. Joining the Army was the only thing that straightened me out, and all I had to show for it was an armful of scars and an unsettling sense of regret.

The wooden doorframe was hard beneath my knuckles. His eyes flicked up, and he pulled one side of the headphones off his ear.

"Hey, Dad." The corner of his mouth tipped up.

My chest squeezed. Sometimes there were still tiny

moments when the little kid with crooked teeth and a big smile peeked through his surly teenage attitude.

Part of me wanted to remind him that he'd messed up and not let me know he'd gotten home. But lately it felt like all I was doing was riding his ass and pointing out the ways he was falling short. Trouble was, he *needed* to be accountable for his actions.

I couldn't win.

Mary had a way with Levi that I just . . . didn't. His therapist assured me I wasn't completely fucking him up, but there were days I wasn't so sure.

His eyebrows lifted as I waged an internal war.

"You need something?" he asked.

I scoffed. "No. Just glad you're home. Love you."

"You too." The words were barely out before his head-phones were back in place and his attention was focused on his phone. I stood in the doorway for half a second longer than I should have, like I was waiting for something.

An opening.

Exhausted and defeated, I walked down the hall to the primary suite. Levi and I lived downstairs, away from the main guest rooms of the inn. There was only one empty bedroom across the hall from Levi, but it was never a room to be rented and was typically only used by friends after a night out.

I never let a stranger that close to where we slept.

Slipping out of my dusty clothes, I tossed everything into the laundry hamper. My fingertips brushed over the bumps and ridges my scars had left behind. They ran from my wrist to my neck as a harsh reminder of the life I had chosen.

A quick, scalding shower was exactly what I needed to wash the day away. My nightly mental gymnastics came back in full force as I ran through everything I needed to prep for the next day. The inn ran like clockwork, but only because I was always on top of it.

After the shower, I carried the clothes basket to the large laundry room off the kitchen. Three washers and dryers stacked on top of one another lined one wall. An oversize washbasin for bleaching and soaking linens was along the other. During the renovation, Mary had decided to keep the oversize windows on the far wall that overlooked Star Harbor Farm.

I gazed into the darkness. Across the yard, something flickered in the distance. A glow. Too steady to be flashlights. Too low to be the moon. And coming from a place that should've been *empty*.

The abandoned cottage was glowing from inside.

My shoulders tensed as my eyes closed and I sighed.

Great.

Either the raccoons had learned how to work a light switch or some idiot was ghost hunting. Again.

After starting my laundry, I grabbed the wooden bat I kept by the side entrance and headed across the yard into the darkness. A breeze coming off Lake Michigan carried the scent of summer. If the clouds would only move out, it would have made for a beautiful, star-filled summer sky.

I stared at the dilapidated cottage. The flimsy curtains were drawn tight, but there didn't seem to be any movement inside. The worn-out porch creaked under my boots as I circumvented the hole I had created earlier in the week.

I knocked.

Nothing.

But I knew better than to trust silence. Silence was just the pause before all hell broke loose.

Another knock, harder this time. "Hey," I called. "You're trespassing."

Still nothing.

I sighed and tried the doorknob. Unlocked.

Fantastic.

I pushed it open, bat at the ready—and something shrieked, a horrible inhuman sound.

Then something collided with my chest.

Soft, warm, and tangled around me in a way that should not feel as good as it did. Bare, feminine legs locked around my thighs, the faint scent of vanilla and something else— something deeper—drifted between us. It was the kind of scent that got under a man's skin.

Dangerous.

From the collision, I lost my footing and slammed backward through the doorway as the bat clattered on the floor and rolled away. I landed on my ass with a woman on top of me—legs flailing, hands gripping my shoulders, a knee dangerously close to my balls.

"What the hell?" I grunted as my military instincts took over, locking my hands around her biceps to keep her from tearing me apart.

"Oh my god! Let me go, you psychopath! You just broke into my house!" the woman shrieked.

I blinked up at a pair of wild green eyes—furious, untamed, and way too pretty for someone currently trying to strangle me. The woman straddling me was an absolute stunner with wavy brown hair, wild from sleep, and she had a death grip on the collar of my T-shirt.

She smelled like exotic vanilla and pure trouble.

And I did not need to be noticing that.

I bucked my hips up slightly, trying to move out from

under her, and my traitorous cock took note. "I didn't break in. *You* are trespassing."

Her eyes narrowed. "I live here," she hissed. My hand flexed against her biceps, heat curling up my spine before I shoved it down.

Nope. Not happening.

The woman ripped her arm out of my grasp and slapped a hand on the floor beside me as she tried to climb off.

My stomach dropped as I sat up. "What?"

"I. Live. Here." She flicked a rogue strand of hair out of her face and stood above me, arms crossed. "Who are *you*?"

A soft glow from the lamp was warm on her skin. She was dressed in an oversize T-shirt and tiny shorts, her skin practically glowing. I couldn't remember the last time I'd seen a woman, rumpled and sleepy, in nothing more than a flimsy pair of pajamas.

My hand flexed at the thought of exploring every inch of that creamy skin. Irritated at myself and her, I bit back a growl.

"No one lives here." I stood, crossing my arms and mirroring her stance.

Fire danced in her eyes at my refusal to leave. "I'm calling the police!"

I held up a hand. "You don't need to do that." I gestured toward the inn. "I'm the owner of the Drifted Spirit. I saw a light on and came to check it out for Stan. Sometimes we get trespassers, and his house is clear across the property."

Relief washed over her before her face twisted in an annoyed grimace. "What are you, the neighborhood watch?" She looked down at her elbow, and I noticed a small spot of blood from where she must have banged it against the floor. "Ow . . ." Her eyes moved back to me. "I'm staying here while I help Mr. Stafford revitalize things around the farm. Not that I owe *you* an explanation."

The air in my lungs seized.

Stan. The farm?

"No," I said, shaking my head. "That's not possible."

"Uh, yeah. Well, it is." Her hands went to her hips. "We shook on it."

My jaw locked. How long had I let myself daydream about the possibilities? I was *this close* to taking over that damn farm. Finally expanding the inn in order to build my own restaurant.

Stan had said it himself—he was ready to give it up. We had walked this fucking property, talked about how it made sense for me to be the one whom it would eventually go to.

It could be yours if you wanted it.

But now some random woman thinks she can snatch it out from under me?

I stepped closer, my frustration leaking into my voice. "You and Stan had a handshake deal?" I let out a sharp, humorless laugh. "That's cute. Because you know who else had one?" I poked a finger into my chest. "Me."

Sure, I was leaving out the part where I hadn't exactly *agreed* to anything, but I knew Stan was a man of his word. He was simply waiting for me to accept it.

"I have no idea what you're talking about." She tilted her head and plastered on a sweet smile, cutting me off. "But, clearly, plans change."

She flashed another sugar-sweet smile that made my blood pressure skyrocket. It made me want to either shake some sense into her or pin her against the wall and see if she'd smile like that for an entirely different reason.

I'm sure to her I sounded completely unhinged, but my blood was boiling. My nostrils flared. This woman was pushing all the right buttons, and after the day I'd had, I was in no mood for her bullshit. I didn't care how pretty or feisty she was.

I exhaled, slow and measured. I had two choices: start a fight with this woman in a barely standing cottage, or keep my cool and figure out what the hell just happened.

I scraped a hand down my face.

Option two won out, though I'd be lying if I didn't acknowledge there was some appeal to going toe-to-toe with a smoking-hot brunette.

She smirked like she'd already won—like she wasn't standing in a house she had no business claiming. Like she hadn't just pulled the rug out from under me without even realizing it. My fists clenched at my sides, and I took a slow breath before I did something really fucking stupid, like kiss her just to shut her up.

Something flickered in my gut. Annoyance. Attraction. A bad idea waiting to happen.

Nope. Nope. Nope. Time to go.

"Fine." I exhaled, turning for the door. "Enjoy the rabid raccoons."

Her eyes darted toward the dark corners of the cottage. Just for a split second, and there it was—the tiniest flicker of hesitation.

I bit back a smirk and picked up my baseball bat with a swipe.

She lifted her chin, recovering fast. "I intend to," she shot back, voice dripping with stubborn pride.

I muttered a curse as I walked away, gripping the bat tighter than necessary.

This summer just got a whole lot more complicated.

FIVE

ELODIE

W HY HAD I opened my big mouth?

I sat up on the thin, sagging mattress and rubbed my temples as the slow, insistent plink of water echoed through the dark, empty cottage. The storm had rolled in fast last night, thick clouds swallowing the sky, and I had spent every minute of it lying awake, staring at the small leak in the ceiling.

Each drop landed in the metal mixing bowl I'd found in one of the cabinets—pinging like an incessant clock, counting down the minutes of my sleepless night.

Drip. Drip. Drip.

I sighed, tossing back the thin blanket. My eyelids felt like sandpaper, my limbs heavy from exhaustion, but I couldn't sit in this critter-filled dungeon a second longer.

The morning wind howled as I stepped onto the front porch, wrapping my arms around myself. The air was thick with the scent of damp earth, petrichor, and pine. The storm had passed, leaving behind a washed-clean sky, the first pale streaks of sunrise peeking over the tree line to the east.

And then I saw it.

A small, beat-up box of Band-Aids perched on the porch railing.

I didn't have Band-Aids, but I had scraped my elbow last night in my highly dramatic collision with Star Harbor's resident asshole, and now, conveniently, a box had appeared overnight.

The storm must have blown them here—or, more likely, the storm in human form next door had dropped them off and didn't want to admit it.

At first I had thought the man was an intruder and I was ready to defend myself, teeth bared and claws out. Instead, I had been met with rich brown eyes, dark hair, and tattoos that seeped onto thick, muscled forearms. A few even leaked onto the backs of his hands and knuckles. He had scars, *lots* of them—trailing up his arm and disappearing beneath the sleeve of his T-shirt.

My stomach flipped at the memory of how my fear had morphed into instant intrigue. He was pure contradiction— dark eyes that saw too much, hands that looked like they'd built a thousand things but also ruined them, a voice that was both gravel and silk.

And then he had to open his mouth and ruin the illusion. He was irritable, and for some reason his clipped, annoyed tone was aimed directly at me.

As if simply existing was some heinous crime.

Shaking my head, I pushed off the railing and took in the wreckage around me. The cottage was in rough shape. The wood-planked walls were weathered and warped from years of neglect. The flower beds were completely overrun, thick vines and early-summer blooms bursting through the mess like nature was reclaiming what was once hers.

Still, it could be beautiful again, and apparently I had

nothing but time to kill. Cleaning the dilapidated cottage was first on the list.

Hours later, I hadn't made much progress on cleaning up the house. I tied my hair into a messy bun, exhaling as I wiped down the grimy kitchen counter. My arms ached from hours of scrubbing, my hands raw from scouring layers of caked-on dirt off the bathroom floor, but I had officially declared war on this house. If I was going to live in a literal horror movie set, the least I could do was not get tetanus while doing it.

I straightened, stretching my sore back, and caught movement out the front window, then grinned as Stan came into view.

I walked to the door and opened it for him with a smile.

He walked toward the porch, hands tucked into his pockets, eyes skimming the cottage like he was assessing whether it was still standing.

"Morning, Miss Elodie," he called, climbing the steps and stepping inside. "You survived the storm, then?"

"*Survived* is a strong word," I muttered, waving a hand toward the dark stain on the ceiling. "Your haunted shack here has a built-in rain feature."

"Sorry about that." Stan chuckled, leaning against the railing. "Could be worse. Could have fallen straight through the floorboards in your sleep."

I leveled him with a look. "Comforting. Thank you."

His grin deepened, but his gaze drifted toward the farmhouse in the distance, his expression going thoughtful.

"Are you planning to take a break from all this?" He gestured toward my cleaning supplies, his lips twitching.

I wiped sweat from my brow, following his gaze to the rolling acres of land stretching toward the farm property. "Maybe. Thought I'd walk around a little today."

Stan nodded approvingly. "Good idea. Helps to see what you're working with." He hesitated, then added, "I know this place is in rough shape. If you're looking for another project, I'd be happy to front the money for supplies to fix it up."

I thought about his offer. Sure, I had a little savings, but it certainly wasn't enough to live off *and* fix up a house that wasn't even technically mine. Day to day would be a whole lot easier if I wasn't worried about uninvited houseguests, like raccoons or annoyingly handsome neighbors.

I smiled at Stan. "I can work with that." I let out a reluctant laugh, then hooked my thumbs into my back pockets as we started walking. "Hey, what's up with that place?" I asked, nodding toward the inn. "It's beautiful."

The Drifted Spirit Inn stood like something out of an old novel—haunting, elegant, the kind of place that carried a thousand untold stories in its bones. A three-story Victorian beauty with a towering turret, crisp white paint, and dark-green shutters that framed its many windows like watchful eyes.

A wraparound porch stretched wide, its rocking chairs swaying gently in the lake breeze. A faded wooden sign swung gently from a wrought iron bracket by the front steps, the words *Drifted Spirit Inn* hand-painted in delicate gold script. Beneath it, a small plaque read: *Established 1886.* Despite its ghostly name, the inn felt *alive* in its own way—holding its breath, waiting for someone to fall in love with it all over again.

It was the kind of place that pulled you in before you even realized you'd stepped closer.

I wasn't sure what surprised me more—that a broody, imposing man ran an inn at all, or that it somehow made perfect sense.

Stan followed my gaze, his eyes crinkling at the edges. "That'd be Callum Blackwood's place. Drifted Spirit Inn."

Callum.

My lips pursed. The infuriating, handsy man whom I had practically tackled last night.

I blinked. "He runs that whole place by himself?" I asked as we walked along the fence line that separated the two properties.

Something about that didn't fit. He didn't seem like the bed-and-breakfast type, the welcoming-and-hospitable kind. He seemed more like the stay-the-hell-out-of-my-way-or-I'll-burn-this-town-to-the-ground type.

Mr. Stafford picked up a stone, inspected it, and tossed it aside. "Helen keeps him from working himself into the ground. But yes, it's his. Has been for years now."

I glanced back at the inn, my curiosity buzzing. "Is Helen his wife?"

Stan sighed, rubbing his jaw. "No, Cal lost his wife several years back. Been raising his son ever since. He and Levi—his boy—live there," Stan added. "Took some time, but Cal made it work after Mary passed. Helen Harris works for him. She's more the mothering type."

Something soft bloomed beneath my ribs, a quiet, unwelcome tug in my chest. A single dad, raising a son alone. Grieving a wife. Keeping a business afloat.

I had no business feeling anything about that. The man was a menace, a walking mood swing wrapped in muscle and a bad attitude. He was also—annoyingly, unfairly, completely—the kind of guy a girl could spend too much time trying to figure out.

Absolutely not.

I was not going to get curious about Callum Blackwood.

Nope. No soft spots for grumpy innkeepers.

I crossed my arms, looking away. The idea of Callum—tall, scowling, built and tattooed like a Norse god—being a single dad was something I was not prepared to process.

The sharp annoyance I'd felt last night was still there, but now it tangled with something else.

I didn't like it.

I also didn't like the way my stomach had a weird little reaction to the thought of him raising a kid alone. I certainly didn't like that the small, silent act of kindness—a stupid box of Band-Aids—had settled into my chest like its own unwelcome houseguest.

I suddenly had a whole lot of questions about a man I absolutely did not need to be thinking about.

So I did what I always did when something made me uncomfortable.

I assigned it a word—*thoughtfulness*—shoved it down, rolled my shoulders, and pasted on a smirk.

"Let's dig into the details." My gaze swept across the rolling hills. "Tell me what I'm working with here."

Love and nostalgia filled Stan's blue eyes. "Back in the nineties, Karen and I purchased fifty-one acres. We were hoping to return to my farming roots, settle in, and live a quiet life." He pointed toward a simple house far across the property. "Never could have children of our own, but we lived there and had a happy life together."

I smiled at how proud the old man was.

"For a time, the farm was doing well. We had families come for outings, pick out their pumpkins, that kind of thing. Karen liked to bake, so she also offered some simple treats."

I hummed with a smile. "I remember."

"Eventually, we also bought the orchard across the way," he continued, "putting us right at 142 acres."

In the distance, scraggly trees were overgrown but still appeared to be flowering and producing fruit.

"Okay." I frowned, my mental to-do list rapidly growing.

"Now I pay some locals to tend to the trees." My eyes tipped to him and he continued: "They do the bare minimum, mind you. I just need someone letting me know if disease spreads or we lose any trees. They're paid in free produce."

I nodded as my brow furrowed. Tackling a project of this scale was going to take time, patience, and lots and lots of money.

"If you can't do this, tell me now," he said, as if reading my thoughts. "You look worried."

"Not at all," I said, turning to Stan. "I don't have to worry when I know this is going to be incredible." My thoughts drifted to Callum. "Is that neighbor of yours going to be a problem?"

Stan sighed, looking back toward the inn in the distance. "I don't think so. Some days it gets to be too much. He knows I've been feeling burned out for a while. I thought he might make an offer one day but . . ." Stan trailed off like the fact Callum wasn't falling over himself to buy the farmland saddened him. "Truth be told, I didn't even realize how much of a future this farm still had in it until you showed up."

Pride expanded in my chest, and I shot him a wide grin. "Then it looks like we have a beautiful family farm to revitalize."

I stretched my arms wide, taking in the overgrown farmland in front of me, holding it in my imaginary embrace.

Stan chuckled, shaking his head. "That we do, Miss Elodie. That we do."

~

I LAY in the middle of an overgrown field, starfish style, staring at the blinding sun. Grounding into the earth, my mind wandered to the farm and its possibilities.

I nearly cried from overwhelm when Stan handed me a banker's box filled with paper. *Nothing* for Star Harbor Farm was digitized. I was, quite literally, starting from scratch.

A devious grin spread across my face. Unencumbered by rules or expectation, this farm could be whatever I dreamed up, and if there was one thing I excelled at, it was dreaming.

I had plans to meet with the accountant later in the week, but Stan assured me that while still operational, the farm had operated in the black and earned enough that, even now, finances weren't a problem.

Community engagement.

That was his problem. Star Harbor didn't realize what a gem the farm was—what it *could* be.

I sat up, plucking dried grass from the back of my hair, before grabbing my sketchbook. Sitting with my legs crossed, I flipped to an open page and started scribbling. A large rectangle with an oval drawn around it was labeled *pumpkin patch—tractor ride to get there.* Another rectangle *—corn maze. Is it too late to plant? Orchard—phase two project.*

Selene was an art teacher, so maybe she knew of a few talented kids who could help with painting, maybe even a mural or posters to spread the word.

With each idea, the sketch, and my excitement, grew. My mind zipped faster than my hand could draw, and one idea tumbled into the next.

I flipped the page to a fresh sheet and began mocking up a poster with stick figures. If I was going to rally the community, I knew building buzz early was key. As it stood, the farm was as much of a ghost as the Lady, but I could bring it back to life.

I stretched my legs, tapping the toes of my hunter green boots together as I thought. Mud clung to the bottoms and sides, but against the bright-green grass, with my jeans rolled at the hem, I already looked the part. Phone in hand, I leaned back, framing my rubber boots in the shot with the dunes and Lake Michigan blurring in the background. An idea took root.

The pumpkin patch.

I shot to my feet, not bothering to dust myself off, and ran toward the old pumpkin patch, my sketchbook tucked under my arm. A huge grin spread across my face as the section of land that once grew pumpkins came into view.

Sprawling, leafy green vines with large broad leaves were woven between tall, overgrown grasses. My heart rate climbed higher as I noted each vine starting to produce multiple yellow flowers, some even showing the first signs of tiny green pumpkins forming at the base of female flowers.

Despite years of neglect, they'd survived and continued to grow on a volunteer basis. When a vine produced a pumpkin, it had been left to rot, spilling its seeds into the land for another year.

With my bare hands, I carefully worked around a small patch of vines, ripping out the unwanted grass from the roots and tossing the clumps aside. I cradled a little pale-green pumpkin as I gently moved it to the side and continued weeding a section of dirt. I turned in a circle, admiring the small clearing I'd created.

Perfect.

Mud was caked under my nails, and a few tiny scratches stung my wrists and forearms. I toed off my boots, not caring that my socks sank into the soft, wet earth. Arranging the wild vines to flow across the toe of my boots, I smiled at the contrast of sunny, yellow blooms against the rich, hunter green of my work boots. Once the arrangement was perfect, I stepped back and quirked my head. Lowering myself to my belly, I held my phone's camera out to frame the picture.

A giddy zip of excitement tickled my ribs as I angled the camera to capture the midmorning light just right. After taking a few photos from various angles, I opened an editing app and filtered the image to be soft and cheerful, yet still moody and interesting.

Rallying the community behind me could start by spreading the word through a social media page. I frowned, staring at the app and thinking of the perfect username for the farm. I wanted something simple yet catchy enough to grab the attention of locals *and* tourists.

@StarHarborRoots

My hands shook so badly I could barely type as I set up the account. I chose the stylized photo and wrote my first caption: *Legendary Roots, Fresh Beginnings. Coming This Autumn.*

I added every hashtag I could think of, including the Star Harbor tourist board and even the local women's historical society. Without hesitation, I hit "Post" and sucked in a lungful of fresh lake water air.

It was publicly official. I had only a few months to make this place ready for the families of Western Michigan.

I crossed my arms and took in the land. Amy's parting words still stung as they snaked through my mind.

I need someone who can follow through, not just get excited about the next project.

Being excited wasn't a bad thing, and I could prove to everyone that I had the follow-through it took to make this project not only happen, but become a resounding success.

Nothing and no one could stop me.

CALLUM

I HAD TO STOP HER.

Irritation rolled through me as I watched my new neighbor leap off the top step of her porch and skip—yes, skip—across the lawn toward a truck that came to a stop near the road. For whatever reason, my new, unwelcome neighbor had burrowed under my skin. More times than I liked to admit, I found myself peeking out of the kitchen window toward the little crumbling cottage. Neither the storm nor the raccoons had scared her off yet, and I was starting to worry that nothing might get her to leave.

She wore dark, straight-leg denim, cuffed at the ankle, and a simple white T-shirt, streaked with dirt. Sunlight caught in her brown hair, highlighting strands of gold that wove through her soft curls. She threw her head back in laughter at something the man said. Despite my distance, I imagined the sound was bright and bubbly, the kind of laughter that had a melodic quality and tickled the hairs on the back of your neck.

Ideally, her laugh would be an ugly, grating sound like a honking goose or a wet, wheezing sound.

I laughed to myself at the mental image of those sounds coming from her as I rinsed a plate and stacked it into the industrial-size dishwasher.

"What, or should I say *who*, has got you smiling like that?" Helen's voice was laced with humor as it floated over my shoulder.

I fixed my face and wiped my hands on a dish towel before turning toward her. "I'm not smiling."

A disbelieving snort pushed out of her nose. "Of course not." She looked at the stack of dishes neatly arranged in the dishwasher. "I thought Levi was taking care of that this morning."

"Yeah, well . . ." I sighed. "Me too."

Helen knew I was struggling to connect with him lately. For the past few months it seemed like my little boy was slipping further and further away and there wasn't a damn thing I could seem to do about it. The more I pushed for connection, the more he pulled away, retreating further into himself.

The boy needed structure. Discipline. Trouble was, the last thing he wanted was to hear it from me.

She came up beside me, patting the back of my shoulder. "It's all a phase. The good parts as well as the not-so-good parts. Don't forget that."

Levi used to follow me around like my shadow. Now? I felt like a stranger in my own damn house. Like I was watching my kid slip through my fingers and had no clue how to grab hold of him before he was gone entirely.

I hung my head, letting the weight of it settle over me. "I got it." I offered a halfhearted smile. "Thanks, Helen."

She shooed me away from the sink with a flick of her wrist. "Now go on. Get out of here. Aren't you supposed to be taking the morning off?" She raised an accusatory eyebrow.

One day a week Helen left early to attend a meeting with the Keepers, and I filled in at the front desk if other staff weren't available to greet our guests.

The Star Harbor Historical Society was a women's group that had been going strong in Star Harbor since the late eighteen hundreds. Informally known as the Keepers, they were a pillar in our small community, bringing in fresh ideas, helping small businesses, and acting as the record keepers for all things related to the Lady of the Dunes—though no one outside of the group actually knew what went on during those meetings.

I looked at Helen and offered a small smile. It was nice that she had an active social life outside of the inn.

At least one of us did.

I never knew what to do with myself outside of work and wrangling Levi. "I'm going," I surrendered, hanging the hand towel off the handle of the dishwasher to dry.

By the time I got to my room, I'd decided on a run to clear my head. A run was a good idea. I needed to shake loose the tightness in my chest, the kind that had been building. It had absolutely nothing to do with my chances of snooping on my new neighbor to see what she was up to.

After changing into a white T-shirt and running shorts, I laced up my shoes and headed out the side door. The path that ran between my property and the farm was quiet, and I shoved down the little pang of disappointment when I didn't see her right away. The cottage was dark inside, with no signs of movement. I pushed myself, running harder than necessary, simply to clear my mind.

It could be yours if you wanted it.

Ever since Stan mentioned, offhand like it was nothing,

that he could see me purchasing the land someday, I'd foolishly assumed that was the plan. Sure, it wasn't official—nothing on paper, no formal offer—but it didn't need to be. I thought Stan had trusted me. I figured that when he was really ready to step back, I'd be the one to step in.

I could have jumped at the chance to expand, but instead I'd hesitated.

A flush of frustration ran through me.

That land was a piece of this town's backbone. It wasn't meant to be somebody's pet project or another half-baked dream. Stan was well past retirement age—there was no way he could manage a fully operational farm again. If she thought she could waltz in and treat it like some cash-cow side hustle, she had another thing coming.

The old man was at risk of someone taking advantage of him. He was smart, but too kind and trusting. My jaw clenched as I thought about the newcomer pulling one over on Stan.

While she didn't appear to be the cold, heartless type, I knew looks could be deceiving. It didn't matter that the woman appeared to be a complicated mixture of cool confidence and warm smiles, wrapping around you like impenetrable sunshine.

It annoyed the fuck out of me.

I strayed from my usual route to swing across the landscape and atop a hill that overlooked the farm. Tucked into the far corner, Stan's house stood like a testament to the man himself. It had been built in the sixties, and though Stan and Karen had breathed new life into the home, its simple, single-story structure and warm brick exterior remained largely unchanged.

I liked that.

I frowned at the new activity that was underway. My

gut twisted. *That should be me out there.* Since our talk, I had been waiting for the right moment to speak to Stan about purchasing the farmland—but I'd waited too damn long. Now he appeared fully invested in giving it a facelift because of *her*.

In the old pumpkin patch, laborers were hunched over, clearing the unruly area with nothing but hand tools and backbreaking effort. If it were me, I would have taken a plow to the entire area.

Started fresh.

It was strange to see so much activity on the long-forgotten farmland. My quiet corner of Star Harbor, disturbed by a naive woman with a determined glint in her eye.

I scanned the faces of the workers, curious whether she was out there among them.

I scoffed. It wouldn't have surprised me. She seemed like the bleeding-heart type.

Determined to run her out of my mind, I forced my legs to get moving again. Curiosity piqued, I wasn't above a little trespassing and ran right through Star Harbor Farm to get a closer look at whatever else she was orchestrating. Outside of attempting to clear the pumpkin patch, everything else looked like the same, neglected farmland.

Holding that knowledge, the last leg of my run was infused with fresh confidence. I pushed harder, ran faster, all with a lightness in each step. There was no way in hell she could pull off whatever scheme she thought she was cooking.

I made a mental note to call my financial planner to discuss my options. Revitalized farm or not, Stan was still getting older and couldn't hold on to it forever. I needed to get my ducks in a row if I planned a full-on hostile takeover and to purchase it before she could. Hell, I had no idea whether that was her plan, but money talked. I needed a handle on the situation before that woman ruined everything for me.

My steps faltered when I circled back toward the inn and saw Wes's truck parked in front of her cottage. Chest heaving, I used my shirt to wipe the sweat from my forehead and scanned the area. Soon the pair came into view and my jaw clenched.

She and Wes walked, side by side, rounding the cottage and coming to a stop in front of the porch steps. She beamed up at him with her bright smile, and something heavy twisted in my gut. Wes was explaining something, his arm sweeping wide to gesture at the cottage.

With her face tipped toward the sun, she reached out to playfully brush her hand against his forearm. Her laughter floated over the lake breeze, sweet and melodic.

I knew it.

A sharp, ugly twist coiled in my gut, like I'd swallowed a mouthful of something sour. I didn't know what irritated me more—how easy she made everything look, or the fact that Wes seemed to be eating it up.

Her attention snagged on me, standing at the edge of the grass, staring like some unhinged madman. Wes must have noticed, because soon he was turning and looking at me too.

His face split into a wide grin as he raised his hand. "Cal."

I shook my head, cursing myself for not minding my own business, and walked toward them. I kept my attention on Wes, but I could feel her stare boring into the side of my face.

I held out my hand. "Morning. What brings you around?"

"Work." Wes owned his own construction company, and, given the state of the cottage, it was safe to assume he was being hired to help fix it up. "You know Elodie?"

The woman's voice cut through our conversation. "Hello, Callum."

My eyes whipped to hers. *How the hell did she know my name?*

The sound of my name coming from her mouth landed like a sucker punch—familiar, like she knew me. Like she had the right to say it with the perfect amount of husky teasing.

My frown deepened as her name rolled around inside my head. *No fucking way.* "Elodie . . . as in Hayes's sister Elodie?" Not only had someone swooped in and hijacked the future I'd been counting on—but it was Hayes's sister? That made it so much worse.

My friend was the oldest sibling in his family and often mentioned his sisters. I had met Selene and Kit, who lived in town, but only knew Elodie and Clara by name.

Her thin-lipped smile was strained. "That would be me. I didn't know you knew Hayes."

My answer was clipped. "Very well, actually."

Hayes was one of the best men I knew. He had good judgment. Smart instincts. But if he thought his sister belonged here, fixing up a farm she had no business touching, maybe he wasn't as sharp as I thought.

She scoffed, a light disgusted noise rattling in the back of her delicate throat. "Not that well, apparently."

Between us, Wes chuckled, and his hand clamped onto my shoulder, giving it a squeeze. "I've got my work cut out for me."

My eyes didn't leave Elodie's, but I grunted, knowing exactly what he meant.

With a shake of his head, Wes turned back to Elodie. "I'll send a quote in a few days and you can decide if you'd like to move forward. You've got my number."

Her face morphed into pure sweetness. "Thank you, Wes."

He nodded. "Anytime, Ellie." He turned to me, my face souring at his use of a nickname for her. "See you at the game."

I nodded, trying to scrape together the remaining bits of my sanity. When Wes was back in the cab of his truck, I turned to her. "How do you know my name?"

A slim shoulder lifted as her chin rose. "I know more than you think." Her bored expression was a challenge I couldn't back away from.

I leaned forward, ever so slightly using my height to my advantage. "This is my town."

This time, a genuine laugh cracked out of her, taking me by surprise. "Okay," she mocked.

I narrowed my eyes. "You can roll your eyes all you want, but I've been here long enough to know when someone's in over their head," I grumbled, fists clenched.

"No. No, by all means, please claim the town that I grew up in as *your town*." Her fingers curled into air quotes, and she laughed again.

Knowing full well I was acting like a gigantic baby, I doubled down. "You don't know the first thing about running a farm."

Her mouth parted like she was about to argue, but I caught it—the flicker of something behind her sharp green eyes. A challenge. A dare. Like she wanted me to underestimate her just so she could prove me wrong.

Her arms crossed, pushing her tits higher beneath the thin white T-shirt. "I don't need to run it. I need to rescue it. Besides, I can learn anything."

Her unbridled confidence was astounding. Elodie fully believed every word. My life had taught me that even with the best of intentions, sometimes life still grabbed you by the balls.

I shrugged, crossing my arms and looking down at the gorgeous, infuriating neighbor. "Fix up the place, I don't care. All that means is less work for me when it comes time to buy it. I'll be taking it over when this little side quest of yours fails."

Her jaw set, her whole body humming with defiance. I'd known plenty of dreamers who thought they could outwork reality, and I knew exactly how their stories ended. It was just a matter of time before the shine wore off, before the hard parts set in and she packed her bags. I wasn't wrong about her. Not yet.

Fire blazed in her green eyes. "You are a self-righteous asshole."

I let my gaze wander lazily over her shoulder to the run-down house behind her. I smirked, slow and deliberate, because I knew it would piss her off more. "And you're a stubborn pain in the ass who's in over her head."

Her stance widened, like she was squaring off despite our significant size difference. "I'll prove you wrong."

My cheek twitched. There was something fun about poking this particular bear. "You can certainly try."

She was fire and fight, all wrapped up in one frustratingly beautiful package. And if she wanted a war? I'd give her one.

I shook my head. Once upon a time I might have been

tempted to see this gorgeous, feisty woman as a friend and ally.

She had walked in and disrupted everything. If she wanted to play farmer, *fine*—I'd let her, but when she crashed and burned? I'd be there, ready to take back what *should* have been mine.

She may be my friend's little sister, but it was official. Elodie Darling just became my fiercest rival.

SEVEN

ELODIE

I REALLY WISH he was ugly.

Even his scowl was attractive in an infuriating, punchable way. But in reality, it did make me feel less guilty for wanting to hit Cal right in his stupid, handsome face.

Didn't matter.

Given the chance, I'd still like to get in a cheap shot, if it weren't for the fact that I'd probably break my hand on that chiseled jawline.

Fuming, I turned away from him and stomped up the stairs. When my foot plowed through another rotted board, I stumbled, ass in the air as I fell forward onto all fours. Cal's soft, husky laugh made my face turn hot.

I straightened, yanking the hem of my T-shirt and ignoring the cavern opening in my stomach. I shot a glare over my shoulder.

He's not that handsome anyway.

THE NEXT DAY, still thoroughly irritated, I collapsed onto the floor of the living room, limbs splayed out like a chalky crime scene outline. If anyone found me, I'd tell them I was mourning the tragic loss of my patience—and the last remaining shreds of my dignity.

Despite what Cal Blackwood thought, I wasn't some directionless mess. Sure, my track record was . . . *chaotic*, but that didn't mean I was incapable. He didn't know a damn thing about me, yet he was so sure I would fail. That man was so certain that I would pack my bags and run.

A small, infuriated part of me wanted to prove him wrong.

KIT

Holy shit! What did you do?

I stared at my phone with a crease in my brow. *Well . . . any number of things, really.*

Twisted my ankle and broke three nails trying to wade through the overgrown orchard.

Contemplated building a Cal voodoo doll out of straw and pure spite. Still considering that one.

Found a newspaper clipping of Cal, standing in front of the inn with a sexy scowl, and poked holes through his eyeballs.

Had a wildly realistic sex dream about the aforementioned grumpy neighbor who hates me.

Though, honestly, maybe I should just set up a damn boxing ring and settle this properly—because, apparently, by helping Stan, he thinks I stole something from him.

That was the kicker, wasn't it? Cal didn't just hate that I was here—he hated that I was standing in the way of whatever future he had envisioned for the farm.

I knew that look. He wanted it. Badly.

I frowned at the thought, turning it over in my head. *Why?*

For a guy who constantly looked like he wanted to be anywhere but here, it didn't make much sense. *What did he want with a pumpkin patch and an overgrown orchard?*

KIT

Literally everyone is talking about the farm!
Are you losing your shit?

A heady zip tore through me. The social media post must have gained some traction with the locals. I quickly opened the app to check, and my phone nearly tumbled from my hand.

Not just *some* attention, *lots* of attention.

There were thousands of likes and comments under the photo of my muddy boots in the pumpkin patch. The page even had real followers.

I was officially losing my shit. If I was going to be a public spectacle, I might as well put on a show.

I dialed my little sister, and she answered on the second ring with a squeal.

Holding the phone from my ear, I grimaced, though a wide smile replaced it.

"Literally everyone is talking about it," Kit said.

"I had no idea . . ." I continued to scroll through the hundreds of comments.

"No going back now, huh?" She laughed.

"This is incredible." I grinned as I scrolled. There was never an option to *not* do what I set out to do. "Do you want to hang out tonight? I heard there's a band playing at the Lantern."

"Can't," she said. "I've got a meeting with the Keepers."

The historical society was 90 percent social club and 10

percent nonprofit organization. With a mix of old and young, being a part of the Keepers was a privilege, and somewhere deep inside me, I had missed connecting with other women.

"She is everywhere and she is nowhere," I said with mock reverence, repeating the warning we'd heard over and over in our childhood. It was practically the mantra of the historical society.

We both giggled. Growing up in Star Harbor meant you were forced to live in the Lady's shadow. *Everything* revolved around her and the legend. A few times I even bought into the idea she was real, but hard evidence of an apparition was hard to come by.

"The meeting starts in an hour, if you want to come. This month we're working on needlepoint, but we just started," she offered.

I didn't know a single thing about needlepoint, but that wouldn't matter. With a resolute nod, I grinned. "Save me a spot. I'll be there."

Without waiting to say goodbye, I ended the call with Kit and scrambled to my feet. A thrill ran through me. I'd missed this—the friendship, our community, the way Star Harbor wrapped around you whether you liked it or not.

After five minutes of scrubbing, I gave up on trying to get all the dirt from under my chipped nails. I slipped on a long, cornflower blue sundress and simple flip-flops. The summer sun was sagging against the tree line when I stepped onto the front porch and frowned at the empty driveway.

I really need a car.

With a determined nod, I turned myself around and kicked off my sandals. It was only a couple of miles to walk into town, but a pair of sneakers would save my already aching feet. After I changed shoes, I slipped the long strap of my purse over my head and headed in the direction of the main road. As I passed the Drifted Spirit Inn, delicate instrumental music floated across the evening air.

I paused, taking in the gorgeous building up close. Set against the trees, its moody exterior was warm and inviting against the slashes of crimson-and-gold sunset. It was the kind of place that welcomed you inside, tempting you with the promise of a well-worn chair and a cracked-spine paperback.

Too bad its owner was such a thorn in my side; otherwise I might have let curiosity get the best of me and walk inside to poke around.

Instead, I filed it away as one more thing Callum Blackwood had ruined for me. Right between *the peace and quiet of my own home* and *the universal appeal of a strong jawline*.

With Cal's brooding face flashing in my mind, I stomped away with freshly renewed determination. I made it only a mile down the road before the overhead trees blocked out any remaining sunlight. The air was warm, but thick with tension. My ears pricked as I listened for any signs of life on the desolate road. The only sounds were the soft thud of my sneakers against the pavement.

Everyone knew that traveling alone on any stretch of quiet country road in Star Harbor was risky. Generally speaking, the town itself was very safe. Crime rates were nearly nonexistent, but it wasn't a lurking madman or criminal mastermind that had me nervously peeking over my shoulder.

It was a ghost.

She is everywhere and she is nowhere.

A chill tickled my back, and I pulled my arms around

my middle. Light was swallowed up by the swaying trees that lined the roadway. My ears tuned to every creak and snap of twigs. A rustle of leaves to my right formed a lump in my throat, and I locked my eyes ahead of me, refusing to peer into the darkened tree line.

"It's a deer, or a mouse, or a stray cat," I whispered to myself, refusing to let my imagination take over. My feet pounded against the pavement, and my legs burned as I quickened my pace.

Ahead, a soft yellow glow peeked through the trees. My eyes widened, struggling to adjust to the change as light slanted through the forest. The bend in the road obscured my view, and I couldn't quite make out what I was seeing.

My jaw clenched as my blood cooled. With a sharp turn, the light flicked across my face, and I released my breath with an unsteady laugh.

A freaking car.

Not a vengeful spirit. Not a harbinger of doom. Just good old-fashioned internalized paranoia.

I chuckled again, feeling silly for thinking it could have been anything else. I stepped off the road onto the gravel shoulder as I continued walking. Instead of passing by, the truck slowed.

Without knowing who it was, I raised my hand in greeting. With my head high, I kept walking, but when I heard the vehicle stop, I glanced over my shoulder. White taillights flashed as the truck began to back up.

Curious, I stopped to look at the driver.

The window lowered and Cal's irritated voice greeted me. "What the hell do you think you're doing?"

Relieved and annoyed, I pasted on a slim smile. A snappy retort was on the tip of my tongue, but I decided I wasn't going to let him sour my mood. Instead of engaging, I shook my head and started walking.

Cal's truck reversed down the road, following beside me as I kept walking. "You're going to get yourself killed."

I scoffed. "Says the man going the *wrong way* down a curvy road." I exaggerated the roll of my eyes and pinned my attention forward. If he wanted to wreck his truck because he was stupid, that was his fault.

With a frustrated grunt, Cal slammed on the brakes, then whipped the truck into gear. He pulled forward, turning in a wide circle to stop beside me.

He leaned across the cab of the truck, pushing the passenger-side door open. "Just get in."

I weighed my options.

One: Be sensible, accept the ride, and avoid unnecessary ghost-related anxiety.

Two: Remain stubborn, walk the rest of the way, and risk becoming the next town legend.

I stared, hands on my hips as I fought reason and temptation. "Why?"

Cal stared out of the windshield. "Don't make me drag you inside."

Heat fluttered low in my belly at the way his words surprised me. I shouldn't like the depraved mental image his agitated growl created.

Feeling defiant, I raised my chin. "That's kidnapping."

His mouth twitched like he was holding back a smirk, which only made my pulse misfire in protest. This man had no right being so annoyingly attractive while issuing threats disguised as favors.

He tipped his chin toward me, his rich brown eyes pinning me in place. "Are you always this difficult?"

My lower lip jutted forward as I considered his question. "Probably." A trait, I decided, that I would take straight to my grave.

When he shifted in the driver's seat, his legs spread in the most obscenely masculine way, my heart rate jumped. Warm notes of *clean man smell* filled my nose. I didn't think Callum intended to kidnap and harm me, but honestly, there were worse ways to go.

He didn't say any more, but his presence *demanded*. His heavy gaze sparked something inside me that made me want to comply and refuse all at once.

With a huff, I climbed into the cab of his truck, sitting as far from him as humanly possible. With crossed arms, I sat, pouting, but not totally sure why. A large part of me hated that he'd won our little standoff . . . and that I liked it.

When he leaned in, reaching across me to pull the seat belt over my body and secure it at my hip, I held my breath. His face was inches from mine as my eyes floated over the planes of his face.

It was wildly unfair how good he smelled—like cedar, coffee, and bad decisions.

Up close, his lips were lush and soft. His five-o'clock shadow was just long enough to make me wonder what it would feel like against my smooth skin.

I swallowed hard. "Thank you," I croaked, shifting even farther away.

What the hell? Why was it so hot in here?

I cracked open the window, trying to breathe. Fresh air. That was what I needed—not a five-minute break from reality where I could press my face against his shirt just to see whether he always smelled this good.

Without another word, Cal pulled onto the roadway, heading toward downtown Star Harbor. The trees whizzed by as we sat in growing silence.

Finally, the deep rumble of his voice filled the cab. "I'm surprised you were willing to walk that stretch of road all by yourself. Especially with it getting dark out."

My eyes narrowed on him. "Don't tell me super-serious Cal Blackwood believes in *ghosts*?"

The corner of his mouth lifted, and for a split second I thought he might actually smile. Instead, his gaze only flicked in my direction before landing on the road in front of us. "I thought everyone from Star Harbor believed in the Lady."

I wasn't about to tell him about my mild internal freak-out only moments before he arrived. Instead, I opted to appear aloof. Totally unaffected. "When you live here long enough, you get used to the weird and unexplained."

"Like what?" he asked.

I considered his question. *Where do you even start?* "Strange noises floating off the lake. Unexplained sightings. The legend is woven into the fabric of this town." My attention landed on the lights of downtown Star Harbor as we rounded the curve that led to the main road. "I mean, who are we without her?"

He nodded, considering my words. "Your brother certainly has reason to believe."

My fingers curled around the hem of my sundress. Of course he was friends with Hayes.

It shouldn't have surprised me, but something about hearing it from his mouth made my chest tighten.

I hadn't been back long, but even I knew the rumors that followed my brother like a shadow. Hayes was cursed. He carried that weight like an anchor, letting it drag him further and further into whatever it was that kept him in Star Harbor, restless and watching.

And now Cal was looking at me like he knew something I didn't.

Star Harbor wasn't just haunted by ghosts—it was haunted by stories. Stories that wove into our bones and refused to let go.

I tracked Cal's eyes, moving across the roadway to where my brother's vehicle was stopped at the train tracks. The crossing bar was down and the lights were flashing, but there was no train in sight. As soon as we got closer, the lights stopped blinking and the bar lifted.

Everyone knew not to get behind Hayes if you needed to cross the tracks. For whatever reason, he *always* got stuck at that exact spot. It was as ridiculous as it was impossible, yet there he was.

Cursed.

The single word flashed through my mind, and my chest squeezed for my older brother. It was impossible to believe, yet his shitty luck was undeniable.

I wondered whether Cal was worried my brother might see us and have questions. If Cal and he were friends, it might seem odd for Hayes to see us together in his truck. Seemingly unaffected, Cal moseyed into town, double-parking in front of the local library.

My eyebrow arched. "How did you know where I was going?"

"Everyone knows where the women around here go when the Keepers meet." He turned to me, a soft expression across his face. "Get out."

I bit back a grin as I climbed out of the cab. "Thanks for kidnapping me."

For a moment something flickered across his features—like he might fire something back and engage in a bit of fun, harmless flirting.

Instead, he nodded once before I closed the door, and without looking back, Callum drove away, leaving me standing there with my own stupid, racing thoughts.

With a deep exhale, I took in downtown Star Harbor.

Homesick.

The word fluttered in my head as I took in the sight of my hometown. I hadn't let myself admit it yet, but something about being here, about standing in the heart of this town, was settling into my bones like I belonged.

The downtown area of Star Harbor was as quaint as it was populated. In the summer months, thousands of visitors flocked to the area to enjoy the hiking trails, towering sand dunes, and pristine beaches of Lake Michigan.

Who needed the tropics when you had Western Michigan?

There were dozens of tourist towns that dotted Lake Michigan, but it was the Lady of the Dunes that drew them to Star Harbor.

I gulped in the warm air, imagining the last dying rays of golden light reaching every corner of my soul.

Staring at the entrance to the library, I lifted my chin and rolled my shoulders back as I grinned.

Here goes nothing.

EIGHT

ELODIE

"Do you think these stitches look crooked?" Kit leaned over, holding a wooden embroidery hoop out to me. The beige canvas stretched over the small circle. The historical society was not only the women who kept the lore of the Lady alive, but a social club steeped in local history. They were responsible for maintaining any records of the Lady and ensuring her memory was kept very much alive. Every few months, as a social project, they took on learning a new skill, doing all the things women in history might do: quilting, dance lessons, croquet.

Their current project was learning needlepoint.

Kit's hoop was stretched tight with a series of small X's printed on black fabric. If I squinted hard enough, I could make out where the floral border would be and a phrase in the center.

"What will it say?" I whispered.

Kit could barely contain her giggle. "It will read *Please don't do coke in the bathroom.*"

A sputtering laugh escaped me as we both dissolved into a fit of giggles. Ribbing her with a poke of my elbow, I gave my sister my most serious look. "That is hideous and totally inappropriate."

She beamed, dimples flashing. "Thank you!" She gestured toward Selene. "So is hers."

Selene's angelic face lifted. Her brows were creased in concentration as her attention focused on us.

"Go on," Kit prodded. "Show her."

With a sly smile, Selene flipped her hoop around. From a distance, it was much easier to make out what she was creating.

A wreath of delicate flowers along the bottom cradled the long, beak-nosed mask of a plague doctor with the words *Wash Thy Accursed Hands* arched over the top.

I had missed this—the silly camaraderie of sisterhood that the Keepers seemed to bring out in everyone. It felt like slipping into a warm, well-worn sweater—frayed in places, but still cozy. Or maybe I just wanted it to feel like home. I wanted to slot back in like I'd never left, like I hadn't spent years chasing a life that suddenly didn't fit anymore.

I was already behind in my needlepoint, but Helen assured me that after a few practice hoops, I'd get the hang of it.

I poked my needle through the canvas, stabbing myself in the finger. "Shit!" I sucked the tip of my finger, gently biting down to distract me from the pain. Needlepoint was officially on my enemies list, right next to humidity, Cal Blackwood, and feral raccoons.

Tara Smithton drew my attention. "So, Ellie. How are things going at the farm? We're all so excited to see what you do with the place."

With my finger still in my mouth, I abandoned my hopeless needlepoint practice. "It's good." I smiled, excited to talk about my new project. "It really is amazing how quickly things get done with a little help and a lot of money."

Tara was one of my mother's best friends and the town's beloved librarian. Mom and Tara had grown up together, and each had created a family in the very town they'd been born in. Her light auburn hair was cropped short in a no-frills bob, her wispy bangs framing a kind face.

"She's back after all this time," she clucked. Tara leaned into my mother, bumping her side. "You must be so proud, Angela."

My eyes flicked to my mother, who smiled at me. We shared the same green eyes and brown hair, though hers was more wiry and wild, like Kit's. Her dimple was deeper on the right side, and I could pull up the memory of sinking a fingertip into it as a little girl, wishing I had inherited just *one* from her.

"No matter what Ellie does, it's done with gusto." Humor and pride swirled together like sweet cream churning into my favorite morning coffee.

Mom was soft and strong. She and Daddy were the roots that kept my family grounded so each of the Darling siblings could find our own wings to fly. They were the sole reason I was wholly unafraid to jump into anything with both feet. No matter what, I knew they'd be there to dust me off if everything blew up in my face.

Mom winked at me before returning her attention to the embroidery hoop in her hands. I had missed her. My parents were the kind of steady, good-hearted people who made you believe anything was possible. It was probably their fault I kept barreling headfirst into impossible ideas, like rescuing this long-forgotten farm.

When I poked myself a third time, I groaned, dropping the hoop into my lap once again. "I officially give up."

Helen chuckled from across the circle. Over time, she had become the heart of the Star Harbor Historical Society. Helen had a knack for fusing our town's little social club into a historical society that was the backbone of Star Harbor. I just couldn't believe she could stand to work with such a cantankerous man as Callum.

I stretched my back as soft conversations folded over me. The meeting room in the library had been updated since I had last seen it, but it had retained its vintage charm. Oil paintings and framed newspaper clippings hung around the room—most related to the town's families and our infamous ghost story.

I sighed, wondering aloud, "Don't you think it's kind of sad?"

A strange chill curled down my spine as I stared at the faded newspaper clipping. It wasn't just sad—it felt wrong. Like a puzzle missing too many pieces to ever see the full picture.

Selene looked up from her lap. "What?"

I gestured toward one of the faded newspaper articles. "The poor woman's likeness is plastered all over town, and no one even knows her name."

My sister hummed. "I never thought about it like that."

"Well, that is mildly depressing," Kit quipped.

I had grown up with the legend, same as everyone else, but something about it hit differently now. Maybe it was the way her face was everywhere, but no one actually knew *her*. Or maybe it was because, for the first time, I was looking at the land around me as something I was responsible for—not just as a pretty backdrop to my childhood.

Helen hummed as she continued working on her project with a smile, until curiosity got the best of me. "Ms. Helen, what do we know about the Lady, *really?*"

Helen's dark-brown eyes crinkled at the edges. Her mother had once been a Keeper, and over time, Helen had assumed the role of matriarch to the tight-knit little club.

"Legends change over time." Helen's voice was low, holding an eerie edge as she continued to work on her needlepoint. "Oftentimes it's difficult to parse out fact from fiction, but we do know that our Lady would have been young—no more than her early twenties, most likely. It's common belief that she was mourning a lost love—perhaps a sailor tragically lost at sea."

Beside me, Kit sighed wistfully.

"But who *was* she?" I pressed.

Helen smiled and set her hoops aside before rising. In the corner of the meeting room, Helen opened a cabinet and pulled out a thick scrapbook. It was old and weathered, with small scraps of paper peeking out at the edges.

"Inside is everything we know." Helen placed the heavy book on a small table and opened it. "In 1903, a young woman's body was found on the dunes. She wore a locket with the initials A.L. engraved on it, but there was no mention of the woman's true identity. The Keepers have gone through many archives and believe that she was likely Alma Lovell." Helen flipped to another page in the book. "We found an engagement announcement that mentions the pending marriage for a young Alma and William Lovell."

All eyes were glued to Helen as her soft voice wove a tale of tragic young love.

"Was it William who was lost at sea?" Selene asked, knowing the legend of the Lady often whispered of a lover lost to the tides.

Helen's bony shoulder lifted. "It's possible. There are no other records of a William Lovell that we have ever found. It seems he disappeared right alongside his lovesick bride-to-be."

I frowned, letting the story settle over me. Call me a cynic, but a young girl is found dead and her boyfriend mysteriously disappears? Something dark and uneasy scratched at my brain.

"The Drifted Spirit was once a family home, owned by a rather successful businessman, Louis Barker. He would have been a multimillionaire by today's standards. He built what is now the inn as his family home and owned all the land around it. No one really knows what secrets those walls are keeping, or what's buried in the land." Helen's gaze settled on me as an unsettling wave of discomfort rolled through me.

The history of Stan's beloved farm may be more than I bargained for.

My plan had been simple, though maybe not entirely well thought out—fix up the farm, bring people in, prove that Stan and the farm were still worth loving.

Suddenly it felt like I was stepping into something bigger—something with roots tangled deep beneath the soil.

My throat was thick, but I swallowed hard. "I love that," I lied, unsure why my voice sounded like peanut butter over sandpaper.

My mother reached for my hand and squeezed, offering silent support. "Elodie knows what she's doing. Working with Stan, bringing a piece of Star Harbor history back to life . . . I know I'm not the only one who's excited to see what she comes up with."

Mom winked at me and a slow exhale escaped my lips.

My heart pounded. "I think as long as I can get people to take a chance on visiting the farm, they'll absolutely love it." I could see every detail perfectly as my uncertainty started to dissolve.

"All I need is time . . . and money, but Stan assured me he was on board. Whatever it takes." I looked around the room, knowing I needed the Keepers to stand behind me. "I won't forget the Lady, I promise. I'm doing this for Stan, but also for our community."

"You can lean into the lore. Draw in more curious tourists," Kit offered.

I smiled at my little sister. "I think I might. Once we're up and running, I just have to get tourists to step out of downtown and come see us."

Helen's deep-brown eyes flickered with mischief. "You could always talk to Callum."

Of all the names in existence, she just *had* to say his.

"Oh, perfect," I grumbled under my breath for only Kit to hear. "Let me just skip over there and ask my least-favorite person in town to help me."

Kit snickered into her hand, leaning in. "Maybe if you flirt a little, he'll cut you some slack."

I gave her a look. "I'd rather eat glass."

"Well . . ." Kit grinned. "That would be on brand for you since you are a farmer now, after all."

I playfully stuck my tongue out at my little sister as Helen continued: "Cal has managed to make the Drifted Spirit one of the most popular destinations despite it not being right in town." Her cheery words grated across my skin.

A disgusted scoff was out before I could stop it. "He's the worst," I grumbled, using my abandoned needlepoint to distract me. I didn't know what his problem was, but the man seemed *determined* to treat me like the villain.

Kit made an obnoxious snort under her breath. I kicked

her under the table as a sea of surprised eyes washed over me. I sat straighter in an attempt to cover my unintentional slip of the tongue.

Apparently I was the only one who could see Callum Blackwood's horns.

Helen's smile was unreadable. "I think I speak for all of us when I say, the Keepers are happy to help however we can."

Murmurs of agreement filled the room as warmth and determination seeped into my soul.

There was no way I was going to fail.

AFTER ANOTHER HOUR of unsuccessful needlepoint practice, my fingertips had taken enough abuse, and Kit drove me home. The inn was quietly bustling as she rolled to a stop in front of my crumbling cottage before saying goodbye and disappearing down the road.

I looked up at my temporary home. Wes would soon be getting to work, patching up and replacing the rotting porch boards. At least I wouldn't have to worry about falling through it and showing my whole ass to Cal . . . again. It would be nice when Wes and his crew made their way inside to spruce up the damp, dingy cottage.

I breathed in the night air and exhaled in a deep sigh. *Home sweet home.*

Or, at least, home for now. I was trying to stay optimistic about that part.

The farmland stretched out before me, silent and waiting. A hundred little decisions loomed in my mind, stacking like bricks. There was no turning back now—not unless I wanted to tuck my tail between my legs and admit I'd bitten off more than I could chew.

I straightened my spine. *Not happening.*

Darkness blanketed the farm, and even when I squinted, I could barely make out where the farm ended and the dunes began. Closing my eyes, I let the soft sound of rolling waves lull me.

A twig snapped to my left and my eyes flew open.

Was it the Lady? A murderer? Raccoons? Whatever it was, it was about to get a very aggressive lesson in personal space.

Instead of discovering yet another critter scurrying across the porch, a lanky shadow skulked behind my cottage.

"Hey!" I shouted into the darkness, masking my surprise with irritation. "Who's there? You come out right now!"

My feet were swift as I stomped around the cottage. I grabbed a fallen branch as a weapon and held it like a baseball bat. After I hurried around the back, my feet stopped short.

A teenage kid had his hands stuffed into his pockets and was trying to get away. Not a ghost. Not a threat. Just a kid with the kind of posture that screamed, *I don't want to get caught, but I also don't want to run because that would look suspicious.*

"Stop!" I could hear a light scoff as he kept walking away from me. "I said *stop!*"

The figure stilled, slowly turning around as I yelled.

My fear instantly dissolved when I recognized his stern, mildly annoyed look. I tried to make out his features in the low lighting. "Hey . . . are you Cal's kid?"

The resemblance was unmistakable—same stubborn

jaw, same broody energy, but with a little less permanent scowl.

His attitude melted, and a scared little boy stood in his shoes. "Please don't tell my dad."

My chest pinched. "What are you doing out here?"

The boy shrugged, but I wasn't letting him off the hook that easily. Instead, I waited him out. Finally, he kicked the dirt with the toe of his sneaker. "I was bored."

"You were bored." My jaw flexed. "You were bored so you thought you'd creep around people's houses?" That logic had *teenager* written all over it.

The boy sputtered. "I wasn't! I went for a walk down the dunes." His arm lifted. "There's a path that runs behind the cottage where the cliffs aren't as steep. It's easier to get to the beach that way."

I looked over my shoulder at the small path worn in the grass. Some spots were so bare the sandy earth beneath it peeked through. "Huh." I shrugged, dropping the tree limb at my feet and dusting off my hands. "Good to know."

I shook my head at the well-worn path he was referring to. Something about the way he knew exactly where to go told me this wasn't his first time sneaking out. "Do you come out here a lot?" I asked, tilting my head.

The boy hesitated, then shrugged like it didn't matter. "Sometimes. There's not much to do at the inn."

I let that settle. Not much to do. It reminded me of being a restless teenager in Star Harbor, looking for something—*anything*—to make the small-town nights feel bigger.

I crossed my arms. "So I take it your dad doesn't know you're out here?"

The boy pulled in his lower lip and shook his head.

My lips twisted. "I should probably tell him."

The boy's eyes jumped to mine. "But—"

I raised my hand to stop him. "I *should*, but since you really weren't doing anything wrong, I guess I don't have to. Just be careful and head straight home."

He nodded enthusiastically, seemingly relieved I wasn't going to rat him out. I had no intention of getting the kid in trouble. Hell, I'd sneaked out to hang with friends at the dunes more times than I could count.

I watched the boy as he started making his way back toward the inn. It was clear he was Cal's son and over time would likely take on his father's impressive frame. If he was already sneaking out, Cal was going to have his hands full with him.

I should've let him go. After all, he was just a kid sneaking around where he wasn't supposed to, and I'd been there, done that. But as he turned, something about the sad, heavy set of his shoulders hit me square in the chest. That stubborn posture, the way his voice had softened at the mention of his dad.

I understood that feeling—the weight of expectation. The need to carve out your own space, even if it meant breaking a few rules.

"Hey, kid," I called out. "Do you need a job? It might suck, but I will pay well. *Really* well," I added to sweeten the offer.

It was an impulse decision, but I'd always trusted my gut. And right now my gut was telling me this kid needed something to keep him occupied that didn't involve sneaking around in the dark like a little haunted Victorian child.

The boy's shoulders perked up. "Yeah, sure."

"Don't you want to know what the job is?" I asked.

His shoulders bounced. "Not really."

Yep. Definitely Callum's kid.

A chuckle rumbled through me. "Fair enough. Come see me in the morning and I'll put you to work. I'm Ellie, by the way."

He lifted his hand. "Levi. And thanks . . . for not telling my dad."

I smirked. "Yet." I pointed at the inn. "Straight home."

Levi nodded. "Yes, ma'am."

I rounded the cottage, watching Levi all the way home to make sure he made it safely. I had a good feeling about the kid, even if his dad was a growly stick-in-the-mud. Levi might be a handful, but at least he was willing to roll with the punches. His dad, on the other hand? He was an entirely different kind of challenge.

NINE

CALLUM

THE SMELL of fried beignet dough filled the kitchen. I tapped the spider strainer against the deep pot to drain the last of the hot oil as I set aside the final batch of beignets. Quickly, I grabbed the sifter and gently tapped its side, dusting the tops with a healthy amount of powdered sugar.

Three glorious mounds of sugar-dusted beignets waited on the prep counter. They were the final element for today's breakfast and best served fresh and hot.

I glanced through the kitchen window, across the lawn. The sun was just coming up, but Wes's construction truck blocked any view of my neighbor. All I could see was the front porch and a few men patching up worn boards on the outside of her house.

Just as well, I supposed. It was probably better I couldn't see what new havoc she was wrecking over there.

I shook my head.

"Hey, Dad." Levi stepped into the kitchen, stealing a beignet and shoving the entire thing into his mouth.

"Careful that's—"

"Hah—hot!" Steam wafted around the pastry like a

dragon's breath as he tried to chew around a mouthful of hot dough.

"Hot," I finished. My eyes flicked to the clock, surprised that it was 7:26 and Levi was not only awake, but bright-eyed and dressed for the day. "What are you up to?"

He shrugged. "I'm going to work."

I looked around, stunned. "Work?"

Levi's face bloomed with a cheeky smile. "I got a job. Sick money too."

Suspicious, my arms crossed. "A job? Doing what?"

He looked past me toward Star Harbor Farm and gestured with his chin. "Helping Ellie."

I dropped the spatula onto the counter with an undignified clatter. I didn't mention that Levi's *job* was supposed to be helping around here. A job he consistently failed to do, I might have added. My molars ground together. "You're helping at the farm? And she's paying you?" My chin lifted. "How much?"

His eyes flicked around the kitchen, avoiding mine. "Well . . . I don't really know yet—but she promised it would be good!"

His sweet, naive little heart. I shook my head. "Son, you need to be careful. Not everyone has good intentions."

Especially dream-stealing harlots with perfect asses and a sassy mouth. Not that I noticed. Not that I cared.

"Now if you need money, we can talk about paying you more for what you help with around here." I pinned him with my best parental look. "But we also need to talk about you actually *doing* the things I ask you to."

I helplessly watched my son's hope and excitement wither in front of me. Levi's sweet eyes went hard, and I hated myself for being the cause of it.

Damn it.

I'd been trying to hold on to him, and all I'd managed to do was push him further away. Again.

"Fine," he pouted. Levi went to turn around and stomp back to his room, where I was almost certain he'd hole up for the foreseeable future.

"Stop," I said, and he slowly turned to look at me, a tiny flicker of hope sparking in his eyes. I pinched the bridge of my nose and exhaled. "Just . . . be careful. Don't let anyone take advantage of you."

Levi brushed past me as he grabbed a baseball cap off the hook by the door. He hesitated, balling his fists inside his hoodie pockets as his eyebrows popped up. "You know, for someone who doesn't like her, you sure do watch her a lot."

My spine went stiff. "Watch it," I warned, though my words lacked any real threat.

Levi was already out the door, his snort of amusement carried away with the morning breeze. "Later, Dad!"

And just like that, I lost him to the enemy.

"And it's too warm for a hoodie!" I shouted at his back, but I doubt he heard me. Levi was already bounding across the lawn toward Elodie's place.

I watched through the window as she stepped out onto the front porch to greet Levi. That soft, easy smile. The kind of smile that could make a person feel like they belonged somewhere—like they were wanted. Her smile was bright and wide for my son, and an aching spot ballooned in my chest. I wondered what it took to earn a smile like that.

Not that I wanted one, or that it would ever be directed at me.

I continued to watch as she said something to Wes, who

was working alongside a few of his men. He got one of her smiles too.

Oh, for fuck's sake. I scrubbed a hand down my face. *I am a pouty little bitch this morning.*

Still, as Levi walked beside Elodie and disappeared behind a rolling hill on the farm, I couldn't stop the nagging feeling in my gut.

One little recon mission. Just enough to confirm what I already knew—she was going to fail spectacularly.

I picked up the phone and rang the reception desk.

"Hello, Drifted Spirit Inn. This is Helen."

"It's me. I need to pop next door for a minute. Breakfast is ready and warming. I set aside two blueberry crumb muffins for you. Be back in ten."

Helen's chuckle floated across the telephone line. "You really are the best boss. Take your time."

I grumbled and hung up.

Brushing the last remnants of powdered sugar from my hands, I removed my apron and hung it on a hook.

If I still had a snowball's chance in hell of making things right with Stan—of proving his best option was to sell the farm to me—I needed to know what Ellie was really up to. It would also make it that much easier to swoop in and rescue it when she inevitably fucked it all up.

It was something that had been beaten into me in the Army. The ends always justified the means. No room for excuses.

If I wanted to take down the enemy, I needed to know her better than I knew myself. Unfortunately for me, the enemy was a five-foot-seven knockout with wild hair and a fiery personality. Knowing the enemy meant stepping straight into the lion's den. Or, more accurately, straight into the orbit of Elodie Darling and her goddamn sunshine.

I stalked toward her cottage.

It was time to find out exactly what Elodie Darling was up to—and how to make damn sure she didn't get too comfortable.

With confident strides, I paced across the lawn toward Wes's truck. His work pants were dusty and well worn from his time working in the construction field. As I swung a leg over the fence that divided the properties, my movements caught Wes's attention.

"There he is!" Wes called as an easy grin spread across his face. He walked toward me, hand out. "Figured you'd be researching chiffon pastry or some shit."

I gripped his hand, pushing into him. "Shove it. You know my cakes are amazing."

He grinned. "I won't argue with that."

My eyes swept over the farmland as it bustled with activity from Wes's crew to laborers clearing the fields. "Sure is busy around here," I grumbled.

Wes rocked on his heels. "Busy is good. I like to work, and this place needs plenty of it."

I harrumphed, glancing at the old cottage and noting that Wes and his team were practically rebuilding it from the inside out.

I jutted my chin toward the cottage. "Heard she's a real battle-ax."

"Ellie?" Wes frowned at me, shaking his head. "No, she's great, man. I've known her since we were kids."

Taken aback, I folded my arms. "You don't think it's odd? Her coming in here and telling Stan how to run things?"

Wes's attention on me made it clear he was trying to figure out what my problem was. "I don't know." His carefree shoulders lifted. "Maybe it's good for old man Stafford to have a project."

I suppressed a snarl. Seemed like Elodie and her *ideas* had put sparkles in everyone's eyes but mine.

I wondered if Mary had known Elodie, and whether they had been friends. "Growing up, was she always so . . . *cheerful?*"

He shrugged again. "I didn't really hang around with her back then. Hayes and I ran in different circles, and the Darling girls are younger than us." He looked out onto the farm, and my irritation grew when his eyes landed on Elodie in the distance. He let out a soft whistle. "Though I don't know, man, maybe I should have been paying better attention."

His arm playfully bumped mine. My eyes darkened, but I didn't say a word.

Wes nudged my arm again. "I mean, c'mon, you have eyes, right?"

"I have a brain too," I grumbled. "And it tells me she's a pain in my ass."

"Sure." Wes stretched the word out, letting it settle between us before adding, "Is that what you were just staring at? Her being a pain in your ass?"

I scowled, shoving him hard enough to send him back a step. "Go build something."

"Unless," he continued, watching me, "you were thinking of going for it."

I scowled. "Going for what?"

Wes rolled his eyes. "Asking her out, dumbass."

I stared at my friend. I had been married to his sister, for fuck's sake. Sure, at the time I had only asked her because she was pregnant, and I thought it was the honorable thing to do, but love and respect had grown there. Mary had been an amazing mother. She deserved better than the hand she had been dealt.

Specifically, better than a man like me.

When I remained silent, Wes shook his head. A seriousness dropped over his features that meant I wasn't going to like what he was about to say. "Mary's been gone a long time. I know things weren't perfect, but you've done right by her."

The throb in my temple was back. Wes knew as well as anyone that a life in Delta Force always meant collateral damage. How he'd ever managed to forgive me for what I'd put his sister through was beyond me.

Hell, I hadn't even forgiven myself.

I shook my head. "I'm not asking anyone out."

His seriousness evaporated and a chuckle rumbled in Wes's chest. "I'm going to hold your hand when I say this." He clamped a hand on my shoulder. "You're an idiot."

I shrugged him off and took a cheap, playful shot with my elbow to his ribs. Wes reacted, pulling me into a headlock. Wes was taller, but I had bulk on him, and we were evenly matched. Despite our military training, this was pure fucking around, and we both knew it.

I laughed as Wes tried to wrestle me to the ground. I changed levels, throwing him off guard until we both tumbled into the grass, splayed out on our backs. Out of breath, we panted, staring up into the bright, cloudless sky.

A genuine laugh broke free, and a lightness I hadn't felt in days rolled through me.

"Want to get a few beers once your housework is done?" Wes teased.

I grinned. "You bet." I sat up and sighed before slapping

the back of my hand against his gut in a cheap shot and running off across the grass.

~

THE LANTERN HAD BEEN CROWDED, a popular local band drawing in a healthy crowd. Brody joined us after work along with his half brother, Austin. Hayes had gotten a flat tire on his way out, but once that was sorted, he came too.

I nursed a beer on the outskirts of the bar, happy to observe a Thursday night in Star Harbor unfold. The warm temperatures drew out the crowds, and the back patio was filled with patrons. I would have been happy finding a quiet corner, but I had been outvoted.

Hayes was content to brood with me while the rest of our group took turns buying rounds and striking out with the tourists. I had no interest.

Then the energy in the room shifted. I didn't even have to turn my head to know she was there—I felt it.

Ellie stepped into the bar like she belonged there. Which, I supposed, she did.

She was laughing, something bright and easy, already caught in conversation as she wove through the crowd. She greeted people as she passed—old classmates, neighbors, familiar faces from her childhood.

"Ellie! I can't wait to bring the kids to the farm," a woman called, raising her wineglass as Elodie passed. Elodie grinned, tossing back something in response, her enthusiastic energy contagious.

Her sister Kit was with her, but Elodie was the one who drew attention without even trying. She reached Hayes first, giving him a quick, familiar squeeze on the arm as she passed. He responded with a nod, smirking slightly. Then she turned toward the rest of us, scanning the table, her eyes flicking to me for a beat too long before moving on.

I should have looked away, but I didn't.

Wes would have a fucking field day with this.

The sound of easy laughter, the unhurried sway of her hips as she moved through the bar, the faint scent of something warm and sweet trailing behind her. My eyes were already tracking her, already noting the way her hair fell in wild waves around her shoulders, already catching on the soft slip of fabric hugging her curves just right, already cursing the way the light caught on the bare skin of her collarbone.

"I'll get the next round," I announced to the table, already moving toward the bar.

I wasn't happy she was here. At least, that was what I told myself.

I wasn't happy that she was invading my space, my night, my town, just like she'd already invaded every corner of my brain. I wasn't happy that she had this effortless way of commanding attention, of turning heads, of making people want to orbit around her like she was the damn sun.

And I sure as hell wasn't happy that I was one of them.

At the bar, I signaled to the bartender and waited, focusing on my drink, my breathing, the game playing on the mounted TVs—anything but her. She was moving past me, close enough that I caught the faintest whiff of vanilla and something floral, something that made my grip tighten around my beer bottle.

And then, before she even realized it, some idiot moved too fast in her direction, not seeing her, not noticing that she was about to get knocked into the barstools.

I saw it before it happened, and my body reacted before my brain caught up.

My hand was on her before I could think better of it. My palm was firm against the small of her back, steadying her, grounding her, feeling the heat of her skin through the thin material of her dress.

She stilled, just for a second—just long enough for her body to register mine, for the warmth of her breath to ghost across my jaw when she turned her head toward me, for her pulse to kick under my touch.

I should have moved my hand. I should have let go.

Instead, my fingers curled ever so slightly against her.

She wasn't looking at me now, not fully. Her gaze had dropped over her shoulder to where my hand was still pressed against her, like she was trying to piece together why I was still touching her.

Then I felt him—the drunk guy who nearly sent her into the bar, still standing too close, still in her space like he had a right to be.

I barely spared him a glance. Just reached out, tapped him on the shoulder.

The guy turned, bleary-eyed and slow. I didn't smile, didn't frown. I didn't even have to raise my voice. I just looked at him.

"Back up." My voice was low and even, with nothing but steel behind it.

He blinked, took one look at me, and immediately moved, his hands lifting in surrender.

Elodie finally looked up, her gaze sharp and searching, trying to pin me down. "What was that about?"

I lifted my beer, flicking my attention back toward the game. "It was nothing."

She didn't buy it, but after a beat, she scoffed under her breath. "Whatever."

Shaking her head, she lingered in my space just a second too long before finally stepping away.

When the bartender returned with our beers, I scooped them up and returned to the table, where I spent an unhealthy number of minutes watching Elodie laugh and dance with Kit. At one point Kit saw Hayes, and I thought the women might join us at our table. Kit cast an invisible fishing line toward him and pretended to reel him in, but when he playfully swatted her away, she laughed before turning around on the dance floor.

He might be as brooding as me, but Hayes had a genuine soft spot for his sisters.

I had a thousand questions for Hayes about one sister in particular, but I kept them to myself. My obsession with Elodie was borderline unhealthy, and the last thing I needed was my friend knowing I was actively rooting for his little sister's downfall.

Elodie moved like she was made to dance, undulating to the beat that proved she had natural rhythm. When the band played a slow, crooning ballad, her eyes fluttered closed. The long column of her neck stretched as she tipped her face toward the ceiling, carried away by the music. My eyes lingered, roaming over her skin, soaking in any scrap of bare flesh as she swayed.

My jaw clenched so tight it ached.

With her head tipped back, exposing the elegant stretch of her throat, I felt a sharp, physical pull, low and insistent, like an invisible tether yanking me toward her.

She was everywhere and I couldn't find an ounce of peace. My beer bottle hit the table a little too hard.

I need to get the fuck out of here.

I gripped my thigh under the table in an attempt to ground myself. I had been too lonely for too long. My physical reaction had nothing to do with the fact that Elodie happened to be the embodiment of my ideal woman—thick curves, taut skin, pouty lips that begged to be wrapped around me.

It wasn't her—it was just shitty luck. At least, that was the lie I had to tell myself to keep from turning into a caveman whenever some schmuck tried to dance with her.

When an upbeat song started, Elodie eagerly bounced on her toes, her tits bouncing along, and I finally lost it.

"Okay, I'm out of here." I stood, the wooden legs of my chair scraping against the floor.

Surprised by my abruptness, Hayes lowered his beer bottle. "You sure?"

I dropped a handful of bills onto the table, abandoning my own drink. "Yep. I'll catch up with everyone later."

Hayes nodded. "Sounds good, man."

As I made my escape, I risked a glance at the dance floor. Elodie's eyes locked with mine and my pulse hammered in my ears. For a split second, time slowed as her doe eyes blinked. Her tongue wetted her lower lip before her lips hooked up in a defiant smirk.

Hot, hostile energy sizzled across the crowded bar.

With her eyes still on mine, she leaned over and whispered something to Kit, who nodded.

Annoyance rattled through me. It took everything inside me not to storm up to her and plant my mouth on hers just to wipe the cocky look off her face.

I tamped down the urge to claim her and prove to everyone that Elodie Darling had no hold over me whatsoever. Need, hot and angry, tore through me. My raging cock pressed against the zipper of my jeans and didn't relent the entire drive home.

The inn was quiet, but I slinked into the side entrance,

avoiding everyone. I needed to get my head on straight. To focus.

I needed a release.

I briefly noted that Levi's door was closed, and the soft glow of light assured me that he was home. I slipped the key into my suite and kicked the door closed, not bothering to lock it behind me. I wasn't turning in for the night, just doing what I needed to get some relief.

I scrubbed a hand down my face and paced the length of my room, dragging my palm over the back of my neck. The air inside felt stifling, thick with something I couldn't shake.

Her.

That fucking smirk. That smug, infuriating look in her eyes when she met my gaze across the bar. Like she knew she was in my head. Like she belonged there.

Once inside the bathroom, I stepped into the shower and let the hot spray scorch the muscles in my back.

I should be thinking about anything else—the breakfast menu for tomorrow, how to be a better parent, the list of repairs waiting at the inn.

Anything but her.

But the second I shut my eyes, she was there—laughing, teasing, moving to music like she was made from it. My breath came heavier. I knew exactly where this was headed, and I hated myself for it.

But not enough to stop.

Heat unfurled inside me as my dick throbbed. Thoughts of Elodie and her gorgeous, infuriating face continued to fill my mind. I had never had a hatred hard-on, but it was a mysterious and powerful thing.

Feeling it, thick and heavy, I hated the fact that it would

be wasted on my hand when it deserved to sink into a warm, wet woman.

But I didn't have a choice.

My hand wrapped around it and I groaned, choking on the sound as need drove me forward. Blood hammered in my veins, and I shut out the world. I let every rational thought leave my head as I lost myself in sensation.

I hadn't been with a woman in years, and stroking my cock had become just another way to appease my base instincts. A means to an end.

But this was different.

Unabashed need danced with something dark and unnamed. The image of Ellie sprawled in front of me, on display for *me*. I groaned at the thought of her hot, wet cunt waiting for me to stretch her open. My cock protested, hating my hand but needing it all the same. I didn't allow myself to touch her, not even in my mind.

Instead, I continued stroking my cock to the image of Elodie, just out of reach. Teasing me. Acute awareness prickled at something in my brain, heightening my already honed senses. The mental imagery was working, because suddenly I could *feel* her in the room, pliant and curious. I could practically smell her spicy vanilla perfume mixing with the steam of the shower. It only fueled the fantasy, bringing it to life as I hurtled closer to the edge.

Tension curled in my lower back as I jutted my hips forward, fucking my hand and imagining what it might be like to paint those perfect tits with my cum.

She would like it, reveling in how undone she made me. I groaned as I tugged. As far as angry jerk-off sessions went, this one was unrivaled.

Pathetic.

My fantasy should have been enough—I had hoped to be left sated, empty, and free of her—but it wasn't.

The water pounded against my skin, but it didn't rinse her from my thoughts. I braced a forearm against the tile, hanging my head as I pumped. Soon thick ropes of cum painted the shower wall as I envisioned it landing across her tits instead. Pointed nipples glistening with my release.

As I came my body jerked, and a single word slipped past my lips: "Elodie."

ELODIE

I really meant to turn around.

Once I had realized that I accidentally walked into the *wrong* room and someone was showering, I had swiveled on my heels to hustle the hell out of there.

Then a single word stopped me in my tracks.

Elodie.

My name, spoken in a choked groan that could only mean *one* thing. One guttural, masculine moan that paralyzed me. One I had felt right down in the soles of my feet.

Heat sparked at the edges of my skin like the first lick of a wildfire.

I wasn't supposed to hear that. I was definitely *not* supposed to feel it. A pulse of heat shot through me, sharp and insistent, pooling low in my belly like my body had rewired itself to respond to him.

No. Not *him*. The situation. The sheer primal sound of it.

I could lie to myself and pretend like I thought the moan on the other side of the door meant he was injured, but I knew better. I knew *exactly* what was happening in that shower.

What I didn't know was why it was *my* name on his lips.

In my defense, I *had* knocked and the door was already cracked when I pushed it the rest of the way open.

I had even called out, for fuck's sake.

Breaths sawed in and out of me as I pressed my back to the wall next to his bathroom door. My nails dug into my palms as a low throb pulsed between my legs. Cal moaned again and I nearly screamed.

I would never be able to look Callum Blackwood in the eye again.

As I scanned the darkened suite, it was clear this was Cal's living space. Masculine traces of him were evident—the king-size bed meticulously made with sharp, military-grade edges. Zero frills on the bedside table, only a lonely clock and a wristwatch. Across the room, his closet was open, his shirts and pants hung with painful organization.

I moved on instinct, legs carrying me forward before I even registered the motion. My pulse pounded in my throat, my breath short and uneven. I needed to get out of there—now, before—

The shower squeaked as it turned off.

"Fuck," I whispered, desperate with the need to escape. In the dark, I tiptoed across the suite, cursing the ancient floorboards that softly creaked underfoot.

When I made it to the door and slipped into the hallway, I let out a sigh of relief. Cracking the door just as it had been, I scurried down the hall, still clutching the whole reason I was lurking around the Drifted Spirit Inn in the first place.

My body was on fire as I scurried as quickly as my feet could take me.

"Elodie." A thick, booming voice stopped me. *His* voice. Only this time it was filled with surprised annoyance rather than the desperate groan of a man about to orgasm.

I jumped with a yelp, turning toward him. His head was poked out of the doorway, bare shoulders on display. He was wearing nothing but a towel, hastily wrapped around his hips. I swallowed hard, envying the terry cloth as it hung on for dear life.

A drop of water tracked the cut V of his waist, slow and deliberate, before soaking into the white cotton. I told myself I wasn't watching. That I wasn't standing here like an idiot, rooted to the floor, pulse hammering in my ears.

Thick water droplets clung to the tips of Cal's hair, darkening it to nearly black. The hall light cast a moody glow, but I could see his sharp gaze freeze on me.

"Oh!" I cleared my throat. "Hey, Cal." *Fancy meeting you here . . .*

His dark gaze narrowed, his eyebrows suspicious slashes across his eyes. For a moment he just stared, his demeanor clouding with intensity as though he knew I had violated his sacred privacy.

Could he tell? Could he read the thoughts tumbling from my mind?

I've been actively imagining your dick in your hands for the last several minutes.

I blinked, hoping that seventh-grade drama class wouldn't fail me and I could act my way out of the world's most awkward encounter. I lifted my hand with a jerky wave.

"What are you doing here?" he demanded. "No one is allowed back here."

My mouth opened, but I snapped it closed again. I pointed in the direction of the front desk. "Helen sent me back here. Levi left his hoodie at my place. I was just returning it."

"It's late." His eyes flicked to the black hoodie and back to my face before he sighed and shook his head. "Why that kid thinks he needs a hoodie in June is beyond me."

I didn't respond because my brain was still back at the bar. I was lost in the memory of how his hand had landed on me, warm and steady, fingers pressing just enough to ground me before curling against the small of my back.

A warning. A claim. A reaction maybe he hadn't even thought through. I'd played it off and acted like it didn't shake me, but it had.

I'd danced for him.

Maybe that was it—the way I moved, the way I let the music carry me, all while knowing exactly where he was in that bar.

I wanted him to look. I wanted him to feel it, but I hadn't expected *this*.

I hadn't expected to come home and hear my name on his lips, groaned like a prayer, like something pulled out of him by force.

My pulse jumped, betraying me.

I gripped the hoodie tighter, hoping he wouldn't see the way my fingers were shaking.

I blinked, willing my brain back to the moment. "That's kids for you, I guess." I reluctantly held the crumple of black fabric out, unable to step forward.

His moody eyes flicked across the hallway as he stepped out of his room, wearing nothing but that low-slung white towel. Heat licked up my spine. He wasn't just built—he was carved, like something meant to be worshipped in dim candlelight. Broad shoulders, every inch of him honed from discipline and something far more dangerous than just hard work at the gym. His chest, all ridges and valleys of muscle, tapered into a trim waist. A constellation of old scars mapped their way across his skin, stark against the ink that wrapped his biceps and climbed the hard cut of his forearm toward his hand.

Not clean, perfect lines—his tattoos wove through rough, jagged scars, ink bleeding into flesh that had been torn and stitched back together more times than I wanted to consider. Some deep and thick, others thin and raised, a history that spoke of battles I would never hear about. The contrast between them—the art and the damage—was staggering. Proof that he had been torn open and put back together again.

I swallowed, pulse hammering. He was devastating, and I hated that I couldn't stop looking. The space between us felt too small, the air too thick.

Cal reached for the hoodie, his fingertips burning a path across the back of my hand as he dragged them across my skin.

An awkward laugh snagged in my throat. "Levi did great today—I worked him hard and he didn't complain once."

What the hell? Why am I making small talk about his son when he's naked?

"Okay, bye!" My cheeks flamed, and I swiveled on my heels to make my escape without looking back. I wound through the maze of the Drifted Spirit, beelining it toward the front door.

"Find what you needed?" Helen's voice was full of honey as I rushed past her.

I paused, facing her. She was perched on a high-backed

stool behind the front desk, absently looking up from a book. The well-worn novel was splayed open on her lap—a vintage Harlequin romance with its long-haired love interest wrapping himself around the waif of a woman beneath him.

My mind instantly pinged to Cal wearing nothing but a towel. *He'd look good with a sword in his hand.*

A real sword. Not his dick—oh my god.

A strangled "Yep!" was all I could muster as a fresh wave of heat crawled up my chest and neck.

Helen chuckled to herself, and I couldn't help but wonder whether her overly vague directions—*the living quarters are down that hallway, past the kitchen and toward the back*—were intentional.

Sure, the elderly woman had no way of knowing exactly what I would walk into, but the mischievous glint in her amber eyes told me she had a feeling I might stumble into her boss.

Maybe the innocent-looking woman really was a troublemaker.

I turned, wrapping my arms around my middle and suppressing a smile.

"You know," Helen said at my back, "you got me thinking."

Curiosity piqued, I turned with a raised eyebrow.

"The Lady," she supplied. "You were right. It feels wrong that we don't know more about who she really was, outside of the legends." Helen leaned forward, pulling an old scrapbook out from behind the desk. It landed with a gentle thud on the thick oak desktop. The book was similar to the one at the library, but bound in cracked leather the color of wine.

"This old house came with a lot of old memories." She nodded toward the book. "Including this."

Drawn forward by intrigue, I stepped closer and gazed at the words *Scrap Book* in swooping cursive printed on the cover and embossed with gold. This kind of distraction was exactly what I needed to forget all about Cal and his thick, masculine groaning.

My fingers hovered over the words. "May I?"

I glanced at Helen, who smiled. "Of course."

The hinges creaked open, and I was assaulted with the slightly sweet, musty smell of almonds. The old-book smell wrapped around me as my fingers floated over the pages, too afraid to touch it. The book seemed to be a record of the Barker household and general goings-on in Star Harbor. Newspaper clippings were glued next to sepia portraits. Faded, hand-written notes included scribbled dates and annotations.

I paused at a photograph of the Drifted Spirit Inn. Though the image was old, the home stood proudly in the background. The trees weren't nearly as imposing as they now were, and the land around the home was undeveloped. At the base of the porch steps, a handsome couple stared at the camera, two children—a young boy and girl—by their sides.

A handwritten date was scribbled beneath it: 1886.

"This is so cool," I whispered, lost in the history of it all.

Helen pointed at the photograph that had captured my imagination. "That is Louis Barker along with his wife and children around the time that construction of the home was completed. He was an intensely private man . . . little is known about his family." She lifted a shoulder. "Most is probably just lost to time, which makes the mystery all the more alluring."

I glanced up and smiled, knowing exactly what she meant.

"There are some pictures of the farmland, a few notes written by who I am guessing was Mrs. Barker." Helen closed the book and slid it toward me. "I thought you might want to borrow this—use some of the old pictures."

My imagination sparked to life. I could already see the social media images of then and now, side by side, showing what the farmland used to be and how Stan and I were honoring it, even today.

I reached for her hand and squeezed. "Thank you."

Carefully, I lifted the book off the counter and hugged it against my chest. Bit by bit my plan for enticing people to Star Harbor Farm was becoming clearer. The most important hurdle was making sure the farm was up and running by the time people showed up.

That included a laundry list of items that made my head spin. It was time to focus. Prove myself.

I was drowning in tasks, and the last thing I needed was to be distracted by moody innkeepers who spent the better part of the evening scowling at me at the Lantern, only to moan my name in the shower.

Besides, Cal never had to know. Not about the hallway. Not about the moan. Not about the fact that for the rest of my damn life, I would hear my name in that voice, in that moment, whispered into the dark like a secret.

He never had to know.

ELEVEN

CALLUM

Oн, I knew.

I 100 *percent* knew Elodie had been in my space and heard me moan her name. The way she blanched and couldn't stop staring at my dick was a dead giveaway.

It was the kind of moment that should have had me crawling into a hole, swearing off humanity for a solid month. Instead, it had me pacing my room half the night, fists clenched, jaw tight, *aching*.

I told myself I was fine—that it didn't matter.

But here I was, standing at the ballpark, still trying to shake her out of my head while going through warm-ups.

I needed to focus on the game. I was supposed to be getting my head on straight, dialing in, settling into the rhythm of the pregame drills, but my brain was still stuck on last week. The knowledge that she'd been there, that she'd heard me, that she *knew* it was her I was thinking about—it made something sharp and restless claw inside me.

I rolled my shoulders back, exhaling hard.

Focus, Blackwood.

I looked around the field as the opposing team ran through their warm-ups.

Hayes was late. Again.

The first pitch was supposed to be in five minutes, and half the team was stretching while the other half stood around waiting for his inevitable excuse.

I whistled to Brody to get his attention. "Any word?"

Brody checked his phone. "He says he's two minutes out. Something about a bird?"

I shook my head, sighing.

Wes arched a brow. "Did he get shat on again?"

Brody smirked. "Worse. Apparently a bird flew straight into his windshield. Just—*bam*—out of nowhere. He had to pull over, check the damage." He looked up, eyes gleaming with amusement. "According to him, the bird even stared him down before flying off."

"It's like they seek him out." I huffed a laugh, stretching my arm across my chest.

Hayes's truck finally pulled into the parking lot, and he climbed out, looking like a man personally wronged by the universe.

Brody grinned, calling out toward the parking lot. "Rough afternoon, bud?"

Hayes slammed the truck door shut and pointed a finger at him. "Do not."

Wes chuckled. "That bad?"

Hayes exhaled through his nose, dragging a hand down his face. "Some damn seagull flew straight into my windshield. Full speed. I thought I killed it. Pulled over, checked the road—the thing just dusted itself off and walked away like *I* was the asshole."

I shook my head, smirking. "You are the asshole."

Hayes scowled but didn't argue, his mood already lifting. The guy never liked to talk about his epically bad luck, but we all knew it hovered over him like a storm cloud.

Brody clapped him on the back. "Yeah, well, worry about it later. We've got a game to win."

Hayes shot him a flat look but said nothing. I turned back toward the field, adjusting my grip on my mitt. That was when I heard it—bright and unmistakable.

Ellie.

A burst of laughter cut through the warm summer air, light and full of something I didn't know how to name. My spine went tight before I could stop myself, my fingers clenching around my glove.

I didn't have to look. I definitely shouldn't have looked.

But of course I did.

She was by the playground, her tanned legs flashing in the sunlight as she chased after Winnie, the kid's high-pitched giggles carrying across the grass.

Elodie lunged, grabbed her niece around the waist, and tumbled into the grass, both of them dissolving into playful laughter.

I clenched my jaw.

She was wearing a stupidly cute red sundress, the hem flaring around her thighs as she rolled onto her back, breathless from chasing her niece.

She had nothing to do with this game. Nothing to do with me.

So why the hell was I still looking?

I exhaled sharply, rolling my shoulders back, turning away.

I shifted my weight at first base, pounding my glove once against my palm, keeping loose. Hayes was at shortstop, scanning the field with that quiet, brooding intensity that made it look like he was plotting something other than softball. Brody, the only guy who took this league semiseriously, was on the pitcher's mound, already talking shit to the batter. Wes, stationed at third, had his hands on his knees, grinning like he was having the time of his life. We rotated positions sometimes, but tonight this was the lineup.

The game started, and I told myself I was done thinking about Elodie, but my body had other plans. I was acutely aware of her, my eyes sneaking glances to see if she was watching me just as intently as I was watching her.

During the game, everything clicked. My swings were clean, my throws were sharp, my reflexes were *on*. I wasn't even thinking—I was just playing. For the first time in weeks, we weren't losing and the team's energy was high.

Every time I glanced up, Ellie was still there. Sitting on the bleachers now, shaded by the old oak trees, watching the game.

She was thigh to thigh with Selene, whispering and smiling as they watched us play. Winnie had lost interest and was twirling in the grass next to the field, completely unaware of where she was standing.

My senses prickled, danger alerting in my brain—the little girl was too close.

Crack.

The unmistakable thwack of a bat connecting with a foul ball.

The sound was too fast, too sharp—and I realized the ball was headed straight for Winnie.

I moved before I could think. My feet pounded against the dirt as I lunged, grabbing Winnie, twisting my body just as the ball slammed into my flank.

A sharp grunt of pain tore through me, but it barely registered. My focus was on the tiny human blinking up at me from the grass.

With a grimace, I looked down at her wide-eyed face. "You okay, kid?" I grunted. "I didn't crush you, did I?"

Winnie, completely unfazed, grinned. "That was *awesome*."

I huffed out a laugh, shaking my head as I steadied her on her feet. "Yeah, awesome. We'll go with that."

I barely had time to process what had happened before Ellie and Selene were there. Selene reached Winnie first, dropping to her knees. "Oh no, Win, are you hurt? You scared me half to death!"

Winnie shook her head. "Mr. Cal saved me."

Selene looked at me, emotion thick in her voice as she held on to Winnie. "Thank you."

I nodded. It's what anyone would have done. I didn't look at Ellie, but I could feel her eyes on me.

Fuck, my side hurts.

Selene glanced between Winnie and Elodie. "Maybe we should go."

Winnie pouted, stamping her little foot in the grass and pointing. "But Uncle Hayes is playing."

Ellie let out a shaky breath, smoothing a hand over Winnie's hair before finally looking up at me. "Are you okay? Man, that must have hurt."

I barely registered the question because her hand was suddenly lifting my shirt to examine where I had been hit.

My entire body locked up, and three things hit me all at once:

One: Her palm was warm against my bare skin, her fingers pressing lightly into the bruised muscle.

Two: My chest went tight, like my body was trying to barricade itself against the effect she had on me.

Three: She smelled like honey and vanilla and something that made my brain short-circuit.

Jesus Christ. I'd taken a direct hit from a softball at full speed, but this was what rattled me?

Before I could even wrap my mind around it, Hayes jogged over, tossing his mitt onto the grass, and the moment shattered.

Ellie pulled her hand back.

I rolled my shoulders, shaking off the tension, but the heat of her touch stayed with me.

Hayes thumped me on the back. "Jesus, I don't think I've ever seen you run so fast. You good, man?"

I stretched my back again, knowing I was going to be sore for at least a few days. "Fine." My attention snagged on Ellie, whose lower lip jutted forward in the tiniest pout.

Was she worried about me?

I cleared my throat and walked toward the field. "Come on, Hayes. We have a game to win."

The game resumed, but for the rest of the night, all I could think about was the feel of Ellie's hand on my skin.

Levi was in a damn good mood.

Which, in theory, should've been a good thing—except when that mood was directly related to *her*.

I watched from the edge of the property as my son moved across the farm with an energy I hadn't seen in years. He was wearing work gloves and carrying a wooden crate full of something—I didn't know what, and I didn't particularly care. All I could see was how relaxed he looked, how much he was smiling.

And worse—how much of that had to do with Elodie Darling.

She was in the middle of the field, clipboard in hand,

barking orders like she'd been running this place for a decade instead of a few weeks. A pair of black sunglasses was perched on top of her head, her hair wild from the coastal wind.

She looked obnoxiously competent.

Annoyance simmered low in my gut.

I didn't want her to be good at this. I wanted her to be overwhelmed. I wanted her to realize she was in way over her head. But, from the way Levi was hanging on her every word, that sure as hell wasn't the case.

Levi hustled toward her, laughing at something she said. She beamed at him, reaching out to squeeze his shoulder. My teeth almost cracked from how hard I ground them.

I started off toward them.

I had no business there, I knew that, but I told myself I was walking over to check on Levi—to make sure she wasn't using him as free labor or feeding him some sugarcoated bullshit about what this farmland was actually worth.

That was the only reason.

It had absolutely nothing to do with the fact that my body had been wound tight ever since she touched me at the game. Ever since I'd turned my head and seen that stupid, worried little pout on her lips when she asked if I was okay.

I exhaled sharply, shoving my hands into my pockets.

This was fine. I was just here for another recon mission.

So why the hell am I already losing my mind?

I stepped onto the property like I wasn't questioning every decision that had led me to this moment. Ellie was in the middle of marking something on a list when she noticed me. Her sunglasses slipped down her nose as she turned her head.

And then she smiled.

Not one of her cocky, taunting smirks. Not one of those smug little grins that made me want to kiss the challenge right off her lips.

No, this was different.

Soft. Open. Warm.

It knocked the damn air out of me.

She adjusted her sunglasses and turned fully toward me. "Well, well, well. If it isn't my favorite grump."

I scowled and gestured toward my son, who was walking toward the barn. "What the hell is he doing?"

Ellie's gaze flicked toward Levi as she smiled. "Learning. Growing. Thriving." She crossed her arms. "So, naturally, you hate it."

"I don't hate it," I bit out.

"Are you sure?" She tilted her head, full of mock sympathy as she pointed toward my face. "Because that vein in your forehead is saying otherwise."

I clenched my jaw and willed my body to not react to her.

It didn't work.

Ellie turned toward Levi, who was hauling something across the field. "He's a hard worker. And he actually listens when I tell him to do something."

I huffed. "Yeah, well, maybe if I paid him a stupid amount of money like you are—"

"I haven't even paid him yet," she cut in with a laugh.

I frowned. "What?"

Ellie grinned, infuriatingly smug. "He hasn't even asked. I think he just likes it here. But don't worry, I've got an envelope full of cash ready and waiting for him."

I hated how much that got under my skin. I hated how easily she was pulling him into her world.

How she was pulling me in too.

Ellie lifted an eyebrow. "Would you like to pitch in, or are you just here to pout at me until you stomp away?"

"I am not pouting." I huffed, but fixed my face.

She clicked her tongue, stepping closer, her voice dropping just enough to send something sharp and hot through my chest. "You sure about that? Now, beat it. It's hard enough without having you lurking around, all broody and hot and miserable."

My pulse hammered in my ears.

I did not like the way she said that.

I also didn't like the fact that my gaze dropped to her mouth against my will.

Her smug smile grew.

Fuck.

She was taunting me.

A sharp whistle cut through the air. Levi waved wildly from across the field, jogging over.

I laughed to myself—saved by my own damn kid.

Levi looked between us, oblivious to the fact that I was having a full-body meltdown over the proximity of a woman I allegedly couldn't stand.

"Ellie, I need to run to the store," Levi said, out of breath. "Stan said we need more stakes for the pumpkin patch setup."

Ellie nodded, checking her clipboard. "And zip ties."

Levi pointed at her. "Yes. Right, zip ties. Got it."

I narrowed my eyes. "You're letting a fourteen-year-old drive into town for supplies?"

Ellie scoffed. "Oh, forgive me, *Father of the Year.* What was I thinking, allowing a teenager without a valid driver's license to drive to a store?"

Levi rolled his eyes. "I'm going with Mr. Stafford, Dad."

I didn't actually think she would allow Levi to drive illegally, and I certainly wasn't worried about him running errands with Stan. I was worried about being left here.

Alone.

With her.

Ellie turned to Levi and grinned. "You're my hero. If you come back with snacks, I'll add ten percent to today's earnings."

"Oh, heck yeah." Levi shot me a grin and jogged off.

And just like that, I was alone with her again.

Ellie let out a deep sigh, stretching her arms over her head. Her white T-shirt lifted just enough to expose a sliver of smooth, sun-kissed skin.

I dragged my eyes away before I did something fucking stupid, like reach out and touch her.

Or fall apart completely.

"So." She exhaled again, twisting her lips in thought. "Are you going to keep glaring at me, or are you going to help?"

"Help?" I scowled. "Help with what?"

She smiled, slow and sweet, stepping into my space. The heat between us crackled.

I held my ground, my muscles going tight as she tapped a finger against my chest.

"Don't worry," she said, voice soft, teasing. "I won't tell anyone you actually like it here."

I grabbed her wrist. Not rough, but not gentle. Just enough to remind both of us that we were walking a razor-thin edge.

Her lips parted.

Despite knowing better, I let my thumb brush over the inside of her wrist, slow and deliberate. Ellie swallowed hard. Her pulse jumped under my touch.

I leaned in, just enough to feel her breath on my skin. The tension coiled so tight, I thought I'd snap.

"Hey!" Levi's voice rang out.

Ellie jerked her wrist free and I took a step back.

Levi jogged toward us again, holding up a yellow bag this time. "I forgot the keys, but I did find some Sour Patch Kids."

Ellie laughed, reaching into her pocket to hand Levi a set of truck keys. He tossed her the candy as she beamed at him. "You do love me."

She shot me one last look—one last smirk that promised I was thoroughly fucked.

And, damn it, I was.

TWELVE

ELODIE

THE MOMENT LEVI LEFT, the tension was unbearable.

Callum stood there, hands in his pockets, watching me with that unreadable, broody expression. He should have left. He should have taken the out, turned right around, and walked home.

But he didn't.

He stayed, and I refused to be the first one to break, so I turned and walked away.

I exhaled sharply, forcing myself to move and ignore the heat simmering beneath my skin. I wasn't about to let some broody, muscle-bound grump make me flustered when I had a to-do list a mile long.

I spun on my heel, heading toward the barn, throwing him a glance over my shoulder. "You coming, or are you just going to stand there and glare at me all day?"

Callum hesitated and his jaw ticced.

Then, after a slow inhale, he exhaled hard through his nose and followed.

I grinned. *That's what I thought.*

The heavy thud of his boots sounded behind me as I

crossed the field toward the old barn. The moment I stepped inside, I was hit by the thick, heady scent of hay, aged wood, and something richer, darker—the unmistakable scent of Callum.

Something about his cologne mixed with the earthiness of the barn was unfair. Like someone had bottled pure testosterone and bad decisions and let it seep into my bloodstream.

I pushed the feeling aside, propping my hands on my hips as I surveyed the space.

"This is where I want to set up the farm stand," I announced, tapping my fingers against the clipboard in my hand. "We'll need a register here, some shelving along the back, and space for display crates."

I turned toward Callum just in time to catch his gaze dragging over the room—not in a casual way, but in a way that looked . . . familiar. Like he was remembering something.

Callum hovered in the entrance, his broad frame silhouetted against the daylight. He looked like he was regretting his choices, but I didn't give him the opportunity to change his mind.

I reached for the nearest crate, shoving aside an old, dusty tarp. "All this junk needs to be cleared out."

I felt his gaze on me, heavy and assessing. Cal didn't move or speak. After a beat, he exhaled through his nose and rolled his shoulders back.

And then—he worked. For all his grumbling, Callum *worked.*

He might be broody, miserable, and allergic to fun, but damn, when he put his body to something, he put his *whole body* into it.

Thick forearms flexed. Broad shoulders shifted under

the pull of each lift. Muscles contracted with each haul of heavy crates and long-forgotten equipment.

I should not have been watching, but I was. Not discreetly either.

I let myself look, let my eyes drag over him like I had every right to. Because *Jesus*—watching him work, watching him use all that power, that strength, and knowing exactly how it would feel pressed against me?

It *did* things to me.

Callum dropped a crate with a loud thud, stretching his neck. His gray tee was damp with sweat and clung to every hard ridge of his stomach. He caught me looking and narrowed his eyes.

"What?" I asked innocently, pretending to catalog and sort through the items on my clipboard.

He grunted, shaking his head before grabbing another heavy bin. The muscles in his arms rippled.

My mouth went dry.

I'd never seen Callum Blackwood fight, but I'd heard the stories from my sisters. He was trained to take down enemies before they even saw him coming. A man who moved through war zones with the kind of quiet, lethal precision that made people hesitate before crossing him. And now, here he was—hauling crates like they weighed nothing, scarred muscles shifting beneath sun-warmed skin, every inch of him honed for battle.

I hadn't meant to objectify him, but good lord, that man was made to carry things.

He moved with effortless power, rolling a shoulder before crouching low and bracing thick, corded arms around the wooden frame. His fingers flexed, forearms taut, veins rising as he lifted like it was nothing.

Muscles pulled, his shirt stretching tight across his back, and I was not prepared.

Warmth unfurled in my stomach, molten and slow, as I watched him carry the heavy crates to the door and set them down outside of the barn, just as I'd asked.

Then he turned, shaking out the tension in his arms. His jeans rode low on his hips as he worked. The heat inside the barn turned thick and heavy, beads of sweat trailing the ridges of his throat.

A lump formed in my throat. Callum should never have been in that barn.

But *damn*, did he look good in it.

We kept working, the quiet stretching long between us, the space between us shrinking by the minute. Callum didn't just move things. He dominated the space, a storm rolling through the barn, determined and commanding, like he belonged there.

And maybe, in some way, he did.

I watched as his fingers absently traced the worn wooden beam beside him, hand gliding over it in a way that almost felt . . . reverent.

Like he was ruminating over the lost possibilities.

I blinked, watching him, as a stark realization washed over me. *He wants it for himself.*

I swallowed hard, wrapping my brain around the fact that I'd possibly uncovered the reason Cal Blackwood was so contentious toward me. Maybe he'd wanted the farm for himself and my restoration plan had gotten in his way.

I didn't say a word. Instead, I yanked a bundle of rope from a dusty crate. "This needs to be tossed," I said, absently throwing it in his direction.

He caught it, scowling. "You needed me here for this?"

"What can I say?" I grinned. "Turns out I like watching you lift heavy things."

Callum sighed through his nose. "Christ, woman."

I smirked and turned back to the stack of crates, reaching for a particularly large one. But the moment I bent over to grab it, Callum was suddenly there, chest at my back, his arms bracketing mine as he reached for it first.

Heat poured off him.

I froze, hands still on the crate, my heart slamming against my ribs, but he didn't move.

Neither did I. I just stared at the tattoos inked across the back of his hand.

I could feel every inch of him behind me—broad chest, solid thighs, the brush of his stomach against my lower back. He hadn't meant to get this close. It had just happened, and now we were both standing there, breathing like we had just run across the field.

"Move," he said, voice low.

I didn't.

Instead, I turned my head slightly, my pulse hammering as I peeked just enough to catch his expression, and *fuck*.

His gaze was heavy, heated, locked on my mouth like he was barely holding himself back.

I licked my lips, which was a mistake. His hands flexed, grip tightening around the edges of the crate, his chest rising and falling in a way that made my thighs press together.

I wanted to press into him and feel all that strength against me.

Instead, I took a slow breath. "You're staring," I whispered.

Callum's jaw ticced. His nostrils flared, but he didn't move, and neither did I.

The barn was hot as hell, the summer heat pressing in, and I could feel sweat prickling at the back of my neck.

I cleared my throat. "Water break," I muttered, ducking from his embrace and adding distance between us so I could breathe.

I reached for the cooler near the barn entrance and cracked open a water bottle. I tilted my head back as I drank deep, desperate for the relief. A stray drop escaped, slipping down my chin, trailing the column of my throat.

I didn't think anything of it, until I felt him watching.

Slow. Intense.

His eyes moved over me like he wanted to lick the drop from my skin.

My breath hitched. My pulse jumped.

I lowered the bottle, swiping my thumb across my damp lower lip, my tongue darting out to catch the moisture.

His hands curled into fists like he was physically restraining himself from tearing me apart.

But I didn't smile or tease—I just stared right back.

Breaking the spell, I twisted the cap onto my water bottle and dropped it back into the cooler with a loud *thunk*.

We had work to do. Old brooms and rogue tools were shoved in every nook and cranny of the barn. Everything needed to be cleared and gone through. I didn't have time for sexy staring contests with a man who was waiting for my downfall.

We worked in heavy silence. The huge barn shrank around us as we practically ignored each other. When my hands became caked in dust and grime, I reached for the old hose coiled near the barn entrance, twisting the spigot with more force than necessary. The second I lifted it, a rogue spray shot from a crack in the hose, dousing me in an icy stream before I could jerk it away.

Water sprayed everywhere—over the dusty barn floor, over the crate, and all down the front of my shirt.

I gasped at the sudden chill of the icy water, the white fabric instantly clinging to my skin.

Callum cursed, and I looked up to find him staring again.

Not at my face, but at my tits, because, of course, the thin, soaked fabric of my tee was obscenely clinging to my skin, leaving nothing to the imagination.

I should have been embarrassed, but I wasn't, because Callum looked *wrecked*.

His throat bobbed as he swallowed, his fists clenching at his sides like he physically had to stop himself from reaching for me. His pupils were blown, jaw locked so tight it could have cracked.

The air between us ignited.

Heat licked up my spine, fire spreading low in my belly as Callum's eyes dragged over me, lingering, devouring.

I knew exactly what he was thinking. I could feel it, and I wanted him to do it.

I had never been so attracted to a man I barely knew, but something about Cal seemed to short-circuit my brain. He exuded confidence and capability—like he was the kind of man who knew how to keep a woman safe in and outside the bedroom.

He was nothing like any other man I'd known—least of all my buttoned-up, cheating-ass ex.

What was his name again? Oh, right. No one cares.

Callum took a sharp step back, like distance was the only thing saving him. "Fucking hell."

I tilted my head, playful and teasing, despite the wild pulse beating at my throat. "Something wrong?"

Callum didn't answer. Just exhaled, hard and uneven, dragging a hand through his already mussed hair.

His fingers flexed at his sides again, like he was fighting himself.

And, damn it, I wanted him to lose that fight.

I took a slow, measured step forward, erasing the distance between us.

His nostrils flared.

I gestured between our bodies. "Are you going to do something about this?" My challenge was barely above a whisper.

Callum's eyes flicked to my mouth, and then, in the span of a breath, he was on me.

His hands grabbed my waist, his body caging me against the stacked crates as his mouth crashed against mine.

Hot.

Hard.

Unyielding.

I gasped, parting for him immediately, and Callum groaned into me. It wasn't a soft kiss. Not tentative. Not testing. It was fire and frustration, all sharp teeth and a rough, claiming pull—like he'd been holding back and finally let go.

Finally.

His fingers dug into my hips, like he needed to anchor himself. I pressed forward, arms winding around his neck, drinking him in, breathing him in.

A rumble came from deep in his chest, and I felt it everywhere.

I fisted his T-shirt, pulling him closer.

Callum growled, pressing me back against a beam. The feel of him—hard muscle, solid heat, pure want—sent a pulse of fire straight through me.

His tongue swept over mine, and I whimpered, my thighs clenching.

Callum groaned like he felt it, too, one hand sliding down, gripping my hip, and dragging me flush against him.

His cock was thick and hard, pressing against my stomach, and I wanted him everywhere.

Wanted his hands up my shirt. Wanted his mouth lower. Wanted to sink against him and never come up for air.

But just as suddenly as it happened, Callum ripped himself away, like he had just realized what he had done. His breaths were ragged, his hands still gripping my hips, like he couldn't let go even if he wanted to.

I licked my swollen lips, swallowing past the ache in my chest. His eyes were still on my mouth, still hungry. He took another step back, and his hands dropped.

Cal ran a hand over his face, exhaling hard. "Fuck."

I just smiled, because, yeah. He was so fucked.

And so was I.

THIRTEEN

CALLUM

THE NEXT THREE weeks blurred together in a haze of working long days, waking early, fixing things that always seemed to be breaking, and trying to forget Elodie Darling existed altogether.

It wasn't working.

I told myself I was busy. That I had better things to think about. That I didn't have time to sit around stewing over a kiss I shouldn't have let happen in the first place.

But damn it—I felt that kiss everywhere.

It was in the restless energy that coiled in my chest every night, in the way my fingers tightened around my coffee mug each morning, like holding on to something solid would keep me from thinking about the softness of her in my hands.

My jaw tightened whenever her name was brought up. Anytime Levi mentioned the farm, my fists clenched. A slow, burning heat crawled up my spine whenever I caught a glimpse of her across town, talking too close to someone who wasn't me.

I was officially losing my mind.

It wasn't just the kiss. It was the way she had smiled against my mouth, like she'd known that kiss would happen all along. The way she had melted into me, fingers twisted in my shirt, like she belonged there.

I was a grown man—a logical, practical man. I had been through war zones, trained to fight in the worst conditions imaginable. I knew how to compartmentalize, how to keep my emotions locked down where they belonged, so why the hell couldn't I get her out of my head?

It wasn't like I wanted her. Not really. I just wanted to stop the urge to kiss the smug look off her face. To stop remembering the way she tasted like honey and heat and recklessness.

Every second I spent not thinking about her was followed by a second where I was gritting my teeth, telling myself I *wasn't* thinking about her. I tried drowning it out with work. Fixing things that didn't need fixing, running until my lungs burned, but it didn't matter. My mind still went back to her—uninvited and unstoppable, like a song I hated but couldn't stop humming.

I wasn't usually the kind of man who got rattled. I didn't lose sleep over things I couldn't control. But Elodie? She had sunk beneath my skin like a sliver, impossible to ignore and impossible to remove without drawing blood.

I was torn from my brooding by a low, scratchy yowl.

The sound scraped against my patience like nails on a chalkboard. I ignored the catlike groans at first, shifting my focus to the busted railing I was reinforcing on the porch. Another yowl. A little closer this time.

I sighed, tightening the drill in my hand.

Then came the third—long and drawn out, like something from a horror movie.

I dropped my head back. "You've got to be kidding me."

I turned, and there it was. A scrappy, battle-worn menace of a cat—patchy fur the color of old rust, one ear half torn, and a single gold eye that gleamed with the kind of knowing patience only a creature who had survived some serious shit could possess.

Its fluffy tail twitched playfully, like it had been summoned by the universe to personally test my patience. One golden eye blinked up at me in blatant expectation.

For a beat we just stared at each other.

It yowled again, even louder this time.

"No." I pointed the drill at it. "Absolutely not."

The cat tilted its head. Blinked. Then it proceeded to take a slow, deliberate step forward.

I scowled. "Don't even think about it. You are not welcome here."

I tried to swat in its general direction, but it took another step.

I set the drill onto the porch. "I mean it."

Another step.

Jesus Christ.

I narrowed my eyes, leaning forward. "Do I look like a cat guy to you?"

The scrawny furball hopped onto the porch, then sat, curling its tail around its feet like it had all the time in the world, letting out a massive, jaw-cracking yawn. The cat yawned like my presence was boring it to death.

"You've got to be kidding me," I muttered, dragging a hand down my face and looking around in disbelief.

The cat just blinked again and licked its paw.

I considered my options. Shooing it away didn't work. It appeared immune to my scowls. I certainly couldn't ignore it—not when it was sitting there like some furry omen of my inevitable downfall.

I settled for intimidation.

Straightening, I took a slow, deliberate step forward, boots scuffing against the wood. The cat didn't move. Another heavy step. Still nothing.

Fine.

I crossed my arms over my chest, leveling it with my best military-grade frown. "Go away."

The cat stretched, arching its bony spine, and then— just to really drive the knife in—rolled to its back, belly in the air as both arms and legs stretched out, like it had lived here its whole damn life.

Unbelievable.

"This isn't happening," I muttered. I had survived worse things than this—literal battles, fistfights, near-death experiences, but apparently my greatest adversary was a cat with one eye and an attitude problem.

The cat rolled back to its belly and flicked its ears, unimpressed with my surly attitude.

I exhaled sharply, looking past it toward the property line and the unmistakable sound of trucks, tires grinding against gravel, engines running too close to my property.

I would have to deal with my furry, uninvited guest later.

I stepped off the porch to peer down the roadway, my already sour mood turning downright lethal.

There was a line of work trucks—on *my* road.

Freshly irritated, I clenched my fists as I watched another truck roll to a stop in front of the inn. I didn't need a sign to know who was responsible for this particular headache.

By the time I got close enough to see her, Elodie was at the end of the roadway, clipboard in hand, hair windblown and wild, and looking like she hadn't a care in the world while chaos unfolded around her.

She was thriving, while I was losing control. I probably should have turned around. Should have let her deal with whatever mess she was creating, but I couldn't.

Because now she was messing with my business, and for the first time since she showed up, I was entirely out of patience. Elodie Darling was encroaching.

Again.

I'd spent the last three weeks avoiding her, but now she was forcing my hand.

"Fine," I muttered, shooting one last glare at the cat. "I'm dealing with this right now."

I stalked across the front yard, boots kicking up dirt, frustration stinging in my chest.

The sun was still high, beating down on my back. The scent of cut grass and summer flowers mixed with the breeze rolling in from the lake. The air smelled like home, and I hated that it felt different now.

Because of her.

Because of this.

The smart move would have been to keep my distance, but instead I was marching toward trouble, shadowed by an unwanted cat hot on my heels. I glanced down at the cat, who looked like it was heading into battle alongside me.

"This is probably your fault," I said gruffly. "I just know it."

The cat didn't disagree. I shook my head and suppressed a smile. I wasn't its friend. I wasn't feeding it. I wasn't keeping it. I sure as hell wasn't naming it.

When I reached the property line, I didn't slow my pace. "Darling," I called, voice sharp.

She turned, shielding her eyes from the sun. And then—

of course—she grinned, wide and welcoming. That sweet, slow, sunshine-smothered smile sent something dark and restless moving through my stomach.

"Good morning, Callum." Her voice was all light and pleasant, like we were friends. Like she hadn't spent the past three weeks haunting my every waking thought. Elodie arched a brow, tilting her head. "A little early in our relationship for sweet nicknames, don't you think?"

I crossed my arms. "That's your last name, isn't it?"

"It sure is." Her grin widened. "But when you say it like that, Cal, it almost sounds like you're sweet on me."

I ignored the warmth spreading low in my stomach and kept my arms crossed. "What the hell is all this?"

"Oh, you know." She gestured vaguely at the mess she was creating. "Just a little facelift to the entrance."

I narrowed my eyes. It was too close. She was too close.

"This road is supposed to stay clear," I said. "You've got trucks blocking access to the inn, and if they keep cutting through, it's going to screw up the entire driveway."

She tilted her head. "So what I'm hearing is that you don't like the road being messed up?"

I exhaled slowly. "That's exactly what I just said."

Elodie made a thoughtful noise, crossing her arms and nodding. "Right. Interesting."

I frowned. "Interesting how?"

She bit her lip, looking entirely too amused. "Just . . . you know. I was expecting you to say something more dramatic. Like, 'Elodie, you're ruining everything' or 'Elodie, I can't stand you' or maybe even—"

"Elodie," I gritted out, my patience hanging by a thread.

She grinned. "Ah. There it is." Her laughter was easy, effortless, and worse—it was nearly contagious.

My lips twitched, and I killed the impulse immediately. There was no way I was giving her that win.

The morning sun hit the golden strands of her hair as she shifted her weight. The hem of her shorts rode up just enough to—

Damn it.

I needed to get my head on straight. I shook her from my thoughts, taking a slow breath, and dragging my focus back to why I was here. "I need the road cleared."

"Mm. I don't know." She tapped a finger against her chin. "That sounds like a *you* problem."

My jaw ticced. "It's a problem for everyone using this road."

Her smile didn't waver. "That's funny, because last I checked, that was your bed-and-breakfast and my farm. Two separate businesses, remember?"

I inhaled through my nose, hands curling into fists. "*Stan's* business is causing my business problems."

Elodie's gaze flicked to my hands, then back to my face. Her own expression softened, just slightly. "I get that this is hard for you."

I scoffed. "This?"

She nodded. "Yeah. The whole . . . me succeeding thing. It must be tough."

My teeth actually ground together. "You're impossible."

"And yet," she mused, "here you are. *Again.*"

She was baiting me. I should have turned around and left.

But she was standing there, all bright eyes and flushed cheeks, the heat from the morning pressing around us, making the air thick and heavy.

And for one terrible, fleeting second, I remembered what it felt like to kiss her.

Did she think about it too?

I didn't know what was worse—the fact I'd lost sleep over a *kiss* or the fact that Elodie seemed completely unfazed by the whole thing.

My pulse pounded.

She tsked. "So grumpy. You know, that's not a good look for tourism."

Before I could fire back, another voice cut through the tension.

"Ah, good! You're both here." Breathless, Helen strode toward us, clipboard tucked under one arm, an eager glint in her eye. "Callum, I've had three guests complain that they can't get up the road. Some trucks are blocking the path—it's a mess out there."

I pinned Elodie with my best *I told you so* look, and she had the decency to look remorseful.

"But what I also needed to tell you both is that the Keepers are hosting the Ghost of Star Harbor walking tour again this year. We've got nearly triple the sign-ups, and we're inviting local businesses to participate—advertising, handing out brochures, that kind of thing." She turned to Elodie. "Star Harbor Farm could be involved . . . get a little free advertising."

Elodie's smile widened. "I'd love that."

I wanted to walk away, but instead I heard myself saying, "The Drifted Spirit Inn will be there too."

Elodie turned, brows lifted in amusement. "Really?"

Helen beamed. "That's fantastic! The inn would be a perfect last stop on the tour." She turned to Elodie with a wink. "Everyone could get an early peek at the farm too."

I had no idea why I'd just agreed to that. Apparently self-preservation had left the chat, because the last thing I needed was another excuse to be around Elodie.

"We'll be ready." The confidence in Elodie's voice was unmistakable.

Helen turned, pausing to smirk at me before she headed in the direction of the inn.

The cat—my unwanted shadow—rubbed against Elodie's leg. She sucked in a surprised gasp, crouching down to greet him—or . . . her?

It.

"I didn't know you had a cat!" Elodie's voice rose several octaves. "Oh, come here, little baby."

She scooped it up like a newborn, letting it rest against her chest as she nuzzled into its scraggly fur.

"Hey, sweet girl," she cooed. "You're so cute." The full force of her smile was beaming at me. "Is she yours?"

I scowled. "No."

Elodie's smile deepened as she continued baby-talking to the cat. "Your daddy is so grumpy. Don't let his mean scary looks fool you. I think he's a big old softie. If he's mean to you, you come tell me and I will yell at him for you. Oh, what a sweet baby."

With an exaggerated eye roll, I turned on my heel, stalking back toward the inn. Elodie's laughter followed me, along with the cat, prancing at my side. I wanted to let it go, but as her laugh curled around me, warm and light as summer, I had the sinking feeling that—like the damn cat— she wasn't going anywhere.

And worse—I didn't hate it.

FOURTEEN

ELODIE

A GIDDY LITTLE thrill zipped through me as I watched Cal stomp back toward the Drifted Spirit. That mangy little cat pranced at his side, and I couldn't have stopped my grin if I tried. Just last week that scrappy barn cat had popped up out of nowhere. While I was finishing the last of the barn clean-out, she'd startled me with a flick of her fluffy tail and a low growl. She was scared, and based on how beat-up she'd looked, the cat had been on her own for a long time.

After proving I wasn't a threat, I bundled her up and headed to the vet. The scratches up my forearms had been worth it. She confirmed that the cat was about a year old, but had been through a lot in her young life. The clip in her ear indicated she had been previously spayed as part of Michigan's animal control program. The vet assured me that she would be a perfect barn cat since she was so accustomed to life outdoors—all she needed was a little love and someone to care for her.

I knew just the person.

That sassy little cat wasn't the only thing that was battle-worn and a little untrusting. All I needed to do was place her new food dish strategically close to the Drifted Spirit. I knew it was only a matter of time before she cozied up to Cal.

Besides, if he was really so heartless that he refused to see past her one-eyed glare, then he didn't deserve her love anyway. I would be more than happy to care for that sweet little cat if he wouldn't.

I watched with a triumphant grin as Cal walked side by side with the cat all the way back to the inn. I'd been right about Cal—he wasn't nearly as cold and heartless as he pretended to be. There was a soft heart beneath all that bluster, and maybe that cat was one way to draw it out.

Cal needed a friend, and he had made it clear that he wasn't interested in that friend being *me*.

Which was a shame, really, because if that kiss was any indication, being *friends* with Cal Blackwood had the potential to be very, very fun.

At first my pride had taken a hit when, after that soul-searing kiss in the barn, Cal had all but disappeared. That changed when I finally did run into him at the hardware store downtown and he looked like he'd seen a ghost.

There was comfort in knowing I had wriggled under his skin.

With an exhale, I spun in a slow circle, taking inventory of the transformations unfolding on the farm. The pumpkin patch was thriving since the vines now had room to spread, a new stone-and-iron entryway would welcome families from all over to Star Harbor Farm, and the orchard was slowly taking shape. I had talked to the man Stan used to tend to the orchard, offering him actual money to carefully trim back the trees. The farm wouldn't be ready to sell apples this season, but I was playing the long game.

When a large truck rolled by, I whistled and lifted my

arm. The driver slowed to a stop and lowered his window. "Ma'am?"

"Morning. I need you and your crew to be mindful of blocking the road. We're getting complaints and I don't want to impact the inn. Can you take care of that or do I need to call the boss?" I asked with a tip of my eyebrow.

The driver let out a low chuckle, shaking his head. "Damn. You're tougher than you look."

I shot him a wink. "And don't you forget it."

The driver nodded and smiled back. "I'll take care of that. We'll be off the road in fifteen minutes."

"Thank you!" Satisfied that I solved that particular problem, I made my way toward the barn. The sun beat down on my shoulders, and I took in the rolling green hills in front of me. I gave myself a mental pat on the back. This place was more than just a project. It was proof that I could build something, that I could take broken, overgrown land and make it into something worth keeping.

In some ways the transformation was proof that Amy was wrong about me. I wasn't some *flake* who couldn't follow through. I was seeing this to the end.

At first it was pure exhaustion that kept me from over-spending and relying on retail therapy, but lately it felt like something more. Day by day, my lifestyle had been pared down to quiet mornings walking the farm, getting my hands dirty with whatever needed fixing, and rebuilding the neglected relationships with my family.

I breathed in the warm coastal air. *Is this what satisfaction and belonging feel like?*

I was proud not only of the strides I'd made in getting Star Harbor Farm ready for the public, but also for thinking about Callum Blackwood only 872 times per day.

By this time next week, I might get it down to 700.

Maybe even 650, if I really put my mind to it. Progress was progress.

Besides, that number was down from the incalculable stream of thoughts since he pressed me against the wall of the barn and delivered the best kiss I'd ever had in my *life*.

A girl just didn't forget something like that . . . even if he did spend the next three weeks actively avoiding me.

My muscles burned as I made long strides across the farmland. The inside of the barn had been scrubbed clean, ready for the shelves that I had designed and ordered for excess pumpkins. A local company was hired to sand the exterior of the barn and give it a fresh coat of cherry red paint.

As I pulled open the door to the barn, my eyes found the exact spot where Cal had rocked my world. I couldn't imagine a universe where I wouldn't feel that unsettling *whoosh* in my stomach every time I stepped inside.

Even now, the scent of sawdust and sun-warmed wood filled my nose, tangling with the ghosts of memory. My skin prickled, my body remembering before my mind even had the chance to stop it.

The interior of the barn may have been mostly empty, but I could see the potential with effortless clarity. I documented everything on social media—stylized images of the budding fruit trees, the barn transformation, and even the down-and-dirty messes of installing the new front gates. As a result, the Star Harbor Farm social media account had steadily taken off. I had even started including myself in the posts, sharing my progress with the followers, highlighting the *steep* learning curve of a city girl returning to her hometown roots.

Sure, I wasn't proud of the fact I twisted an ankle or got muddy when I fell on my ass or had to ask the followers what certain barn equipment even *was*, but the positive response and outpouring of support was well worth it.

Recently I had even been fielding phone calls from local artists asking if there would be spaces available to rent in order to sell to our customers. I tucked that little nugget in the back of my mind, remembering to talk to Stan about even more expansion opportunities.

But first things first—my main goal was transforming the old farm into a premier family destination. Star Harbor Farm wasn't going to be just any old farm. It would be a place where families came year after year, making new memories. It would be fun and nostalgic all at once.

If Cal had his way, nothing would change, but I knew that what the farm needed was *fun*.

A honk outside drew my attention, and I stepped from the shadows inside the barn into the afternoon sun. Stan drove a tow truck with Levi grinning in the front seat. My heart squeezed for the kid—he'd been smiling more days than not, and I knew I'd had a hand in that.

He'd been through so much in losing his mother, and somehow this farm had become a safe place for him too. Seeing him light up over something as simple as an old farm made me want to protect that spark at all costs.

"Ellie!" Levi shouted. "I had an idea!"

My hand shielded my eyes from the sun, and I could just make out an old vehicle being pulled behind the tow truck. It was black and rusted in spots, but it was the kind of farm truck from the 1950s that *screamed* nostalgia.

When Stan parked, he and Levi got out to greet me.

Stan clamped a hand on Levi's shoulder. "This kid's got a head full of ideas." Stan's eyes twinkled. "If only he got this excited about remembering to eat breakfast."

Levi huffed. "It's not my fault the coffee you make is terrible."

My brow creased. "You're fourteen! Why are you drinking coffee?" I shook my head. Some battles were hard-won, and this conversation was going off the rails. "Okay, focus. So what's the idea?"

Stan gestured toward the old truck. "He saw this pile of scrap metal behind my house and insisted we drag it up here."

Levi walked toward the ancient truck. "Isn't it awesome? Stan says it doesn't run and all the tires are flat, but I thought we could put it up here, near the barn. People could take pictures near it or you could fill it with pumpkins or whatever." His brows were lifted, waiting for me to see his vision.

"Levi . . ." I shook my head, pulling my lower lip between my teeth. "I don't know what to say. This is—I mean, it's . . . *perfect!*" As my voice climbed higher alongside my excitement, Levi's grin split wider. I grabbed his shoulders as I bounced up and down in front of him.

"Stan, can you drag it around this side?" I pointed to where the truck could be near the barn without blocking the roadway or any entrances. Stan nodded, and we took a step back as he adjusted the tow truck to place our new centerpiece in the perfect spot. It took some time to get it unhooked, but once it was in place, I framed it with my hands like a photographer. I already knew the perfect way to style the truck for a new social media post—maybe I'd even get Levi to be in it, if he wanted to.

"This really is perfect." I bumped my shoulder into Levi's, emotion burning at the bridge of my nose. "Thanks, kid."

His face turned eight shades of red, but he only ducked

his head, kicking at the dirt with his boot and smiling. "Just figured it could make people happy."

"It will, Levi." My throat tightened. "*You* do too."

Stan hung out the driver's-side door, standing above the tow truck. "I swear I can't see it the same way you do, but I'm glad it makes you two happy. You've both got that same creative spirit as my Karen." Stan's eyes went wistful for a moment before he thumped his hand on the roof of the truck. "Better go see Phil at the junkyard." Stan pointed to the four, sad flat tires on the antique truck. "If she's going to be photographed, might as well fix her up a bit, and Lord knows Phil's got tire mountain over there."

My eyes went wide as a thought clicked into place. *Tire Mountain. Tire. Freaking. Mountain.*

"That's it!" I bounced on my heels. "You know how I was saying there's that big empty chunk of land over here?" I spread my arms to the large hill to my left. "Tire Mountain! Stacks of old semitruck tires that are built into the hillside. Kids can climb up and maybe even have a potato-sack slide down the side or something!" My mind was moving faster than I could talk. My energy was bubbling. "Okay! I have to go draw this up before I forget it!"

I spun in a circle, my brain firing off faster than I could keep up. This was it. This was *exactly* the kind of thing that would make Star Harbor Farm different. *Memorable.* It was fun and nostalgic and a little bit ridiculous—just like the best childhood memories always were.

I pointed at Stan. "Talk to Phil. See what kind of deal you can make to take a butt-load of those tires off his hands!"

I ran back toward the barn as Stan laughed and shook his head. "You got it, boss."

FIFTEEN

ELODIE

THERE ARE few days that go down in history as truly *perfect*.

Today was not one of them by any stretch of the imagination. I was filthy, tired, and frustrated that sometimes I had to exercise patience.

I hated that.

Tire Mountain was a wild idea but would help the town reduce its waste while adding an attraction to the farm. Trouble was, getting thirty gigantic semitruck tires dug into the side of a hill was a hell of a lot more work than I'd bargained for.

But it didn't matter, because it was for the kids. I really wanted it to be complete before the Ghost of Star Harbor tour gave people a peek into what we were creating on the farm. I would have to settle for half built and hope everyone else could see how great it was going to be.

The night of the tour was thick with mist, hanging low along the streets of downtown Star Harbor like something alive, creeping into the cracks of old buildings, stretching long fingers into the hollows of the trees.

The ghost walk had started off as fun, an excuse to get tangled up in the town's past, but somewhere along the way the atmosphere had shifted. Now at the end of the tour, standing at the entrance to the farm, looking at the shadows stretching long and lean across the dirt road, I felt the weight of something I couldn't name pressing against my skin. A tingle danced up my spine.

The scent of damp earth and lake water clung to the air, mingling with the faintest trace of something else—cedar and smoke, something sharp and clean, something unmistakably *him*.

Callum.

He wasn't looking at me, but I could feel him. The way his presence took up space, the way my body had been attuned to him all evening, tracking his movements without even meaning to.

I exhaled slowly, rubbing my arms against the sudden chill.

The tour was wrapping up, the lingering guests listening to the last stories woven by the Keepers, but I didn't move.

Because he was still here and because I still hadn't stopped thinking about what I'd heard.

Not the kiss—that came later—but the private moment I hadn't been prepared for. An image that still rattled through me at the worst times, creeping up my spine, pooling warm and restless low in my stomach.

I hadn't meant to intrude, and I certainly hadn't meant to walk into his house that day, catching him in the kind of moment that can't be undone—can't be unfelt once it had settled under the skin.

And now?

Now I stood in the dark and wondered—*had Cal done it*

again? Had he thought about me like that since the first time? Had he muttered my name in the dark the way I'd heard it spill from his mouth that night, rough and wrecked, nothing like the cold detachment he pretended to wear like armor?

Lately, I had become obsessed with the thought. A slow burn started in my stomach, crawling lower, settling deep.

I swallowed hard, pressing my nails into my palms, forcing the thought away before it dragged me under.

"Okay, this is way spookier than I expected," Kit said, suddenly appearing at my side, rubbing her arms. "I thought this was gonna be like a campfire-story situation, but this is legit terrifying. I feel like we should be holding hands."

I huffed out a laugh but looped my arm with hers. "You need me to protect you?"

Kit scoffed. "You, protecting me? Okay, tough guy."

Her tone was teasing, but I took the opportunity to shift the conversation before my thoughts wandered back where they shouldn't.

In the evening light, against the dune cliff, the farm looked moody and menacing, not at all the memory-making family destination I was striving toward. I sighed, looking out over the fields. "I feel like it's all coming together, you know? Like the hard work is finally paying off."

From the corner of my eye, I saw my little sister make a face. "Yeah, Stan's place is great . . ."

I stopped to look at her. "What?"

Kit went to speak but paused. I pinned her with my best older-sister look so she'd continue. "Well, come on—I mean, you're giving him ideas, but you're not actually *doing* the work, right?"

I blinked at her, momentarily stunned. *What the heck? Even my little sister doesn't think I can do it?*

I swallowed back the sharp pang of tears before I let my emotions overtake me.

"I'm doing a lot of work, actually. Almost *all* of it, to be exact. Sure, I have help, but I'm not sitting on my ass eating bonbons while everyone else gets their hands dirty." I held up my mangled manicure. "Do these look like they've seen the inside of a spa?"

Kit held up her hands in defense. "Whoa. I'm sorry. I didn't realize the sweat equity you were putting into the place. *Noted.*"

"Sorry." I softened. "I'm just a little tired and grumpy."

Clearly my defensiveness was also indicative of some inner sore subject . . . maybe I needed to work on that.

As we followed the group across the grass toward the dune cliff, I pointed to the front porch of the inn, where the cat was curled on the top step. "Speaking of things that need protecting . . . I may or may not have manipulated Callum into adopting a stray cat."

"I'm sorry, what?" Kit blinked, holding back her laughter.

I crossed my arms, tilting my chin up. "She's scrappy and one-eyed and has the attitude of someone who's survived a war. It seemed like a perfect pairing."

Kit stared at me for a long second before her lips curled into an absolutely evil grin. "Wait—you thought he needed some pussy and brought him an actual cat instead of"—she gestured toward me—"dishing yourself up on a platter?"

My laughter and eye roll were immediate. "Trust me. Callum doesn't want anything I have to offer."

Kit hummed, unconvinced.

And now I was lying to myself and *my little sister. Great.*

The truth was, I still remembered exactly how it felt

when he kissed me. How his hands had tightened on my waist, how his body had pressed firm and unyielding against mine, how his features had darkened before he—

"Hello." Kit waved a hand in front of my face. "You okay?"

I forced a very unbothered, completely fine, not-at-all-horny nod. "Yep!"

Kit's knowing smile made it clear she wasn't buying it.

The distant wail of wind cut through the night, sending a ripple of unease through the thinning crowd. I swallowed, shifting closer to the group of Keepers standing off to the side.

Helen's voice dropped lower, spinning the final part of the legend.

". . . and on nights like this, when the fog rolls in and the moon is hidden, some say you can hear her crying—the Lady of the Dunes, still waiting for the man she lost to the sea."

Another gust of wind whispered through the trees.

I wasn't scared, not really, but when another low, eerie sound rolled through the night, my stomach clenched, and I reached out, gripping something hard beneath my hand.

I looked down to see my fingers curled around Cal's scarred, tattooed forearm.

Solid, warm, and unmovable.

I expected him to jerk away, to tease or to smirk, but instead, he went still. So still I could feel the shift in his breathing, feel the slight, tense flex of his muscles beneath my grip.

The warmth of him sank into my palm, searing my skin.

A slow, excruciating beat passed.

Then his voice came, low and unreadable. "Scared, Darling?"

I swallowed hard. Too hard. "Pfft." I let go too fast, crossing my arms. "No. Just"—I cleared my throat—"making sure I didn't trip on those rocks."

His gaze dragged slowly from my legs back up to my face. "Right."

I turned away, pulse hammering, heart lodged somewhere in my throat. Kit snickered beside me and I jabbed her ribs with my elbow.

A familiar voice cut in. "Hey," Austin said, stepping up beside Callum. We exchanged smiles and head nods as he stepped in line with us.

Helen and my sister Selene started passing out information about the Lady of the Dunes as the tour came to a close.

Austin leaned toward Cal. "Hey, that woman over there? What do you know about her?"

Kit perked up immediately, glancing between them to find Austin looking right at our sister Selene.

Callum flicked his gaze toward Austin. "Why?"

Austin shrugged, casual but a little too interested. "She seems . . . interesting. Thought maybe you could introduce me."

Kit's eyebrows shot up, and she leaned toward me to whisper, "Ooooh. Selene's got a hot younger man on her tail."

I bit back a giggle but shushed her. "Leave her alone," I whispered, but I would tuck that interesting little nugget away for later.

Callum, however, didn't react beyond a slow exhale. "Maybe another time, man." Cal turned to walk toward the inn.

Kit and I hung around near the fence line while the tour

dispersed. When it ended, I hugged my sisters goodbye and lingered outside as the last of the crowd disappeared.

Crossing my arms, I breathed in a lungful of night air before glancing toward the Drifted Spirit. Cal was staring at me, his cat weaving a path between his legs.

I stared back, watching Callum watch me.

I rested my butt against the new porch railing of the cottage. With the dunes at my back, I watched and waited.

The cat twined herself around Cal's legs again, rubbing her face against his pant leg.

Callum didn't kick her away or shove her off. Instead, he reached down and scratched behind her ears as I fought a smile.

I wonder if he named her.

When he looked up, his eyes were softer, but intense. A lump formed in my throat, but before I could escape, Cal was already off the front porch and walking right toward me.

SIXTEEN

CALLUM

I STALKED toward Elodie without any real objective in mind. All I knew was that I had spent the last two hours keenly aware of her every movement. The dampness in the night air added a slight chill, and my brain kept wondering whether her jeans were enough to keep her warm. Her little T-shirt, knotted at her belly button and revealing a sliver of toned, tanned skin, certainly wasn't doing fuck all.

I had no idea what I planned to say to her once I reached her cottage. All I knew was that I was pissed off, keyed up, and downright irritated.

A trilling meow sounded at my feet, and I looked down to see the cat trotting alongside me.

I paused. "Scratch."

Fine. Yes, I had caved and named her.

I turned and pointed toward the Drifted Spirit Inn. "Go home."

She glared at me with one golden eye and plunked down onto her furry bottom next to my boot.

I lowered my voice so she understood just how serious I was. "Go."

I never knew a cat could harrumph, but that was exactly the sound that came from her tiny furry body, but she did listen.

At least someone around here does.

Satisfied I was entering this battle alone, I continued on my warpath toward Elodie Darling. In one easy stride, I hooked a leg over the cedar fence that separated our properties and vaulted myself over. Elodie stood at the base of her porch steps with her arms crossed and her chin lifted in the air.

Her exaggerated eye roll only ticked my heart rate higher. "What now?" she grumbled as I got within earshot. Her piercing emerald eyes held mine, but even in the low lighting, I could see they held no malice.

No, this was just what we did—poked and prodded at each other for sport. I complained about whatever new idea for the farm she came up with, stomping my feet and acting like a baby. She pretended to listen and take my concerns into consideration before smiling that sultry, devastating smile and doing whatever the fuck she wanted anyway.

I had come to live for those little back-and-forth moments when I could volley petty insults and low-level complaints simply so I could watch her pout that pretty little mouth and call me an insufferable ape.

With her arms crossed like that, Elodie's tits swelled higher, stretching the limits of the cotton fabric of her shirt. My hand twitched at my side, desperately wanting to feel the shape and weight of her. I curled it into a fist as my cock raged against the zipper of my jeans.

Somewhere along the lines, our bitter banter had become my twisted version of foreplay, and I had missed it.

Part of me wondered whether I argued with her for the

sole excuse of using the image of those flushed cheeks and pouty lips to jack off to every night.

I bit down on my molars as frustration rippled through me.

"What is it now, Mr. Blackwood?"

Oh, that was a new one.

I couldn't say I hated it—the formal sound of my name rolling off her pouty lips.

The tip of my tongue pressed against my teeth as I suppressed a smile. "Just making sure you made it home safely. I saw you were awfully scared out there tonight. So scared you had to grab my arm." I brushed a dismissive hand across the skin on my forearm, where I could still feel the branding heat of her touch. "You know in some places, that's assault."

A disgusted scoff rattled in the back of her throat. "You are the *worst*." She dragged out the last word for emphasis. "Besides, I didn't even know it was *you* next to me." A mischievous grin hooked at the corner of her mouth as she blinked innocently. "I thought it was Austin."

My nostrils flared. I knew she was lying, poking at me just to get me riled up, and I hated that it worked so easily.

Austin was twenty-eight, built like a tank and with a metabolism that hadn't seen the dark side of thirty, and his cocky smirk proved that he knew it too. He may be Brody's half brother, but I'd still lay the kid flat out if he thought he had a chance with Elodie.

Besides, I reminded myself that it was her sister Selene that Austin was asking about.

I scoffed in her direction. "If you think that kid can kiss you well enough to make your toes curl, then by all means have at it." I took a step toward her, closing the gap between us as primal instinct took over. "But don't forget, I could smell how badly you wanted me when I kissed you. Admit it . . ." My voice lowered. "You were dripping for me, weren't you?"

Her cheeks flushed, but my words hadn't scared her off yet. "Tell me, Cal. Tell me exactly what it is you hate about me."

I couldn't do what I wanted to, so instead I let her have it. "I hate that there are workers stomping all over this place. I hate that my kid would rather spend time with you than me. I hate that I can't get a *second* of peace and quiet anymore. I hate that if you somehow manage to pull this off, the place will be crawling with tourists. I hate that you think you've got what it takes to actually pull this off, and I really hate that I know you're fucking right."

The last part had slipped out, but once it did, tension charged the space between us.

She swallowed hard, knowing she'd won. Her chin lifted. "You are the most insufferable man on the planet."

I shook my head, letting a lie roll off my tongue. "You and your opinions mean nothing to me."

She blanked and her lips pursed. I knew my shitty comment had wounded her, at least a little bit. "Is that why you came all the way over here? To prove to me exactly how *unaffected* you are by my presence?" Her eyes flicked to my dick and he twitched at her attention.

I opened my mouth to fire back a retort when her hands gripped the sides of my face, pulling my mouth to hers.

For a millisecond I was stunned, but I didn't hesitate.

I took control.

My arm banded around her slim little waist as I pulled her roughly into me. Her body melted into mine as her breath hitched, opening her mouth just enough for my tongue to delve in and explore. I couldn't think straight with the way her leg hitched up against my hip, pressing her heat into me.

My cock throbbed, begging to take her in every way possible. My body moved as my thoughts scrambled to keep up. My hands gripped the round globes of her ass, lifting her up so she could straddle me. Our mouths moved in sync, her tongue sliding against mine as little moans pumped out of her and into my bloodstream.

I had never felt such a clawing, aching need for someone.

I ripped my mouth from hers. "Tell me to stop."

She was breathless, her eyes searching mine as I stomped up the porch steps toward the front door of her cottage. "Why the hell would I do that?"

My mouth clamped onto her neck, my teeth dragging a path along the smooth column of her windpipe, stopping just below her ear to whisper, "Because if you don't, I'm going to hate fuck you until you learn to do what I say."

A wicked grin flashed across her features. It was a challenge, and I think a part of her knew I was full of shit—that she was the one completely and utterly in control of me.

Elodie's tongue slid across her upper lip as she stared down at me. "I hate you too," she whispered, then pulled my lip into her mouth, gently biting down on it. "Don't you dare fucking stop."

It was all the permission I needed. Her consent was the last thread keeping me from completely unraveling. With one free hand I turned the knob and kicked open the front door of her cottage with my boot.

It swung open, rattling on its hinges and slamming into the wall with a crack.

Elodie giggled as she arched against me. "Ooh . . . Wes is going to be pissed at you. He'll have to fix that hole."

I growled up at her. "I don't give a shit what Wes thinks. He can bill me for it."

"Oh, Daddy with the deep pockets," Elodie teased.

Such a fucking brat.

She climbed higher on my waist, making it impossible not to feel her heat pressed against me. I deposited her onto the kitchen table with an ungraceful thump. Her tits bounced, and my throat went dry. My fingertips found the collar of her T-shirt, and without hesitation I ripped it open, admiring the creamy, sheer lace bra underneath.

"You're paying for that too," she said, breathless.

Her fingers grabbed my belt buckle, yanking me forward until my thighs hit the table. She jerked and pulled until my belt came loose.

As she went for the button of my jeans, I covered her hands with mine. "Mm-mm, Darling. You're not running the show here." I gripped underneath her thighs and hauled her to the edge of the table. "I am."

She sat back on her elbows, tipping her knees open and putting herself on display just for me. I slipped off her green rubber boots and socks before unbuttoning her jeans and lowering her zipper with an aching slowness.

As the teeth of the zipper separated, I kept my eyes locked on hers. I wanted her to know *exactly* whom she belonged to. We were both panting as I peeled the denim away from her smooth, tanned thighs.

Her long hours of work rebuilding the farm had toned her legs and given her some added bulk. I fucking loved her fullness as my fingertips dimpled her skin with my tight grip.

All that separated me from her was a flimsy scrap of the same sheer material that covered her breasts. The thong covered her pussy but disappeared between her ass cheeks, and I ran a finger down her seam, letting it disappear alongside it.

She inhaled and arched her back, nipples pebbling beneath the sheer fabric of her bra. My fingers plucked at one taut little bud as I groaned.

My hand teased the fabric covering her, relishing the hot, wet mess beneath my hand. "I knew this cunt would be dripping for me."

"Oh. Oh my—" she panted.

"Open your eyes," I demanded. She complied and my back wound tighter. "Say it. Tell me who makes this greedy little pussy wet."

"You." She gasped as one finger slipped inside her thong. Her head fell back, revealing the slim column of her neck, and my hand ached to wrap around it. "Fuck, Cal. It's only wet for you."

I grinned. "That's right, Darling."

She was soaked for me and I was going to ruin her for anyone else.

SEVENTEEN

ELODIE

My legs were spread, exposing my most private area to a man I was supposed to hate. His hungry eyes were locked on my pussy as one finger, then two, teased the edge of my panties. My hips moved, silently begging for him to shift.

To fill me.

His calloused hands gripped the sides of my thong, dragging it down my thighs as he stepped away to stuff them into the pocket of his jeans.

"Touch yourself. Just your fingers." Cal licked his lips as he unbuttoned his jeans. My senses prickled as he slid one hand into the denim, pulling out the biggest dick I'd ever seen in real life.

Apparently the veins in his forearms weren't the only veiny, glorious things he possessed.

I shifted my hips, parting my legs to glide my fingers through my pussy. Cal's fist gripped his cock as he slowly began to work up and down. I dipped one finger, then two, inside of me. Cal matched my rhythm with his strokes as I moved my fingers in and out with slow, seductive pumps.

His moan was low and guttural as he watched me. Using my fingers, I parted my lips, exposing my clit and massaging it. A moan escaped me as my head tilted back, eyes closed.

The warm heat of Cal's mouth clamped on my pussy sent shock waves through my system. I looked up to see his head buried between my thighs. The flat of his tongue ran across me, stopping to tease and suck my sensitive bud. His groan vibrated through my center, ratcheting the heat in my veins higher.

I stared at the glorious sight of Cal Blackwood on his knees for me. I bit my bottom lip, eyes widening, when his fingers plunged into me—slow, sensual movements that worked in time with his mouth. Delicious friction brought me closer and closer to orgasm.

My breasts ached to be touched, my hands finding my nipples to pinch and add to the assault on my senses. A breathy moan escaped me.

"Come for me. Show me you're mine." The command in his voice was my undoing.

"No," I whined, not wanting to give in to him just yet. But despite my protest, my toes curled as the first wave of a full-body orgasm crashed over me.

"That's my girl." Cal's dark, soothing words rolled over me as my pussy clenched around his fingers. His head dipped low, and he lapped up my orgasm as I rode the wave.

Another whimper escaped me, and I knew I was done for. I would have done just about anything for Cal to keep touching me and to stretch me open again and again.

My throat was dry as I gulped for air. A thin sheen of sweat coated my skin. Cal stood, still nestled between my legs, and slid the hard length of his cock through my pussy.

Long and thick, I wanted to grind into him, make him give me every inch.

I moaned and shifted my hips—a silent plea for more.

"Greedy, aren't you?" he teased as his fist tightened around himself. Our eyes met, and I stared into the caramel browns of his intense gaze. "Tell me you want it."

I swallowed and nodded.

A beautiful smirk twitched at his cheek. "You know I'm going to make you say it."

I bit back a frustrated growl as Cal rubbed the head of his cock against my clit. "I won't beg."

His cock slid through my lips, pausing at my entrance. My hips shifted forward in a needy flex, and his eyebrows popped up. "You sure about that?"

"Callum." His name rolled from my tongue like a needy, frustrated grunt. My hand wound around the back of his neck, holding him in place while supporting my weight. My body was *screaming* to leave the limbo of almost-sex and feel the full girth of him. My legs wrapped around his hips, pulling him forward.

"I've been tested," I whimpered, unashamed to reveal I wanted nothing more than for him to fuck me bare. "And I'm on the pill."

Beneath my palm, I could feel the tension in his neck. He was as out of control as I was. "I'm clean." He leaned back to look me in the eye. "You're good with this?"

"Please," I begged, arching backward and inching my hips forward.

I was so wet when Cal slid inside me. Inch by inch I stretched to accommodate him. I was so full it burned, and I hissed in a breath.

"I'll go slow," he assured me, gently feeding me another inch as I struggled to accommodate his length.

I stared down at the spot where he disappeared inside me, and warmth bloomed low in my belly.

Fuck, he was only halfway in.

My eyes flicked to his face, and I caught him staring at me. A curious tug of emotion tightened in my chest as his features softened.

With slowness and care, Cal moved, easing out and thrusting back in with a steady rhythm. My body buzzed with every movement. When I was finally able to take all of him, I braced my arms behind me.

"Okay," I exhaled. "Now fuck me like you hate me."

A devious spark glinted in Cal's eyes. He knew a challenge when he heard one. I didn't need delicate. What I needed was for him to claim me, put me in my place. Remind me why we were even at odds to begin with.

His hips started to piston, thrusting into me as my breasts bounced. Cal's hands clamped onto my hips, holding me in place while he fucked. His dark eyebrows pinched down, and the image of his grumpy face sent a ripple of pleasure down my spine. Another orgasm was dangerously close, and watching Cal use my body for his own pleasure was enough to send me careening over another cliff.

As I came again, our eyes met. A tug of emotion squeezed in my chest. My jaw was slack as pleasure rolled over me.

Cal leaned forward, filling my view with only him as his thick, gravelly voice whispered, "You're so pretty when you come."

His eyes moved to my lips seconds before he leaned forward and captured my mouth with a ravenous kiss. My arms wound around his neck, holding him to me as he kissed me and pumped in and out of me.

He groaned, and his hips shuddered as his body covered mine. His cock pulsed, emptying inside me, and I was overcome with pure, crackling satisfaction. Cal Blackwood knew how to fuck, but I had fucked him right back.

His cologne clung to my skin, and I reveled in the fact that his body was safe and warm as it draped over me. Kisses trailed up my neck until his mouth met mine again. Gentle this time, he planted a chaste kiss on my lips.

When he lifted his head, his eyes were searching mine. Before he spoke, the tip of his nose brushed the side of mine. "Are you okay?"

My chest swelled. The simple question made my heart clang against the inside of my ribs. "I'm fantastic." I grinned, taking inventory of my slack and sated limbs.

He eased his weight off me, carefully pulling his cock from inside me. I watched the muscles in his throat work as he swallowed, his eyes locked on the space between my legs. A warm, wet trickle of cum seeped out of me, and my knees instinctively moved together.

Cal's wide palm gripped my thigh, pressing me back open. Without a word, he swiped his thumb through the gap, pushing his cum back inside. A hot, full-body blush warmed me.

I had just been thoroughly and properly fucked on my kitchen table, hadn't even fully undressed, and I couldn't wait to do it again.

Our eyes met, the heat from the fight long forgotten. A smile bloomed across my face. His grin matched mine—a devastatingly charming arch of his full lips as his attention solely pinned on *me*.

My heart pounded in my ears as we stayed locked, staring at each other and grinning like fools. I pushed away the nagging reminder that he was my rival.

My enemy.

An enemy that might have just accidentally become a friend.

EIGHTEEN

CALLUM

She was so wet for me.

I didn't want her, but something inside me *needed* her. I had lost control, not thinking about the consequences, and instead thinking only of *her*. Spread out on the table, Elodie's ripped T-shirt hung open, exposing her sheer bra.

I hadn't even had the decency to properly undress her.

I cleared my throat, taking a step back to pull up my pants and give her space to close her legs. She scooted to the edge of the table, holding her tattered shirt together and looking at the pile of discarded clothes on the floor.

"Well," she said, humor laced in her voice as she surveyed the mess.

I bent down and scooped up her jeans, holding them out to her. "Sorry."

Her face twisted. "Sorry? For what?" Elodie shook out her hair. She kicked her legs as she sat at the edge of the table, totally unaffected by the fact she was still naked from the waist down.

I gestured toward her. "Your shirt."

She plucked at the ripped cotton and hit me with a devious smile. "I already told you, you're paying for that."

I bit back a grin as my eyes met hers. "Noted."

I looked around. These were dangerous waters—the lines between what we were and what we'd become were getting murkier by the second.

Elodie hopped off the table, holding her discarded clothing in front of her. Her head tipped to the side, a cute little pout forming on her lips. "We still hate each other, right?"

"Yes," I lied.

I wanted to hate her. It would certainly be easier, but there was no way I could. Who could possibly hate a woman who walked around like a literal ray of sunshine?

"Good." She padded toward the bathroom before turning to look at me over her shoulder. "Now get out of my house."

I chuckled and stuffed my hands into my pockets.

It was nothing more than two consenting adults working out a little frustration. That was all it was.

All it could be.

It was only a matter of time before she truly did hate me —not because of the incredible sex, but because of the kind of man I was. The kind who knew the ends always justified the means.

The farmland should have been mine. I had thought about it—hell, I'd almost convinced myself I wanted it. It was a chance to build something bigger, something lasting— the perfect opportunity to feed people my way.

I had let doubt creep in, let the past whisper that I wasn't meant to want more, and in the time it took me to get my head on straight, Elodie had swooped in, turning it into something I barely recognized.

My dream was muddied now—a dream that certainly didn't include Tire fucking Mountain.

Stan was already set. He had Elodie keeping the farm afloat, and she was making something real out of it.

Me? The only thing tying me to this place was an inn I never wanted in the first place. My son's happier, sure, but how long would that last? How long before this town started feeling too small, before he started asking questions I couldn't answer?

Questions about why we stayed. About why I acted like this place was temporary, even though I've been here long enough that it shouldn't feel that way anymore. About why, when I looked at Elodie, it felt like I was standing on the edge of something I didn't know how to name.

How long before I got too damn comfortable?

That was the part that scared me the most, because I didn't want to be comfortable. If the Army had taught me anything, it was that getting comfortable was how you started thinking you belonged somewhere. That was how you forgot what happened when it all got ripped away.

Deep down, I knew the only way to hold on to my sanity while keeping Levi in Star Harbor would be to move forward with acquiring the farmland. Weeks ago, before things had gotten complicated with Elodie Darling, I'd made the call. The course to make Stan an offer he couldn't refuse was already set in motion. My financial adviser and I had gone over the numbers—really took a look at what it would take to buy the farm from Stan and create the farm-to-table destination I had dreamed of.

We agreed that it was too risky to take on by myself, but that a solid venture capitalist was a plausible way to make the restaurant happen. He'd put me in touch with the owner of Tower Business Ventures, JP King, and I was eagerly awaiting his return phone call.

As Elodie disappeared into the bathroom, I watched her walk away, wondering why a pinch beneath my ribs wouldn't go away.

At an emotional impasse, I surveyed the cottage. The air was still heavy with the scent of her—vanilla, sun-warmed skin, and the lingering trace of sweat from the heat between us. My body was loose, spent, my mind replaying how our fight had turned into the single hottest moment of my life.

The room was warm, thick with the quiet hum of contentment, the kind that felt dangerous in its ability to lull a man into believing, just for a second, that he belonged in a moment like that.

I walked toward the front door, smiling at the small hole the door handle had created in the wall when I'd shoved it open. I opened the front door and let the evening's darkness fold over me. Outside, the night was deep, the farm silent save for the rhythmic chirping of crickets and the distant rustle of the wind through the trees and the waves lapping at the shore.

I opened my mouth to say goodbye when the smell hit me. Sharp. Acrid. Wrong.

Smoke.

Frowning, I lifted my head, sniffing the air. At first I thought I was imagining it. Maybe the scent had drifted in from a neighbor burning brush, but then Elodie's face appeared from the bathroom, her brow furrowed. "Do you smell that?"

I held up a hand to her as I strained to listen for something. Anything.

Shouting.

I listened again to hear the faint crackle of fire eating

through something dry. And then the glow—bright, violent orange licking at the inky darkness on the far edge of the farm.

Adrenaline hit me like a hammer to the chest. After zipping my jeans and shoving my feet into my boots, I was out the door in an instant.

Elodie was right behind me, pulling on a new shirt, her voice sharp with panic. "Oh shit, Callum—"

We tore down the porch steps, running across the field, and that was when I saw it. Not just fire. A fucking inferno.

Flames devoured the old barn in hungry, snapping bursts of heat and light, throwing shadows across the field. Smoke billowed into the night sky, thick and choking, but it wasn't the fire itself that had my stomach plummeting into freefall.

It was the figures silhouetted against the blaze.

Levi.

"Dad!" His voice was high, panicked, barely audible over the roar of the fire. He was coughing, one arm thrown over his face while trying to pull another kid away from the flames. They weren't moving fast enough.

Jesus, they aren't moving fast enough.

Every inch of my body went cold.

I didn't think. I just ran faster.

The heat was suffocating as I tore across the field, my boots kicking up dirt. Smoke stung my eyes, filled my lungs, but I couldn't slow down. I reached them just as Levi stumbled, dragging his friend with him, their faces pale and streaked with soot.

I grabbed Levi first, gripping his shoulders hard enough to bruise. "Are you hurt?"

He shook his head, eyes wide, terrified. "We—we tried

to put it out, but—" He coughed, his whole body trembling. "I didn't mean—"

"Later." I hauled him up, shoving him toward the field. "Run. Go to Elodie. Now."

His friend was coughing, eyes watering, his legs barely holding him up. I threw his arm over my shoulder and half carried him, half dragged him away from the flames, feeling the heat licking at my back. Every muscle screamed, but I didn't stop until I knew we were clear.

The second I let go, Levi was on me, gripping my arm, his breath coming in ragged, tearful gasps. "Dad, I—"

"Shut up." My voice came out raw, harsher than I intended, but I couldn't think past the blood pounding in my ears. I turned, scanning the yard. "Elodie?"

"I'm here." She was at my side, eyes wild with fear, hands trembling as she reached for Levi. "Jesus, are you okay?"

Sirens wailed in the distance, flashing red and blue cutting through the firelight. The cavalry had arrived, but it was too late to save the barn. The fire had already claimed it, the roof groaning as it collapsed inward, sending another plume of embers rising into the night.

Elodie flinched, tears welling in her eyes as she stared at the blazing inferno. I clenched my jaw so hard my teeth ached.

The fire department took over, shouting orders and dragging hoses across the field. The air was thick with smoke, the scent of burning wood and charred metal heavy in my throat. I stood frozen, staring at what was left of the barn, feeling the weight of what Levi had done settle like lead in my chest.

A figure stepped toward us. Brody came into view, his

badge glinting in the firelight. His expression was grim. "I need to ask some questions."

Levi's whole body stiffened beside me. His breath came in short, choppy bursts, his face pale beneath the layer of soot streaking his skin. He looked up at me, then at Brody, his throat bobbing as he swallowed hard.

I could feel the weight of his panic, the way it sat on his chest like a stone, but that didn't matter. He had to explain.

Brody shifted his weight, his expression unreadable, but there was something in his stance—something that wasn't just a cop doing his job. It was the same thing I felt clawing at the inside of my ribs—the fear of what could have happened.

"Levi." My voice came out rough, too sharp, but I didn't have the patience to soften it. "Tell us exactly what the hell happened."

Levi flinched but didn't look away. His fingers clenched into fists at his sides. "We didn't mean to—" He exhaled hard, his voice shaking. "We weren't trying to start a fire. We just—" His hands lifted, then dropped helplessly. "We were just messing around."

I felt my stomach drop. "Messing around?"

Levi nodded quickly, words tumbling out, desperate now. "We were just hanging out in the barn. Me, Jamie, and a couple of the guys. They—they brought some beer, but I didn't—" His voice cracked. "I wasn't drinking. I swear. I was just there."

Brody sighed, shifting his weight. "Levi, just tell us exactly what happened. How did the fire start?"

Levi's jaw tightened, his gaze darting toward the wreckage, the collapsed beams still hissing where the fire hoses had drenched them. He looked sick. "Jamie found some old fireworks in his brother's truck. Just stupid Roman candles and bottle rockets. He lit one, but it tipped over, and—and it hit a pile of old papers or something in the back of the barn. The fire caught so fast. We tried to stomp it out, but the wood—" He shook his head, his voice rising in panic. "It spread too fast. I told them we needed to call someone, but the others ran. Jamie was scared. He froze. I was trying to get him out when you—" His voice wobbled, and he sucked in a breath. "When you got there."

I didn't realize my hands were clenched until I felt my nails biting into my palms.

Fireworks.

Fucking fireworks.

The kind of mistake that was so fucking stupid, so reckless, so easily avoided—but still one that could have cost my son his life.

I scraped a hand down my face, trying to get a grip on my own temper. Yelling at him wouldn't fix this. But damn it, I wanted to shake him.

I wouldn't survive losing you.

Brody let out a long breath, his expression carefully neutral as he turned to me. "The other kids?"

"Gone," Levi muttered, looking at his feet. "They bolted as soon as the fire caught."

Of course they had. Bad-influence kids never stuck around to deal with the fallout.

Brody nodded like he expected that answer, his fingers tapping against his belt. Then he turned to Elodie, who had been silent, her lips rolled tight as she fought back whatever emotion was rising in her throat.

"Elodie," Brody said gently. "Would you like to press charges?"

Silence stretched between us, thick and suffocating.

Elodie's gaze locked onto Levi's, her expression unreadable. He looked so damn young in that moment. Just a kid who'd made a bad call, who had lost control of a situation he thought he could handle.

But that didn't change the fact that something was gone now.

Something special that she couldn't get back.

The fire had taken more than just an old barn.

It had taken her trust.

And it was a damn good possibility that it had taken whatever fragile thing had been forming between Elodie and me too.

Elodie's gaze lingered on Levi, the weight of everything unsaid hanging between them. She exhaled sharply, arms crossed over her chest, her body tense as if bracing against a storm.

"No," she said finally, her voice quieter than I expected. Not soft, not forgiving, just empty—like the fire had burned up whatever she had left to give. "It's not my place to press charges, but I doubt Stan will want to either."

Relief flashed across Levi's face, but it was short-lived. Elodie wasn't looking at him anymore. She turned on her heel, her rubber boots crunching over the damp grass as she walked away. "I need to talk to Stan," she said flatly as she headed in the direction of his house.

She needed space. Hell, I couldn't blame her.

The guilt inside me twisted, gnawing at my ribs, but there was nothing I could do to fix this.

At least, not tonight.

Brody cleared his throat. "I'll take Jamie home, talk to his parents, and file a report." His gaze flicked to me, steady but edged with something else. A warning. "Levi's lucky, you know. This could've ended a hell of a lot worse."

I nodded, clenching my jaw. I fucking knew that. I'd

been picturing the worst-case scenario since the moment I saw him standing in front of the fire.

Brody gave Levi a long, stern look, then nodded toward his cruiser, where Jamie was waiting. "Get him inside, Cal. He's had enough for tonight."

Levi didn't argue. He didn't even fight me on it. My distraught son just stood there, shoving his hands into his pockets as Brody walked off. We listened to the low murmur of Brody's voice as he spoke to Jamie, watched as he opened the passenger door, and then they were gone, red and blue lights flashing in the distance before disappearing into the dark.

The night air was quiet now, save for the occasional hiss of steam as embers cooled beneath the weight of dampened wood.

I turned toward Levi. He wouldn't meet my gaze.

"Let's go," I muttered.

We started toward the Drifted Spirit, the grass wet beneath our feet, the smell of smoke clinging to our clothes, our skin, our bones.

Neither of us spoke.

I glanced at him from the corner of my eye. He was staring straight ahead, shoulders hunched, his face unreadable, but I knew what he was feeling. It was the kind of shame that sat heavy in your gut, twisting until it felt like you might choke on it.

Maybe I should've said something then—reassured him that he wasn't a bad kid, that he wasn't ruined just because he'd fucked up. But I couldn't. Not yet. Not when I was still utterly rattled by the thought of losing him.

As much as I wanted to truly believe that he was going to be okay, there was a part of me that couldn't shake the fear that I was failing him.

The niggling thought that, somehow, staying in this town and merely pretending I was happy was making it worse.

Guilt washed over me. The only way I could see myself truly happy here would be to create something new, like the restaurant. Trouble was, that path meant I'd have to see the devastated look on Elodie's face when it happened.

The ends always justify the means.

I bit back a frustrated growl.

I swallowed hard, forcing the words out before I could think better of them. "Maybe working at the farm isn't a good idea."

Levi's head jerked toward me, his eyes wide and brimming with tears. He hesitated for a beat, then muttered, "I guess."

NINETEEN

ELODIE

I REALLY NEED MY PARENTS.

The early-morning light felt too bright, too indifferent to the wreckage left behind by the fire. Golden sunbeams stretched long across the fields, glinting off the lingering remnants of charred wood and blackened earth, highlighting just how much had been lost. The air still carried the acrid scent of smoke, mixing with the usual crispness of morning dew, and it made my stomach turn.

It wasn't my farm, not really, but in many ways it *felt* like it was. Every inch of this land had woven itself into my skin and become as much a part of me as my own breath. And now, looking at the smoldering ruin where the barn used to stand, where Levi and his friends had nearly burned the whole place down, something inside me ached like it had been carved out with a dull knife.

It could have been so much worse.

I swallowed hard, forcing myself to exhale slowly as I raked my hands through my wild hair. The worst was over. No one had died. That was supposed to be the silver lining, but somehow it still felt like I was standing in the aftermath of a disaster, picking through the bones of what used to be whole.

Footsteps crunched behind me. I turned to see my parents approaching, my mom slipping on work gloves, my dad already rolling up his sleeves, ready to help. I hadn't even needed to ask. They just knew. Tears welled in my eyes as I walked toward them.

"Oh, sweetheart." My mother's voice was thick with sympathy, her arms already opening for me.

I let myself lean into her for just a second, the warmth of her embrace grounding me. My dad was less vocal, but I felt the solid weight of his hand squeeze my shoulder.

That was enough. Their presence was everything.

Movement caught my eye and I saw Levi sulking across the grass in our direction. I half expected him to show up, knowing Cal would probably make him atone for his mistakes. He stood off to the side, hands shoved deep in his pockets, shoulders hunched like he was waiting for someone to bark angry words at him and tell him to leave.

For a long moment I didn't know the right words to say. Part of me wanted to be angry. Part of me wanted to tell him to go home and think about what he'd done. But mostly I just felt bad for the kid.

When he finally had the guts to look me in the eye, I winked. He stood, stunned, before the tiniest smile ghosted on his lips.

"We'll get it cleaned up," Dad said simply. No wasted words, just action. That was how he'd always been.

I nodded and straightened, swallowing past the lump of tears lodged in my throat. If ever there was a moment to hike up my big-girl panties, it was then.

"Stan's already moving some of the larger beams." I gestured toward where he and a few of the farmhands were hauling away twisted metal and the charred remains of the farm stand. The barn was supposed to be the heart of Star Harbor Farm, but it was gone. "I don't want to sit around feeling sorry for myself. I just want it done."

Mom gave me a knowing look but didn't argue. "Then let's get to work."

I had turned to say something to my dad when I caught movement in my periphery—Levi had stepped forward, grabbing a shovel from the pile of tools without a word.

He didn't look at me again, just adjusted his grip and walked toward the wreckage with purpose, like he needed to be there.

The morning passed in a blur of movement. Hands blackened with soot. The sting of sweat in my eyes. The rhythmic scrape of shovels and the occasional low murmur of conversation. There was no space for dwelling, just the simple, repetitive act of cleaning up what was left. I took a few moments to document the wreckage. I posted a few slides with images of what was left of the barn, us working to clean everything up. The images were real and raw. There was something cathartic about documenting the setback, letting the world know I wasn't giving up that easily.

My eyes burned from lack of sleep and my shoulders ached from use as I looked out over the glittering Lake Michigan waters.

I felt Cal before I saw him, his presence a weight at the edge of my awareness. I turned, and there he was— moving through the wreckage like he belonged there, too, boots kicking up ash, sleeves pushed over his forearms as he lifted a fallen beam with that same effortless strength that made my stomach twist in ways I didn't want to examine.

He hadn't said he was coming and hadn't asked whether I needed help. He was just *there*.

I tried not to watch him, tried not to notice the way the sunlight caught the damp edges of his hair, the way his muscles flexed beneath his shirt as he worked, but it was impossible not to.

At some point we ended up next to each other, neither of us speaking. The fire had done more than burn wood. I had a sinking feeling it had burned something else, too— something fragile and undefined that had been forming between us.

I didn't know whether that tenuous *something* could be rebuilt.

I reached for a charred board at the same time Cal did, and our hands brushed. I sucked in a sharp breath, but he didn't move away.

He just exhaled slowly, his fingers curling around the wood as he lifted it, his voice rough when he finally spoke. "You holding up?"

I hesitated. A million responses flickered through my mind. I could lie, say I was fine. I could say that it wasn't a big deal, that it wasn't breaking my heart to see this place damaged like this when we'd made so much progress on the farm. But when I looked at him, at the quiet, steady way he was looking back, the lie wouldn't come.

Instead, I said, "It just sucks."

He nodded once, as if he understood exactly what I meant. "Yeah, I know."

We worked in silence after that, but it wasn't uncomfortable. It never really was with him, and that was the worst part.

I spotted Levi across the barn, shoveling a pile of scorched debris, his movements stiff and too careful—like he thought if he did this right, if he worked hard enough, it would erase the events of the previous night. It was so obvious that the poor kid was beating himself up over what had happened.

I walked toward him, stopping just a few feet away. He stilled, like he knew I was coming but didn't know what to expect.

"Hey," I offered softly, to not scare him off.

"Hi." His eyes flicked up and he swallowed. "I know you're mad."

I nodded, not ignoring the fact that, yeah, a part of me was *big* mad. But it was more than that, and Levi deserved to understand the complicated emotions I was feeling.

"I thought we had an understanding, kid," I said quietly, making sure my voice wasn't too harsh. "I trusted you."

Levi's shoulders curled inward. He kept his eyes down, focused on the burned wood at his feet.

For a long second, he said nothing. Then, finally, he exhaled and forced himself to meet my gaze. His voice was barely above a whisper. "I know I messed up."

I nodded, placing a gentle hand on his shoulder. "Yeah."

His throat bobbed. "I didn't mean to—"

I stepped forward, wrapping him in an awkward hug, his shovel pressed between us. "I know. We all mess up sometimes."

Silence stretched between us. Then Levi's arms wrapped around me, squeezing me back. "I'll fix it," he muttered through tears.

For a moment, I simply held him. "You already are." A lump formed in my throat, making it hard to swallow. I straightened to look at him, trying not to cry. "I'm just so glad you weren't hurt."

I squeezed him again, reassuring him that he was still

cared for. After I let him go, I reached for my own shovel, exhaling past my emotions. "Okay, let's do this. Teamwork makes the dream work."

From across the barn, I caught Cal staring at us with an unreadable expression. I swallowed hard and tried not to imagine what he was thinking.

A few hours later, just as the worst of the wreckage had been cleared, Stan called out: "Ellie, come take a look at this."

I wiped the back of my gloved hand across my forehead and walked over, Callum following without a word.

Stan was standing beside a section of the barn floor that had been warped by the fire and water damage. A portion of it had caved in slightly, revealing a dark space beneath.

"What is that?" I asked, kneeling to get a better look.

"I'd venture to guess it's a root cellar, but I've never seen it before." Stan frowned.

I looked into the hole. "It looks like there might be something in there."

I glanced at Callum, who shrugged. "Only one way to find out."

We pried up the loose floorboards, revealing a small underground space lined with stone. It was mostly empty, save for a single, battered steamer trunk sitting in the shadows, its leather edges singed, its brass lock rusted.

A strange shiver crawled up my spine. I reached out, running my fingers over the lid. "How long do you think this has been down here?"

Stan whistled low. "Could be a hundred years or more."

I swallowed, my pulse ticking faster. "Help me get it out."

It took some maneuvering, but we managed to haul the trunk out onto solid ground. The metal clasps were weak from heat exposure, and with a little effort, we pried it open.

Inside, the trunk was filled with old fabric, bits of lace, and a broken pocket watch. But it was the bundle of letters tucked in the corner that caught my attention.

Most were ruined—the ink blurred, the paper falling apart in my hands—but a few were mostly intact.

I lifted one carefully, my breath catching as I read the date at the top: *September 3, 1903.*

I skimmed the first few lines, my pulse thrumming louder with every word.

My Darling, I cannot stay here any longer. Every day, I wake with the feeling that I am being watched . . .

I read the rest, my hands tingling around the paper.

I should have left when I had the chance. Now, I fear it is too late for us . . . I will be at the lighthouse before the tide turns. Meet me there before the moon is high, and we will go —far from this place, far from the eyes that follow me. If you love me, do not believe what they say.

At the bottom, the signature. Two simple initials. *A.B.*

The world around me faded. The ruined barn, the sweat and soot clinging to my skin, the exhaustion pressing behind my eyes.

Callum crouched beside me, peering over my shoulder to read the letter. His voice was a low grumble in my ear. "Well, that's creepy as hell."

I licked my lips, still staring at the letter. My fingers trembled slightly. "It's a love letter."

His gaze flicked to me, something unreadable passing through his expression. "You really believe that?"

I didn't know, but I wanted to.

I wanted to believe that love—real, desperate, reckless love—left an imprint strong enough to last more than a century. That even after all this time, after all the loss, some part of her story had survived.

It gave me hope that maybe some part of mine would too.

THE SUN HUNG low over the horizon, bleeding gold and orange across the sky, casting long shadows over the farm. The scent of smoke still clung to the air, but the worst of it had faded, replaced by the rich, earthy scent of damp soil and the cooling breeze rolling off the fields.

I sat on the porch steps of the cottage, turning the letter over in my hands, the ink smudged but still legible. The words had burned themselves into my mind, looping over and over: *If you love me, do not believe what they say.*

Questions raced through my mind.

Who was she? Who had she been writing to? What had she been running from?

And why, despite everything, did it feel like I understood her?

Movement caught my eye, and I felt Cal approach the cottage. His boots scuffed against the gravel as he crossed the grass, his steps slow, deliberate. I didn't look up, not even when the porch creaked beneath his weight as he climbed the steps and settled beside me.

Neither of us spoke.

I could see him from the corner of my eye—his forearms streaked with soot, his shirt damp at the collar, a smudge of ash along his jaw. He braced his forearms against his knees, exhaling low and steady, like he was carrying something heavy and trying not to let it show.

I never thanked him for staying.

For being the kind of dad that helped his kid be accountable.

For helping me when he didn't have to.

But the words felt inadequate and caught somewhere in my throat.

Instead, I lifted the letter slightly, staring at the faded ink. "I think you might be right."

Callum's gaze flicked to the paper, then to me. "About what?"

"That it's a little bit creepy. I've read it a few thousand times. I get the feeling she was *running*. Hiding." I ran my thumb along the frayed edge. My voice dropped slightly. "Whoever wrote this . . . I don't think she was waiting for someone. She was trying to get away."

The words tasted strange as I said them, like they held more weight than I understood. Like I was on the edge of something, just shy of grasping it.

Callum was quiet for a long moment. Then his voice came low, thoughtful. "People believe the stories they want to believe. Maybe there are a few more clues in the trunk to help you parse out what happened."

I frowned slightly, turning the letter over in my hands again. *Who was she running from?*

I turned my head just enough to meet his gaze. His eyes were shadowed in the fading light, unreadable.

Something between us had shifted. I could feel it, thick and uncertain, settling into the spaces neither of us had the nerve to fill.

I didn't thank him for staying, and he didn't say he was going to leave.

Instead I sighed, resting my head against his shoulder and looking out onto the dunes.

TWENTY

CALLUM

I should have kissed her, sitting side by side with her on the porch steps, both of us covered in smoke and ash.

I should have turned my head, pressed my mouth to hers, and tasted the exhaustion and quiet relief that had settled between us. I should have traced the soot-smudged curve of her jaw with my thumb, let her breath ghost against my lips, let myself believe—for just a second—that she would have let me.

But I didn't.

I just sat there like a fucking idiot, letting the moment slip through my fingers, letting the warmth of her body fade as the night deepened.

The walk back to the Drifted Spirit felt longer than usual, my boots dragging against the dirt path. The air was thick, sticky with the last traces of summer heat, cicadas droning in the distance. All I wanted was a hot shower and a cold beer, but when I saw Elodie, looking so small and fragile, sitting on those porch steps alone, I found myself walking right up to her and sitting down without a word.

When she sighed and rested her head on my shoulder, I

nearly broke. A part of me wanted to scoop her in my arms, clean her up, and hold her. I wanted to press my mouth against hers and do whatever it took to erase the sad, defeated look from her face.

That would be thinking with my dick, and she deserved more than that.

I hated to admit it, but there was no denying that Elodie Darling had grown far more attached to the idea of Star Harbor Farm than I ever had. She *ached* from the loss of the barn.

A ripple of annoyance rolled through me. The problem was, I wasn't sure whether I was annoyed at her—or at myself. For not keeping my distance. For letting her get under my skin.

I needed to concentrate on the restaurant, on Stan, and Levi. But instead all I could think about was the way she had felt against me, warm and soft, like she belonged there.

Now, almost twenty-four hours after sitting on her porch steps, I could still pull from memory the soft sound of her sighs, her sweet vanilla scent, and the weight of her exhausted body sagging against me.

"Blackwood, snap out of it." Pulled from my thoughts, I glanced up to see Wes grinning at me, his hands spread open. "We've got a game to win, old man."

I shot him a dirty look. "I'm younger than you, asshole."

He jogged past me, slapping me on the ass before assuming his position at second base.

Despite the evening hour, July's oppressive heat and humidity clung to the air. The WarDogs were a bunch of hot shots from a few towns over, and most of them looked barely old enough to be in the adult league.

They may have an undefeated record, but us Star Harbor Phantoms were scrappy and ready to fight. I massaged the leather of my mitt, thumping my fist into it as I shifted on my feet.

Those kids liked to shit talk from the bench, but we were about to give them a lesson in not underestimating your elders. On the backs of their T-shirts, instead of last names, were cheeky, slightly inappropriate names like Swalls, Switties, and Swuts.

When Swalls—a play on *Sweaty Balls*, I assumed—stood and stepped up to the plate, Brody's intense stare glanced around at our team before winding up for the first pitch.

"All right, place your bets," Wes called out, adjusting his cap. "Does Swalls knock it out of the park, or does Brody humble him?"

"Depends," I said, shifting on my feet. "Are we counting Hayes as part of our defense, or is he just here for moral support?"

Hayes scoffed from third base. "The game hasn't even started."

"Yet," Brody called from the mound.

"Yeah, man," Wes added, shaking his head. "I swear your bad luck is rubbing off on us. We were winning games before you showed up."

"Oh, come on," Hayes groaned. "You seriously believe that bullshit?"

"I don't know," I mused, stretching out my shoulder. "This season has been in the shitter. Kinda makes you think."

Hayes flipped us off without firing back.

Brody grinned and readied his first pitch. "All right, let's show these kids how it's done." His throw was steady and even, hurtling toward the batter.

The kid swung, the bat cracking against the ball.

My head whipped as I followed the movement of the ball flying high into the outfield, sailing over the home run wall without stopping.

I shook my head. "Fuck me."

So much for respecting their elders. The WarDogs dominated, beating us in a pathetic 12–2 game.

Nursing our sore muscles and wounded pride at the Lantern was our only option.

In the dugout, I slipped off my dusty cleats, wiggling my toes and stretching out the muscles in my legs before they had the opportunity to cramp. As I leaned forward and tried desperately to reach my toes, I flipped my phone over to see if Levi had called to check in.

After the incident with the barn, he was grounded indefinitely. So far he was accepting the consequences like a champ.

As I stretched, I held the phone to my ear, listening to a voicemail from an unknown number. "Good evening, Mr. Blackwood. This is JP King from Tower Business Ventures."

My jaw clenched as the voicemail continued: "I'm calling in regard to the Drifted Spirit Inn. I understand you're seeking a partnership to expand the Drifted Spirit to the neighboring farm property. I have to say, a farm-to-table restaurant with on-site accommodations and views like that are highly intriguing. That little farm is already generating some buzz on social media. My office is only a short drive away. Let's meet."

I flipped my phone into my duffel bag, not bothering to listen to him rattle off his telephone number. A slow coil twisted in my gut, though I wasn't exactly sure why.

All the attention Star Harbor was getting thanks to Ellie's recent popularity on social media was only helping my cause. As far as I knew, Elodie was helping Stan revitalize the farm and would return to her glitzy life in the city. I wasn't sure how long Stan planned to continue operating the farm by himself, but when the time came for him to officially retire—*again*—I'd be ready.

Maybe the unease in my gut was a latent worry that Elodie Darling was the new face of Star Harbor Farm. Maybe she had plans I wasn't aware of—plans that included her operating the farm herself. Or maybe my unease was because I could perfectly picture the hurt on her face when I purchased the farm and upended her plans entirely.

But the reality was, my restaurant wasn't just a shot in the dark. With a partner like JP King, it was entirely possible. The only thing that stood in my way was Elodie Darling and the gnawing guilt that even *thinking* about it made me a total asshole.

When Brody whistled to get my attention, I shook off the guilt, packaging it into a little box and shoving it into the recesses of my mind. We were sore, sweaty, and more than a little humiliated.

Someone had brought a cooler, so we cracked it open in the dugout, passing around water bottles while we licked our wounds. The mood was lighter than it should have been for a team that just got their asses handed to them, but that was the thing about these guys—no one took themselves too seriously. Brody ribbed Hayes about his curse, Wes made a case that we should start recruiting under-twenty-five players, and I mostly just listened, stretching out my leg as I sipped my water.

"Lantern?" Brody finally asked, already knowing the answer.

"Hell. Yes," I muttered, tossing the empty plastic bottle into the bed of my truck.

The Lantern was only a few blocks from the park, so we

fell into step, our sneakers scuffing against pavement as we walked toward the bar.

"You were off today," Hayes said, falling into step beside me. "That bad mood got a name?"

"It's called getting my ass kicked by a bunch of twenty-year-olds," I muttered.

Hayes snorted. "Nah. That's just old age."

I flipped him off, but he wasn't done. "It's a woman, isn't it?"

"No." *Absolutely yes.*

As I opened the front door of the Lantern, I saw her. Elodie was there, because of course she was. I couldn't catch a break in this small town.

As we filed into the Lantern, Brody slowed his pace just enough to glance at the bar in the back, his expression shifting—just for a second—before he covered it up with a brooding scowl. I followed his line of sight and spotted Kit Darling behind the wooden bar top, moving fast, her curly ponytail swinging as she poured drinks. She hadn't even looked our way, but Brody ran a hand over the back of his neck anyway, like something about her presence got under his damn skin.

Elodie was sitting at the bar, laughing at something Kit said, her own chestnut waves spilling over one shoulder, her fingers wrapped around a sweating glass of something that looked too sweet.

The place was packed for a Wednesday, the usual crowd a little rowdier than normal. A cluster of older women near the jukebox were cackling over something, waving what looked like neon-colored bingo cards in the air.

Elodie hadn't noticed me yet, but that didn't stop the familiar punch to the gut, the same one I'd been trying—and failing—to ignore since the second she blew into town like a hurricane.

Her jeans hugged the curves of her hips and ass—an ass I could too easily recall sinking my fingertips into. I ignored the uncomfortable swell behind my zipper as we crossed the room.

I nodded as we walked up to the bar. "Kit. I didn't know you worked here."

"Hey, fellas," Kit greeted with a grin. "I don't. Rusty was flailing behind here so I hopped over the bar to help." Her head bounced toward Rusty, the Lantern's resident crab-ass behind the bar who only grumbled at her. Kit cleared away some glasses as our group huddled around the barstools. "Heard the WarDogs didn't go easy on you."

Beside me, Brody scoffed. "More like bent us over the table and made us call them Daddy."

Kit's eyes flew to Brody, a hot flush staining her cheeks as Elodie, mid-sip, coughed and sputtered beside me. My temperature spiked. I could so easily recall Elodie on display atop her own kitchen table, wet and ready for me. My jaw flexed at the memory.

Was she thinking about it too?

With a half-smile, I thumped a hand on her back as she tried to clear her throat.

"Thanks." She coughed again and offered a shy smile as I pulled back my traitorous hand. Our eyes locked, lingering far too long for a couple of people who were supposed to hate each other.

Before I could do something stupid, like give in to the pull between us, Hayes walked up. "We've got a table over there."

Kit slid a bucket of beers to her older brother. He pulled one from the ice, taking a long drink.

"Get out of here," she teased. "I need to flirt for some fat tips, and I don't need my older brother lurking around. I told Rusty he can have my help for an hour, so the clock's a-ticking." Her eyebrows bounced playfully. "Then I'm going to go find some trouble."

Hayes shook his head and sighed. I laughed at how easily Kit could get under her brother's skin. "What about you?" My attention flicked to Ellie. "You looking for trouble?"

She hid the hint of a coy smile by rolling her lips and focusing her attention on the empty drink in front of her. "That's the plan."

Kit slid a fresh cocktail in front of Elodie, one that looked suspiciously like Sailor's Doom. Elodie held out a small, crisp stack of twenty-dollar bills. "I'm a big winner already. Two hundred bucks!" Her eyes sparkled with a triumphant grin.

Kit laughed, wiping down the bar. "You won one round, and it was only because that one lady misheard the numbers."

Elodie gasped, clutching her chest. "How *dare* you undermine my victory?"

Kit discarded an empty beer bottle and stole a fresh one from Hayes's bucket. When he scowled, she playfully stuck out her tongue. "I'll give it back when you're done being so grumpy."

Hayes laughed and shook his head as we turned to walk toward the table. "Sisters, man."

I laughed and nodded, taking a pull from my beer bottle. "I'll have to take your word for it."

Hayes leaned back into his seat as he watched his sisters talk at the bar, mingling with friends and enjoying their night. It was rare to see the storm cloud above his head break, but there was no denying that Hayes Darling adored his sisters.

An uncomfortable twinge pinched beneath my ribs at the memory of how I had *adored* one particular sister of his.

"I'm not kidding," he said. "One is so fiercely independent, she's raising her own little hellcat. Another is engaged to a douche canoe who thinks he's better than everyone else. Kit's never met a stranger in her damn life, and then there's Elodie."

And then there's Elodie.

I watched her as Hayes continued talking. "Since she was in high school, I had to watch the idiots fall hard and crash at her feet." Hayes shook his head and chuckled. "It would have been a hell of a lot easier if they were all spinsters."

I chuckled and shook my head with him. "Yeah, that's probably so."

Even a blind man could see the Darling sisters were all beautiful in their own right.

My eyes settled on one specific knockout.

Elodie wasn't just beautiful. She was the kind of woman who got under your skin. The kind you couldn't shake no matter how many reasons you gave yourself to stay the hell away. She had put on makeup and tried to tame the unruly curls by pinning one side behind her ear, but I could see evidence of exhaustion. Tiny half-moon shadows peeked under her eyes, and the tight, slightly strained smile proved she hadn't gotten much sleep last night.

I hadn't, either, but I assumed it was for an entirely different reason.

Hayes's low voice shook me from my thoughts. "You're different, you know."

I frowned at him in question.

Hayes rolled his eyes. "Different from all the other assholes who tried to fall at her feet." He jutted his chin toward Elodie.

"Oh." It was all I could muster. *Shit. I* am *an asshole.*

But what the hell was I supposed to say? That Hayes was wrong? That I hadn't spent the past twenty-four hours trying not to think about her? That the only reason I was even there, pretending like everything was fine, was because sitting next to her on that porch—being the one to support her, even in silence—felt too damn good?

Hayes chuckled again. "Yeah. *Oh.*"

I finished my beer and blew out a stream of breath. "I don't know, man. There's just something about her that . . . irritates me."

Hayes clamped a hand on my shoulder. "She'll do that to you. But listen, I don't want to lose a friendship over whatever"—his fingers flicked between me and Ellie—"*thing* this is between you two, but you're both adults and don't need my permission. Just be sure and don't hurt her."

I could have argued with my friend—immediately told him that there was absolutely nothing going on between Elodie and me—but Hayes was a good guy and had been a friend for a long time. He deserved more than some asshole lying to his face.

I settled on a noncommittal *Yep*, hoping it was enough to alleviate his misplaced worry.

An hour later, I clocked Elodie's fourth shot of something hot pink and closed out my tab.

She was laughing, head thrown back, her eyes already glassy with alcohol and whatever joke Kit had just cracked. Her cheeks were flushed, her movements loose, with the kind of easy sway that told me she was well past tipsy.

There was no way in hell she was getting herself home.

I scrubbed a hand over my jaw, exhaling slowly. I wasn't looking for a reason to stay, but I'd be damned if I let her stumble through the dark alone.

Tossing a few bills on the table, I muttered a goodbye to the guys, but my attention was on the front door. Elodie was already walking out of the bar, and there wasn't a chance in hell I was letting her go alone.

TWENTY-ONE

CALLUM

I AM NOT drunk enough for this.

Elodie was barefoot, her sandals long abandoned, weaving her way down the sidewalk with all the grace of a baby deer on ice. Her wrap shirt had come untied at some point, billowing out behind her like the damn Lady of the Dunes herself, to reveal the sheer lace of her bra beneath it.

My jaw locked, heat flashing through me in a way that was both completely unwelcome and entirely unavoidable.

Elodie was attempting to walk down the sidewalk with two older female companions from the bar. She swayed, a loose-limbed kind of stumble that sent her straight into one of the older women, who caught her with a laugh.

But I wasn't laughing.

My eyes dragged back to her, to the way she was completely oblivious to what she was putting on display, to the hungry looks from a couple of drunk assholes lingering outside the Lantern.

A sharp, possessive edge swirled in my gut. She had no clue—no clue what kind of attention she was drawing, no clue how easy it would be for someone to take advantage of her like this.

One of the men nudged his buddy, nodding in her direction, and something primal snapped in my chest. I stepped forward without thinking, my entire body coiling tight as I stared him down.

Say something. Just say something so I have an excuse.

The guy must have sensed it, because he looked away real quick.

Smart.

Elodie had no clue how badly I wanted to haul her against me and cover her up—because if anyone was getting a view of what was mine, it sure as hell wasn't going to be them.

She was still grinning when her gaze lifted, locking onto me. Her smile faltered for half a second, her brows knitting like she was trying to piece together why I was here, and why I was following.

"Mr. Blackwood," she breathed, swaying slightly before propping a hand on her hip. "Are you stalking me?"

She squinted, blinking slowly, like she was trying to force her brain to connect the dots. Then her lips parted in dramatic realization. "Oh my god," she gasped. "You *are.* You're totally obsessed with me."

I crossed my arms, leveling her with a look. "I'm making sure you don't face-plant in the middle of Main Street."

She huffed, but there was no real heat behind it. "That's sweet, but unnecessary. I have Rose and Betty."

"It's Sheila," the dark-haired woman corrected, lips twitching with a smile.

Elodie gasped, pressing a hand to her chest. "No."

"Yes," Sheila deadpanned.

She turned to Rose, eyes wide. "Did you know about this?"

Rose patted her arm. "We were going to break it to you gently."

Elodie looked around like she'd been personally betrayed. "Since when?"

Sheila let out a delighted cackle. "Since birth, sweetheart."

I ignored them. "Where's Kit?"

Elodie blinked, then waved a dismissive hand. "Oh, she's fine. She went home with her *own* bad decisions."

I muttered a curse, raking a hand through my hair. Of course she did. Kit was a handful in her own right, but at least she was capable of getting herself home without stripping down to her underwear in the middle of town.

The three of them were linked at the elbows, a drunk, giggling tangle of limbs as they swayed down the street. Elodie wasn't the only one whose clothing was coming undone.

Rose was wearing a lace-trimmed camisole and what looked like a slip instead of an actual shirt, and Sheila—well, Sheila had completely ditched her blouse and was parading down Main Street in a leopard-print bra like it was a Mardi Gras parade.

I pinched the bridge of my nose. "Where the hell are your tops?"

Sheila flung her arms out, nearly taking Elodie down with her. "Too restrictive. The universe wants us to be free."

Rose clapped. "Preach."

"You guys." Elodie gasped dramatically. "I love you."

Oh, for fuck's sake.

"Elodie," I ground out, already feeling the headache brewing, "where exactly are you going?"

She turned in a slow, exaggerated circle, as if that might help her find the answer. "The Drifted Spirit Inn."

I stared at her.

"*Your* inn," she clarified, like I was the idiot in this situation. "They're staying there, so we're walking together."

I looked at Sheila. She nodded. "Yep. Girls' night!"

I took a deep breath, then let it out slowly. "You're not walking anywhere like this."

Elodie pouted. "Why not? My legs work just fine."

I gestured broadly. "Because this is not walking attire."

Sheila shimmied her shoulders. "Oh, honey, don't act like you're mad about it."

My jaw flexed, heat creeping up the back of my neck when I thought about Elodie. I wasn't going to admit they had a point, but for the sake of what was left of my sanity, I needed to get them all out of public view before half the town saw this shit show.

I rubbed a hand down my face. "All right, let's go, ladies. I'm driving you."

It took way too much effort to wrangle all three of them toward the park and into the cab of my truck. Rose climbed in first, taking over the passenger seat, but Sheila took one look at the setup and declared, "Oh, sweetheart, I need leg room," before crawling, ass in the air, over the seat and into the back.

Which left Elodie with the middle seat next to me, practically in my lap.

She wiggled, trying to adjust, and I tensed as her thigh pressed firmly against mine. She leaned forward, her nose inches from the side of my face as she looked me over.

She was too close. Too warm. Too damn tempting.

The worst part was that she didn't even realize what she was doing to me. The way she sighed, content, like sitting beside me in the truck was the most natural thing in the world.

Like she belonged there.

My hand flexed against the steering wheel, fighting the urge to touch her, to pull her closer instead of keeping her at a distance.

"You're so *tense*, Callum," she murmured, her voice full of tipsy amusement.

I swallowed hard, gripping the wheel until my knuckles went white.

Yeah, sweetheart. No shit.

My attention flicked up and Sheila grinned at me through the rearview mirror. "Oh, this poor boy is *struggling*."

I put the truck in gear and focused on the road.

Get them home safely.

I ignored the fact that Elodie smelled like vanilla and tequila and something softer, something that always seemed to remind me of her.

I ignored the fact that I could still feel the ghost of her head on my shoulder from the night before.

I ignored the way her breath was warm against my neck.

I gritted my teeth.

Just get them home.

By the time I got Sheila and Rose safely deposited into their rooms, Elodie was slumped against the passenger door, blinking slowly, like she was trying to remember exactly where she was and how she got there.

"El," I said softly, nudging her shoulder.

She blinked up at me, then beamed a smile like it was the first time she was seeing me that night. "Hey, you."

I sighed. "Come on, Darling, let's get you home."

She hummed, stretching like a damn cat, her open wrap top slipping farther down one shoulder.

I turned away in an attempt to be respectful. Without looking, I adjusted the shirt to cover her breasts.

Her cottage sat in the darkness, just beyond the inn, the stretch of cedar fencing between them a quiet reminder of boundaries—ones I should have been paying more attention to.

Elodie was already attempting to climb out of the truck, her balance not great, and I didn't have time for smart choices. Before she could face-plant into the gravel, I scooped her up, one arm under her knees, the other around her back.

She gasped as I pulled her from the cab and into my arms. "Callum!"

Instead of protesting, she curled into me, fingers fisting in my shirt, her breath warm against my throat. "*Mmm.* You smell good," she murmured.

I swallowed hard. "You smell like tequila and bad decisions."

"Those are my two favorite things." She hummed a chuckle and her hands roamed. "You know, I like the muscles under all that grump."

I bit back a groan. She was not making this easy.

I grunted. "Unless you want to wake up tomorrow with road rash, just hold on to me."

She curled against me with zero argument, and *fuck*, I felt that everywhere.

When I reached the property line, I muttered a curse under my breath as I stared at the fence. "I'm the idiot who fixed this damn thing, and now I've got to haul you over it?"

She nuzzled her face against my shoulder, completely unbothered.

I sighed. "Of course you don't have any complaints now."

It took some maneuvering, but I managed to get us over without dropping her, which was a damn miracle.

I carried her up the porch steps, nudging the door handle with my elbow. It swung open without resistance—unlocked, just like I figured—before I kicked it shut behind me.

Wes had completed the interior renovation—keeping it simple and functional. The kind of renovation that made it livable, but nothing more.

It was Elodie that had made it beautiful. When I had been inside before, I was more concerned with getting her naked than really taking it in.

Soft, golden light spilled from mismatched lamps, casting shadows that made the place feel warm and worn in. The furniture was secondhand, but she'd thrown knit blankets over the backs of chairs, covered the scuffed coffee table with books. There were fresh flowers on the kitchen counter, some kind of lavender scent lingering in the air.

Elodie made things better.

I shouldn't be here.

Ignoring the thought, I carefully carried her to the back bedroom and sat her down on the bed. When I went to move away, she fisted my shirt and whispered, "Why are you doing this?"

I swallowed hard, brushing a loose curl from her face. "I want to apologize in the only way I know how."

Her lashes fluttered as she battled sleep. "Apologize for what?"

For being an asshole. For not resisting the pull between us. For my kid burning down your barn.

I wasn't even sure why I felt the need to apologize and

make things right with her. All I knew was that she deserved it.

I stayed quiet, pulling back the comforter and sheets. Carefully, I guided her legs into the bed.

Ellie snuggled into her pillow without resisting. "You're apologizing by tucking me in?"

I smoothed my thumb across her cheekbone, my throat tightening. "Yeah, something like that."

Her smile was slow and sultry as her tequila-soaked gaze wobbled on mine. "You could stay."

I froze. Her eyes were half lidded, her fingers curled loosely against my chest. I knew I should go.

I knew.

Instead, I left her in the bedroom and stalked toward the kitchen. I filled a glass of water and rifled through a few drawers before finding some Tylenol. I placed the glass and tablets on her nightstand, setting them within reach. Elodie's breaths were heavy, and her eyes were closed.

Then, before I could change my mind, I toed off my shoes and slid onto the bed next to her. The second I lay down, she burrowed into me, her warm breath hitting the side of my throat as she pressed her face against my shoulder.

My pulse thundered. *This is a very bad idea—I should definitely go.*

But then she sighed against my skin, fingers curling into my shirt like she didn't want me to leave, and suddenly I didn't want to either.

I exhaled, my fingers slipping through the tangle of her hair, grounding myself in the feel of her. I shouldn't have let it happen—I knew better. I'd told myself a hundred times this meant nothing, but my heart called me a liar every time she was close enough to touch.

Elodie shifted, her lips brushing the edge of my jaw, her voice a sleepy murmur. "You're thinking too much."

I huffed out something between a laugh and a sigh. "Is it that obvious?"

She made a soft sound, her fingers tightening on my shirt. "Mm-hmm."

She sighed, losing the battle for sleep. "I need to figure it out. For her."

"What?" I frowned, looking down, unsure what she was talking about. "For who?"

Her lashes fluttered. "The Lady."

Before I could ask what she meant, she was already lost to sleep, her fingers still curled in my shirt. I had a dozen more questions but instead of asking, I held her and let myself pretend, for just one night, that I wouldn't have to let her go.

Elodie stayed curled into me, warm and soft, unguarded in a way that made something tighten in my chest. I wanted to believe this was real, but I knew better than to hold on to things that weren't meant for me.

TWENTY-TWO

ELODIE

With a groan, I awoke to the sound of a woodpecker hammering outside my window. Only it wasn't outside; it was much, much closer—the hammering was coming from inside my skull.

I cracked one eye open, only to immediately regret it. The bedroom was too bright, the air too still. My tongue felt like sandpaper, my stomach a fragile, treacherous thing, as if one wrong move would send me over the edge.

I groaned, pressing my palms against my face. "I am never drinking again."

The silence in the cottage expanded.

"Okay, maybe that's a lie, but I am never drinking *that much* again."

A wave of nausea rippled over me as I squeezed my eyes tight. My mouth was still dry and sticky and tasted faintly of tequila and a reckless night. Stark morning sunlight filtered through the gauzy white curtains in my bedroom.

Normally, waking to the warm sun on my face had me stretching my toes, yearning to bake in the warm light, but today that was not the case.

I was cold, but sticky. My dry lips smacked together.

Why did I think that bingo and three too many shots of tequila were a good idea?

I assumed drowning my sorrows over the burned-out shell of the barn was a good idea, but I had failed to remember how brutal a tequila hangover could be.

I planted my face into the pillow, breathing slowly and willing the contents of my empty stomach to stay down. I sucked in a long, slow breath.

Warm cedar. Musk. *Him.*

My breath hitched.

The scent wasn't just in my pillow—it was clinging to me, woven into the very fibers of my sheets like he had been here, wrapped around me, real and solid and impossible to forget.

A hazy flash of memory surfaced—strong arms lifting me, the solid press of muscle against my side, warmth cocooning me in the dark.

My stomach flipped.

Hazy images of the line between Cal's dark eyebrows deepening flashed in my mind. I filtered through my foggy memory of the night before.

Cal showing up to the Lantern, dusty and looking fine as hell after his softball game. The way those baseball pants clung to his ass was downright criminal. It had taken effort to pretend I hadn't noticed the way his biceps peeked out from under the hem of his shirtsleeves.

More so, it was a concerted effort to not constantly look in his direction, but all night I could feel his attention on me. After Kit was done working her magic behind the bar, we had really doubled down on our night out, and somewhere after the third or fourth shot of Electric Cooter, things started getting fuzzy.

Kit grabbing me and kissing me right on the mouth as she laughed and said goodbye.

Stumbling out of the Lantern with two new friends in tow, feeling like I was too damn hot in the outfit I had picked out—the one I had chosen with the sole purpose of driving Cal Blackwood up a wall, if by chance I ran into him.

But who was I kidding? Of course I was going to run into him. The postgame beers at the Lantern had always been a tradition for the Star Harbor Phantoms.

I let out a shaky exhale, trying desperately to breathe as my stomach tightened again. Cal . . . why did I vaguely remember being carried in his arms? Or the way his body, hard and warm and protective, felt wrapped around me?

I cracked one eye open and saw the small glass of water and neatly arranged pills on my bedside table—items drunk Elodie *definitely* hadn't had the wherewithal to set out.

I exhaled, rolling to my back. "Shit."

I patted my body, fingers skimming down my torso like a forensic investigator trying to piece together the evidence of my own crime.

"Still dressed. No mysterious bruises. No wedding ring. This is a good start."

I continued to pat down my body, gently exploring, and let out a sigh of relief when I realized I was still fully clothed in last night's outfit.

At least we hadn't had sex.

But I felt it, deep in my bones, that Cal wasn't the type of man who would take advantage of a woman in my precarious situation. I squeezed my eyes closed again, pressing my fingertips into my eye sockets.

Thank goodness it was Cal who wrangled me and brought me home.

Stupid, stupid, stupid.

Now I would have to add *Gentle Caretaking* into the column of things I didn't hate about Callum Blackwood. It was concerning how rapidly that column was outpacing the other column affectionately titled *Reasons Callum Black-wood Is a Dick.* It was also worth noting that his dick—and the masterful use of it—did not fall neatly into that column either.

I grabbed the Tylenol on the bedside table and carefully sipped just enough water to get the pills down. The morning sun was too bright, a clear indication that I'd likely overslept. I sat up and the room spun. I blinked away the dizziness in search of something—*anything*—to put in my stomach so I might claw my way through this miserable day.

His scent clung to the air like a ghost. Besides the Tylenol and glass of water, there was no other evidence of him.

Maybe I had dreamed it up—a whimsical, horny fantasy that included a tender side to Cal. I pushed the sweaty curls away from my face, laughing at the thought as I padded toward the kitchen.

As I looked up, I stopped.

In the center of the table was a white paper bag, and in front of it, a scrap of paper with blocky masculine hand-writing scrawled on it.

Way to tie one on, Darling. Sugar and carbs ought to help. — Cal

I could almost hear the teasing rumble of his voice, that gravelly amusement edged with something softer. I unrolled the top of the paper bag and found several homemade-looking pastries inside. My stomach grumbled like a petu-lant child stomping its feet and demanding to be fed imme-diately. I reached in and pulled out a pastry from the top. It was round with a flaky, buttery crust. The center was filled with what looked like raspberry jam, and slivered almonds were sprinkled on the top.

Despite knowing I should probably take it easy, I took a generous bite, moaning at how the buttery crust melted inside my mouth. The crust crumbled at the edges but dissolved on my tongue, rich with butter and just a whisper of vanilla. The raspberry jam was thick, sticky sweet, with a tang that made my taste buds sing.

I chewed slowly, savoring, and let my eyes flutter shut in ecstasy.

No man had ever brought me pastries before.

"So freaking good," I mumbled out loud around the bite of pastry.

For a fleeting moment it didn't matter that Cal had seen me acting like a reckless woman, because apparently it meant him taking care of me in the form of protective embraces and next-day pastries.

You couldn't convince me that a hot shower and that raspberry tart couldn't cure 90 percent of my problems. By the time I limped through that hot shower and another three pastries—apricot, lemon, and cheese Danish that time—I was feeling a thousand times better.

Half the day had already been spent trying to pull up any other memories of the night before, to no avail.

Hot coffee in hand, I stepped out onto the front porch of my cottage and looked in the direction of the Drifted Spirit. A pair of old men were sitting on the front porch, deep in a game of chess. Another couple chatted while enjoying the porch swing on the far side of the inn. Cal's cat was basking in the sun, curled into a content little ball. Walking down the steps of the porch were two elderly women with vaguely familiar faces.

Betty?

No, Sheila and Rose, I think—though my recollection was unquestionably fuzzy.

"Yoo-hoo!" one called out, waving her arm above her head. "You still owe me a shot, honey!" she called, her laughter full bellied and shameless.

I tentatively lifted my free hand in greeting when the woman reached down, grabbed the hem of her shirt, and flashed me, her hot-pink bra visible for a millisecond. I choked on my coffee as the woman and her friend dissolved into a fit of laughter as I stared in shock. A laugh burst from my chest as a flood of patchwork memories came back to me.

Sheila and Rose had been my bingo accomplices, and Cal had made sure we had all gotten home safely. I lifted my coffee mug in solidarity and shook my head, taking a sip.

The day was definitely salvageable.

I looked out onto the farm and its rolling hills. Star Harbor Farm was in various states of progress, but our biggest setback had been the fire at the barn. The barn was meant to be the welcoming showpiece, a grand testament to everything Star Harbor Farm stood for—community, agriculture, and good old family fun. What stood in its place was the blackened remains of charred wood and heartbreak.

I reached for my phone, capturing a panoramic image of Star Harbor Farm, the burned remains of the barn clearly visible. People were so enthusiastic to see our progress, and this would continue to be a part of it. The wind whispered through the skeleton of the barn, rattling the charred beams like bones. A place that once held so much potential had been reduced to nothing but blackened ruin.

I clenched my fists. This place deserved more than my grief.

It deserved rebuilding.

In my green boots, I trudged across the farm, noting that there was still so much hope and potential in the lush pumpkin vines that grew stronger every single day. I couldn't let one setback, no matter how devastating it seemed, ruin what we were going for.

Stan was counting on me. The community was counting on me.

In the light of day, the barn was just as bad as it had felt on the night of the fire. Nothing had been salvageable except for a few thick beams that had only minor charring. Those had been placed to the side, but the rest had been hauled away.

With my phone, I captured a few more pictures, attempting to be artful in the way I explained exactly what had happened and where we would go from there. I left out the boys' involvement, of course, but shared that the tragic accident had claimed the heart of Star Harbor Farm.

When I looked back through the pictures, I had somehow used moody lighting and elegant angles to capture the heartbreak and loss I had felt settle into my bones.

I typed out a heartfelt caption: *Sometimes, something has to be taken away for something better to grow in its place.*

I wanted it to be true. As I looked around the expanse of the farm, for the first time I wondered whether this feat was too large to pull off. I stared at the rubble so long that my chest hurt.

"Beautiful, isn't it?" Stan's voice floated over my shoulder and I turned, my face twisting in confusion at his comment.

I exhaled, kicking a rock in the general direction of the barn. "I'm not sure we're looking at the same thing," I pouted.

Stan sucked in a deep, cleansing breath, his arms accentuating the movement. "Look at this view." One hand swept out to the sand dune cliff beyond the barn and the glittering waters of Lake Michigan. "Where else in the world can you get a view like this?"

A smile tickled my cheek. I closed my eyes and let the soft breeze wash over me, just as a group of sandhill cranes flew overhead, their dinosaur-like squawking making my smile blossom.

"It's a beautiful summer day. We all woke up safe in our beds. Some people in someone else's bed." I peeked to find Stan hitting me with a knowing look, and I could feel my cheeks get hot as he feigned ignorance. "Sure was an early morning for Cal to be walking out of your cottage . . ." He raised both his hands. "But I'll leave that between the two of you."

I let out a nervous laugh. "He was just checking on me." I glanced up at the old man who had become more of a grandfather than I had ever known. "I let loose a little too hard last night, but he made sure I made it home safe."

Stan nodded. "That sure sounds like the Cal I know. He likes to pretend the cold exterior is who he is, but every so often you get a glimpse of the man beneath all that. And that . . . is another miracle in itself."

My smile warmed. Stan had such a simple, yet eloquent, way with words. The world deserved to experience it. They deserved to see the vision of Star Harbor Farm I had sold him come to life. Feeling sorry for myself or letting something as simple as a totally devastating, almost life-threatening barn fire get in my way seemed downright silly.

I squinted against the sun, feeling more determined

than ever. My eyes shifted to Stan. "Think there's a YouTube video on how to build a barn?"

A hearty chuckle rumbled through him as he threw one arm around my shoulder and pulled me in for a side hug.

TWENTY-THREE

THERE WERE, in fact, *lots* of YouTube videos on how to build a barn.

Unfortunately for me, and much to my dismay, I slowly came to the realization that building an entire barn from scratch would be *slightly* outside of my wheelhouse. After unending calls to local contractors, I also learned that it would be several months before construction could even begin, given that the summer months were the busiest in the profession.

As much as I hated to admit defeat, it looked as though Star Harbor Farm would have to open without the barn as its heart and showpiece. Undeterred and knowing there was no rest for the weary, I moved down to the next best thing on my to-do list: *Source a stupid number of straw bales.*

After borrowing the keys to Stan's farm truck, I climbed inside the cab of the old square-body Ford. I turned the key and the engine cranked to life. Surely someone in town knew of a local farmer looking to sell off some straw. The truck's seat rumbled beneath me as I bounced across the gravel road that led to the main roadway.

When I rounded the bend on the way toward town, I noticed a horse and buggy pulled off to the side of the road. Growing up in Western Michigan, Amish and Mennonite communities were a part of life. It wasn't uncommon to see a horse-drawn carriage trotting down the main roadway, the drivers lifting a hand in greeting as you passed.

As I slowed to give them ample room, I realized their carriage had a broken wheel. I eased on the brake, coming to a stop next to the buggy, and rolled down my window. "Hi there. Do you need some help?"

The oldest man in their group, dressed in a pale-blue shirt, black trousers, and black suspenders, looked at me, his eyes roaming over the old truck. "Are you Stan Stafford's kin?" he asked while making only minimal eye contact.

"Uh, kind of," I answered with a shrug. "I'm his friend. Borrowing his truck. It looks like your vehicle is in a bit of a bind. Can I give you a ride somewhere?"

The man hesitated. "That is kind of you. We do not usually take rides, but this time, it appears to be needed. We have a damaged wheel," he answered. "Your help would be much appreciated."

I unlocked the door, and he pulled it open.

The man dipped his chin. "I am Gideon."

I waved. "Elodie."

"If it's all right, we would all like to take you up on your offer," he stated.

"Of course," I said. "Hop on in."

Gideon motioned to the others. "Sarah, Jonah, in the back."

I glanced in the back seat of the cab, hoping that Stan's greasy tool bag didn't dirty Sarah's beautiful dress. Gideon then instructed the oldest boy, Samuel, to stay behind with the horses. The younger children, instead of climbing in the back seat as I expected, climbed into the bed of the truck. Sarah climbed in carefully, smoothing her dark-blue dress over her lap, her white kapp fluttering in the breeze. She pressed her hands together, folding them neatly, her bare feet tucked beneath her.

Unbothered, Gideon sat in the front, next to me. From the back, I could hear the children speak a language I didn't understand, but I recognized the melodic lilt of Pennsylvania Dutch.

I gripped the steering wheel. "Okay. Here we go."

Gideon pointed out directions, taking me down a winding country road that led to the outskirts of the county. We reached a long narrow road, and the truck bounced along until we came to a stunning white farmhouse. Crisp white sheets pinned to clotheslines billowed in the breeze, baking in the afternoon sunlight.

A woman stopped, setting down the laundry basket and lifting a hand to wave. Two smaller children were running through the clotheslines, a yappy dog nipping at their heels.

The air around their homestead was peaceful—that of simple elegance and pride in the lifestyle they had maintained, despite modern progress all around them. In a way, I envied them, that they valued their culture and traditions so much that they refused to bend to the will of man and time.

In the distance, the sound of rhythmic hammering caught my attention, and I glanced toward a neighboring farm property where at least thirty men were nearly finished hammering the trusses of a massive barn.

"Wow," I said, completely entranced with how the men straddled the wood without any safety equipment at all. "It's masterful, isn't it? The skill that must take is really impressive."

Gideon only offered a dip of his chin and a small but proud smile. "It is simply what must be done."

A seed of curiosity grew until, finally, it got the best of me. "How long does something like that take you?"

A slight frown pulled down Gideon's mouth. "About two, I'd say. For that one, going on three."

"Months?" I asked, with an exhale. "Wow, that seems pretty fast."

Beside me, Gideon chuckled as he climbed out of the truck. "Days."

"Days?" I couldn't help the shock seeping into my voice. I pointed across the field. "They built that barn in *two days?*"

"That's not a mighty feat when the community works together. It's just our way."

The hammering was rhythmic, a steady song of labor and craftsmanship, of hands working in tandem like some unspoken symphony. The sheer number of people—all moving, lifting, working—was staggering.

A barn. An entire *barn*, rising from the dust in mere days.

My throat tightened. *This* was what true community looked like.

"Are you for hire?" A burst of embarrassed laughter escaped my lips before I could help it.

Gideon pursed his lips as though he was seriously considering my question. "You say you're Stan Stafford's kin? Word traveled about what happened to his barn. I take it that's what you're referencing."

I swallowed hard and nodded. "The barn was completely destroyed," I said glumly. "There's nothing left and we have to start over. Every construction company I called can't even start for at least a few months, let alone get it done in a matter of days." The mere thought of it had frustration simmering beneath my skin, but there was no use in crying over it—again.

I sighed and gripped the steering wheel. "Okay, well, best of luck with your carriage."

"We do not ask for much, only that we may serve where we are needed. The Lord provides, but neighbors must also do their part." Before he closed the door, Gideon reached into the back pocket of his slacks, pulled a small white rectangle from his pocket, and reached across the cab to hand it to me. "The business is roofing, but as you can see" —he gestured toward the barn raising in the distance— "there's more than that we can do. The number on there is for a business line—voicemail only—and it gets checked once every few days. If you're needing our services, you know how to reach us."

"I—I couldn't possibly—" I stammered as I turned the card over in my hand.

"Around here, community is everything. Seven people passed us before you stopped to offer your aid. Returning the kindness would be the neighborly thing to do. You're not one to give back a miracle, are you?" His words hearkened back to when Stan called the morning sunlight and a burned-out barn, the simplicity of it all, a miracle.

I swallowed hard. "No, sir, I'm not," I answered with a smile.

He nodded. "Then I suppose I'll be hearing from you." With that, he closed the door and walked away.

I ran my thumb over the edge of the card, tracing the embossed print like it held some kind of secret magic.

A barn in a matter of days. A second chance. A miracle.

I looked up at Gideon, at the quiet certainty in his expression, and grinned.

TWENTY-FOUR

ELODIE

SOMETHING about the morning felt off before I even opened the cottage door.

It was the kind of stillness that didn't belong to a farm in midsummer. Too quiet, too weighted. Not the peaceful kind of quiet that wrapped around you like a soft blanket, but the kind that made you feel like the world was holding its breath—like something had already changed and was just waiting for you to notice.

I stepped outside anyway, because what else was I going to do? Sit inside and pretend that I wasn't waking up in a place that still smelled faintly of smoke and soot? Pretend the barn wasn't still a blackened memory visible from my front porch?

The mug in my hand was warm, but my fingers drummed lightly on the ceramic. I stared out at the field, across the hill where the barn used to stand. The wind tugged at my curls, but I didn't lift a hand to fix them. I didn't move at all until I heard the crunch of gravel beside me.

My smile widened as I sipped my morning coffee. "You're lurking now?" I teased without turning.

"I brought coffee. Thought it might help keep you from murdering the next contractor that tells you to wait six months."

I glanced over my shoulder to see Cal standing there, holding out a second mug of coffee. Not his usual scowl, but not soft, either, his expression was somewhere in between.

I glanced at the mug of crappy instant coffee in my hand before tossing the entire thing, mug and all, into the grass. "Perfect."

Cal shook his head in disbelief before inching forward to pass me the ceramic mug.

"Thanks." I smiled, wrapping my hands around the cup and letting the steam curl around my face.

Cal sat and leaned against the railing beside me. Our shoulders didn't touch, but the space between us felt electric.

For long moments we both looked out onto the sprawling farmland in front of us. "You're quiet," he finally said.

I glanced sideways, smiling into my coffee. It was bitter and a little underwhelming, but it seemed like he tossed in some cream and sugar and hoped for the best.

It's the thought that counts, I reminded myself. "Being quiet isn't a bad thing."

He grunted beside me. "For a woman like you it means trouble. It means you're plotting, and that's when you're most dangerous."

I snorted softly, but the sound felt hollow. The wind shifted again. And this time it carried more than just the scent of damp earth and woodsmoke. It carried the sound of footsteps.

I smiled as Helen approached us, but I didn't even need to see her face to know something was terribly wrong. Her stride was too slow, her hands clasped tightly in front of her. Cal straightened beside me, reading the same thing I was.

"Good morning, Helen. Are you okay?" I asked, setting my mug down on the railing as I stood.

She stopped in front of us, her eyes red-rimmed and wet. "We just got a call. Stan passed away last night. In his sleep."

I blinked, my uncaffeinated brain moving too slow to process the information. "Wait, what?"

"Stan," she said softly. "He's gone. He was supposed to meet with the orchard workers, but when he didn't show, they got worried. One went into the house and found him. Police and the medical examiner are on the way. Officer Brody called for Cal, but I answered."

My legs wobbled. Cal swore under his breath.

I sat down hard on the porch step, coffee forgotten, just as a line of police cars and an ambulance filed onto the farm property, bypassing us entirely and heading toward his home.

No, Stan.

I waited for the sobs, for the rush of grief to crash over me like a tidal wave. I felt it in a dull, hollow ache, like something had been scooped out of me without warning. My hands trembled as they covered my mouth.

Helen sat beside me, placing her arm around my shoulder and a hand over mine. "He went peacefully. There was no pain."

I nodded, though I didn't really hear her. My mind was already spinning. Sadness swirled with confusion and disbelief.

I looked up, eyes finding Cal's. He was standing rigid,

jaw clenched. Pain flashed in his eyes, but a stoic mask quickly replaced it.

"This changes a lot," I said aloud to no one in particular. "The farm, the renovation." A thousand thoughts flipped through my mind. "Did he have any other family?"

"No." He shook his head, voice rough and thick when he sighed. "Stan was a pillar in this community. He was a good man."

I didn't know the extent of their relationship, but I knew Stan had a soft spot for Cal. His shoulders were rigid and my fingers flexed, wanting to reach out and offer some sort of comfort. Despite my nerves, I rested my hand on his forearm. I sneaked a glance up, our eyes meeting. When his brown eyes softened, I allowed myself to lean into him, resting my head on the side of his shoulder with a soft, sad smile.

Standing side by side, we looked out onto the property as the scene in the distance unfolded like a movie. Helen sniffed and stood. "I just can't watch. I'll be at the inn if you need anything." I wasn't sure whether she was speaking to me or Cal, but I reached for her.

I stepped forward and wrapped her in my arms. "Thank you." My heart squeezed for her and the loss of her old friend.

As Helen walked away, Cal and I stood in stunned silence, a tear slipping from my eye before I could angrily swipe it away. I couldn't get a read on Cal as he stood, stone still, with his arms crossed over that broad chest of his.

Was he thinking about the land? My project? The plans he so vocally hated?

It hit me that the one person who had believed in both of us wasn't here anymore.

Uncertainty rattled through me as I took a deep gulp of

morning air. *Don't be selfish. This was never about you. It's about Stan and his dream.*

The edges of my vision blurred and narrowed with tears and the weight of what Stan's passing meant. Star Harbor Farm would be in limbo now.

No one, least of all me, knew what came next.

STAN'S FUNERAL was a sight to behold. So many people from the Star Harbor community came out to honor him. During the service, I couldn't help but notice how good Cal looked. I had daydreamed about how he filled out a pair of jeans, but he was downright devastating in a black tailored suit and tie.

Stan was buried at the local cemetery, and during the service many stepped up to talk about the kind of man Stan had been. He always lent a hand, gave back to the community, and cared about every person who'd ever worked for him. The loss of Stan Stafford was a hefty blow to the residents of Star Harbor.

I was proud to have known him, even if it was only for a little while.

Word about the fate of his farm buzzed through his graveside services as gossip spread. Stan had a last will and testament, and if rumors were to be true, he had asked that the community gather to all hear his wishes at once.

My knee bounced as I sat in the community room of the Star Harbor Library. The Keepers were gathered in the circle of cozy chairs that usually held knitting needles and plans for upcoming town events.

Today, the air was different. Charged.

Helen stood at the front of the room alongside a formal-looking man in an ill-fitting suit. Eager ears had gathered, since the information regarding Stan Stafford's will somehow directly affected the Keepers. Helen's voice was steady, even though her hands weren't as she welcomed the group.

The man took a step forward, wasting no time with chitchat or introductions. "Thank you for joining us. It is my duty to discuss the assets outlined in Stan Stafford's will. It is important to note that when a business owner dies, the ownership and assets of the business become a part of their estate and are distributed according to their will. Mr. Stafford has outlined portions of his assets to be divided among various causes, including the Remington County Humane Society, the Women's Resource Center of Western Michigan, and other charitable organizations. The majority of his assets, however, are tied to the property known as Star Harbor Farm. Monetary allocations for general upkeep, maintenance, staff salaries, et cetera have been earmarked." He paused as the room buzzed with silent tension. The man shifted in his loafers. "Mr. Stafford wishes the fate of Star Harbor Farm to lie in the hands of the Star Harbor Historical Society." He nodded toward Helen. "A preservation easement has been filed, ensuring the land will remain agricultural and community focused in perpetuity."

Soft, confused gasps and low murmurs undulated through the room as I looked around, trying to understand and gauge the reactions of the group.

"What exactly does that mean?" Helen asked, a deep furrow settling between her brows.

"This means that the historical society is responsible for either running the farm themselves or selling it. If the property were to be sold," he continued, "the proceeds are to be donated directly back to the town of Star Harbor, earmarked for public works and education, as dictated by the deceased."

Helen's lips pressed into a thin line. "So, as a group, it is up to us to decide the best path forward?"

The man nodded. "It is. Stan's final notation reads: 'This land belongs to all of us, but someone's got to carry the torch, might as well be the smartest bunch of women I know.'"

I pressed my lips together, fighting a fresh wave of grief. That someone carrying the torch was supposed to be *us*, but of course, not everyone saw it that way.

"When must the decision be made?" one of the town council members asked from the back.

"Hopefully not before I might be able to throw my hat into the ring." Cal's voice had my head whipping behind me. His frame filled the doorway as a sea of eyes tracked him.

Still dressed in his suit, he walked down the center aisle toward the front of the room.

He nodded terse greetings to some but avoided my gaze entirely. "Mr. Stafford's land borders the Drifted Spirit Inn. It's my understanding that at one time, the property was one parcel of land. I would like to purchase the farm to reunite the properties."

I stiffened, my blood running hot as my cheeks flamed and my mind raced.

"But Elodie is the one who's been working the land with Mr. Stafford," Selene said, voice sharp. "She's the one who has put in the time. She had the vision—the vision Stan himself wanted to bring to life."

Her eyes blazed in Cal's direction, and my chest squeezed for my sister's loyalty. *Bless her.*

The group broke into murmurs of agreement and dissent. I tried to keep my face blank, but inside I was vibrating with panic.

After steeling myself, I stood. "It's not about who wants it," I said, my voice cutting through the noise as I lifted my chin and willed my voice to be strong and clear. "It's about what is best for this community. *My* community." The dig was petty considering Cal had lived in Star Harbor for a long time, but he wasn't *from* here. This decision was huge—bigger than any soft feelings I had been starting to develop for my new neighbor.

I set my shoulders. "It's about who has earned the right to purchase it."

Cal tilted his head as he studied me, his gaze locking with mine. "And who decides that?"

"You want it for your inn," I shot back. "I want it for the farm—for what Stan believed in. A family destination that brings people together."

His eyes heated, and a tingle raced up my back. "You think I don't give a damn about that land? I've lived next to it for ten years. I've made Star Harbor my home. Have you?"

Fire burned in my lungs, but I stood tall. "And you had plenty of time to make an offer while Stan was still here. You didn't."

His mouth twisted as his jaw flexed. "Careful, Darling. You don't know what you're talking about."

I pulled my shoulders back and set my jaw, hoping he wouldn't call my bluff. "I know enough." I raised an accusatory eyebrow, hoping no one else could see my fingers tremble at my sides.

"Enough to bankrupt yourself trying to turn a crumbling farm into a fairy tale?" he huffed.

I hadn't intended to publicly argue with Cal, but I wasn't giving up on Stan's dream without a fight.

A disgusted noise rattled in the back of my throat. "Better than using it as a marketing ploy for overpriced brunch."

Helen clapped her hands once, sharp. We both stood at attention like the tantrum-throwing children we were acting like. "Enough. This isn't the time *or* the place."

I shook my head, biting back tears as shame washed over me. I was embarrassed for how I'd acted, but Cal had pushed—just as stubborn as I was.

The damage was done. Lines had been drawn.

When the meeting adjourned, I grabbed my purse and avoided Cal's gaze altogether. Outside the library, I stormed down the steps, the midsummer sun scorching the back of my neck. Cal followed, his dress shoes loud on the pavement.

"You really think I'm the enemy here?" he called to my back.

I stopped short and turned, hurt and shame bubbling to the surface. "Aren't you?" I gestured toward the library. "What *was* that in there?"

He closed the distance, heat rolling off him like a storm. "You think I don't respect what you've done here? I do. But don't pretend this is just about a legacy for you. You want that land because it feels like something you can fix. I'm not the only one with something to prove."

I flinched. He wasn't entirely wrong, and that made it a thousand times worse.

My arms crossed. "And why do you suddenly want it so badly, Callum? I would *love* to know what magical dream you're fulfilling by taking this away from me."

Emotion flickered over his dark features, but they were

gone before I could decipher them. Then he smiled, slow and dangerous. "Maybe I just don't like losing."

I barked out a laugh as my eyes rolled. "Fine. May the best *woman* win."

Cal leaned in, voice low. "The historical society will decide, but it doesn't really matter, does it? You don't have the money."

"And you don't have the charm. Like you said, the *Keepers* decide, and they're already Team Ellie." I narrowed my eyes at him in playful mocking. "Ooh, I bet knowing that pisses you off."

The tension crackled between us like a live wire, but neither of us moved. His lips hovered inches from mine. His dark eyes bore into me. When his gaze flicked to my lips, they parted on an inhale. Instead of moving forward, he scoffed and turned on his heels.

I watched, swallowing past the grit in my throat as I watched him walk away.

A flash of hurt tweaked beneath my ribs. Sure, poking at Cal had become my new favorite pastime, but this felt different. *Personal.* Watching him walk away struck a chord that I didn't particularly want to examine. Instead, I needed to focus on convincing the Keepers that I was the best choice for Star Harbor Farm.

It's just money. I could find it anywhere.

THAT NIGHT, I stood at the edge of the field, the moonlight turning everything silver and strange. I could hardly believe that it was just over a month ago that my wild ideas had accidentally gotten me in over my head with Stan. I never anticipated how it would feel to build something bigger than myself, to feel as though I was setting down roots, to finally have a *purpose*.

I held Gideon's business card between my fingers, the paper soft and worn from where I had run my thumb over it a hundred times.

The land was quiet. The kind of quiet I had quickly grown to love. Now it felt like a challenge hung in the air.

I was keen enough to recognize that Cal was hiding something—his strong reaction to my ideas was more than a man protecting his peace and quiet. His angry glare had hurt and disappointment written all over it. Cal had plans for the land that he hadn't shared, I was sure of it.

A tender part of me felt guilty for making things harder on him. Whatever his plans were, he was keeping that information close to the vest. For Cal, this was personal.

I sucked in a lungful of night air and reminded myself that the whole point of this adventure was to help Stan honor the land he had loved for decades. The farm was bigger than the both of us.

Stan was gone and the future of the farm wasn't guaranteed, but one thing had become abundantly clear—if I wanted it, I was going to have to fight like hell.

In the distance, across the dunes, my eyes snagged on a flash of white as a cold shiver raced up my back. My arms crossed over my middle.

I didn't know what the future held for me, but I couldn't give up. Not on Stan and not on myself. I wasn't just going to build a barn. I was going to build something no one could take from me.

TWENTY-FIVE

CALLUM

My kitchen was too quiet.

Not the kind of silence that settled in with the night and wrapped itself around your shoulders. This silence felt sharp. Hollow. The kind that made you feel like the walls were waiting for something that wasn't coming.

I didn't know what to do with it.

So I scrubbed the same damn coffee mug three times before finally setting it on the drying rack and grabbing a dish towel. I wasn't really thirsty, but I filled a glass with water anyway. Then I emptied it into the sink. Then filled it again.

Stan would've told me I was being an "overthinking bastard" and shoved a beer into my hand.

He would've laughed at how long I'd been putting off fixing the wobbly leg on the kitchen island, calling me out for walking past it every day like it wasn't mocking me.

"You see the problem. You've got hands. Fix it," he'd said once when I complained about a leaky faucet.

I pulled the stool out and crouched beside the island, wrench in hand. The bolt wasn't even that loose, just enough to give it a little wobble when you leaned too far left. Still, I tightened it like it might keep the whole damn building from falling down.

The wrench bit into my palm harder than it needed to.

I could still hear Stan's voice. Still see the way he leaned back with an easy grin, feet up on the porch rail, calling me "son" like it was a casual afterthought. He never knew how deep that word could cut when it came from someone who meant it.

And hell, I didn't even correct him. Not once.

Something inside me knocked loose then, but I didn't let it fall apart. Just held on tighter to the wrench and gave the bolt one more unnecessary turn.

By the time I made it outside, the sky was starting to burn with the colors of early evening—orange bleeding into a rich indigo that clung to the edges of the hills. I grabbed a beer from the fridge, popped the cap, and made my way toward the fence line, letting the quiet wrap around me.

Levi was already there.

Perched on the fence, arms draped over the top rung, gaze locked on the far edge of Stan's property like he was trying to will the old man back into view.

His silence didn't surprise me. What did surprise me was how long it took him to realize I was there.

"You think Stan knew?" he asked finally, without looking over. "That he was dying?"

I exhaled through my nose. "He was old. Sometimes that's just what happens."

Levi nodded slowly, swiping at his nose. "He was the only guy who ever called me 'bud' like he meant it."

My grip tightened around the bottle.

"He didn't treat me like a screwup," he added, quieter now. "Not once."

"I miss him too." My chest ached, and words caught in my throat as I looked at my boy. "And you aren't a screwup. Do you understand me?"

Levi's eyes sank to the ground, and he only nodded. My words were forced, but he deserved to understand. "I'm serious. You're a good kid. I don't know what I'd do if anything ever—" I didn't dare complete that thought. My words choked on tears, but I wrapped Levi in a fierce hug.

Silence stretched again, heavy and close.

Levi finally pulled back and asked, "What happens now with the farm?"

"I don't know." The truth tasted bitter. "But a lot of people are going to have opinions about it."

Levi's head dipped in acknowledgment. Then he turned to look at me, eyes steady. "It's okay to miss him, Dad."

I didn't say anything. I couldn't. I just stood there like a man trying to stay upright in a world that felt tilted.

And then Levi—this kid who used to throw tantrums over Pop-Tarts—reached out and set a hand on my shoulder. Steady. Sure.

It hit harder than anything I'd been ready for. I gripped my son, pulling him into a hug while we both cried over the old man who'd always been more than just a neighbor.

That night, long after Levi had gone to bed, I found myself on the couch with my phone in my hand and the volume low. I wasn't even sure why I had opened Instagram. Maybe I wanted to mindlessly scroll and forget about the day. Maybe I wanted to see whether anyone else was posting about Stan or the farm.

To my surprise, the first thing to pop up was a reel, posted by Kit Darling.

The caption read *Let's help make Stan and Elodie's*

dream a reality! Donate here! A link followed, bright and shiny and irritatingly enthusiastic.

My thumb tapped the reel before my brain caught up.

Elodie's smile filled the screen.

She wore a floppy, wide-brimmed hat that made her look like she'd wandered out of a Hallmark movie and onto a farm by accident. The video must have been older because Stan was in the background, laughing alongside her.

Elodie's face was split into a wide grin as a baby goat clambered into her lap, and she let out a laugh—loud, unfiltered, pure joy. Her nose was smudged with dirt, her cheeks flushed, and she looked so alive it hurt to watch.

Elodie looked like summer, like the kind of warmth you could drown in if you weren't careful.

"How do we feel about goat yoga, Star Harbor?" she asked the camera with a teasing grin.

In the background, Winnie shouted, "She's not a yoga goat! She's a jumping goat!"

The video cut with perfect comedic timing, and I found myself gritting my teeth when I saw the likes: 12.7K.

Then I read the flood of comments: "This girl is magic." "Stan knew what he was doing leaving that farm in her hands." "I'd go to goat yoga even if it broke me."

I stared at her face frozen mid-laugh, her hand wrapped around that silly goat like she'd known it forever.

Damn it, she is beautiful.

Not just the way she looked, though that didn't help, but the way she didn't even have to try. She was beautiful in the way she pulled people in just by being exactly who she was.

The community loved her.

They *believed* in her.

Hell, I might have too . . . if she hadn't been standing in my way.

The next morning I stopped at the bakery to grab a coffee and hear myself think, but that didn't happen—I barely made it through the entrance before I heard them.

Three Keepers—Cora, Harriet, and Lorraine—were seated at the back near the window, chatting like they were on stage.

"That Darling girl is something else," Harriet said, folding her napkin like origami.

"She's going to bring this town back to life," Cora agreed, nodding toward her phone, where the goat yoga video played on a loop.

"I donated. Did you?" Lorraine asked, sipping her tea like she hadn't just stabbed me in the gut.

I didn't say a word, I didn't need to. Cora glanced up, spotted me at the counter, and nudged the others. Their conversation slowed, lowered, but didn't stop and that made it worse.

I paid for my coffee, muttered a tight thanks, and walked out with my jaw clenched. I was used to respect in this town, used to being someone people trusted with things that mattered.

Now? Now I was the guy standing in the way of the beloved local hero and her dream.

That night, I told myself I was just taking the long way home. I told myself I needed the drive to clear my head.

Instead, I ended up coasting up the road that ran alongside Star Harbor Farm, windows down, the air thick with the smell of cut grass and dusk, until I found her.

In cutoff shorts and a tank top, Elodie's hair twisted into a messy knot, dirt smeared across her cheek like war paint. She was standing by an equipment shed with Winnie, stringing sparkly banners between the posts while the kid sang something that sounded like a cross between the "ABC Song" and a Taylor Swift chorus.

Elodie's laugh rang out, and I swore I felt it in my ribs.

She looked so damn happy.

So grounded. So *certain*.

This is what Stan saw—not just charm, but heart. Grit. A whole damn future with Elodie at the helm.

I got out of the truck before I even realized I was doing it. I took one step toward the fence, toward her.

Elodie didn't see me; she was too busy living in that little golden moment with her niece.

I stood there, heart hammering in my chest like it might shake something loose.

I yearned to go to her. A huge part of me wanted to cross that line, start a conversation that might not end where either of us expected. I could tell her I missed Stan—that I didn't know what to do next. That I couldn't stop thinking about her no matter how hard I tried.

But I didn't.

Because if I crossed that line now . . . I didn't know if I'd ever come back.

I swallowed hard and kept driving until I got back to the inn. I parked the truck and didn't look back.

CALLUM

YOU'VE GOT *to stop stalking this poor woman.*

That was the thought running through my head as I rolled to a slow halt in front of Star Harbor Farm, my fingers drumming against the worn leather of my steering wheel. I had places to be. Things to do.

But instead I sat there, watching her.

Again.

I had no damn business being there, but I couldn't shake the feeling that I owed her an apology. At the meeting with the Keepers, I had panicked. Without a plan, I had inserted myself, stomping all over Elodie in the process, and I had been beating myself up over it ever since.

Trouble was, I didn't know how to explain to her that the only thing keeping me together was the prospect of the restaurant—something that she was standing directly in the way of. Still, my callous treatment of her at the meeting gnawed at me until I couldn't stand to be away from her.

I knew my responsibility was back at the inn, fixing the busted latch on the back door, making sure the new guests had everything they needed, checking on the sourdough starter I had going in the kitchen. I could have been occupying myself with any number of things that had absolutely nothing to do with her, but I found myself lingering at the edge of the farm.

I watched her like some idiot who hadn't already made this mistake before. I was a fool who hadn't already learned that wanting Elodie Darling led straight to trouble.

But trouble sure looked good.

She was kneeling in the dirt, wrists deep in soil, her brow furrowed in concentration. Elodie was barefoot, because of course she was, her green rubber boots cast off haphazardly to the side. Her legs were tucked under her, the curve of her calves dusted in dirt, her cutoff shorts riding up just enough to show sun-warmed skin. The sun cast a golden glow over her shoulders, and when she lifted a hand to tuck a wayward curl behind her ear, my jaw flexed.

It should have irritated me, the way she got under my skin. A part of me hated the way she made me notice things. I shouldn't be able to recall how she always smelled like vanilla and something softer. I didn't need to know the way she could light up a room just by existing in it. It was none of my business that her determination was the most frustratingly beautiful thing I'd ever seen.

Any other version of me would have been annoyed, but at that moment, I wasn't.

Elodie, her sister, and her niece were working near the entrance—right beside the new sign. Freshly painted, clean and crisp, "Star Harbor Farm" was spelled out in a welcoming script, the colors bright against the pristine wood.

I sighed, raking a hand through my hair, cursing myself for stopping in the first place. But before I could throw the truck into reverse, my gaze flicked past her to the others—her family. Her mom and dad, her sisters—and Levi.

My gut twisted.

My son stood off to the side, shifting his weight like he wasn't sure what he was doing there. Elodie's mom was talking to Levi, her voice warm and easy, and whatever she said made him stand a little straighter. Levi's shoulders squared like he was being given something real, a job that was simple, but important.

I climbed out of the truck before I could talk myself out of it, and the crunch of gravel beneath my boots gave me away. Levi glanced up, his eyes landing on me.

His expression flickered with something uncertain before he lifted his chin. "Am I supposed to go?"

Elodie's mom turned to look at me, her green eyes crinkling at the edges. "Of course not, sweetheart." She patted Levi's shoulder with the same casual affection I'd seen her give her own kids. "We could use all the extra hands we can get."

Levi brightened, just enough that I felt it in my chest.

I didn't know what to do with that—with how easily they made room for him. There was no suspicion, no hesitation, just . . . warmth. Levi hadn't had the luxury of grandparents. Mine were across the country in my home state of Nevada, and Mary's parents had been older, both passing away when Levi was an infant.

It was something I hadn't even known Levi needed until I saw him stand a little taller, his hands tucked in his pockets like he was trying to be cool, but his face said it all. He wasn't used to this, and neither was I. Something about the way they were with him—the way they welcomed him without an ounce of judgment—settled deep in my ribs.

He wasn't a kid who got a lot of that, and it hit me harder than I was expecting.

Elodie glanced up from her spot in the dirt, watching the exchange with quiet interest. Her gaze flicked to me, eyes narrowing just a little, like she wasn't sure what I was still doing there either.

Hell, if she figured it out, maybe she could clue me in.

Her mother's voice rang out before I could decide whether to stay or go. "Since you're standing there looking so capable, why don't you make yourself useful and carry that crate of flowers over here?"

I turned, spotting the wooden crate filled with flower flats bursting with bright, heavy blooms. I determined part one of my apology could come in the form of manual labor.

A slow grin tugged at my mouth as I looked at her mother. "Was that a compliment, Mrs. Darling?"

"I'm just saying, a man with strong hands is a man who gets things done," she said airily, lifting an eyebrow in a way that told me she might get under her daughter's skin and have a little fun while doing it.

"Mom, please," Elodie groaned. "I am begging you to stop flirting with my—" She clamped her mouth shut, her cheeks flushing pink.

"No, go on." I leaned back on my heels. "Finish that sentence."

She shot me a look that could have leveled a lesser man. "Neighbor."

Mrs. Darling grinned, patting my arm like she'd known me for years. "I'm just saying, Callum looks like a man who could put those muscles to good use."

Elodie let out a quiet groan, pressing her fingertips to her temples. "Mother, please. He's the enemy, remember?"

Selene stifled a chuckle, shaking her head as she worked in the dirt.

I reached for the crate. "Where do you want it?"

"Right over here, handsome," Mrs. Darling called, and I bit back a laugh at the way Elodie shot her mother with another murderous glare.

I carried the crate to where Elodie was kneeling, setting it down beside her.

"Your family always this much fun?" I muttered under my breath.

Elodie exhaled sharply, reaching for a trowel. "You have no idea. What are you doing here?"

"Trying to apologize." My eyes traveled over her gorgeous face. "I'm sorry I jumped in at the meeting without having a conversation with you first."

She swallowed, absorbing my words. "I do not accept." Her cheek twitched as she fought a smile.

"That's okay," I whispered. "You will eventually."

I crouched beside her, our knees brushing. She smelled like fresh earth and something sweet, like vanilla sugar warmed by the sun. When she reached for the trowel, I intentionally reached for the same one, my fingertips brushing over the back of her hand. Sparks danced up my arm. She did too—I saw it in the way her breath hitched, the way she hesitated, her lashes flicking up just long enough to meet my gaze before she dropped them again.

I crouched, reaching for one of the flowers, gently loosening its roots. "You know, you're doing it wrong."

Her head whipped toward me, eyes narrowing. "Excuse me?"

I gestured to the plant she was about to stick in the ground. "You've got to rough up the roots a little first. Otherwise, they won't root as well."

She arched her brow, unimpressed, but still listening. "Since when are you an expert on gardening?"

I worked the soil between my fingers. "Since I was a kid. My mom loved to garden—vegetables, flowers, you name it."

That gave her pause. Her lips parted slightly, like she wanted to ask more about my childhood. Instead, she took the plant from my hand, mimicking the motion, her shoulder bumping against mine as she worked.

I could have pulled back, but I didn't.

"Better?" she murmured, glancing up at me through her lashes.

Something low and tight curled in my chest. I cleared my throat. "Better."

A small, sticky hand suddenly smacked against my knee. I looked down to find Elodie's niece, Winnie, peering up at me, her face smeared with what looked like chocolate and an alarming amount of dirt.

"You're still so big," she announced, tilting her head like she was trying to solve a puzzle.

I arched my brow. "Yeah? And you're still small."

She gasped, eyes going wide with amusement. "I *am* small!" She grinned and turned to Elodie, tugging on her shirt. "Aunt Ellie, does Mr. Cal look bigger to you?"

Elodie bit her lip, her eyes full of laughter. "Hmm . . . I guess that's how growing works, Win. If we're not paying attention, Mr. Cal might just keep getting bigger and bigger." She gestured toward me. "Especially that big old ego of his."

Winnie turned back to me, inspecting me with the same level of scrutiny she probably gave her stuffed animals when she decided they needed a checkup. "I think you could pick up a whole cow."

"Really?" I smirked. "A whole cow?"

She nodded, very serious. "A *big* cow."

Selene chuckled from where she was kneeling a few feet away. "Careful, Win. If you tell a man he's strong, he'll start lifting random stuff just to prove it."

Elodie grinned up at me, eyes full of mischief as she spoke to her precocious niece. "I mean, now I kind of want to see if he can pick up a whole cow."

I shook my head, amused. "That's not happening, Darling."

Winnie gasped dramatically, her little hands flying to her cheeks. "You called her darling!"

I stilled, glancing down at her with a crinkle of my nose. "I did."

Her little mouth twisted. "But that's her last name."

Elodie scoffed, pressed a hand to her heart, and looked at her niece. "Rude, isn't he?"

Winnie giggled, twirling a curl around her finger. "Darling is also Mama's last name. She let me pick and I wanted it to be mine, too. She even let me get a brand new middle name!"

I watched the tiny tornado as we followed the dancing trail of her thoughts. "Is that so?"

Winnie straightened her shoulders and put out her hand. "Winifred Elizabeth *Amaryllis* Darling. Amaryllis means sparkle."

My eyes popped to Selene who was smiling at her precocious daughter. "That's right."

I shrugged. "Maybe Elodie needs a cool new name, too." Personally I'd thought of several choice names any time Elodie had popped into my head: *Trouble. Pain in the Ass. Irresistible.*

Elodie waggled her eyebrows at Winnie, then tilted her head at me. "I guess I'll have to think about that."

I gave her a slow, deliberate once-over, fighting a smile as my gaze landed on the streak of soil across her cheek. "You do that."

She rolled her eyes at my intensity, but I didn't miss the way her lips curled at the corners, the warmth in her gaze.

Winnie, satisfied with our attention on her, beamed up at me. "You're staying to help us."

Selene snorted. "It's polite to ask first, Win."

I winked at Winnie. "If the boss says to stay, I'll stay."

I huffed a quiet laugh, shaking my head at the easy, lighthearted exchange. As Elodie met my gaze, something shifted in my chest. I got to my knees and started filling holes with the flowers from the crate.

We fell into a rhythm, our hands moving in tandem. Our shoulders brushed too many times for it to be accidental. She smelled like lavender and earth and summer heat, and I tried not to think about it.

Winnie had gotten bored, so Selene took her for a walk around the farm. Mr. Darling was working with a crew to create new walking paths, and Mrs. Darling had taken the role of foreman, gently giving directions and suggestions on how to make the walking paths more inviting for guests.

We finished the last of the planting, and a smudge of dirt remained streaked across Elodie's cheek. Without thinking, I reached out, swiping my thumb over the smear.

Her breath hitched.

I froze.

Her skin was warm beneath my touch, the faintest flush dusting her cheekbones. I couldn't hold back and let the moment pass. My thumb lingered, just a second too long, my pulse a steady drumbeat against my ribs. Her lips parted, her breath catching, and for one reckless moment, I wanted to feel her soft mouth against mine again.

Bad idea. Very, very bad idea.

The air between us shifted, thickening, stretching tight.

Her gaze flicked to mine, wide, startled, like she hadn't expected me to touch her. Like she wasn't sure what to do with the way it made her feel.

Like she wasn't sure what to do with the way it made *me* feel.

I swallowed hard, dropping my hand. "You had something on your face."

The back of her hand slid over her cheek, wiping where my thumb had been.

I pointed with my trowel. "Stack those empty plastic containers and I can take them to be recycled."

She blinked, recovering, then rolled her eyes. "You're bossy."

I reached for the empty crate. "You love it."

Her lips parted, like she was about to argue, but then she just shook her head, going back to work, stacking the black plastic containers.

And somehow we just . . . kept going and working side by side. The sun warmed our backs, the scent of fresh soil and blooming flowers thick in the air. I worked with the sound of Selene teasing Elodie, of Levi's quiet laughter blending in, of Elodie's mom humming some song I only half recognized.

There was an ease there that shouldn't have existed between us, but it did.

When Elodie finally sat back on her heels, hands on her hips, surveying the work we had done, she smiled.

Really smiled.

Fuck me, that smile settled into my chest. It felt like getting hit with a two-by-four, and something cracked open inside me.

I should have walked away and let this be enough. The afternoon, the way her family had accepted Levi, the way Elodie had looked at me—this should have been the line. Trouble was, standing there with the smell of fresh dirt and summer clinging to my skin, with Elodie looking up at me like she was waiting for something . . . I stepped right over that line.

I turned to her, brushing the dirt from my palms. "I'm picking you up at six," I said, voice rougher and more demanding than I meant it to be.

Elodie blinked. "What?"

I met her gaze, unwavering. "Tonight. Six o'clock. Wear something you don't mind getting dirty."

She opened her mouth, then closed it, tilting her head. "Is this a date or more of that apology?"

I didn't answer right away. Instead, I let my gaze drop, slow and deliberate, dragging over the curve of her mouth, the slope of her throat, the way her pulse fluttered there like a secret. When I met her eyes again, I saw exactly when she stopped breathing.

I finally said, my voice rough, "It's both. Be ready at six."

Her eyes narrowed, like she was looking for some kind of loophole. "I don't remember agreeing to a date."

I smirked, liking this new shift between us. "You will."

Her mouth parted, probably to tell me off, but then Selene let out a low snicker. "Ohhh, I like him."

Elodie groaned, dropping her head into her hands, but I caught a glimpse of her smile.

Levi shook his head, looking thoroughly embarrassed of his dad.

Elodie's mom just beamed and kept on working.

I stood, dusting my hands off on my jeans, and turned toward my truck, leaving her sitting there in the dirt.

Sure, Elodie could think about it, and she could argue all she wanted, but that date was happening.

ELODIE

WEAR SOMETHING *you don't mind getting dirty.*

Cal's words rolled through my mind as a delicious shiver crept up my back. He had surprised me when he'd asked me out on a date, but then again, the entire afternoon had been surreal.

Cal had apologized for his reaction at the Keepers' meeting. I hadn't realized how much I needed him to say those words until they were out. It wasn't that I was surprised Cal was interested in the farm—I knew that—but such a public display against my plans felt so *personal*.

A part of me was still irritated at him, but the more curious part won out. Cal was so confident I would eventually accept his apology that I was curious to see what other ways he might want to apologize.

It was so on brand for him to just show up, frowning and watching what I was doing, as though he was trying to figure out all the ways in which I was doing it wrong. But then he softened, his hackles lowering until we found a quiet, steady rhythm of working side by side.

Once the planting was completed, he and Levi

retreated back to the inn, and I spent the rest of the time cleaning up the trowels and empty planting containers while dodging sidelong glances and snickers from my sister and parents.

My parents had the uncanny knack of seeing the good in everyone, so of course they were already half in love with Callum Blackwood. A strange pressure built beneath my breastbone. I was starting to see it too—not just the good in him, but the quiet steadiness beneath all that gruffness.

Anyone who cared to look would see the way he took care of the people in his orbit without asking for anything in return. It was dangerous, the way he could slip past my guard when I wasn't paying attention.

Dad had taken Levi under his wing, patting him on the shoulder and showing him the best way to use the square shovel to cut a new walking path into the earth. It was grueling, sweaty work, but Levi worked hard and my dad, always free with his praise, encouraged Levi every step of the way. The sullen moody teenager I had met only weeks ago still clung to the edges, but over time Levi was relaxing into a quiet, confident young man.

Despite his mistake, somewhere along the line I had fallen for that kid, and I couldn't help but smile anytime he came to mind.

I glanced at my reflection in the bathroom mirror. "And now you've got a date with his dad," I said aloud, my excitement growing.

My reflection beamed back at me, eyes bright, cheeks a little flushed—not from nerves, but from something dangerously close to giddiness. I pressed my fingertips against my lips like I could hold it in, but there was no stopping it.

I was excited.

I reveled in the sensations—the way my skin hummed in

anticipation, the way my stomach did that ridiculous little swoop. I wasn't just hoping for a good time with Cal—I was genuinely looking forward to it, and hell if that didn't make my heart trip over itself.

It wasn't just the idea of Cal seeing me like this—it was the way I wanted him to see me. *To notice.*

Anyone could see that Cal Blackwood was the hottest bachelor in Star Harbor. Sure, he was grumpy and kept to himself, but he was also kind—the type of man who showed up when you needed him, who took care of things without making a show of it, who watched over the people he cared about even when he pretended not to. A man who spoke with passion but apologized when he was wrong.

His looks might have caught people's attention, but it was that quiet, unwavering steadiness that held it.

With a sigh, I surveyed my outfit—a simple heather gray V-neck T-shirt cuffed at the sleeves. The front was tucked into a pair of jeans that made my ass look incredible. They weren't exactly work jeans, but I was willing to get them dirty if that meant Cal might also appreciate the way the denim hugged my curves.

My toenails were painted a hot pink, not that I expected Cal to see them—oh hell, who was I kidding? A very large part of me was hoping he might.

I spritzed on a few pumps of the expensive perfume I reserved for special occasions and secured a simple pair of gold studs in my ears. We may be getting dirty, but it was still a date.

Nerves tickled my tummy, and I pressed a palm against it to settle the butterflies, blowing out a steady stream of breath through my pursed lips. Cal had nearly seen me naked already, and we had even spent the night spooning in my bed after the Lantern.

So why the heck was I so nervous?

That was when I realized it wasn't just about the sex. Yes, I certainly was hoping Cal and I might find ourselves in a tangle of limbs and panting breaths, but what was more, I actually wanted Cal to like me.

I smoothed my hair, twirling a loose, frizzy curl around my finger in hopes of forcing it into shape. When I released it, it sprang back up, doing whatever the hell it wanted.

This pick-me energy was new and unsettling. Cal had been a thorn in my side, actively cheering for my failure in revitalizing Star Harbor Farm, all for the sake of his precious *peace and quiet*. But somewhere along the way, something had shifted. He wasn't quite so cantankerous, and more than a few times he had been actually helpful.

Maybe I liked that unexpected and interesting side to Cal, or maybe the bratty side of me liked knowing I had the power to get under his skin and into his head. A low thrum pulsed at my core, and I chuckled to myself.

Yep, that was definitely a part of it.

A hard knock at the front door made me jump and I stifled a yelp, the remainder of my nerves skittering across the floor.

"Coming," I called out, giving myself one last once-over before hopping toward the door as I stuffed my feet into a fresh pair of socks.

I pulled open the wooden door. "Hi!" I exclaimed on an exhale.

Cal stood at my front door freshly showered and looking like a fantasy come to life. My eyes started at his scuffed work boots, traveling higher, appreciating how the well-worn denim of his jeans stretched across his thighs. The hem of his T-shirt covered his tapered hips but flared out with the V of his torso. The gray material stretched across his chest, and his arms tested the strength of the fabric as his arms flexed beneath it. My gaze dragged across the column of his throat. He hadn't bothered with a fresh shave and my legs pressed together at the thought of that scruff tickling my inner thigh.

When I finally reached his face, his eyes were playful and a smirk teased his lips. "Are you eye fucking me, Darling?" he teased.

A chuckle rumbled out of me. "One *thousand* percent," I admitted with a full belly laugh.

His eyes flicked between his shirt and mine. "Nice outfit."

My shoulders shimmied, noting the nearly identical light-gray colors. "We're twins."

I held my hands open to my sides. "Is this what you had in mind?" I asked.

Cal didn't answer right away. His gaze dragged over me, slow and unhurried, like he was memorizing every inch. The heat in his eyes sent a shiver rolling down my spine, my skin prickling under the weight of his attention. His jaw ticced, the muscle there flexing like he was holding something back. His fingers twitched at his sides, and I had the distinct feeling he wanted to touch me but was using every ounce of restraint not to.

"You're perfect." His voice dipped an octave, and I could feel the low timbre hit me in the chest.

A heady thrill at his approval zipped through me. "Let me just throw on my boots, and I'll be ready to go."

"I said be ready at six."

I rolled my eyes. "It's six-oh-three," I shot back, loving that whatever tension had pulled tight between us didn't ruin our playful banter.

Cal took a step back, allowing me room to step out of the cottage and pull the front door closed.

He pointed at the door. "Lock up," he demanded.

I shook my head and turned. "Yes, sir," I teased.

A firm *thwack* struck me right in the ass, and I yelped.

"That's right," he rumbled in my ear with a playful edge in his voice.

I swallowed a giggle as heat flooded my system. With a smile, I bent down to slip a foot into one of my green boots. Cal's arm reached out and I grabbed it, steadying myself as I tugged on the first boot, then the other. His forearm flexed under my grip, the muscle jumping slightly, but he didn't pull away from my touch.

Damn it, why are forearms so hot?

Cal didn't move and didn't say a word, but stood there, letting me balance, his jaw tight like he was thinking very, very carefully about something. I straightened, pulling my hand from his arm and tucking a rogue hair behind my ear to try to hide the blush I felt creeping onto my cheeks.

I looked up to see a large 4-wheeler parked in front of the cottage. I looked at Cal in question.

His arm swept wide. "Your chariot, my lady."

My eyes went wide as my breath hitched. "Can I drive?" I asked, practically bouncing on my toes with excitement.

Cal's eyes narrowed. "How about I get us to where we're going first, and then if you're up for it, you can take it for a joyride."

I stuck out my hand between us. "You've got yourself a deal."

His large palm enclosed mine, warmth crawling from my palm all the way up my arm.

With a delighted squeal, I left Cal standing there and

climbed onto the 4-wheeler and patted the seat. "Well, saddle up, cowboy."

Cal chuckled and shook his head. He moved to the back of the vehicle, then reached for something near the tires. A black helmet settled on my head, and he adjusted the straps. His fingers brushed my jaw as he fastened the strap, his touch firm but careful. I swallowed, my skin burning any place his fingers touched me. Cal was too close—or maybe not close enough. For a moment our eyes locked and my gaze shifted across his warm, brown eyes.

His voice was soft and low. "Got to keep you safe."

My throat was thick. Before I could come back with a witty response, he was gone, moving around the vehicle. Cal slipped his arms through a backpack and settled himself onto the seat behind me.

His thighs were thick and warm on the outside of mine. His arms caged me in as he reached for the handlebars. His cologne wrapped around me as my brain went fuzzy. It took every ounce of control not to arch back and wiggle my butt against him like a cat in heat.

I took a deep breath. "No helmet for you?"

The corner of his mouth lifted. "I'm not the precious cargo, Darling." He turned the key, and the vehicle roared to life.

The words landed low in my stomach, unfurling like something slow and molten.

Precious cargo.

He had said it so easily, like it was a simple fact—like he actually meant it. I swallowed hard, trying to ignore the way my pulse tripped over itself.

We bounced along the hilly terrain of the farm, hugging the property line between the Drifted Spirit Inn and Star Harbor Farm until we popped out onto a quiet county road.

After checking that the roadway was clear, Cal pressed forward, guiding us across the asphalt and into the tree line, where the forest swallowed us whole.

The early-evening sun hung heavy in the sky, its amber glow stretching long shadows across the ground, slipping like molten gold through the canopy. The air thickened as we ventured deeper. Cooler beneath the towering oaks and maples, the scent of damp earth and pine settling into my lungs. The tires crunched over fallen twigs and scattered stones, the steady hum of the engine blending with the rustling leaves, a whispered promise that night was closing in.

The woods felt alive out there—untamed and breathing. It was a place where time moved differently, where the world beyond the trees didn't seem to exist. A breeze rustled through the branches, carrying the crisp bite of early evening. Everything felt quieter, like the rest of the world had blurred at the edges.

Cal slowed, and when the vehicle stopped, I looked around. As far as the eye could see there was nothing but trees and greenery and a few foot paths made by either animals or hikers. Birds chirped and leaves rustled, but there was no other sign of human activity.

Curiosity piqued, I followed Cal as he got off of the 4-wheeler and walked to the back. "So what's the plan, man?"

Cal adjusted the backpack onto his shoulders and accepted the helmet, placing it on the back rack. He turned and looked out into the trees. "The plan is to make you dinner, but first we forage."

My eyes went round. "Mushroom hunting?" I asked. "I haven't done that since I was a kid!"

Cal nodded, adjusting the straps of his backpack before turning to me. "But there are rules first."

"Of course there are, *Daddy*." I enjoyed the way my silly teasing always got under his skin, making the tiniest hint of a blush color his cheeks.

Cal sighed and leveled me with the most *Daddy* look ever. A bubble of laughter tickled my chest.

"I'm serious," he said. "I can't have you getting poisoned on our first date. We are probably past the morel season, though with the recent rain we could get lucky. But when it comes to mushrooms, don't eat anything unless you are one hundred percent sure of what it is. I know most of our native species, poisonous and not, so I still want you to double-check with me first before you put *anything* in your mouth."

My eyebrow crept higher. *"Anything?"*

A flash of desire rippled across his features as he smiled. "Anything."

My belly fluttered, but I nodded, giving him a break because I knew he was right. Ingesting mushrooms you thought were safe without being absolutely certain could be deadly, and I had no intention of dying before getting to experience a full date with Callum Blackwood.

I raised both palms. "I won't touch anything. I promise."

Cal chuckled, his shoulders softening as he started walking down the trail with me at his side. "You can touch things, mycotoxins are absorbed through your gut, not your skin."

Grumpy Cal was hot. Intelligent, protective, grumpy Cal was downright irresistible.

Keeping in step with each other, we wandered from the path, letting the forest envelop us as we stepped over fallen trees and rotted logs. Cal crouched first, his broad shoulders dipping low, his forearm brushing against my knee. I swallowed, suddenly hyperaware of how close we were, of the warmth of his skin even through the fabric of his shirt.

Cal grabbed my hand, encouraging me to crouch beside him. His hand held on to mine as his other pointed in the distance. "See that white mound on the log over there?"

I nodded, but it was hard to concentrate on anything besides Cal's large hand wrapped around mine.

"Early mornings and early evenings make the light better for seeing the contrast of the mushrooms against the earth. Plus, they prefer cooler, damper temperatures, and sometimes the summer sun just gets too damn hot . . . looks like we got lucky."

I walked with him hand in hand as we approached the fallen log. "What is it?" I asked, examining the strange-looking mushroom. It was a creamy yellow color with a trumpetlike cap and wavy edges.

"These are my favorite. Chanterelles." He plucked one and twirled it between his fingers. "Their flavor is kind of nutty . . . almost peppery. They hold up really well to cooking."

Swoon.

I helped Cal pluck a few from the log, and he placed them in a small mesh bag inside his backpack. "Always leave some for the next foragers," he instructed. "Could be other humans like us, or animals or bugs."

My heart squeezed—only he would think about the animals and bugs. My eyes caught on something bright orange clinging to the side of a tree. "Oh, what about that?" I pointed.

Cal's smile stretched across his face, hitting me with its full, devastating power. "Good eye."

We walked toward my find. "Do you see how it grows together like a shelf? The color is really special too. Look here." He pointed to the underside. "There aren't any gills. This one's called chicken of the woods. I like it with pasta."

I kept my expression perfectly serious. "Is it a bad time to tell you I'm allergic to mushrooms?" I asked, and watched as Cal's face fell, visible heartbreak washing over his features. His whole body tensed. His mouth parted slightly, his brows drawing together.

I tossed my head back in a cackle. "I'm kidding," I laughed. "Oh man, you were *really* bummed there for a second."

Cal's jaw flexed before he wrapped an arm around the back of my neck, pulling me into him. "You are such a little shit."

His arm was solid around me, his body a wall of heat against mine. My breath stuttered, caught between laughter and something heavier, something I wasn't sure how to name. His thumb skimmed along my jaw, the rough edge sending a delicious shiver through me.

For a moment I stood, staring up at him, our bodies flush, our breathing sawing in and out in tandem. His thumb moved to brush across my eyebrow, then down the side of my face, as though his fingertips were memorizing every plane and curve of my features. My lips parted, begging to feel his mouth on mine.

"Do you hear that?" he asked, staring into my eyes.

I blinked up at him, trying to stay in the moment while my senses were on overload. All I could hear was the pounding of my own heart. I could have pulled away. I could have made some joke, or teased him like I always did, but I just stood there, looking up at him with my pulse in my throat.

His thick fingers laced through mine.

"Come here," he said, his voice lower than before. "Let me show you something."

TWENTY-EIGHT

CALLUM

The creek water was warmer than I expected.

Not warm, exactly—cool enough to take the edge off the heat of the day—but with the sun dipping lower, the shallows had absorbed just enough of the July warmth to be comfortable.

Elodie bent down, brushing her hand through the running water. She toed off her boots with quick, practiced motions, then balanced on one foot as she peeled off her socks.

She shot me a mischievous look over her shoulder. "Come on, Blackwood. Live a little."

I huffed out a breath but followed suit, stepping out of my boots, rolling my socks down, and shoving them inside my boots before following her into the water. The smooth river rocks were slick beneath my bare feet, but Elodie moved like she belonged there, like the water had always been a part of her.

Elodie waded in deeper, the hem of her jeans darkening as the water lapped against her calves. She tilted her head back, letting the last golden rays of sunlight spill over her face, and *fuck* if it didn't do something to me.

I wasn't the kind of man to talk about beautiful moments. I'd seen too many things, lost too many people to believe that life handed those moments out freely. But standing there, watching her with bare feet in the creek, laughter on her lips, water glistening on her skin—hell, I wanted to believe in them.

"El," I called, my voice rougher than I meant it to be.

She turned, blinking those big bright eyes at me, and smiled. "Yeah?"

I didn't answer right away. Instead, I took my time, drinking her in. The curls that had escaped from her bun, damp at the edges. The flush high on her cheekbones from the warmth of the day. The way she fit here so damn easily, like she was always meant to be part of this place, like she belonged right there—with me.

I wanted to reach for her. Pull her into me. I wanted to get my hands on her skin and feel the soft, wet press of her against me in the water.

"Shh." My finger pressed to my lips when a sound broke through the stillness and my ears pricked. "Do you hear that?" I whispered, searching for the source of the sound.

She stilled, concentrating on the sounds of the forest.

A low, breathy moan. A woman's voice, punctuated by the sharp, repetitive grunts of a man.

Elodie's eyes went wide. "Oh my god," she whisper-shouted.

I didn't have to look far to find them—tucked just off the trail, only half hidden by the trees, was a couple who apparently hadn't been able to wait until they were back in town to tear each other's clothes off.

Elodie's shoulders shook with silent laughter as she

covered her mouth, but when she looked at me, her gaze turned wicked, and she waded toward me. "Well, well. Star Harbor sure is . . . lively tonight." Her eyebrows bounced.

I exhaled sharply, dragging a hand down my face. I knew exactly what she was thinking. That damn sparkle in her eye told me everything I needed to know.

"Don't even think about it," I warned as my attention narrowed on her pretty face.

She gasped, all false innocence and blinking lashes. "Think about what, Cal?"

I stepped closer, slow and deliberate, until I was right in front of her, looking down at her. My mouth hovered over hers. "About giving them some competition."

Her breath hitched. Just a little—just enough, and fuck if I wasn't tempted.

I took one step forward, then another. Elodie's body stayed flush with mine, her steps mirroring mine as I moved forward.

I could have backed her up against the nearest tree, pressed my body into hers, let my hands and mouth explore all the ways I already knew she would fit against me. I could have let her feel how badly I wanted her—how close I was to losing my grip.

But the second she made a move like she might actually push me on it—just the tiniest shift in her stance, watching her teeth sink into the plush pillow of her lower lip—I curled my fingers around her wrist and yanked her toward me, lowering my mouth to her ear.

"Not here," I murmured, my voice low and rough. "Your moans are for me, Darling. No one else gets to hear them."

Her sharp inhale sent a thrill down my spine. Her body softened, just for a moment, before she covered it up with a grin. "Possessive much?"

I shrugged, not bothering to deny it. "Get on the damn 4-wheeler."

She laughed, but she obeyed, turning toward the bank, sloshing through the shallows toward dry land.

I followed, my eyes trailing the way her wet jeans clung to her legs, appreciating the way the denim hugged the curve of her ass. My pulse ticked against my throat, something low and raw coiling in my gut.

The woods around us were quieter now, the lovers in the distance coming down from whatever high they'd chased. The air was still except for the occasional rustling of leaves, the distant croak of a bullfrog, and the rhythmic sound of water spilling over smooth stones.

Elodie reached the muddy bank first, hesitating for half a second before planting her foot and pushing herself up.

She made it halfway before her bare foot slid on the damp earth.

I caught her before she went down, my hands clamping around her hips, jerking her back against me.

Her sharp inhale hit the humid air, and suddenly there wasn't enough space between us.

My fingers flexed against her hip bones, anchoring her there, every inch of her ass pressed into me. The heat of the day had faded, but she was still warm—her body molded against mine like she belonged there.

Like she *knew* she belonged there.

Her breath was uneven, her body tensed in my grip, but she didn't pull away.

I dipped my head lower, my lips a fraction away from the curve where her shoulder met her throat. I could feel her pulse there, a quick, rapid beat. She smelled like earth and river water, like something wild and untouchable, and for a split second I wanted to bite down, mark her, brand her as mine.

Instead, I exhaled slow, deliberate. "Careful, Darling."

She shivered.

Then she turned her head slightly, just enough for our eyes to meet in the dim light. A challenge flickered there, dark and teasing. "Or what?"

My jaw ticced. I tightened my grip, then just as quickly released her, stepping back.

She let out a breath, something close to disappointment flickering in her expression before she masked it with a bratty look. "I knew you didn't have it in you."

My nostrils flared. "Keep pushing and you'll see what happens."

She grinned, and before I could stop her, she was scrambling up the rest of the incline, laughing under her breath. "Are you gonna stare at my ass all night, or are you coming?"

My hands fisted at my sides. "Brat."

She only laughed harder, but I could hear the tightness in it, the way she wasn't quite as unaffected as she wanted me to believe.

We walked the rest of the way in silence, the 4-wheeler still a ways off. The woods had swallowed it in darkness, but I knew where it was. She moved ahead of me, her bare feet padding over damp earth and scattered leaves. After pulling on our socks and boots, I hauled the backpack over my shoulder.

Every few steps, Elodie glanced over her shoulder, her eyes catching mine, something electric humming between us. By the time our ride came into view, I wasn't sure who was chasing whom.

She reached it first, running her fingers along the seat

like she was considering something. Then she turned, leaning back against it, waiting.

Her chest rose and fell, her breath shallow. Her shirt was clinging to places it had no business clinging to, and I let my gaze drag over her, slow and thorough, making sure she saw it.

Her lips parted.

I stopped in front of her, close enough that my body heat licked against her skin.

I wanted to press her against the metal, slot my thigh between hers and make her moan my name. I only resisted because the slow torture of teasing anticipation was far better. I'd promised Elodie a proper date, and I'd be damned if I didn't give it to her.

Instead of acting on impulse, I reached past her, grabbing the helmet from where I'd stashed it on the rack.

She let out a breath that sounded a lot like frustration.

I smirked.

She scowled.

I held the helmet out, waiting.

After a long beat, she snatched it, shoving it onto her head. "You're impossible."

I stepped back with a grin and winked. "And you like it."

Her eyes narrowed, but she climbed onto the seat without another word.

I dragged a hand down my face and released a slow exhale, trying to shake off whatever the hell this was. The heat, the adrenaline, the way she looked at me like she already knew what buttons to push and exactly how hard to press.

I needed a distraction.

So, like an idiot, I tossed her the keys. "Scoot up. It's your turn to drive."

Her eyes lit up, mischief sparking like a damn firework as she caught them midair and scrambled to make room for me behind her.

Turns out, letting her drive was a mistake—or maybe it was the best decision I'd made all night. I couldn't tell.

Elodie had always been wild energy, but behind the wheel, she was something else entirely. She took the trails fast, kicking up dust, letting out sharp, delighted gasps whenever we caught air over a hill. Every time I looked at her, she was grinning like she'd just found some new kind of freedom.

And me? I was grinning right alongside her.

I didn't realize how much tension I was carrying until she laughed—full, unrestrained, and effortlessly happy. The tension I was carrying unfurled itself from my ribs.

She threw me a playful look over her shoulder. "Admit it. You're having fun."

I just shook my head, a full smile spreading across my face as I gripped her thighs. "Drive before you crash us, Darling."

Her laughter rang out into the night.

The Drifted Spirit was quiet when we rolled up, the last stretch of evening painting the sky in hues of deep violet and burnt gold. A few guests sat on the porch, rocking in chairs, murmuring in low voices as the cicadas hummed their summer song. Scratch perked up from her favorite chair as we got closer, but she stayed put.

After she parked, I reached over to cut the engine. Elodie's fingers flexed against the worn handlebars. She was still buzzing with energy from the drive, a live wire of adrenaline and something else—something thick and charged that neither of us acknowledged out loud.

I turned to her, my voice low. "Hungry?"

Her eyes darkened, lips parting slightly as she glanced at my mouth. "Starving."

Fuck.

The way she said it—like she wasn't just talking about food—sent a slow roll of heat through my bloodstream.

I got out before I did something impulsive, like haul her into my lap and take her right there on the seat with an audience. The 4-wheeler was silent, leaving only the sound of the wind off the lake and the crunch of gravel under our boots as we made our way inside.

Elodie followed me through the back entrance, where the kitchen was already dimly lit with warm light. The space smelled like the remnants of whatever meal Helen had reheated earlier—garlic, roasted herbs, the faintest trace of something sweet. I grabbed the pack of mushrooms we'd foraged and tossed them onto the counter, rolling my shoulders to shake off the tension crawling up my spine.

"Where's my bestie?" she asked, referring to Levi. Over the years plenty of women showed interest, but having Ellie so casually and fully embrace my son was entirely new. It was clear she cared for him as a person, not just tolerated him to get to me. Her care and genuine interest in my son made my heart crank into overdrive.

"Community service with Brody. It was part of his penance for the incident at the barn." I moved around her, careful not to touch her. I knew once I started, it was going to be nearly impossible to control myself.

Elodie hummed acknowledgment as she looked around the kitchen. Everything was cleaned and organized with military precision, just as I liked it. She slid onto a high stool, watching me like she was trying to figure something out. "You do this a lot?" she asked, voice lazy, teasing. "Cook for women after dark?"

I tried not to smile as I set a pan on the burner and turned on the flame. "Nope."

She bit her lip, tapping a slow rhythm against the countertop with her fingers. "So I'm special then."

My hands stilled for half a beat before I reached for the oil. "Seems that way."

Her teeth caught her lower lip again, and for a long moment we just . . . looked at each other.

That was how I knew I was in trouble—because this date wasn't just about sex. This wasn't just about wanting her. It was about the fact that she could read me too easily, crawl into my damn head and make herself comfortable.

And I was letting her.

Our teasing was still there, but underneath it, something heavier. Something neither of us had the energy to fight off anymore.

"I just want to make you dinner." Really, I wanted to take care of her, and I didn't know what the fuck to do with that.

So I did what I always did—I focused on the task in front of me. First I filled a pot and set it to boil before taking a damp paper towel to clean our foraged mushrooms. My face heated as her eyes clocked every movement, silently observing without judgment.

The steady scrape of my knife against the cutting board filled the quiet as I chopped the mushrooms, working fast, needing something to keep my hands busy. The scent of butter and garlic bloomed in the air as I added them to the pan, the sizzle breaking the silence like a gunshot.

Elodie let out a soft, pleased hum. "You know, a man who can cook is a dangerous thing."

I glanced over my shoulder. "Oh, yeah?"

"Yes," she said, watching the way my hands moved, the way my forearms flexed as I worked. "You make it look easy. Casual. Like you're not over there looking entirely too good while doing it."

I huffed out a laugh, shaking my head as I reached for the pasta, adding it to the water. "So now I'm dangerous because I can cook?"

She leaned forward, propping her chin on her fist. "It's the fact that you can cook without a recipe and look so good doing it. That's double homicide, really."

The corner of my mouth twitched. "Sounds like you should be more careful, then."

She exhaled a slow breath, dragging her fingers across the marble countertop. "You keep saying that, Callum, but here I am."

Yeah. There she fucking was.

I looked at her—*really looked*. A curl slipped from the twist she'd put it in, framing her face and making her green eyes look impossibly large. She wasn't just pretty, she was

. . .

"Stunning." I hadn't meant to say it aloud, but when her eyes whipped to mine, the blush on her cheeks had me biting back a smile.

A shy hand tucked the curl behind her ear. "Thank you."

The room tightened. The air turned thick, charged with something molten and hot.

We stared at each other for a beat before I cleared my throat and gave the pasta a quick stir. "So do you miss it?" I asked. "The city."

Elodie kicked her feet as she considered my question. "Honestly? Not even a little." She let out a tiny laugh. "I mean, sure. I miss a *few* things like this one little bakery that made the most divine oat milk lattes." Her eyes went dreamy. "You know the kind with the fluffy foam on top and a drizzle of caramel? *Mmm . . .*"

The way her throat hummed had my stomach swooping. She mistook my awestruck silence for judgment because her nose crinkled. "It's silly."

I shook my head. "I don't think life's simple pleasures are silly."

"Is that so, Mr. Blackwood?" Her eyebrow rose. "How do you enjoy your coffee?"

"Black," I deadpanned, earning me her hearty, genuine laugh—my favorite one.

Elodie raised her shoulders and sighed. "Honestly, I don't miss the life I had there. Being here, working on bringing Stan's dream to life? It's . . ." Her hands motioned in front of her chest. "Changing me."

My head tipped, eager to glean any insight into the complex woman in front of me. "How so?"

"I built my entire life around *fun*—events, planning, being effortlessly charming." She batted her lashes. "You know," she said, her voice deepening as her brow furrowed, "damn the man and just have fun!" She laughed, eyes going soft. "Now? I don't know. I've never had to *work* for something. Suddenly all the hard labor on the farm doesn't feel so restrictive. It's freeing. I don't think anyone ever used to think I was someone they could count on, and now it feels like I have an entire community waiting with bated breath to see me make something of the place."

I stepped forward, cupping her face in my palm. My

thumb stroked across her high cheekbone. "As much as I hate to admit it, you don't suck at this."

Elodie gasped and flattened a hand to her chest. "Sir, your compliments make me blush."

I bit back a smile as I rolled my eyes. "You know what I mean—you're talented. You have business mogul written all over you."

Her grin widened. "You think so?"

I jerked my chin in a firm nod. While I didn't like the fact Elodie was damn good at this and it made my dream infinitely harder to achieve, I couldn't lie to her either.

Ellie smiled shyly. "Maybe one day." She looked around the kitchen and hummed. "My very own place where people could stay, eat, hike, and play?" Her wistful sigh knotted in my chest. "Yeah . . . maybe one day."

Silence stretched between us. Finally, Elodie's voice came out in a small whisper. "I guess we have to wait and see what happens with the Keepers—what they'll decide with the farm."

I hummed, drowning in my own thoughts about how my own dreams of running a kitchen were diluted down to morning muffins and strawberry scones. My jaw tensed. Thinking about how close I had been only riled me up, so I shoved it down and focused on her instead. Somehow I found myself making dinner for the one person whose dream was in direct competition with mine.

It was best not to think about it before I burst a blood vessel right in front of her.

I drained the pasta and finished plating the food, setting it in front of her, watching as she twirled a forkful of pasta and took her first bite.

The second the flavors hit her tongue, her lashes fluttered, and she let out a quiet, sinful little moan. "Cal."

Jesus Christ. My name on her lips.

I swallowed hard, my fingers curling against the counter, my voice thick with gravel. "That good?"

She swallowed and licked her lips, slow and deliberate. "I told you, you're dangerous."

I stepped forward, bracing my hands on the counter, caging her in. "You have no idea."

She set down her fork, tilting her face up to mine. "Then show me."

I didn't hesitate.

One hand threaded through the curls at the nape of her neck, the other gripping her hip as I dragged her forward. Her breath hitched, her fingers fisting the fabric of my shirt as I dipped my head, hovering just above her lips.

"Is this what you want?" I murmured.

She exhaled, shaky but sure. "Yes."

I claimed her mouth with mine, and there was nothing slow or tentative about it. It was a collision, all heat and teeth and breathless want, like we'd both been starving for too long and finally, finally, had something to sink our teeth into.

Her hands roamed, gripping my shoulders, my arms, pulling me closer like she wanted to climb inside my skin. I let her, let her take whatever she needed, because *fuck*, I needed it too.

I wasn't sure how we were supposed to come back from this.

I wasn't sure I cared.

Elodie broke the kiss first, barely, her breath uneven against my lips. "We should—" She swallowed, blinking like she was trying to clear the fog from her brain. "I mean, we can't just—"

I studied her, rubbing my thumb along her jaw, feeling

the way her pulse jumped beneath my touch. "What? Have a full-blown health code violation in my kitchen?"

She let out a breathless laugh, her fingers still fisted in my shirt. "I was going to say 'defile this countertop,' but yeah, that too."

"I guess we'll have to find somewhere more suitable then." I grabbed her hips, hoisting her off the stool and over my shoulder. I carried her toward the hallway, the lights dim and the inn quiet around us as she giggled.

Her grip tightened around mine, and when we reached my bedroom door, I placed her on her feet.

She arched a brow, eyes bright with mischief. "Are you sure this place is up to code, Mr. Blackwood?"

I turned the handle, pulling her inside, my voice a low rasp. "Let's find out."

TWENTY-NINE

CALLUM

I BACKED her into the bedroom, my hands gripping her waist, her breath coming faster, matching my own. The door clicked shut behind us, the only sound in the space aside from the low hum of the night beyond the windows and the heavy, uneven rhythm of our breathing.

Elodie's lips were parted, swollen from my kisses, her pupils wide as she tipped her head back to look at me. "Cal—"

"Yes, Darling?" My voice was low, rough with everything I was holding back.

She swallowed hard, but she didn't look away. Didn't waver. "Touch me."

Fuck.

Heat surged through me, blazing and fervent, but I reined it in. She deserved more than rushing. More than a frantic fuck against the nearest surface—though the temptation was there.

Instead, I slid my hands up her sides, slow, deliberate, feeling the way she shivered beneath my palms. Her body melted against mine as I pulled her closer, pressing my mouth to the curve of her jaw, then lower, tracing my lips down the column of her throat.

Her fingers curled into my shirt, gripping tight like she was anchoring herself to me.

I wanted her desperate for me. I wanted her wrecked, and I wanted to be the only man who ever got to see her like this.

I took my time stripping her bare, pushing the fabric of her gray T-shirt up, baring smooth, golden skin inch by inch. She trembled as I peeled it over her head, her chest rising and falling in uneven breaths.

"You're beautiful," I murmured, running my thumbs along the delicate dip of her waist.

A slow smile curled her lips, teasing and warm. "I know."

I chuckled, my mouth finding hers in a deep, slow kiss, one hand sliding up to cup the weight of her breast through her sheer bra, feeling the hard peak of her nipple against my thumb. Her breath hitched, and I swallowed the sound, deepening the kiss, learning exactly how she liked to be touched from the way her body responded.

She arched into me, pressing closer, chasing the friction.

"You're also impatient," I murmured against her lips.

Her fingers fisted in my hair, tugging just enough to send fire down my spine. "I've waited long enough, Callum."

Christ.

I lifted her, wrapped her legs around my waist, and carried her to the bed, laying her down against the soft sheets.

I hovered above her, drinking her in. Elodie's skin was warm beneath my hands, her breath uneven, her pupils blown wide with something that echoed in my own chest.

I trailed my fingers down her side, savoring the smooth skin and the delicate curve of her ribs. She lifted her arms to stretch, her breath hitching as my fingers explored. My hands skimmed lower, brushing over lace, a barrier I had no patience for.

My fingers slid beneath the band of her bra, unhooking it in one smooth motion. The straps slipped from her shoulders, and I caught my breath at the sight of her—bare, flushed, and perfect.

"Elodie," I murmured, reverence thick in my voice.

She reached for me, fingers skating over my chest, the ridges of my stomach, making my restraint damn near impossible. I pushed up onto my knees, watching her as I made quick work of her jeans, dragging them down her legs, along with those tiny socks she always wore around the farm. She shivered as the cool air kissed her skin, but I was already warming her, my hands gliding back up, slow and deliberate, teasing.

"Look at you," I muttered, my gaze sweeping over her.

Her lips parted, her body arching into my touch, a silent plea. I was more than happy to answer it.

I stood just long enough to shed my own jeans, my boxer briefs, every last barrier between us. Her eyes followed the movement, dark and hungry, a flush spreading across her neck.

I climbed back over her, caging her in with my arms. "Like what you see, Darling?"

She didn't answer with words—just a slow, sinfully satisfied smile as her fingers slid over my stomach, down, wrapping around my cock in a way that had my body locking tight.

Fuck.

I gritted my teeth, leaning in, brushing my lips over hers.

"Careful," I warned, my voice rough. "Or this is going to be over before it even starts."

Her laughter was soft, breathless, but it cut off into a sharp inhale as I rolled my hips, pressing against her heat, teasing the edge of something inevitable. My fingers found her pussy, wet and waiting for me. I tested and teased, gliding through her before circling her clit. By the time I slid in one finger, then two, she was gasping and arching into my hand. I watched as my tattooed fingers disappeared inside her. My thumb applied pressure to her clit as my fingers pumped in and out, drawing her orgasm out of its cocoon.

Her fingers curled around my biceps, nails pressing into my skin as she arched, inviting me in. I didn't rush—not yet. I wanted to savor this. The way her body moved, the way her lips parted on a sharp inhale as I adjusted. My cock teased her entrance, tracing and savoring her softness with languid strokes.

Slowly, I pressed into her, inch by inch. She stretched around me, and her breath shuddered against my neck.

Her hands slid up my arms, over my shoulders, tangling in my hair as she gasped. And then, *finally*, I sank deeper until I was fully seated, and nothing else in the world existed.

Heat met heat, bare skin on bare skin. Her hands mapped my back like she needed to memorize every inch, her touch confident and claiming.

She gasped again as I rolled my hips, letting her feel exactly how much I wanted her.

"Cal—"

"I've got you," I rasped, trailing my lips down her body, tasting her, teasing her, driving her to the edge before pulling her back just to do it again. I wanted her shaking, gasping, coming apart beneath me.

Heat pooled low in my spine as her pretty little cunt clenched around me, tight and perfect, like she was made for me—like she had been waiting for this as long as I had.

I pulled back, just enough to watch her. Her eyes were dark, her lips swollen, her chest rising and falling in uneven breaths.

"You okay?" I was barely holding on, my control fraying at the edges.

She nodded, breathless, her fingers tightening against my skin. "More."

I let out a low curse, pressing my forehead against hers as I pulled out just to sink back in, slow and steady. A drawn-out, torturous rhythm that had her moaning, her body rolling up into mine, desperate for more.

"You feel so good," I murmured, my lips brushing her cheek, her jaw. "So fucking perfect."

Her arms wrapped around my neck, pulling me closer, her body arching to meet every deep thrust.

I wanted to make this last. I wanted to drag her over the edge and follow her down. I wanted to stay wrapped in her warmth, her softness, her fire.

Her breath hitched again, her nails biting into my back as she tightened around me and came apart. Her body trembled, pleasure unfurling between us, wrapping around my spine, and pulling me under.

"Elodie," I groaned, my head dropping to the curve of her shoulder as I gave in, let go, let myself feel everything.

The last thing I knew was her whispering my name, her lips pressing against my temple, her body shaking beneath mine.

The tremors racked through her, little aftershocks that

made her breath wash over my skin. My own heart was still hammering, my body heavy, sated, yet unwilling to move away from her warmth.

I pressed my forehead against hers, trying to steady my breathing, to ground myself in the feel of her—soft and pliant beneath me, her legs still loosely wrapped around my hips, her fingers tracing slow, lazy circles over my back.

I exhaled, pressing a lingering kiss against her temple before rolling us onto our sides, bringing her with me, not willing to separate from her just yet. The sheets tangled around us, a sheen of sweat cooling on our skin, but neither of us moved to fix it.

She tucked herself against my chest, her lips brushing over my collarbone, her breath still uneven. "Holy shit," she whispered, voice husky and warm.

I let out a low chuckle, tucking a damp curl behind her ear. "Not bad, huh?"

Her hand smacked against my chest, but there was no real force behind it. Just warmth. Just something that felt dangerously close to contentment.

We stayed like that for a while, just breathing, just existing in the quiet aftermath of something that neither of us had expected but both of us had needed. I ran my fingers up and down the curve of her spine, and she sighed, melting deeper into me.

Then, softly, almost absently, she traced her fingers over one of many old scars on my chest. Elodie's fingers ghosted over my skin, tracing the jagged line of the scars that ran over my shoulder and down the length of my arm. They were reminders of a past life, a past version of me I had stuffed into a box and hadn't thought about in a long time.

"Where are you from?" she murmured, like she wasn't just asking about geography, but about who I used to be.

I swallowed, exhaling through my nose. "Somewhere you've never been. A little nowhere town in Nevada."

She was quiet for a beat, absorbing that, before she said, "And you came here because of Mary."

It wasn't a question.

I stared at the ceiling, my fingers stilling on her bare back. "Her family was here—Wes, her parents. When she got pregnant, it made sense to put down roots."

Elodie stilled, her fingers no longer moving over my chest. "You loved her." There was no jealousy, only warmth in her voice.

I hesitated, not because I didn't know the answer, but because the truth was complicated. It always had been.

"It was complicated," I admitted, my voice rougher than I intended.

Elodie didn't push. She didn't fill the silence with meaningless words or try to fix something that didn't need fixing. Instead, she reached up, cupping my face in her hands, tilting my chin so I had no choice but to meet her gaze.

Her eyes searched mine, not demanding, not expecting—just waiting.

So I told her.

I told her how Mary and I had been a moment, not an epic love story. How we'd been young and reckless, caught up in something easy, something that was never meant to be permanent. How we weren't even seriously dating when she got pregnant.

I told her how I didn't hesitate when she told me.

"She wanted to do it alone," I admitted, my voice quiet. "But I wasn't going to let that happen. I made a promise. To her. To the baby. To my best friend. I promised that I'd show up, that I'd be there no matter what, and there was no going back on that."

Elodie listened, her fingertips brushing slow, absent-minded circles over my shoulder. She didn't judge. She didn't even flinch. She just absorbed my words, the way she seemed to absorb everything—fully and completely.

"I grew to love her," I finally said. "But maybe not in the way I was supposed to. Certainly not in the way she deserved, but she was my family. And Levi . . . I have loved him from the second I knew he existed. That's never changed."

She studied me for a long moment, like she was trying to see the cracks, the pieces of me that had been reshaped by the weight of my past.

Then, softly, she asked, "Do you ever regret it?"

I didn't even have to think. "Not for a single second."

Her lips parted, something unreadable flashing in her expression. "You are such a good man, Cal."

Imagine that—the one woman I had set out to hate, thinking I'm a good man.

I huffed a quiet laugh, shaking my head. "I don't know about that."

"I do." She pressed a kiss to my chest, right over my heart. "I think the only thing I actually hate about you is how impossible you make it to actually hate you. Especially after that first night you barged in on me with a baseball bat, but left me Band-Aids after."

A laugh bubbled in my chest. I couldn't hold back anymore, because she saw me, because she didn't just listen —she understood—I kissed her again.

This time, there was nothing careful about it. This time, I poured myself into the kiss and showed her exactly how much she was changing everything.

THIRTY

ELODIE

My body buzzed with energy.

Hours had passed since Cal had kissed me breathless, since he had pressed me into the mattress and taken me apart with slow, devastating precision. But lying in the tangle of his sheets, my skin still flushed and my breath still uneven, sleep felt impossible.

My fingers traced lazy patterns along his chest, feeling the steady rise and fall beneath my palm. He was warm, solid, and so deeply *here*. That was the part that scared me, because Callum Blackwood wasn't just some guy I had fallen into bed with.

Somewhere between our arguing, our banter, our stubborn refusal to give each other an inch—I'd started to fall for him.

And that was dangerous.

Because men like Cal? They didn't fall.

His fingers ghosted over the bare skin of my back, his voice a deep, sleepy rumble. "What's going on in that head of yours, Darling?"

Darling. Why did I love it when he called me that?

I turned my face to look up at him, our noses nearly touching. "Just thinking."

One of his brows lifted. "That sounds dangerous."

My fingers dragged lower over his stomach. "Says the man who just spent the last two hours proving he's very, very dangerous."

A low, satisfied chuckle rumbled through him. "Are you still in one piece?"

I grinned. "Barely."

His hand drifted down my spine, a lazy, possessive stroke, like he was still claiming me, even in the afterglow.

"Do you ever think it's strange?" I asked, letting my words wander alongside my thoughts.

Cal's brow furrowed as he looked down at me.

"That you live with a bunch of strangers," I clarified with a gentle laugh.

"Ah." He nodded, thinking about my question. "Sometimes, but it's a part of the gig."

The gig.

Hearing Cal talk about how he came to run the inn was heartbreaking. He blamed himself for so much he couldn't control.

Feeling brave wrapped in Cal's arms, I snuggled closer. "If you didn't run the Drifted Spirit, what would you do? Anything in the whole world."

"Own a restaurant." Cal didn't even hesitate.

I propped myself onto an elbow and looked at him with wide, excited eyes. "Really? That's so fun!" My brain was wired to make plans, find a way, and execute them flawlessly. "Well, why don't you? I'm sure the guests you host would flock to something like that, especially if it was close. You could draw people in and also have a place for them to stay." I sighed into him. "It would be dreamy."

His stare lingered as realization dawned on me. *Oh, shit. That was it.*

Cal's plan for the farm property was exactly what I described . . . something that couldn't happen if Star Harbor Farm was next door instead.

My cheeks flushed and guilt swarmed my brain. I swallowed hard, my eyes bouncing across his as I searched for the right words.

Cal's hand reached up, and a soft smile touched his lips. He brushed a stray strand of hair away from my face. "Maybe in another version of some other life."

Cal shifted, rolling on top of me and commandeering the conversation. "But right now, this is exactly the version of my life I want to be living."

His body was warm as it pressed into me. Desire flooded my system, but I sighed, burrowing closer for just one more minute. "I think I should go."

Cal grunted, wholly unimpressed with the idea. "You could stay."

The offer sent a ridiculous little thrill through me, but I shook my head. "It's late, and if I don't go now, I won't go at all."

He made a deep, thoughtful sound, then smirked. "Is that a promise?"

I rolled my eyes and shoved at his chest, but he just caught my hand and brought it to his lips, brushing a slow kiss against my knuckles.

Warmth bloomed in my chest as I dragged myself out of bed, finding my scattered clothes across the room. I tugged on my jeans, my shirt, my socks, stuffing my feet into my boots and swearing under my breath when I nearly tipped over in the process.

Cal leaned against the headboard, watching me with an

expression that was way too satisfied for a man who had just wrecked me so completely.

I pointed at him. "Not a word."

He chuckled. "I didn't say a damn thing."

I narrowed my eyes, but his grin only deepened as he pulled himself from the bed to get dressed.

Sneaking out of Callum Blackwood's bedroom should have been easy.

He lived on the first floor, tucked away from the main part of the inn. There was no one else awake. No one to witness me tiptoe across the wood floors.

That was, until we opened the door and found Levi standing in the hallway with wide eyes and an equally guilty expression.

Levi had his own shoes in his hands like he had just taken them off—like he'd just been caught sneaking in at the exact moment we were sneaking out.

For a long, frozen moment, the three of us just stared at one another.

Realization dawned on the teenager as a red flush crept up his neck. "Oh, you've gotta be shitting me," Levi muttered, scrubbing a hand over his face.

Cal's brows lifted, and he crossed his arms over his very bare, very muscular chest. "Language."

"Are you serious?" Levi snorted. "You're gonna parent *me* right now?"

Cal didn't flinch. "Where were you?"

Levi exhaled, rubbing the back of his neck. "Brody asked me to stay late. He needed an extra set of hands closing up the station. I was helping with paperwork and inventory. I forgot to text you." He shrugged. "And, then, uh . . . we went over some basic self-defense stuff. Brody's been showing me a few things."

Cal's brows lifted slightly, his stance shifting just enough to show he wasn't entirely unimpressed. "Is that so?"

Levi nodded, looking down at his sneakers, like he didn't want to make a big deal out of it. "Yeah."

"So, let's get this straight." I fought a smile, crossing my arms like I was siding with Cal, but really? I was 1,000 percent on Levi's side. "You were out late because you were being . . . responsible?"

Levi shot me a look, catching on fast. His lips twitched like he wanted to smile but knew better. "That's right."

Amusement flickered in his gaze before he leaned against the doorjamb. "And what exactly did Brody teach you?"

Levi's nerves tittered to the surface, and he shifted his weight before lifting a hand. "A few basic moves. Blocking, wrist escapes. I don't know . . . things that might be useful in a fight."

Cal hummed, clearly weighing something in his head before nodding once. "Good. We'll go over what you learned tomorrow."

Levi blinked. "Wait, really?"

Cal gave his son a soft smile. "You think Brody's the only one who knows how to throw a punch or defend himself?"

Levi huffed a noise out of his nose, but this time it wasn't entirely miserable, more . . . surprised than anything. His eyes flicked between Cal and me, and I caught the quick spark of something almost pleased. Like maybe he actually liked the idea of his dad giving a damn about what he was up to.

"Great," he muttered as if the entire conversation was

mortifying. "Does that mean I'll get a training session *and* a lecture?"

Cal chuckled. "Probably."

Levi nodded. "Awesome."

He started to walk away, but then his body shifted back toward us—brows lifting a fraction, like something had just clicked. His arms dropped to his sides, and a slow, knowing horror tugged at the corner of his mouth.

"Oh, wait a second," he said, dragging the words out. "Why are we focusing on me? You're the one sneaking a woman out of your bedroom."

Cal cleared his throat, shifting on his feet. "Not sneaking. Just . . . escorting."

Levi rolled his eyes. "Bro, what are you on about?"

A slow grin tugged at my lips as Cal shifted uncomfortably. "Well, son, when you're with a woman, it's important to . . ."

I didn't help at all while Cal struggled for the correct, age-appropriate words. The entire interaction was cute, hilarious even.

"Okay, I for sure do not need this mental image." Levi made a gagging noise and turned away. "Can I please go now?"

Cal clamped a hand on Levi's shoulder. "Welcome to adulthood, *bro.*"

Levi groaned, shaking his head as he disappeared down the hall, leaving just the two of us in the quiet hallway of the inn.

I turned to Cal, crossing my arms. "Well, that wasn't awkward at all."

"Eh," he mused, slipping his arms around my waist, tugging me closer. "Could've been worse."

I tilted my head, squinting up at him. "How so?"

Cal's voice dropped an octave. "It could've been your parents who caught us."

I laughed, playfully shoving at his chest. I may have been a grown woman, but the thought of coming face-to-face with my parents after the things we did made my cheeks flame.

He laughed, then dipped down, brushing a lingering kiss against my lips before leading me out the side door.

Warm night air wrapped around us, the sound of crickets filling the silence. His hand found the small of my back, guiding me toward my cottage, and I let him. I let myself sink into the quiet, into the moment, and into him.

The night air carried the lingering scent of pine and earth, but my skin still held the warmth of his. My lips tingled, my body still humming with the memory of his touch, and yet we walked slow, unhurried, as if neither of us was quite ready to let the night end.

Behind us, the Drifted Spirit stood quiet under the moonlight, the soft glow of a porch light stretching long shadows across the grass. Beside me, Cal's walk was easy, one hand tucked into his pocket, his body loose in a way that made my chest ache a little—like he was truly comfortable. Like he wasn't thinking about whatever weight he always seemed to carry.

In the distance, past the tree line behind my cottage, a familiar rustling reached my ears—light, scurrying footsteps, chittering sounds.

I bit my lip, trying to smother a smile as the mama raccoon and her babies came into view.

Cal groaned, scrubbing a hand down his face. "You're still feeding them, aren't you?"

I pressed my lips together, feigning innocence. "I don't know what you mean."

"Elodie." He shot me a look, and I shot one right back.

I lifted a shoulder in a casual shrug. "They're cute."

He sighed. "They're criminals."

I gasped, clutching my chest. "How dare you. They're family."

Cal exhaled, long and suffering but laced with humor. "They tried to steal my dinner two nights ago."

I jutted my lower lip out in a pout. "Maybe they were just hungry."

He shook his head. "Maybe *I* was hungry."

I bit back a grin as he muttered something under his breath about "woodland bandits" and "absolute menace behavior," but before I could argue their case further, a sleek, familiar shape slunk out of the shadows, winding through the soft glow of the porch light.

Cal's attention darted to the shadows. His cat Scratch trotted right up to him, weaving between his legs like she owned the damn place—which, honestly, she kind of did.

Cal sighed, bending down to rub behind Scratch's ears. "You just can't help yourself, can you, little troublemaker?" His voice was softer now, full of something that made my chest ache.

With a confident grin, I crossed my arms. "She loves you."

Cal gave me an unimpressed look, but when he crouched down, I saw it—the moment his entire demeanor softened, the way his hand instinctively reached out to stroke over her sleek, scraggly fur.

"Damn cat," he murmured, voice dropping into something warm, something private.

Scratch purred like an engine, arching into his touch, blinking up at him like he hung the moon.

Cal scooped up the cat, holding Scratch like a baby. His

voice dipped even lower, smoothing into something that was almost . . . baby talk. "Who's my little troublemaker, huh? Are you causing problems out here, sweetheart?"

I sucked in a breath, my lips parting. *Did he—did Callum Blackwood just coo at his cat?*

I arched a brow, and when Cal glanced up and saw my expression, he immediately cleared his throat and straightened, like he hadn't just been sweet-talking the feral murder machine who'd been leaving dead mice as gifts on my porch.

I let the silence stretch just long enough for him to feel it.

His jaw flexed as he set her on the ground. "Not a word."

I grinned. "I don't know what you mean."

Scratch rubbed against his leg again, and I swore I saw the corner of his mouth twitch, like he was fighting a smile.

Damn. He is so gone for that cat.

Cal straightened, watching me, his expression unreadable.

I swallowed hard. "Good night, Callum."

For a second I thought he was going to kiss me again. Instead, his fingers brushed my jaw, his thumb ghosting over my cheekbone, his touch so soft, so reverent, my breath caught in my throat.

His voice was low, rough. "Good night, Darling."

Something clicked in my brain and a tiny laugh rumbled in my chest. "I thought you said that was just my last name," I teased.

His face was inches from mine, his deep eyes intensifying in the darkness. One finger slid down my nose with the gentlest touch. "It never really was."

Before I could respond, he cupped my jaw, tilting my

face up as his mouth claimed mine. It wasn't hurried or desperate—it was deep, lingering, full of something I couldn't name but felt down to my bones. His lips moved over mine with purpose, with quiet possession, like he was memorizing the shape of me, like he was staking his claim.

By the time he pulled back, my breath was uneven, my lips tingling, my thoughts scattered and wanting *more*.

Cal paused, brushing his thumb over my bottom lip before stepping away. With a click of his tongue, he barely had to glance down before Scratch trotted after him like she'd been waiting for the cue. Scratch purred, entirely unbothered, as if she had already decided where she belonged.

I stood there, stunned, watching them disappear into the night, my lips still tingling, my heart still racing.

That man was going to ruin me.

I shut the door behind me, leaning against it for a long beat, letting out a slow breath. My lips still tingled, my skin still warm from Cal's touch. My body hummed with the weight of everything that had happened tonight—the intimacy, the way he had opened up, the way I had let him in.

Who was I kidding? I had fallen for Callum Blackwood. Hard.

Shaking my head, I moved toward the bed, peeling back the covers before finding a pair of cozy pajamas. I needed a hot shower and a deep sleep to recover from my evening with Cal. As I stripped off my jeans, I caught sight of my discarded phone on the nightstand. The screen glowed with a string of missed texts, one from Selene.

SELENE

I don't know why I am surprised you pulled it off, but the Keepers are all in for helping with the barn raising. Are you ready for Star Harbor to descend on you like a well-meaning hurricane?

I EXHALED SHARPLY, my pulse skipping.

It's really happening.

My mind spun as I typed out a response. I set the phone down, the weight of it pressing into my chest. This farm, this wild dream—it was coming together, piece by piece, and not just because of me, but because of them. The people of this town, the Keepers, my family. Even Cal.

I ran my hands over my face, overwhelmed, but in the best way.

For the first time since I'd come back to Star Harbor, I wasn't just trying to hold on to someone else's dream. The dream had become my own, and I was building something real. Something lasting and meaningful.

And for the first time in a long time, I wasn't doing it alone.

CALLUM

I woke before sunrise.

The Drifted Spirit was quiet, the kind of stillness that only existed in those fragile moments before the rest of the world woke up. I moved through the inn on instinct—bare feet against worn hardwood, the soft creak of the floorboards beneath my weight, the faint scent of coffee beans filling the air as I started a fresh pot.

It was muscle memory at this point. My routine. Brew the coffee. Look out over the land. Pretend like I wasn't aching for something more.

The air was cool against my skin as I poured a travel mug for myself. And then, without thinking, I grabbed a second one.

For her.

I stared at it for a long beat, watching the steam curl into the air. It was ridiculous. She could pour her own damn coffee, but I set it on the counter anyway. In a paper bag, I gathered a few baked items that I had made, just in case anyone got hungry.

Steam curled from the mugs as I leaned against the

counter, staring out the kitchen window toward Star Harbor Farm. The sky was just beginning to shift, navy giving way to shades of deep purple and dusky pink, streaks of gold breaking over the horizon.

It would be a good day for barn raising.

I exhaled slowly, rubbing a hand over my jaw. The land was still now, but in a few hours, it would be crawling with people. The Amish. The Keepers. The whole damn town.

Elodie.

She consumed my thoughts. I glanced toward the counter. Our two mugs sat there, both filled to the brim. One black, the way I always drank it. The other fixed just the way she liked—oat milk, a thick layer of foam, and a drizzle of caramel over the top.

In the quiet of the kitchen, I allowed myself to smile. A new, hopeful feeling settled between my ribs.

I hadn't stopped to consider why I was making two cups of coffee like it was pure instinct—like she was an inevitable part of my morning now.

I ran a hand over my face, shaking my head as I popped the tops on the mugs to keep them warm. I grabbed both coffees and made my way out onto the porch. The air was cool, thick with the scent of earth and damp grass. A mist curled low over the fields, a quiet hush over everything as if the land itself was holding its breath, waiting for the day to begin.

And I stood there, waiting with it.

Outside, the land stretched before me in muted shades of blue and gray, waiting for the sun. In a few hours, it would be crawling with workers, the quiet replaced with hammering, shouting, the rhythmic hum of a town coming together to build something permanent.

The farm was changing.

She was changing it.

And hell, she was changing me.

I ran a hand over my jaw, exhaling. I should be worried about that, and maybe I was. The fate of the farmland rested in the Keepers' hands. With every improvement, I could feel my dream slip further and further away. It was a strange sensation——to be sad about something but also vaguely okay with it.

I settled onto the porch steps just as the first golden streaks cut across the sky.

The first to arrive were the Amish. They moved quietly, efficiently, their horse-drawn buggies rolling in just as the sky began to warm from deep navy to soft pink. They worked without preamble, unloading tools, stacking wood, making their preparations without a single wasted move-ment. There was something steadying about their presence, their deep-rooted tradition turning what could have been chaos into something structured and precise. There was no wasted movement, no hesitation. It was like watching a well-practiced team fall into place, lifting beams, lining up supports, an entire framework taking shape before my eyes.

Then the rest of Star Harbor started rolling in.

Trucks and SUVs pulled into the drive, kicking up dust, doors slamming as people spilled out—neighbors, friends, old-timers with more opinions than muscle, young families eager to be part of something bigger than themselves. The quiet hum of work was joined by a familiar mix of voices and laughter.

There was an easy camaraderie as they all greeted one another, laughter mixing with the sounds of shifting lumber and rolling toolboxes. The kind of small-town unity that didn't need to be spoken aloud to be understood.

And in the thick of it all was Elodie.

She moved through the crowd like she was born for this, all bright eyes and easy smiles, her hair twisted into some kind of messy knot on top of her head, the loose tendrils catching the golden morning light. She wore jeans that clung to the curves of her hips and a faded blue T-shirt that had probably been soft since the day it was made. She wasn't directing—Elodie never seemed to do that—but she was everywhere at once, delegating with ease, checking in on the workers, making sure people had what they needed, capturing pictures with her phone and laughing.

It suited her.

All of it. The way she threw herself into things. The way she built a community around her without even trying. The way she'd turned that broken-down farm into something that people wanted to rally behind.

I tried to look away. I needed to focus on the work, the logistics, on the fact that they were about to build an entire barn in a single day.

Instead, I watched her.

She must have felt it because, in the middle of whatever she was saying to Selene, she turned, catching my gaze across the crowd. A slow, knowing smile tugged at the corner of her lips. I lifted her coffee mug, and her grin widened as her head bobbed in an enthusiastic nod.

I smiled and looked away first.

"Jesus," a voice beside me drawled. "You are down *bad*."

I scowled, turning to find Wes standing there, arms crossed, watching me with a smirk that was way too pleased with itself. Unease rolled through me, as though I'd been caught cheating on his beloved sister.

"It looks good on you," he finally said, and the knot in my chest loosened. "For a while there, I was worried your dick was broken."

I shot him a droll look as Hayes, Brody, and his younger brother Austin walked up.

"His dick is fine," Brody chimed in. "He's just been busy becoming a less-handsome equivalent to Julia Child." He looked past me at the porch. "Speaking of . . . I need a sweet treat."

I laughed, reaching behind me for the bag. I tossed it at him, and he caught it midair before tearing it open.

"See," I said to Wes, "I'm multitalented, unlike you uncultured cavemen."

Hayes chuckled, glancing around and shaking his head. "Hell of a turnout."

It really was.

Austin's gaze flicked across the gathering crowd, and I caught the subtle way his eyes lingered when they landed on Elodie's sister Selene. The flicker of something unreadable before he masked it with an easy grin.

Interesting.

I filed that away to ask Elodie about it later and focused on the task in front of us.

I slapped my hands on my knees as I stood. "Well, that barn isn't going to build itself."

"Helping the enemy?" Brody asked with a raised eyebrow.

My molars clenched as I fought a sly smile. "We've come to an understanding."

Namely, not talking about the fact the fate of the farm was still in the air while I fucked her senseless.

Together we walked toward the fray, each of the men splintering off to make themselves useful. Elodie was right in the middle of it, bright and buzzing, short sleeves rolled up, hair pulled back, a smudge already streaked across her cheek. She was pure light and energy, and I didn't think she even realized how everyone gravitated toward her.

She caught me looking and reached for the coffee mug I offered her. "Thank you." When she saw the foam and caramel swirl on top, her eyes flew to mine. "You remembered?"

I winked at her, and her cheeks flamed a pretty shade of pink.

Without another word, we got to work.

Lumber moved like clockwork, hands gripping beams, steadying posts, securing frames. The morning air filled with the rhythmic thunk of hammers and the steady murmur of voices. It was an old way of doing things, but an honest way. No heavy machinery. Just sweat, skill, and the knowledge passed down from one generation to the next.

I found my rhythm in the work, the solid weight of wood beneath my palms, the satisfying scrape of nails biting into grain. It was grounding, losing myself in something that required precision but not thought.

Levi worked beside one of the Amish men, his face set in quiet concentration as he listened to the instructions given to him. His movements were careful, his posture straighter than usual, like he was trying to prove himself.

Something in my chest tightened.

My kid belongs here.

I wasn't sure when it had happened—when the sullen, angry boy who had been adrift in Star Harbor had started settling in, but it was finally happening. I could see it in the way he worked, in the way he bantered with the guys, in the way he bumped fists with Austin like they'd known each other for longer than a few weeks.

And I had no idea what the fuck to do with that. Any lingering thoughts of moving on, or dumping the inn to work in a restaurant, evaporated. Levi needed to be here, even if that meant me fully letting go of the last thread of my own dreams.

For him, I would do anything.

A sharp whistle cut through the air.

I turned to see Elodie. She was standing on the outskirts of the barn, hands on her hips, calling out for a break. "If I don't force you people to eat, you'll drop before the barn is even finished," she called out with a grin. "And I am not explaining that to your wives or mothers."

A rumble of laughter rippled through the crowd.

All morning, the Amish women had been working just as steadily. In partnership with the Keepers, they had set up long wooden tables covered with linen. The spread was simple but rich—warm bread, roasted chicken, fresh preserves, and thick slabs of pie.

I hadn't realized how hungry I was until I smelled it.

Apparently I also hadn't realized how determined Elodie was to make me eat until she was dragging me toward one of the tables. I sat, more to appease her than anything else, but the second she set a plate in front of me, my stomach twisted in protest.

She rolled her eyes, settling beside me on the bench. "Don't make that face."

I frowned. "What face?"

Her smile widened. "The one that says you think sitting down and having lunch is some kind of personal weakness."

I huffed a laugh, shaking my head.

She nudged my knee with hers. "Eat, Callum. Please. You've been working hard."

I picked up a piece of bread, tearing it absently. The food was warm in my hands, the scent curling into my senses, but my attention wasn't on the meal.

It was on her.

I focused on the way she looked out at the half-built barn with something like awe. Her attention wandered, like this moment, this day, was so much bigger than her.

The frame of the barn stood tall, its bones solid, its presence undeniable.

"You're really doing this," I murmured, watching pleasure wash over her features.

She smiled, but it wasn't just pride—it was something warmer. Softer. "*We* are doing this."

I knew that by *we*, she likely meant the community, but I looked away before she could see what that word did to me. Something tightened low in my gut. I took a bite of the bread just to keep from blurting in front of everyone that I was falling in love with her.

Before I could face the reality of it—the way watching her in this place was shifting things inside me—I focused on the food. After lunch, work began again, and we didn't stop until exhaustion started to set in. By the time the sun had started its slow descent, the entirety of the barn was up, standing strong against the sky, ready for paint and windows.

The town was still buzzing with a low hum of laughter and conversation, kids running through the grass, people lingering like they weren't ready to go home yet.

The Amish women and the Keepers moved in tandem, setting out what remained of the food, tidying up, making sure everything was in order before calling the day a resounding success.

Elodie stood in the middle of it all, soaking it in.

I watched her. I watched the way she took a deep breath, eyes skimming over the barn, the people, the land—

like she was trying to memorize it. Like she knew, deep down, that this was something special.

Something rare.

Something worth holding on to.

I had spent years convincing myself I didn't truly belong anywhere. That the inn was a quiet existence I could slip into in order to keep Mary's dream alive.

I had never allowed my own dreams to come to fruition. That was my penance for not loving her in the way she had deserved. Resentment soured my stomach. It was rare to allow myself to sulk with the resentment that I was truly unsatisfied with the inn. Expanding would have allowed my dream of a restaurant to live in tandem with Mary's.

It was within reach. I knew in my gut that the Keepers were going to sell—it would be foolish not to. All I had to do was sign the paperwork and I would have more than enough money to purchase the land, but it would completely fuck Elodie over in the process.

It would mean I had to sacrifice her dream for my own.

When Elodie's gaze caught mine again, something fell into place. For the first time in my life, I thought about what it would mean to choose something else.

To choose someone. To choose *her*.

The thought burrowed deep, settling low in my ribs, the weight of everything shifting around me.

I started to wonder what it would mean if I did.

THIRTY-TWO

ELODIE

It was blue.

Not just any blue, but electric, riotously, unapologetically *blue*. The kind of blue that caught sunlight and flung it back like a dare. The kind of blue you couldn't ignore, even if you wanted to.

I stood in the freshly leveled gravel driveway, arms crossed over my chest, chin tipped up to drink in the sight of it. The paint was still tacky in some places, and the scent was sharp and raw in the warm summer air, like the whole building had been reborn and hadn't quite dried yet. A smudge of it streaked across my forearm, proof that I'd been part of the resurrection, that I'd wielded a brush and stood on a ladder and chosen this wild, impossible color on purpose.

For Stan.

In many ways, it felt like the last thing I could do for him with the little time I had left there. It was like closing a book you didn't want to end, but you knew you had to. The barn was finished, but my promise to him wasn't kept. I had promised Stan that we could turn Star Harbor Farm into the best family destination in Western Michigan.

But now, the rest of that dream wasn't mine.

I swallowed past a lump in my throat as I fought back tears. "Hey, Levi."

I battled the sun as I looked up at the big, beautiful barn.

"What's up?" he answered, carrying the last of our five-gallon paint buckets to the front of the barn.

I bit back a smile. "What's red and smells like blue paint?"

His dark brows pinched together. "Um . . ." At a loss, his shoulders lifted.

I grinned. "Red paint."

"Oh, wow." Levi shook his head and started to walk away. "That was bad."

I cackled at my own terrible joke. "Come on. It's *hilarious*." On impulse I glanced at the paintbrush in my hand before throwing it in his direction. The brush tumbled end over end through the air and landed smack-dab in the middle of his back, leaving a massive smear of cheery, blue paint.

Levi froze. When he turned, childlike mischief sparkled in his eyes. Fighting laughter, my hands flew up. "It was a joke. I'm sorry."

His eyes flicked to the nearly empty five-gallon bucket at his feet.

"No. Levi . . . no." I had already started backing up as he lowered to grab the handle of the bucket. I was fucked.

Quickening my steps, panic rose in my chest as he started walking toward me. "Levi. I was messing around. Don't you dare—I'll fire you!"

With every step, my flight impulse ratcheted higher.

When Levi took off in a sprint toward me, I turned and ran. The kid was fast, I'd give him that. Reaching into the bucket, he pulled out a soaked paintbrush, flinging electric-blue paint in my direction as I screamed, laughed, and ran like hell.

His youthful laughter rang out behind me as he shouted, "You can't fire me. I quit!"

With wide eyes I turned, stunned. My mouth fell open. "Levi . . ."

A grin hooked the side of his mouth as he shrugged. "Nah, I'm just playing." He dropped the paintbrush back into the bucket, both of us laughing and breathless. I slung my arm around him, pulling him into an affectionate side hug. We were covered in blue, splatters slashing across our clothes and faces, but we didn't care.

"*Ahem.*" The stern throat clearing behind us had Levi and I whipping around.

Cal had his phone held up, capturing a picture and shaking his head. I'm certain my eyes were wide, mouth open like a fish as I was surprised into silence.

With a smile, Cal pocketed his phone. He jerked his head over his shoulder as he spoke to Levi. "Jamie is here to get you for community service. You should clean up."

Levi nodded, the easy smile never leaving his face. "Yes, sir."

As he walked away, I called after him. "There will be payback for this!"

Levi jogged away, laughing. My attention rested on Cal. His expression was hard to read—like he was studying me and not quite sure what to make of me.

His eyes flicked up to the barn. "It sure is something."

I sighed. "I know. Isn't it beautiful?"

"Yeah. Sure is." His gruff voice had me turning. He

wasn't even looking at the barn, but instead staring right at me. A smile bloomed on my face as I hugged my middle.

Cal cleared his throat, shifting my attention to the brooding look on his face. "Can we go for a walk? I'd like to talk with you for a bit."

Dread pooled in my stomach. Cal and I hadn't addressed the massive elephant in the room—when the summer had started, an unspoken rivalry blossomed between us and we were both fighting for the farm.

Now everything was . . . different.

Unable to find my voice, I nodded and walked in step with Callum. His long strides slowed to allow me to keep pace with him. His wide palms were stuffed into the pockets of his jeans, shoulders hunkered forward like the weight of whatever he needed to tell me was pressing down on him.

"Helen came to tell me today that the Keepers have come to a decision." The gravel in his voice pricked my skin as tears burned behind my eyelids. I didn't think I could look at him without falling apart. He gently cleared his throat. "The preservation easement went through, meaning the land itself is protected from outside developers."

The knot in my chest eased the tiniest bit.

"But," he continued, looking at his boots, "that doesn't keep just anyone from bidding on the property."

My chin lifted. "Bidding?"

His jaw flexed, and he dipped his chin with a nod. "They put it to a vote. Since Stan's wishes were for any proceeds of sale to go back to Star Harbor's public works and education systems, an auction would garner the highest profit."

Panic rose, burning my throat and causing my words to come out choked. "I see."

Cal paused, the dunes at his back and a breeze ruffling his dark hair. "We're all so proud of what you and Stan have done here. It's just—"

My hand flew up to stop him. I wiped under my nose in an effort to hold myself together. "No, I get it."

I could feel Cal's gaze on my face, but I focused my attention on the farmland that stretched in front of me. *So much potential. So much more I wanted to do.*

"I asked Helen to let me be the one to tell you."

A man who could communicate should have been a dream, but what no one tells you is that sometimes you don't want to hear it.

I gathered the courage to finally look at him. "So you're bidding on it then?"

His expression was tortured, but he didn't lie. "Yes."

My lip trembled, but I nodded.

Cal exhaled. "Look, if I don't, anyone can take it for themselves. Sure, the easement helps, but if I don't purchase it, there's no telling who will and what they'll do with it."

My eyes whipped to him. "Please don't do that. Don't lie to me now. I know you've wanted it since the beginning. Just admit it."

His warm, brown eyes bore into mine. "I've wanted it from the beginning. I still want it."

His brutal honesty sucked the air from my lungs. Deep down, I had always known it, but finally hearing it out loud made it *real.* Cal wanted the land for his restaurant, and a part of me knew he deserved that.

I was certain I could never outbid Cal, but stubborn pride bubbled inside me as my chin lifted. "But what if I still want it too?"

I started to walk away. I was too afraid to hear his

answer. My boots crunched on the freshly laid walking paths, defeat echoing in my ears.

"El, please don't walk away," he called after me. "The last thing I want to do is hurt you."

I turned to face him, not bothering to wipe away the fat tears that streaked down my face. "I know, Cal, and I don't want to hurt you either . . . but no matter who wins here, someone is getting hurt. Neither of us can get what we want without hurting the other. How is that fair?"

Cal's arms crossed, his expression unreadable. "It isn't, but if someone else—some corporation or greedy businessman swoops in—" Cal dragged a hand through his hair before gesturing at the barn. Frustration seeped from his every pore.

"What?" I demanded, my voice rising into the evening air.

"You sold them all the dream, El!" he shouted. "Everyone knows exactly how magical this place could be. You documented every step, shared every plan you had. Now all someone has to do is buy the land and profit off *your* ideas! You handed it to them on a silver fucking platter!"

Realization was a sucker punch.

Hurt laced with shame as I fired back. "Well excuse the fuck out of me! I was *happy* and having fun and, and—did you think I knew Stan was going to *die*?" My voice broke on the last word, and I swayed on my feet.

In all my enthusiastic oversharing on social media, I never imagined that I was detailing all the plans to anyone who was paying attention. I had never dreamed that the plans Stan and I were creating wouldn't happen or that someone could come in and take that dream for themselves.

Instantly Cal's strong arms wrapped around me, holding me steady.

Grounding me.

I leaned into his embrace, closing my eyes. I knew in my heart that Cal wasn't the enemy. Emotions were high, and shoving down my sadness for losing Stan had been a losing battle.

I let the grief in.

I let it wash over me in waves, pulled under by the tide of everything I couldn't say—that I loved this place. That I missed Stan. That I was deeply in love with Cal. That I didn't know who I was without this dream, and I wasn't sure I'd survive watching it belong to someone else.

When the heaviest of sobs racked out of me, Cal stayed sitting on the walking path, wrapped around me like a blanket. "It's okay," he soothed, smoothing my curls away from my face. "I won't let anything bad happen to the farm. I promise you."

It was something, but it wasn't enough. I nodded and sniffed, staring at the wet spots staining Cal's shirt. I used the heel of my hand to wipe my tears. "I can't give up again," I whispered.

His arms tightened. "For what it's worth, I don't think you should give up. You need to give this your best shot."

After a moment, I risked a peek at Cal's face. "What about you? Won't you hate me if I still try to buy it for myself?"

His jaw flexed, his dark eyes unreadable as he swallowed and shook his head. "No, Darling. Nothing could make me hate you."

THIRTY-THREE

ELODIE

I was emotionally wrung the fuck out.

After my total meltdown, Cal had carried me in his arms back to the cottage. He was gentle and soothing as he tucked me into bed and kissed me good night. Despite the heaviness and uncertainty between us, I was still utterly, deeply in love with him.

I only hoped it would be enough for him to forgive me for not admitting defeat already.

A few days later, the lawyer's office smelled like coffee that had been reheated too many times and something vaguely citrus, like someone had tried to mask the scent of despair with a cheap lemon-scented candle. I sat in the stiff chair across from his desk, fingers twisting the silver ring I wore on my middle finger. It had been my grandmother's. She was one of the boldest women I'd ever met and, right then, I needed some of her tenacity.

When Mr. Richardson stepped into his office, he got right to the point.

"Mr. Stafford left the farm in the care of the Keepers," he repeated gently, like I hadn't already been told those exact words in the letter the day the will was read. "With a preservation easement, meaning the land itself can't be developed. It is reasonable to believe that they will sell the property."

"Right," I said. "I understand." My voice sounded like it was coming from the other side of a wind tunnel. "And the proceeds from that sale go to the town."

He nodded, clasping his hands together like he was sorry but also very used to delivering this kind of news. "I think he understood the likelihood that, after his passing, the farm would be sold, but Mr. Stafford wanted to ensure the property was in trusted hands. Historic hands that shared his values."

I nodded and looked down at my lap. "And the only thing I can do is purchase it myself?"

His pause was small but mighty. "It appears that way, miss."

I blinked, knowing my only option was so far-fetched it was laughable. I could size up any situation in a matter of seconds and make a plan, but I still hadn't figured out how to make money fall from the sky. "For how much?"

"Well . . ." He clicked through his computer screen. "Back in 1992, the land was purchased for about thirty-five thousand, but with the orchard added, and the easement in place, it's . . . a lot more now. Millions."

I laughed. I actually laughed. It burst out of me unbidden, like a sharp, humorless thing.

I pressed a hand over my mouth like that would keep everything else from spilling out—my hope, my grief, the ragged little dreams I had nursed so close to my heart they'd fused with my ribs.

Millions.

Mr. Richardson didn't laugh. He only offered me a

strained smile, the kind people wore at funerals and divorce proceedings. "I understand this is a shock."

There wasn't a more perfect word for it.

I left his office feeling like I'd been hollowed out, like someone had scraped my insides clean with an ice-cream scoop and forgotten to put them back.

Outside, the world had the audacity to keep turning. Traffic moved. A woman pushed a stroller past the aging office building. A couple laughed and hugged across the street.

And me? I stood on the sidewalk with a file folder tucked under my arm and no idea what to do next.

When I made my way back, the cottage sat quiet, wrapped in the sleepy stillness of a Wednesday afternoon. Before long, someone would purchase the land—the cottage along with it—and I would start over.

I sat on the porch steps, folder unopened beside me, and stared out at the blossoming pumpkin patch. By now it was overflowing with vines, early-stage pumpkins growing larger every day.

This was where it all started. Where Stan leaped with blind faith and believed I could make something of this place. On our meandering walks, I had listened while Stan talked. I had learned the rhythm of bees and seasons. I had imagined a fall festival and cider tastings and starry movie nights with kids curled up in lawn chairs and parents holding paper cups of mulled wine.

This was supposed to be ours. *Mine.*

I hated the idea of someone else profiting off our dreams. I'd poured my heart and soul into the Star Harbor Farm social media pages and worked to create an online community that was unique and exciting. Sharing every step of my journey had been cathartic, and I never imagined that someone could take those dreams for themselves.

I wiped at my cheek before the tear had a chance to fall.

Back inside, I paced. I made tea but couldn't drink it. I needed something to take my mind off the inevitable, aching loss of Star Harbor Farm.

I needed a distraction from the utter ache of hopelessness.

From my dresser drawer, I dragged out the letter I had found tucked inside the old trunk. The faded ink and broken promises were folded neatly between the yellowing pages of her letter.

Meet me at the lighthouse before it's too late.

He is watching.

The words were cryptic, romantic. Slightly terrifying.

I wasn't sure which part I believed more.

That night I had spent the evening combing through the trunk again, desperate for more clues. The woman had clearly been planning to run, and I was more convinced than ever that she was the woman they'd found on the beach all those years ago—was she the nameless ghost whispered about in diner booths and porch swings? Was this the Lady of the Dunes?

But what if her story wasn't the soft-edged tragedy the locals spun it into?

What if it really was something darker?

Something that whispered warnings across time?

I shivered and rubbed at my arms. The cottage felt colder than it should have.

I looked through the window toward the Drifted Spirit. As always, it was a quiet calm of soft lighting and welcoming windows. It was ethereal and dreamy. The thought of running a place like the Drifted Spirit, with its stream of new faces and fresh stories, seemed like a dream come true. Every day would be spent daydreaming, curating the perfect Star Harbor experience for each new guest.

But Cal was proof that not everyone saw things in the same romantic, gold-filtered light. Sometimes that same dream was like wearing someone else's too-small shoes.

Cal hadn't been around all day, and I imagined he was giving me some space after my complete meltdown. We had texted a few short things, like boring updates and half-hearted questions about Levi.

I got the sticky feeling that Cal was somewhere inside himself—a place I didn't have a map for. I wasn't sure whether having space to think made everything easier or infinitely harder.

I missed him, and I hated that I missed him when I was supposed to be figuring out how to save the farm, how to save myself.

Because wasn't that the whole point?

This was supposed to be the version of me who didn't quit. Who didn't run at the first sign of discomfort. Who didn't shrug and float and tell herself the universe would figure it out eventually.

That girl wasn't here.

Not yet.

But damn it if she wasn't trying like hell to show up. If Cal—the man with the most to lose from my winning—didn't think I should give up, then how could I? So much had changed between us. It was like we were standing on opposing sides of a canyon, tied to opposite ends of the same rope. Neither of us wanted to intentionally harm the other, but we couldn't manage to drop the rope either.

I didn't have all the answers, but if I could ensure the

farm was in safe hands, Cal and I could figure the rest out later, together.

How could I live with myself if I didn't find a way to make this work?

I tucked away the letter and focused my attention. I made a messy, sprawling list of every person I could call. Every contact I'd ever made who might have a line on funding, grants, investors, or fairy godmothers. I emailed the state historical commission. I left messages for a business start-up incubator. I reached out to grant writers who might be interested in helping.

There had to be *someone* who could help me.

ONE BY ONE, the doors closed.

"Too risky."

"Wrong kind of nonprofit."

"No ROI."

Every rejection was a paper cut, small and mean and stinging more than it should. By the fifth one, I didn't even bother to respond. Instead, I just dropped my phone on the kitchen table and went out back to cry in the empty barn.

It was the paint that got me really rolling. The stupid, brilliant blue was so bright that it felt like hope, like a glorious middle finger to the idea that this place wasn't worth saving.

"Dang it, Stan," I whispered, dragging my fingers along the interior wall. "Why couldn't you have just given it to me?"

I laughed at my own ridiculous thoughts. Stan wasn't the kind of man who believed in handouts. He valued hard work. Grit. Pulling yourself up by your bootstraps.

Feeling sorry for myself, I stepped out of the barn and stared at Lake Michigan, tracking the distant caw of a crow overhead, as I made my way back to the cottage.

By the time I got back inside, my crummy black coffee was cold, but I forced it down anyway.

I was utterly exhausted. Not just physically, but bone-deep tired. The kind that made your soul feel like wet sand, heavy and clinging to everything.

And yet, underneath the ache, under the grief and rejection and fear, something small and bright and furious was surviving, like a weed that refused to die no matter how many times you stepped on it.

I wasn't ready to give up.

Not yet.

Even if I didn't know how to win. Even if I didn't have a plan or a partner or a dollar to my name, I wasn't walking away.

Because I knew this dream was worth fighting for. That *I* was worth fighting for.

I stared at the stack of rejection emails, at the empty grant applications and loan documents spread across the table like battle plans, and I exhaled slow and steady.

I could do this. I *would* do this.

Even if it broke my heart. Even if I lost Cal in the process.

The truth I didn't want to face was the fact that there might not be a way for both of us to get what we wanted. Cal was right—if someone else bought the farm, there was no telling what they would do to it. I just knew that if I *somehow* scraped together enough to buy it, it would solve everything.

I took a deep breath as the house settled back into its usual quiet, and I opened my eyes.

I started again. *There has to be a way.*

THIRTY-FOUR

CALLUM

SHE WAS TENACIOUS, I'd give her that.

Elodie was still tending the pumpkins. From the edge of the orchard, I watched her crouch in the dirt, her fingers curled around the stem of a vine like it might slip away if she let go. The hem of her T-shirt rode up just enough to expose the slope of her back, and I could see a smudge of blue paint on her skin, dried now but still defiant. She wiped sweat from her brow with the back of her wrist, leaving a streak of dirt across her temple, and I swear, it unraveled me.

The sun hung low in the sky, warm and syrupy, casting her in that golden glow that made everything on the farm look like it belonged in a painting. The cottage. The barn. Her.

Especially her.

It wasn't just that she looked beautiful. It was that she looked like she belonged. Elodie was still fighting for this place even though every logical reason told her not to. Most people would've given up by now—hell, they would've packed up and gone the second the will was read.

But Elodie was out there with her hands in the soil, probably whispering soft encouragements to vines like they were old friends or acting like pumpkins needed pep talks and stubborn hope to grow.

She was breaking my damn heart.

I scrubbed a hand over my face and turned away, the backs of my boots crunching through the gravel as I walked. I didn't want her to see me watching. I certainly didn't want her to catch the look on my face and realize what it meant.

I was on the cusp of a final decision. I wasn't exactly certain of the details, but my mind was dangerously close to being made up.

A part of my brain rioted against the only option that didn't make me ill at the thought of it.

Back at the inn, I moved through the kitchen on autopilot, checking that the sourdough starter hadn't collapsed, that Levi's snack stash hadn't been raided, that the walk-in fridge was holding its temp. Mundane things. Easy things. Things I could control.

The air inside smelled like rosemary and burned sugar from the morning's failed scone experiment. I opened a window to let in the breeze and leaned on the counter, staring out across the property. From here, you could just barely make out the edge of her pumpkin patch.

My throat tightened.

I'd spent the last five years holding things together—for Levi, for the inn, for the memory of a life that had cracked wide open and never quite healed right. I kept thinking if I just worked harder, if I just stayed steady, the rest would fall into place.

And now?

The opportunity I'd always wanted was sitting in front of me . . . and I wasn't sure I could take it.

Not without the risk of losing her.

EARLY EVENINGS at the Drifted Spirit always had a quiet rhythm to them. The lobby glowed with lamplight, warm and familiar. The fire in the hearth crackled low, a soft hiss echoing off polished wood floors. Most guests were coming in from their adventures, stopping in their rooms, and the hum of conversation from the common areas was slowly growing.

JP King didn't belong here.

He sat in one of the armchairs by the window, his posture straight, phone in hand, a suit sharp enough to slice through the quiet. He looked like a man used to closing deals in boardrooms, not small-town inns. His watch caught the firelight when he reached for his espresso, the gold glinting like it had something to prove.

I crossed the room slowly, wiping my hands on the towel tucked into my back pocket. I hadn't even had time to change after the day's work—boots still muddy from a walk around the orchard, shirt clinging to the sweat of midsummer. I probably smelled like cedar and kitchen grease.

He smelled like money.

He stood when I approached, extending a hand like we weren't already sizing each other up. JP had the kind of cool confidence that screamed *money*. His dark hair was styled neatly, and his eyes were a cloudy bluish-green that added to the confident air about him. The corner of his mouth twitched in a half smile as he extended his hand.

"Callum," he said smoothly, like he'd already decided I was someone worth investing in.

I shook his hand. Firm. No bullshit.

"Mr. King."

"JP, please." He gestured for me to sit, but I stayed standing a beat too long, just to feel the weight of control settle somewhere closer to even. Then I dropped into the chair opposite him, legs wide, arms resting heavy on my thighs.

He wasted no time. "You want to own something. Build it from the ground up. Something with roots."

I didn't respond, but let him talk.

"I've looked at the numbers. Your concept—a farm-to-table restaurant, built on heritage and sustainability—it's very smart. Timely. Romantic enough for tourists, real enough for the locals."

"You got all that from a few conversations over the phone?" I asked, not bothering to hide the skepticism.

JP's smile didn't waver. "I make it my business to know potential when I see it. Tower Business Ventures invests in ideas that last, and you've got one."

I leaned back, letting the chair creak under the weight of the moment. "So you're on board with being a silent partner?"

"I want a stake in something meaningful." His gaze was sharp and assessing. "I think you want a way to make this dream happen without selling your soul or drowning in loans." JP set down his cup with precision. "I'll front the capital. You secure the property. We structure it so you maintain operational control, and my company sees returns over time."

I stared at him. "Tower Business Ventures is not exactly known for small-town charity."

He scoffed. "This isn't charity. It's business. You win. I win. The town wins." He said it matter-of-factly, without apology. There were no strings in his voice—but I knew better.

There were always strings. Sometimes they were just invisible.

I exhaled, nodding once. "Sounds like you've thought it all through."

His slow, confident smile grew. "I have."

My brows pinched down, searching for the catch. "What happens when I want to change the menu? When I decide we're going to give away every Friday meal to a local food pantry? Or shut down for a week to host a family who lost everything in a fire?"

He tilted his head. "Are you telling me that's your plan?"

I didn't answer, but held his stare.

JP gave a small laugh. "You're not the kind of man who can be owned, Cal. I'm betting on that."

He stood. Brushed an imaginary wrinkle from his cuff. "I don't need an answer tonight. But you should know—I'm not in the business of waiting around. When that property goes to auction, you need to be ready. You've got a window to act and to be prepared that someone else will move on it if you don't."

I stood, extending my hand. "I understand."

JP's handshake was firm, and he held it for a beat too long, as if he was still trying to figure me out. "I look forward to hearing from you."

He offered a final nod and walked toward the door, his footfalls quiet but unmistakably confident. "Good luck, Cal."

The room settled back into stillness, the fire crackling low behind me. Outside, the wind stirred the branches of the trees lining the driveway. I stared at the empty cup he'd left on the table, the faint ring of espresso still marking the rim.

On paper, the plan was perfect. The restaurant I'd dreamed of, the land I'd grown to love, a business partner who knew how to play the long game. All of it was sitting in my lap, waiting to be claimed.

As the silence thickened, curling around the corners of the inn like fog off the lake, something in my chest refused to settle.

Maybe it was the way Elodie still tended that pumpkin patch like it might save her. Maybe it was the way Levi had started talking about her in the plural—like we were a *we* now, and not just two separate people orbiting the same four walls of this home.

Maybe it was the part of me that knew, deep down, that dreams built on someone else's ashes never tasted the way you imagined. I sat there for a long time, staring at the dying fire, thinking of all the ways a man could love something enough to let it go.

And how sometimes, that was the only way to make it real.

THIRTY-FIVE

CALLUM

By the time I made it to the cottage, the sun had already slipped behind the tree line, casting long, lilac-colored shadows over the pumpkin patch. A soft light glowed from the cottage window, golden and warm, like the place itself had a heartbeat. It was the kind of light that made you slow down, the kind that felt like an invitation you didn't deserve but couldn't walk away from.

I shifted the paper grocery bags in my hands and knocked with my boot.

The door creaked open. Elodie appeared in the doorway, wearing leggings and an oversize sweatshirt that had a faint streak of paint along the sleeve. Her curls were piled in a messy knot at the top of her head, and her eyes looked tired—but vibrant.

She was still there. Still trying, and that did something to my chest.

"Dinner delivery?" she asked, eyeing the bags with cautious optimism.

"I thought maybe I could cook for you," I said, holding

up the bags like a peace offering. "Figured you could use a night off—and I could use an excuse to see you."

Elodie grinned as she stepped aside for me to enter.

The cottage smelled like lavender and something faintly citrusy. A record played low and scratchy in the background—Otis Redding, if I wasn't mistaken. The air felt thick with something I couldn't name, like maybe she'd been crying earlier. I shook my head. I was probably just projecting and overly worried about her.

I caught sight of the wall just beyond the dining table and stopped short. Bright Post-it Notes—pink, yellow, green—lined up like tiny soldiers. Scribbled names. Phone numbers. A few were crossed out. Others had full paragraphs crammed onto them in her looping scrawl. Below them, pages from her notebook and a few printed emails sat tacked up like battle trophies.

My breath caught.

Elodie's small desk had become a war room composed of stationery and shattered hopes—and still, she was there. Still showing up. Still fighting.

"El . . ." I murmured.

She glanced over her shoulder, eyes flicking toward the desk, and shrugged like the sight hadn't just rearranged my entire chest.

She blinked and forced a smile. "Just a visual reminder that I haven't run out of ideas yet."

I didn't have words, only the heavy thud of admiration and guilt settling deeper into my ribs.

She gently cleared her throat and took one of the grocery bags from my arms. "So, are you gonna tell me what dinner is?" she asked, trailing after me as I moved into the kitchen.

"Chicken pot pie," I said, setting a paper bag on the counter. "Comfort food. Seemed appropriate."

She raised a brow, mouth twitching. "You're aware that's like . . . a whole thing to make, right? Not just throwing ingredients into a pan and hoping for the best?"

I pulled out the precooked chicken and homemade puff pastry like a man with a plan. "Don't underestimate me. I have layers of flakiness prepared."

That got a genuine laugh out of her. Elodie leaned back against the counter, watching me with her arms crossed over her chest and her hip cocked in that way that always made me lose my place mid-thought.

As I chopped onions and peeled carrots, her silence grew more weighted—not cold or distant, just thoughtful. I caught her watching me more than once, eyes drifting to my tattooed hands, the scars trailing up my arm, my back, when I moved around the stove.

"You really like cooking, huh?" she asked softly.

I nodded, focusing on not slicing my fingers. "It's quiet. Ordered. You follow the steps, and most of the time you get something good at the end. It doesn't always work that way with people."

"Or farms," she said with a dry laugh, and I glanced at her.

She wasn't smiling anymore. "No," I said. "Or farms."

I stirred the filling and added a splash of cream that instantly looked like a mistake. Too much. It thinned out the sauce more than I meant to.

I grumbled and focused on salvaging the mess I'd made.

"Are you good over there?" Elodie asked, clearly biting back a grin.

I stared down at the pan like it had betrayed me. "It's fine. This is totally intentional."

"Oh, I see," she said, sauntering closer to peek over my shoulder. "Is this your famous 'chicken pot soup'?"

I gave her a sharp look as I attempted to fix the situation, throwing in a few spoonfuls of flour to thicken it up.

"This'll bake fine," I mumbled, feeling off my game. "Trust me."

She didn't answer, just stepped beside me and reached up to tuck a loose curl behind her ear. Her shoulder brushed mine, and it was like getting shocked—small, electric, and enough to make me yearn for more.

While the pot pie baked, we moved around each other like we'd been doing so for years. She poured drinks. I burned the garlic bread. She laughed. I threw a dish towel over my shoulder like I was ready to throw it in entirely. Somehow we set the table, even if the whole place smelled vaguely of scorched toast and onion.

"Moment of truth," I said, sliding a scoop of the pot pie onto her plate. One look at it and I knew I'd fucked it up.

Elodie took a bite, chewed, and paused before swallowing.

My heart sank as she made a face.

"Okay," she said. "It's . . . different."

"Wow." I dropped my fork with a laugh. I rested my forearms on the table and gestured with my hands. "Come on, give it to me. Brutal honesty."

Her gaze flicked up. "I mean, the carrots are mostly raw, the sauce is sort of . . . glue adjacent, and I think there's a clump of flour in here that might qualify as a dumpling."

I laughed, half defeated, and completely in love. "You could lie to me, you know."

She pointed at me. "You said *brutal honesty*. Besides, anything less would rob you of the chance to grow."

I looked up at her and found her smiling, that teasing

glint in her eye softened by something else—something warmer. She reached across the table and tapped her spoon against mine. "But you get points for showing up. That counts for something."

We ate in silence after that—well, she ate. I pushed food around my plate and tried to figure out how to say everything I wasn't supposed to say. The longer we sat, the heavier it all became. The music in the background had long since faded into quiet, and the sun had disappeared completely.

After clearing the dishes—both of us studiously ignoring how bad the food had been—I stood at the sink, rinsing off the plates. Elodie stepped beside me and handed over the dish soap, her fingers grazing mine.

We both froze, but neither of us moved away.

"I miss you," she said suddenly, barely above a whisper.

I turned, her hand still in mine, our bodies inches apart.

"I'm right here," I said.

"You know what I mean." Her voice broke on the last word and *fuck*, I hated that.

I hated the hurt in her eyes. I hated the way we both wanted everything and didn't know how to want it without breaking the other.

"El . . ."

She looked up at me, and for a moment neither of us breathed.

Then her hand slid up to my chest, fingers curling in my shirt, and I kissed her.

Not rushed or reckless. Just . . . deep and long, like a promise I wasn't sure I could keep.

When we pulled back, her forehead pressed against mine. I held her there, anchoring both of us in the quiet. I wanted to tell her everything, but I couldn't.

Not yet.

Instead, I whispered, "I told you, I'm right here."

Elodie didn't say a word—just took my hand and led me down the hall.

Floorboards creaked beneath us, and the soft scuff of her bare feet on the hardwood sounded louder than it should have.

Her hand never left mine, but her grip tightened like she was afraid I would vanish before we reached the bedroom. Like she didn't know my heart had already decided to stay.

Elodie pushed open the door and stepped inside, letting go only to reach for the lamp on the nightstand. Warm light spilled across the bed—rumpled sheets, a half-folded blanket, the soft imprint of where she had slept alone for too long.

I stood in the doorway, watching her, and for a second I didn't move because I needed to remember this.

The way she stood with her back to me, fingers toying with the hem of her shirt like she didn't know what to do with her hands. The way her shoulders rose and fell with the rhythm of a breath she was trying to steady. The way her curls had started to come undone at the nape of her neck.

She turned and I stepped forward.

She didn't say a word as I reached out and traced my fingers down her arm. Her breath was shaky and soft. When my hand slid beneath the hem of her shirt, her eyes fluttered shut.

"Elodie." Her name felt like a prayer on my tongue.

She looked up at me, cheeks flushed, lips parted. "Yes, Callum?"

My voice floated over her ear. "I'm not going to be

gentle," I said, my voice a low rasp. "But I will be careful. I promise, I will always be careful with you."

Something shattered in her gaze as she turned and pulled my face to hers.

The kiss was slow, but nothing about it was soft. It was teeth and tongue and that desperate edge of need we had been circling for weeks. Her fingers fisted in my shirt, dragging me closer. I pressed her back against the edge of the bed and swallowed the soft sound she made when her knees hit the mattress and gave way.

Her soft skin was burning under my hands. Warm and wild and so damn responsive it made my knees go weak. I kissed down her neck, tasting salt and citrus and the faint trace of her shampoo.

She arched into me as I slipped her shirt off, every inch of her revealed like a secret I had been dying to learn.

"Cal," she whispered, her hands sliding up beneath my shirt.

"Yeah?"

"I don't want slow tonight. I want—" Her breath caught. "I want you to show me I'm still yours."

My restraint broke wide open.

I stripped my shirt over my head and pushed her down onto the mattress, following her like gravity. My hands skimmed up her thighs, her waist, memorizing every curve, every shiver. She was flushed, pupils blown wide, chest rising and falling in quick, shallow breaths.

"You are," I said roughly, kissing the corner of her mouth, then her jaw, then lower. "You always were."

When her nails dug into my back and her hips lifted to meet me, I knew there was no going slow.

Only going deep.

We moved together like we'd been made for it—like

every argument, every misstep, every aching moment of *almost* had been leading here. Her legs wrapped around my waist, anchoring me to the earth. Her hands tangled in my hair, in the sheets, in me.

She whispered my name like a tether. I answered with her name like a vow.

There was nothing rushed about it, but everything was urgent. Everything mattered.

Every gasp.

Every bite.

Every time her hips lifted to meet mine like we couldn't get close enough.

I watched her fall apart, her eyes locked on mine, her lips parted in a soundless cry. When I followed, I buried my face in her neck and let go.

Let everything go.

When it was over, we didn't move. Just lay tangled together in the sweat-damp sheets, her breath warm on my shoulder, my heartbeat slowly steadying under her palm.

I kissed her temple, then her cheek, then her jaw. Each brush of my lips was a silent promise that everything would be okay.

Elodie's sated breath was still warm against my shoulder when my phone rang.

For a moment I ignored it—eyes closed, body tangled with hers in the quiet aftermath of everything that had been building between us. Her legs were looped loosely with mine beneath the sheets, her fingers still skimming gentle lines along my ribs.

The phone buzzed again and my body tensed.

"Don't," she murmured, sleep-soft and unwilling to move.

The second I saw Brody's name, the haze cleared. "El," I said, my voice too quiet. "I have to take this."

She was already sitting up, clutching the blanket to her chest.

I answered on the second ring. "What is it, man?"

Brody didn't waste time. "There was an accident. Hayes and Wes. It's bad."

Everything in my mind went still, but my body was moving, searching for my clothes and tugging up my jeans. "An accident?"

I put the phone on speaker so Elodie could hear.

"From what I could gather, Hayes's truck was broken down. Wes came to help and a driver hit them. Hayes is pretty banged up. A few minor cuts, shaken up. They're still checking him out now, but Wes—he took the brunt of it. He got hit protecting Hayes."

I closed my eyes. "Fuck."

Brody's voice was grim. "They're both at the hospital. I'm here now."

"I'll be there." I ended the call and looked at Elodie, who was already pulling on her own clothes.

"I'm calling Selene and Kit. Someone needs to be there for Hayes. I can stay with Levi until we figure it out," she said, her voice calm but tight. "Wes needs you and Levi shouldn't be alone tonight."

I nodded, reaching for her hand. "Thank you. I'll call as soon as I know anything."

She leaned in and kissed me softly—no pretense, no hesitation. Just us.

Then she slipped out, and I was left with nothing but the echo of her kiss and the sick feeling in my gut. I watched as Elodie pulled her phone to her ear, already making calls as she hurried across the grass toward the Drifted Spirit. She ducked through the fence and was swallowed by the darkness.

I dragged a hand over my face and took a breath. Wes and Hayes didn't need me freaking out. I made my way to my truck, pulling a wide circle and driving as fast as I could toward the hospital.

The hospital waiting room always smelled the same—sterile, metallic, and exhausted.

I walked in to find Brody standing near the vending machines, arms crossed tight over his chest, his police radio clipped to his shoulder like a second skin. His expression was grim.

He didn't bother with preamble. "Hayes has a few bruises and a busted lip. Lucky, all things considered. Wes pushed him out of the way when the driver came around the bend too fast."

My throat burned.

"Fuck." Brody scrubbed a hand over his jaw. "Wes took the hit straight on. Broken ribs, punctured lung. His leg is in bad shape, but they won't say much until the surgeon sees it."

I sank into one of the hard plastic chairs like my bones had given out.

"He just . . . reacted?" I asked.

Brody nodded. "Didn't think. Just moved."

Of course he did. That was Wes. In the Army, he'd had this calm about him, like he was built for chaos and pain. Wes was always the first to jump in, never waiting to see whether someone else would do it.

Brody sat down beside me. His movements were slower than usual. Measured.

For a long minute, we didn't speak.

Finally, he said, "You okay?"

I exhaled, shaking my head once. "No."

"Same."

The silence between us was thick. Not awkward—just full. It was the kind of quiet that came when you'd seen too much, felt too much, and still didn't know what to do with any of it.

"What else is eating you?" Brody finally asked.

"I don't even know where to start." I stared at a scuff mark on the linoleum.

When Brody sat patiently, I started prattling on. "I've been holding on to this idea. Of who I was supposed to be. What I was supposed to do with my life."

Brody didn't interrupt.

I looked over at him. "But what the fuck are we even doing? All it takes is one distracted driver and everything's gone?" My thoughts spiraled as my anxiety crept higher. "What if I've been gripping so tight that I can't see what's right in front of me?"

His brow creased. "Are you talking about the farm?"

I hesitated, then nodded. "I thought if I could just make this one thing happen—if I could get it right—it would mean something. That my life would make sense."

Brody studied me for a second. "There's nothing wrong with chasing a dream, Cal."

"No," I said, my voice low. "But maybe it was never the right dream. Or maybe it's the right one for someone else." I exhaled, not making sense. "Fuck, I don't even know . . ."

Brody's expression softened, the corners of his mouth tipping into something that wasn't quite a smile. "You know what Wes said to me last week? We were sitting on his porch, talking about nothing. He looked out at the lake and said, 'I think sometimes we wait too long to start living like it's already ours.'"

My throat closed up. If Wes didn't make it out of this okay, I was going to lose my shit.

"He's right, you know," Brody added. "We keep waiting for the moment things fall into place. But sometimes we have to choose it first."

Silence stretched between us as I let his words settle over me.

I didn't say what I was thinking. I had already made my choice. What mattered most to me had nothing to do with real estate or menus or a return on investment.

Elodie had let me in, and I was going to fight like hell to keep that door open—for her, for us. Even if she never knew what it cost me.

A nurse stepped into the waiting room, calling Brody's name. He stood slowly and glanced down at me.

"You coming?"

"I just need a minute," I said.

When he disappeared down the hallway, I leaned back in the chair and stared at the stained ceiling tiles. My heart thudded out a rhythm I'd heard in a thousand different ways before—on long marches, in active combat, in moments when everything was about to shift.

And I knew.

I knew with everything in me what I had to do next.

The dream I had imagined was beautiful, but it wasn't mine anymore.

She was.

THIRTY-SIX

ELODIE

The inn was still and warm, bathed in golden light that stretched long and slow across the hardwood floors. I sat in the oversize armchair in the Drifted Spirit's kitchen, one leg curled under me, the other bouncing in time with my nerves. Levi sat at the table beside me, fidgeting with the edge of a paper napkin, his shoulders stiff, his silence louder than usual.

I had brought him here an hour ago after the call from Cal, just past midnight. Wes was in surgery. Hayes was alive. But the words kept ringing like church bells in my head, over and over until I wanted to scream just to silence the echo.

It's bad.

There was something cruel about how beautiful the Drifted Spirit was in the dark hours of night. The fireplace crackled low. The soft scent of cinnamon and something woodsy—maybe cedar—floated through the air. Cal's touch was in every detail, from the hooks by the door to the blanket tossed neatly over the back of the couch. It was the kind of place people dreamed of staying in. The kind of place people paid good money to visit.

And Cal had built it. He'd worked for it. He'd earned this.

I was just borrowing the peace for a moment.

My phone buzzed again. I grabbed it so fast it nearly flew out of my hand.

CAL

With Hayes. Wes is in surgery. I'll call soon.

I PRESSED the screen to my chest and closed my eyes.

Please. Please, please, please let him be okay.

"I don't get it," Levi murmured. His voice was so quiet I almost missed it. "Wes is like . . . invincible."

I opened my eyes and looked at him. His face was pale, drawn tight in a way that made him look younger than he ever let himself act. My heart twisted.

"He's still fighting," I said, my voice thick. "That matters."

Levi nodded but didn't look convinced.

I stood. "Come on. Let's do something."

Together, we gathered blankets, stacked muffins from the pantry, and made cocoa that neither of us drank. We didn't talk much. We didn't have to. The silence between us wasn't empty—it was full of fear, of waiting, of love we didn't know how to show but couldn't stop feeling.

A soft knock on the glass door broke the stillness.

Helen stepped into the kitchen, her arms wrapped

around a cardigan that didn't match her dress, her eyes warm but lined with worry. "Hey, sweetheart."

Levi looked up quickly, relief flickering across his face before he masked it with a shrug and looked away. I rose from the chair and met her halfway.

"I didn't know who else to call," I murmured.

"You called the right person," she said, giving my hand a squeeze. "Go. He'll be okay with me."

I nodded, brushing a hand over Levi's shoulder as I grabbed my bag from the counter. But before I could step away, Levi stood too.

"Wait." He shifted his weight awkwardly, his eyes darting between us. "Can you tell my dad something?"

"Of course," I said gently.

"Tell him that I—" He looked down, fingers curling into the hem of his shirt. "Tell him that I love him."

My throat went tight. "I will," I promised, then reached out and pulled him into a quick, fierce hug.

Helen waited until he let go before placing a hand on my arm. Her voice was quiet but firm. "Be strong. He'll need to see your face and not your fear."

I nodded, fighting the sting behind my eyes.

Helen leaned closer, her voice dropping even lower. "And no matter what you see tonight, remember, people are more than their worst days. That boy in there"—she nodded toward Levi—"he gets that strength from somewhere. Cal is tough, but he'll need a shoulder to lean on too."

Tears burned, but I blinked them back and forced a shaky smile. "Thank you."

"Now go," she said, ushering me toward the door. "We've got things handled here."

~

THE SLIDING glass doors of the hospital parted with a whoosh that sounded too gentle for what waited inside.

It smelled like antiseptic and sorrow.

Fluorescent lights hummed overhead as I moved past the front desk, barely hearing the nurse who pointed me down the corridor toward the surgical waiting room. I knew this hospital, had come here once for a broken ankle in high school and again when Kit had sliced open her hand with a pruning shear. But tonight it felt entirely foreign. Too bright. Too quiet. Too full of the kind of waiting that stripped the air bare.

Voices murmured down the hall. Familiar ones.

The waiting room was full. Kit stood near the window, arms wrapped tightly around herself. Austin sat on one of the plastic chairs, hunched forward, elbows on his knees, worry carved into the lines of his face. Brody, still in uniform, prowled across the space like a tiger. My parents were perched on the other side of the room—Dad clutching a foam cup of coffee, Mom rubbing his back in slow, even strokes, like she was trying to keep him grounded.

Cal stood near the hallway entrance, pacing with his hands on his hips and his mouth set in a grim, unreadable line.

The moment I stepped in, every head turned. Kit crossed the room in two strides, pulling me into a tight hug.

"El," she whispered into my hair, "thank goodness you're here."

I clung to her. "How bad?"

She pulled back just enough to look me in the eye. Her own were bloodshot and tired. "Hayes is banged up but stable. He has a concussion and a few bruises. Mom and Dad just saw him." Her voice cracked. "Wes is still in surgery. His leg is badly injured."

I sucked in a breath, my heart bottoming out. "Do they know anything yet?"

She shook her head. "They won't tell us much. Just that it's . . . serious. And long."

I nodded, arms still around her, grounding us both for a moment longer. "Can I see Hayes?"

Kit's mouth pressed into a line. "He's beating himself up pretty badly. Maybe you can talk some sense into him."

I squeezed her hand and moved across the room to my parents first. My dad stood when he saw me, pulling me into a quiet, fierce hug. No words. Just solid warmth and trembling strength. My mom's eyes were glossy as she touched my cheek.

"We're holding it together," she said softly. "But I don't think Hayes is."

I swallowed hard, nodding. "I'll go see him."

I felt Cal's gaze on me as I turned, but I wasn't ready for him yet. Not until I saw my brother and knew for myself that he was okay.

The hallway leading to Hayes's room was silent, every step echoing in my ears like a heartbeat. I knocked gently before pushing the door open.

Hayes sat on the edge of the hospital bed, a white bandage on his temple, his hands clasped tightly between his knees. His eyes were bloodshot, his jaw clenched so tight I could see the muscles twitch. He didn't look up when I entered.

"Hey," I said, keeping my voice soft.

He didn't move.

I took two steps closer, hoping my movements wouldn't scare him away.

Finally, his gruff voice broke through the silence. "I should've seen the car coming."

I walked closer, resting a hand on the metal bed rail. "Sounded to me like you didn't have time."

He shook his head once. "That's not true. I saw it. I froze." His voice cracked like something fragile and furious. "He pushed me out of the way, El. I didn't even warn him. He just . . . reacted."

I moved around the bed and sat beside him.

"You're alive," I whispered. "That means something."

Hayes dragged a hand through his hair. "Not if he loses his leg because of me."

I didn't argue. I didn't tell him it wasn't his fault or try to offer comfort that would feel like sand in his mouth. I just reached for his hand and held it.

We sat in silence, shoulder to shoulder, the beep of the heart monitor next door the only sound between us. Eventually, Hayes leaned against me like he used to when we were kids and the world felt too sharp.

I didn't move. I just let him lean.

When I made my way back to the waiting room, the ache in my chest had bloomed into something unbearable. I needed air.

Cal was still near the hallway. His eyes tracked me the second I reappeared. I nodded for him to follow and stepped into a small alcove just off the main corridor, a quiet nook near a vending machine and a gumball machine with a crack in the globe.

He followed, the lines in his face deeper than I'd ever seen them.

"I saw Hayes," I said.

Cal's jaw flexed. "How is he?"

"Broken. But trying." I exhaled toward the ceiling. "He blames himself."

He nodded once, looking down at his hands.

"What about you?" I asked. "How are you holding up?"

His eyes lifted to mine, and something inside me twisted.

"I keep thinking about the last time I saw Wes," he said, voice hoarse. "We were at the inn. He was teasing Levi. Calm, quiet. Typical Wes."

He paused, then rubbed his hands over his face. "I know people say this shit happens in an instant, but it doesn't hit until it's someone you know. Someone solid. Someone who's been through hell already."

I reached for his hand and held it.

Cal stared at our joined hands, then back at me.

"I can't lose him," he said, the words barely audible.

"You won't." I swallowed hard. "He's still fighting."

He nodded but didn't speak again. Just pulled me into his arms and held me like the world was slipping sideways.

And I let him. I held on with everything I had.

When we returned to the waiting room, the nurse was there. "Family of Wesley Vaughn?"

Every head lifted.

"He's out of surgery. Stable. We'll know more when he wakes, but the amputation went as planned."

The room fell silent.

Amputation.

Kit choked back a sob. Brody stepped forward to steady her. My parents clung to each other. Austin sank into a chair and covered his face with his hands.

Cal just stood there, still as stone.

I felt the bottom drop out of the world.

The doctor's words barely registered. Wes's amputation was above the knee. It would change everything for Wes, but he was alive.

And that was something.

THE NEXT FORTY-EIGHT HOURS BLURRED.

Kit organized meal drop-offs, Selene collected clean blankets and comfort items, and I found myself flitting between hospital rooms and hardware stores, trying to keep busy. Cal wouldn't leave Wes. Helen and I assured him that we could look after Levi while he sat by his best friend's bedside.

I took Levi to the arcade, then dropped him off with friends. I helped clean Hayes's kitchen, even though no one had asked.

I didn't sleep.

Every time I closed my eyes, I saw Wes's leg, saw Hayes's guilt, saw the look on Cal's face when he'd carried me back to the cottage just days ago. Everything felt broken. Like someone had knocked over the world's most delicate mosaic and we were all scrambling to find the right pieces to glue it back together.

And then, on a warm, sunny morning that felt impossibly normal, I sat on my front porch, legs curled beneath me, journal in my lap and a mug of stale coffee clutched in both hands. The air smelled like fresh soil and blooming lilacs. It should have been comforting.

Instead, it felt like a lull before a storm.

I tried to write, but the words wouldn't come. My mind spun with rejection letters, invoices, what-ifs, and a thousand unanswered prayers. The Post-it Notes in my living room had started to feel like a mockery, like all my dreams had been written in invisible ink.

A low rumble caught my attention, and I watched as a luxury SUV rolled slowly down the gravel drive.

I stood, blinking in the sunlight, shielding my eyes with one hand. The car parked in front of the cottage, and a man stepped out—tall, clean-cut, dressed in business-casual slacks and a collared shirt that probably cost more than my whole wardrobe.

He walked toward me with a coffee tray in one hand and the kind of self-assured ease that said he was used to walking into rooms and making decisions that changed people's lives.

I braced myself. "Can I help you?"

He smiled—charming but practiced. "I hope so."

I narrowed my eyes. "You're either very lost or very brave."

He laughed, then held out the coffee. "I brought peace offerings. Not poisoned, I promise."

I stared at him for a beat, then took the cup.

"Thanks," I said warily. "Who are you?"

"My name is JP King," he said with the air of someone used to their name meaning something.

Blank stare.

He chuckled. "I own Tower Business Ventures. I would like to speak with you about Star Harbor Farm."

I blinked, trying to parse together what was happening.

JP smiled, handing me a small business card. "I'm the guy who shows up when someone's trying to build something and needs a little help making it happen."

It struck me as funny how something as simple as a business card could scream *wealth*. It was thick, textured paper with Tower Business Ventures in blocky gold font. JP King's name was beneath it.

I frowned. "So you're like a real estate fairy godfather?"

His lips pressed into a flat smile, a bit of humanity leaking into his blue-green eyes. "I've been called worse."

I crossed my arms. "And what does the real estate fairy godfather want with me?"

JP walked up the steps and sat on the edge of my porch like he belonged there. He gestured over his shoulder. "I want to help you buy the farm."

I laughed. I couldn't help it. It burst out of me like a punch line I hadn't seen coming. "Okay. Sure. And I'm the Lady of the Dunes."

He clicked his tongue. "I'm afraid this is serious."

"So am I. This land is worth millions. I have approximately forty-seven dollars in my bank account and a drawer full of rejection letters."

He sipped his coffee, unfazed. "And yet you're still here. Still working. Still trying."

I stared at him. "Why does that matter?"

He didn't answer right away, but let the quiet settle between us until the birdsong took over.

"Let's call it a favor," he said finally. "From someone who thinks you belong here."

My stomach dropped. "Who?"

JP tilted his head, smiled like he knew every secret in the universe. "Someone who believes in second chances."

I looked him up and down. "Is this some kind of scam?"

"Nope."

My eyes narrowed. "A mean joke?"

He scoffed. "Not even a little."

I searched his face for anything that would give him away—some twitch, some glimmer of a tell, but all I saw was patience. Calm. A kind of knowing that made me want to run and stay all at once.

"Why me?" I asked, my voice a whisper.

Why not Cal?

My thoughts raced. Excitement and disbelief warred with uncertainty. This man was giving me exactly what I needed to purchase the farm and make Star Harbor Farm a reality, but all I could think about was Cal.

What about his dream?

"Sometimes the right person just needs a little push." JP smiled, his words pulling me from my thoughts. "All I am asking is for you to think about it, Ms. Darling."

I blinked. "Umm . . . okay."

He stood, urging me to accept his peace offering in the form of coffee. "If it's all right with you, I'd like to take a walk and hear about your plans for Star Harbor Farm."

So we walked.

Side by side JP King and I walked every acre of the farm while I rambled on about the vision Stan and I had had for the farm. He didn't interrupt, but only paused to ask clarifying questions. If I didn't know the answer, he simply shook his head and assured me not to worry—some details could be worried about later. Then we got back to the cottage and he walked back to his car, got in, and drove away—leaving nothing but dust and questions in his wake.

I didn't move.

Not for a long time.

I sat there with my long-empty coffee cup, staring out at the barn and the pumpkins and the fluttering notes in my window, and I felt something shift. Something huge. Like a puzzle piece had clicked into place—but upside down.

Who would do that for me?

Who would believe in me enough to make this happen?

The answer danced just out of reach. But the feeling it left behind burned hot and aching in my chest.

It didn't make sense.

None of it did.

When I closed my eyes and exhaled, I knew one thing with aching certainty: Someone had opened a door.

Now it was up to me to walk through it.

THIRTY-SEVEN

CALLUM

THE SKY WAS the color of old pewter, streaked with the watery light of a sun not quite ready to rise.

I couldn't sleep.

I hadn't, really, for two nights now, stuffed into a bedside chair as I sat with Wes in the hospital. Every time I closed my eyes, I saw Wes's face—his expression slack with pain, his voice a whisper through gritted teeth as they wheeled him past me in the hall. I saw Hayes, too, pale and too still in that hospital chair, his hands shaking when he thought no one was watching.

For Wes, the road to recovery would be long but he wasn't going to walk it alone. I finally came up for air when the nurse told me I stank and insisted I get at least one good night's sleep away from the hospital.

And a shower.

Back at the inn, the dark sky hung heavy. Damp. Still. In the distance, the lake was quiet in a way that felt sacred.

I had needed that shower more than I realized. After I'd let the water run cold, I pulled a T-shirt over my head and shoved my feet into my boots, not bothering with laces. The screen door of the inn creaked open behind me as I stepped into the thick early-morning air, my breath forming ghostly clouds in front of me. Everything was silvered with dew—the grass, the fence posts, the lower branches of the trees, like the world had been dipped in silence and sealed in glass.

I didn't have a destination in mind. Just a pull. Like if I kept walking, I might find something worth holding on to out there. Stan walked the land every single morning he was alive, and something about that called to me, so I set out walking.

The orchard stretched ahead of me in neat, winding rows. The fog hung low between the rows, thick and unmoving, like grief with no place to go. The damp air clung to my skin. It didn't smell like apples yet—not quite—but the earth was sweet with the memory of last year's harvest. All around me, it felt like everything was holding its breath.

Every scraggly tree felt familiar now, even though I hadn't planted them. They'd been Stan's, then Elodie's. Maybe someday they'd be someone else's, but for the moment, in the haze of dawn and grief, they felt like mine too.

My boots left dark prints in the grass, wet with dew and regret.

I thought about Wes—strong, loyal Wes—hooked up to machines, unaware that his entire life had just shifted sideways. I thought about the way he'd looked out for me in the Army. The way he still did, even when I didn't ask.

He hadn't hesitated.

He'd just shoved Hayes out of the way and taken the hit himself.

I stopped walking, swallowing hard, and leaned a hand against the closest tree.

It was never supposed to be this way. Wes was supposed to be invincible. I remembered him crouched beside me in the dark, desert wind whipping through a busted-out window in Kandahar, his voice low and even as he dressed a bullet graze on my side. "You'll be fine," he'd said, steady as hell. "You're too stubborn to die."

And now? He was in a hospital bed while the rest of us fell apart. Wes was steady. Reliable. But my friend would never be the same.

None of us would.

I tilted my head back and stared up at the starless morning sky. The fog clung to the air like it belonged there.

I thought about Levi and how he'd looked at me when I told him what had happened—scared but steady. He hadn't said much when I told him. Just nodded, jaw tight, eyes wide and haunted. I caught him watching me when he thought I wasn't looking, like he wasn't sure how to be a kid when the adults around him couldn't promise they'd keep standing. That scared me more than anything.

I thought about the Drifted Spirit, how hard I'd worked to keep it afloat. And I thought about the restaurant. The big dream. The one that had kept me moving all this time.

But it didn't shine the same way anymore.

Not since her.

Not since Elodie Darling and her hideous green boots and oversize shirts and the way she looked at this land like it was something holy.

I wondered whether Elodie had slept. The crunch of gravel behind me was soft but certain. I didn't need to turn to know exactly who it was.

Her scent hit me first—floral and lemon and something

sweeter underneath. Then came the warmth of her presence, the subtle shift of air as she stepped up beside me.

Elodie didn't speak but instead held out a steaming mug. Her fingers lingered against mine, just long enough to make the air between us buzz. She looked up at me like she wanted to say something but didn't trust her voice, so she let the heat from the mug do the talking.

I took it without a word, letting our fingers brush. Her hands were cold from the morning air, but mine were colder.

We stood there for a long minute. Shoulder to shoulder. Two silhouettes in the fog.

The coffee burned my tongue, but I didn't care.

"You okay?" she asked, her voice soft and low.

I thought about lying and giving her a nod and a smile and telling her everything was fine, but I was tired of pretending.

"No," I said. "Not really."

She exhaled quietly. "Me neither."

We stood like that, not talking, not moving. Just breathing. The fog was starting to lift, the orchard slowly taking shape again in the early light.

I glanced sideways at her. She was wearing a hoodie that swallowed her whole, bare legs peeking out from beneath it, the toes of her boots damp from the grass. Her bare legs were dusted with dew, and the curve of her neck disappeared into the oversize collar. She looked like a dream painted in muted watercolors—and all I could think was how badly I wanted to keep her safe.

To keep her.

Her curls were pulled back into a loose knot, and there were smudges under her eyes, like she hadn't slept much either.

"Didn't expect to see you out here," I said finally.

She sipped her coffee. "Didn't expect to find you either. But . . . I sort of hoped."

That pulled something loose in my chest. Something I hadn't realized I'd been clinging to.

The words hovered behind my teeth, burning for release. I almost said them then—*I love you*—but it didn't feel right. Not yet. Not until I was certain I could give her everything she deserved.

"El," I said, and my voice broke a little. I cleared my throat. "I've been thinking a lot about . . . everything."

She didn't interrupt, but tilted her head toward me, listening.

"I keep looking at all the versions of life I've tried to build," I continued. "Levi. The inn. The restaurant. I thought if I could just get one thing right, everything else would settle."

The breeze stirred the leaves above us, a low rustling sound that felt like it was listening too.

"But my time with you? That's the only thing that's ever made me feel . . . alive."

Her breath hitched and *fuck it*, I was too exhausted to keep denying it.

"I love you," I said.

Her head whipped toward me, eyes wide, mouth parting like she hadn't been ready for it. She swayed slightly, like I'd knocked the wind out of her with three little words. Her lips remained parted, breath shallow, and her fingers went slack around the coffee mug.

"I've been holding it in," I said, the truth catching in my throat. "Every time you laugh. Every time you fight like hell for this place. Every time you look at me like maybe I'm enough. I've been falling, Elodie. I love you and not in a someday, maybe kind of way. Not if things work out or when the timing's better. I love you now. Completely."

I turned to face her fully.

"Even if all I get to do is bring you coffee and fix fences, Elodie, I'm in. I'm all in."

She blinked. Once. Twice, and then her coffee slipped from her hand into the grass, forgotten.

My heart pounded like a war drum. I'd said too much. Maybe it was too soon. Maybe I'd broken something that had only just started to heal.

I started to step back—to apologize—when she stepped forward and wrapped her arms around my waist, pressing her cheek to my chest like she needed to hear the truth in my heartbeat. I held her there, fingers curling into the fabric of her hoodie, burying my nose in her hair. The orchard stretched out around us, glowing gold with the morning light.

She clutched the front of my shirt like she was afraid I'd disappear. Elodie's voice was flooded with emotion. Her voice shook. "You wrecked me, Callum Blackwood. And I don't even care. I love you so damn much I can't see straight." Her eyes blazed as they searched mine. "I got the money. I don't know how or why, but it's happening. I can't stand the idea of some stranger taking it away from us." Her words ran into one another as she rambled. "But I don't want you to think that I'm taking this lightly. I know what it means for you to not have the restaurant, I—"

My mouth found hers and I squeezed her tight, willing the moment to stretch on forever. No matter what came next, that moment was special. It was ours. Everything else could be figured out later.

For the first time in forever, I didn't feel like I was standing in someone else's story. I felt like I was home.

THIRTY-EIGHT

ELODIE

The Drifted Spirit smelled like butter and cinnamon and a little bit of chaos.

I stood at the far end of the wide farmhouse kitchen, elbow-deep in a bowl of biscuit dough and wearing one of Cal's spare aprons. The hem brushed my knees, and the strings were looped twice around my waist, tied in a bow that kept coming undone.

"Flour's in the bin under the counter," Helen called from behind the stovetop, where she was managing three sizzling cast-iron pans with the grace and precision of a woman who'd been raised on Sunday brunch and strong coffee. I could feel the warmth of the oven at my back and the cool marble counter under my fingertips. The scent of clove and rising dough clung to my sleeves, the kind of comfort that made you close your eyes and just *breathe*.

"I found it," I said, brushing a rogue curl out of my face with the back of my hand. A smudge of flour ended up across my cheek, but I didn't bother to wipe it away.

We'd already served the first wave of guests—retired teachers from Kalamazoo who'd eaten their weight in pecan waffles and maple-glazed sausage—and now we were prep-ping for round two. There were a few late sleepers trickling down from their rooms upstairs, and Helen said we might as well keep the griddle going.

The morning light filtered through the kitchen windows, catching in the hanging copper pots and the glass canisters lined up like sentries on the counter. It was peaceful. The kind of slow, cozy morning that felt stitched together by hand.

Cal had been at the hospital since dawn, checking on Wes. The surgery had gone as well as it could have, but healing didn't follow a timeline, and I knew he was still struggling to wrap his mind around it.

I missed him, but it wasn't the restless, aching kind of missing. It was softer now. Steady.

Because I knew he'd be back.

Because he'd told me he loved me. And I believed him. There was a quiet strength in being loved out loud. Not begged for. Not bargained. Just . . . offered, freely. I hadn't known how much I needed that until Cal gave it to me.

"How are the biscuits coming?" Helen asked, sliding a golden waffle onto a plate and topping it with a dollop of honey butter.

"They're going to be ugly," I warned, lifting a misshapen lump of dough onto the baking sheet.

"As long as they taste good." Helen gave me a wink.

We worked in tandem for a while, moving around each other like we'd done this a hundred times. She passed me the jam without asking, and I restocked the clean mugs by the coffee bar while she flipped bacon with a practiced flick of her wrist.

There was something grounding about mornings like this. The scent of yeast and fruit preserves. The hum of conversation from the front porch. The sound of the kettle whistling in the background.

I loved everything about it.

"Hey, Helen?" I asked.

She turned, lifting a brow. "Mm?"

"I think I want to keep looking into her."

Helen wiped her hands on a dish towel, then leaned a hip against the counter. "Into who, dear?"

"The woman," I said. "The Lady of the Dunes. I can't stop thinking about her. What if we've been telling the wrong story all along?"

Helen's expression shifted. Not surprised, exactly. Just thoughtful. "What makes you say that?"

"I keep circling back to that letter I found in the trunk," I said, lowering my voice even though we were alone. "The one that said 'meet me at the lighthouse' and 'he is watching.' Everyone says she was Alma Lovell, but what if she wasn't?"

Helen frowned. "What do you mean?"

"What if Alma's last name wasn't Lovell?" I said, the words tumbling out. My fingers gripped the edge of the counter, knuckles whitening. I couldn't help but feel as though this wasn't just about solving a mystery, but about setting something right. It was about finishing the story of a woman who never got to write her ending. "What if her last name was really Barker?"

Helen frowned again, deep in thought. "The locket had the initials A.L. That piece doesn't really fit."

"It fits if the locket was a gift from her future husband. Maybe it was an engagement gift or a token of their future life together." My mind was swirling with possibilities. "The engagement announcement you had shown me never listed a last name for her. It only said *Alma and William Lovell*."

Helen's eyes widened just slightly, and then she looked past me toward the hallway, like she was seeing all of the old ghost stories in a strange, new light.

"Alma could have been one of the Barker children," she murmured. "Now that's an interesting angle."

"You even said there wasn't much known about them, right?" I asked. "They lived here, in the Drifted Spirit, and at one time the inn and the farm were part of the same land. What if Alma was their daughter, had some kind of secret lover, and *she* hid the trunk in the root cellar in the barn?"

"You're right about that." Helen nodded slowly. "The Barker children were a boy and a girl. Or, at least, that's what the old records and photographs tell us. A lot of those details are spotty at best. But there was always some speculation about what happened to the children after the family moved away."

I set the tray of biscuits aside, my pulse kicking up. "I know it sounds like a wild theory, but something about it just . . . fits."

Helen studied me, then smiled—soft and proud. "Well, if anyone can give the Lady's story a real ending, I suppose it's you."

I blinked. "You don't think it's silly?"

"Honey." She shook her head. "Half the people who come to Star Harbor do so because of that ghost story. But you're the only one who's ever cared about the real woman behind it. I think that says something."

I swallowed, the warmth of her words hitting harder than I expected.

"If you want to dig, then dig," she added. "There are old

albums in the storage room—stuff from before the inn was even the Drifted Spirit. Who knows what you'll find."

I stepped forward and hugged her on impulse, flour and all.

She made a grumpy sound but hugged me back. "Just don't burn the biscuits."

I laughed. "Noted."

As we pulled apart, Helen returned to the stove. "So how's your mystery investor working out?"

I scrunched my nose. "Cal told you?"

Helen's smile softened as she nodded. "He's so happy for you."

I swallowed hard. The past few days were a whirlwind of paperwork and deadlines and dreams coming true, but I was also still wrapping my brain around the fact that if all went according to plan, Star Harbor Farm would be mine.

Well, *ours*.

I still had one last trick up my sleeve and was relieved Cal had been occupied at the hospital with Wes. I didn't need him getting suspicious. Despite calling JP at 2:15 in the morning, he'd taken my call and seemed just as on board with my idea as ever.

"What can I say about JP King?" I turned to grab the tray, my stomach doing a little somersault as I tamped down my giddiness. "He's . . . professional. Generous. A little intimidating. He's not the least bit worried that someone will outbid us at the auction."

"He can freeze hell with one look, that one." Helen chuckled. "He came out here before, you know."

I paused, my face scrunching. "He did?"

She flipped the last of the bacon, not looking at me. "Yeah, not too long ago. Cal's financial adviser set up the meeting, I think. He said he wanted to see the place. I didn't think much of it—figured he was considering investing in the inn."

I went completely still. The tray in my hands felt suddenly too heavy, the room around me too quiet. A spark lit in my chest—something that felt like disbelief, followed by a swell of knowing so visceral I nearly dropped the biscuits. The breath caught in my lungs.

"Wait a minute," I said carefully, setting the tray back down. "JP King was here before I ever met him?"

Helen nodded. "Mm-hmm. Can't mistake that looker. Tall. Crisp shirt hiding some muscles. Fancy shoes. Not the type we usually see out here."

My heart thudded once. Twice. "And you said Cal's adviser sent him?"

"Pretty sure. Mentioned something about food ventures or hospitality investments." She glanced over her shoulder. "Why?"

But I didn't answer—I couldn't—because my brain was already sprinting ahead—connecting the dots, one by one.

Cal.

He had known.

He'd known all along that JP had the power to help me. JP's offer hadn't been luck or fate or some happy accident.

It had been Callum.

And he'd never said a word.

The kettle screamed behind me, a shrill whistle that yanked me back to the present.

I turned it off with a trembling hand and stared out the window, past the orchard, past the barn, to the land that had somehow become home.

He hadn't done it for credit.

He'd done it for *me*.

Just quiet, radical love in the background of my life. I

pressed a hand to my sternum, like maybe I could hold my heart in place before it split open entirely. I had never loved him more than I did in that exact moment.

"Are you okay?" Helen called, but I was already moving out of the kitchen, desperate for air.

A breeze rolled in from the lake, rustling through the orchard behind me. I turned toward the barn, now glowing soft and blue in the late-morning sun, and felt the full weight of what I'd just learned settle over me like a blanket of starlight.

The man I loved had given up his dream to protect mine.

I closed my eyes and let the emotions wash over me—gratitude, awe, and something deeper. Something that tasted like wonder. Like coming home to the kind of love I hadn't believed existed.

He saw me. All of me. And he chose to lift me up anyway.

As soon as I walked out of the kitchen, I saw him.

Fresh from the hospital, Cal was already wielding an axe, grunting and ripping down the fence between the Drifted Spirit and the cottage.

Splintered wood lay in piles around his boots, the posts yanked clean from the ground and tossed like bones. His flannel sleeves were shoved up to his elbows, exposing his forearms—tan and flecked with dirt, veins tight from the grip of a crowbar. His jaw was clenched, his movements rough and deliberate, like each plank he tore away was a confession.

I didn't say anything at first.

Just watched in stunned awe.

This was the man who had built walls his whole life—between who he was and what he wanted, between the inn and the land, between me and the idea of staying. Now he was tearing one of them down, board by board, like he couldn't live with it standing there another second.

My heart cracked open.

I stepped forward, boots crunching over gravel and broken fence posts, until I was close enough to see the sweat clinging to his hairline, the way his chest rose and fell like he'd run a marathon.

"Busy morning?" I asked. "You look like shit."

He looked up, startled, eyes wild for half a second before they softened.

"Elodie," he said, his voice low and raw.

I pointed at the wreckage at his feet. "This is a little dramatic, don't you think?"

He dragged a hand across his forehead, eyes scanning mine. "I couldn't look at it anymore. That fence—it was never about keeping things neat. It was about pretending I could hold two lives separate. The inn. The farm. Me. You." He sighed. "But they're all tied together now. Whether I like it or not." He shook his head, shoulders dropping, before he flashed me a playful wink.

I exhaled, my breath catching on something too big to name.

"I know about JP," I said quietly.

His expression didn't flicker. It didn't shift into guilt or deflection, but he stilled. Soft and so heartbreakingly open.

"I figured you might figure it out," he said with a shrug. "Eventually."

"You pointed him to me," I said, voice breaking on the last word. "You knew what he could do. You had the chance to take it for yourself, and instead . . ."

I couldn't finish the sentence. My throat was too tight.

Cal stepped forward slowly, carefully, like he wasn't

sure if he had permission. "I wanted you to win, El. Even if it meant I didn't."

I stared at him, this man who'd given up a dream so I could chase mine, and I felt my knees weaken under the weight of it.

"You didn't say anything," I whispered.

He nodded once. "Because it wasn't about me."

I laughed. Just a little. It sounded broken, but bright. "Damn it, you're infuriating."

Cal smiled, handsome and genuine. "I know."

There were too many words in my chest. Too many things I needed to tell him, but they all scrambled together, tripping over each other in the rush to get out.

So I did the only thing I could—I started building.

"I don't know anything about farms," I said, stepping toward him, wiping my sleeve across my damp cheeks. "I can't tell you what soil is best for apples or how to fix irrigation lines. But I know people. I know comfort. And I know how to make a place feel like home."

His brow furrowed, confused—but he didn't interrupt as I kept rambling.

"I want Star Harbor Farm to have a farm-to-table restaurant," I said. "A real one. Cozy. Local. Booked-out-every-weekend kind of place."

His lips parted, but I pressed on.

"And I want you to run it. A true farm-to-table setup. Your food. Your vision. Something we build together."

Cal went still. So still I wasn't sure he was breathing.

"I want the inn and the orchard and the ghosts in the trees and all of it. I want you. I want Levi. I want early mornings and burned toast and a place where people come to slow down and fall in love."

Tears gathered in my eyes, but I blinked them away.

"Love doesn't have to mean someone loses," I said, voice barely above a whisper. "It can mean we both win."

The wind shifted, carrying the scent of lavender from the patch near the porch. The fog had finally lifted. The rickety cottage stood behind me, light spilling through the windows, as if it already knew what came next.

"I'm not scared anymore," I said. "Not of staying. Not of failing. I want to build something with you, Cal. Not because I need you to fix me, but because I'm finally ready to create something that lasts. Besides, I already talked to JP, and he loves the idea so you better get on board."

He didn't answer, not at first.

Cal reached out and pulled me into his arms, holding me like I was the answer to every question he'd ever asked.

His mouth brushed my temple, and he exhaled into my hair.

"You saved me," he murmured. "I just wanted to return the favor."

And that was it.

I smiled up at him. "I think we saved each other."

Just a man and a woman, standing in the dirt, chasing the sunlight, with wreckage at their feet and the future in their hands.

Not an ending, but the beginning of everything.

EPILOGUE

Callum

THE SUN WAS low and slow, stretching gold across the orchard like it knew we needed one more perfect day.

I stood just outside the barn, my boots planted in the dirt, arms crossed as I watched a group of kids charge Tire Mountain like it was Everest. One of them lost a shoe halfway up. Another screamed with delight and launched into a dive-roll. Nobody cried. Nobody got hurt. The kind of chaos that made a place feel alive.

And it was alive—every inch of it.

It was perfect. Chaotic, a little sticky, probably two safety violations away from a lawsuit—but utterly perfect.

A year ago, this farmland was just overgrown hills and a distant what-if. I didn't even believe in forever back then—not until a fiery brunette in muddy boots showed up and refused to leave.

The scents of woodsmoke and warm cider curled through the air. Someone had spilled kettle corn near the firepit, and a trail of toddlers were treating it like a buffet.

The hayride was packed, the tractor rattling down the path behind the barn while laughter and squeals echoed behind it. The bluegrass trio had set up beside the pumpkin patch and was strumming into the late-afternoon light.

A golden retriever with a bandanna labeled "Hank" was doing laps between tables, joyfully stealing doughnuts off paper plates like it was his personal fall buffet. Someone yelled "Hank, no!" and he responded by snagging another one and bolting toward the hayride.

And Elodie?

She was in the middle of it all. Barefoot in the grass, curls wild from the breeze, her laugh carrying farther than the music. She was leaning down to tie a child's shoe, waving at a family she'd met ten minutes ago, smoothing a plaid tablecloth that refused to behave. Her flannel was too big—because it was mine. Her cheeks flushed pink from the chill.

And she was the most beautiful damn thing I'd ever seen. Barefoot and radiant, curls like wildfire, her laugh lifting above the music. She looked like chaos and comfort wrapped in plaid.

And she was mine.

I could've stayed back, just watched her in that golden hour glow like a fool—but I had things to do.

The new sign hung at the front gate, wood-grain lettering carved deep and clean:

Star Harbor Farm & The Drifted Spirit Inn

Est. (again) 2025

Two pieces finally made whole.

We'd closed on the land weeks ago. With JP's help, Elodie had purchased the farm outright, but not just the farm and orchard or the cottage. With the historic easement in place, we were able to fold the Drifted Spirit and the acreage into one—just like it had been before time had torn it apart with lines and paperwork and poorly maintained recordkeeping.

Now it was whole again.

And so were we.

The big blue barn was under renovation, one wall already stripped to the studs, the scent of sawdust clinging to the air like possibility. Construction would pick up in the winter when the events slowed down, and by spring, it would be ready. Our restaurant. Her design. My food. Our dream.

I turned from the barn to help an elderly woman with her bag of apples—Elodie's friend Sheila from bingo, who'd already threatened to steal one of our scarecrows—and walked her to her car. When I turned back around, I saw Elodie standing with Levi at the edge of the bustling pumpkin patch.

His hoodie sleeves were too long, and his sneakers were muddy, but he looked lighter somehow. More settled. Taller.

I watched them talk. She bumped his shoulder, and he rolled his eyes in the exaggerated way that only a teenage boy could. Then she knelt and adjusted something on his boot—probably his laces—and whatever he said made her laugh. That belly-deep, messy laugh I never got tired of.

He looked older.

She looked like home.

They looked like they belonged to each other. Not in the way people say when there was shared blood—but in the way souls just know. Watching them, I had a lump in my throat and no idea what to do with it.

I made my way over just as Levi was biting into a cinnamon doughnut the size of his face.

"You have one?" he asked me, powdered sugar already dusting his hoodie.

I shook my head. "Waiting for the cider slush line to die down."

Elodie grinned up at me, her face flushed. "You're gonna be waiting forever. It's chaos over there."

"That's what happens when your secret recipe gets out," I said, nudging her.

Levi wiped his mouth with the back of his sleeve. "You guys are gross."

But there was a smile hiding in the corners of his mouth, and I caught the way he lingered when Elodie pulled him in for a hug.

"You sticking around for the bonfire?" I asked.

He shrugged. "Maybe. Or I might go hang at Hayes's for a bit. Thought I'd give the two of you a break before someone makes me sing 'Kumbaya' or whatever."

Elodie ruffled his curls, and he ducked away with a grin.

After he wandered off, she leaned into me. "He's okay."

"Yeah." I swallowed around the lump in my throat. "He is."

We stood in silence for a beat, watching the sun dip lower behind the orchard, turning the sky to fire.

Then I reached for her hand.

"You trust me?"

She turned to look at me, brow lifted. "Always."

"Come with me."

I led her past the cider tents and the bonfire pit, past the barn and down the gravel path that wound through the trees. The farther we went, the quieter it got. Just the crunch of leaves underfoot, the hum of crickets waking up in the grass, the crackle of a fire in the distance.

She looked up at the sky and smiled, soft and secret.

And for a split second I almost backed out. Because how the hell do you give someone the world when they've already handed it to you first? But I knew, deep down, the perfect moment I'd been waiting for was something I was already living. Every moment with her was perfect.

When we reached the old oak—the one she loved, with the crooked spine and the wooden swing—I stopped.

She looked around. "Cal?"

"I've been trying to find the right moment," I said, "to do this."

"To do what?"

I dropped to one knee.

Elodie froze.

And then her hands flew to her mouth, eyes already glassy with tears.

"Elodie Darling," I said, my voice low and steady despite the way my heart was trying to punch a hole through my ribs, "this land might be what brought us together, but you're what made it matter."

She let out a tiny sob and immediately covered her mouth again.

"You're the first thing I've ever wanted that didn't come with a blueprint. You didn't just walk into my life like a storm, you rewrote every line I thought I'd already figured out. And thank god you did, because the life I was building before you? It didn't hold a candle to this. If you'll let me, I want to spend the rest of my life building something that doesn't need plans or fences or backup options."

I pulled the ring from my pocket and opened the velvet box.

It wasn't flashy. A thin, antique gold band, a marquise-cut sapphire hugged by tiny diamonds on either side. Simple. Vintage. Unmistakably her.

"It may seem quick, but I'm done waiting for my life to start. I want to chase the sun with you," I said, voice cracking. "Every damn day."

For a long second, she didn't move.

Then she dropped to her knees and threw her arms around my neck, tears warm against my skin.

"You jerk," she whispered, laughing and crying at the same time. "You actual, unfair, impossibly good man."

I held my breath and waited.

"Yes," she whispered into my collarbone. "Yes. Of course, yes."

I held her there, buried in the scent of orchard wind and of the woman who cracked me open and made me whole.

Later, when the stars came out and the fire burned low, she stood next to me with my flannel draped around her shoulders, ring sparkling like starlight as she waved to the last stragglers headed to their cars.

I pressed a kiss to her temple, heart full to bursting.

Some people waited their whole lives for a love that felt like safety.

My safety was wildfire and wonder and warmth.

Elodie was the reason I tore down every fence I'd ever built.

She was the sun.

And loving her?

That was the only thing worth chasing.

WANT TO SEE WHERE CAL & Elodie end up in 15 years? (Hint: there's a very special farm wedding!)

Get it here: lenahendrix.com/get-cal-and-elodies-bonus-scene

BOOK 2 SNEAK PEEK

WHEN WE FALL

I NEED A NANNY. Not a distraction.

I certainly do not need a twenty-something man with a devastating smile, tattooed forearms, and the kind of easy charm that could unravel a woman twice as composed as I pretend to be.

But when my daughter gets kicked out of after-school care (again), and my flaky nanny ghosts us (again), Austin Calloway moves into the duplex next door—and right into our lives.

Now he's helping with homework, cooking dinner shirtless, and showing up with coffee like he's always belonged here.

He's too young.

Too familiar.

Too good with my daughter.

Too close.

And the worst part? He sees through me—the cracks, the stress, the walls I've built to protect what's mine.

The more I try to keep him out, the more I ache to let him in.

But letting someone in means risking everything.

He's the wrong choice . . . unless we're finally ready to see what comes after we fall.

~

Read on Amazon!

ACKNOWLEDGMENTS

To my readers, none of this would be possible without you. I was nervous to leave such a beloved town, but I am so grateful for each of you for trusting me to take you to someplace new and exciting. I know you're going to love it here.

This book felt like a love letter to summertime and all of the hope that comes along with it. As someone who often has big, seemingly unattainable dreams, I *felt* for Elodie. That girl got in over her head, but pulled herself up by her bootstraps and create the reality of her dreams. I hope one day we're all lucky enough to feel that brave!

A huge thank you to my cover designer Cat for taking my long, rambling texts and creating the most gorgeous, cohesive covers. I am so in love with them!

To my beta readers Trinity and Ashley, I hope you loved falling for Star Harbor as much as I did. Your thoughts and insights were so helpful in making sure our new town felt just right in the Lena-verse.

Ashley, you get a second shout-out because I wouldn't have the time or sanity to get HALF as much done if I didn't have your help. I am so thankful to have your support!

I cannot thank Dawn and James enough for outstanding editing and help with creating a brand new town that felt fresh and funky, but still like *me*. Your insights and guidance means more than I could ever say!

To the friends who are in the writing trenches with me,
I could never have written this without you! Sometimes I
was the cheerleader and other times I was beating my head
against the keyboard but knowing you had my back made all
the difference.

Want to connect? Come hang out with the Hendrix Heartthrobs on Facebook to laugh & chat with Lena! Special sneak peeks, announcements, exclusive content, & general shenanigans all happen there.

Come join us!

ABOUT THE AUTHOR

Lena Hendrix is a *USA Today* and Amazon Top 5 Bestselling contemporary romance author living in the Midwest. Her love for romance stared with sneaking racy Harlequin paperbacks and now she writes her own hot-as-sin small town romance novels. Lena has a soft spot for strong alphas with marshmallow insides, heroines who clap back, and sizzling tension. Her novels pack in small town heart with a whole lotta heat.

When she's not writing or devouring new novels, you can find her hiking, camping, fishing, and sipping a spicy margarita!

Want to hang out? Find Lena on Tiktok or IG!

ALSO BY LENA HENDRIX

Chikalu Falls

Finding You

Keeping You

Protecting You

Choosing You (origin novella)

Redemption Ranch

The Badge

The Alias

The Rebel

The Target

The Sullivans

One Look

One Touch

One Chance

One Night

One Taste (prequel novella)

The Kings

Just This Once

Just My Luck

Just Between Us

Just Like That

Just Say Yes

Star Harbor

Chasing the Sun

When We Fall

www.ingramcontent.com/pod-product-compliance
Lightning Source LLC
Chambersburg PA
CBHW030337010826
48973CB00004B/1042